Sunset of the Almond

A. Sappington II

Jadybug Press—Ararat, Virginia
Paperback ISBN: 979-8-218-66120-5
eBook ISBN: 979-8-3493-0553-5
Library of Congress Control Number: 2025907745
Title: *Sunset of the Almond*
Author: A. Sappington II
Digital distribution | 2025
Paperback | 2025

Published in the United States by New Book Authors Publishing

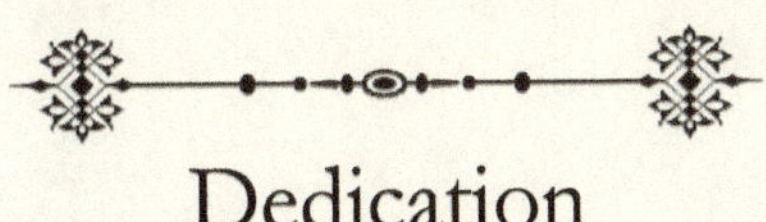

Dedication

I need to express some thanks. First and foremost, I would like to thank God for giving me the words and the drive to write a second book. He blesses me with the strength I need each and every second of the day, one second at a time. All glory to Him. To my wife Faye, who supports my every endeavor with strength, love and kindness. To Ashley and Jayden, my daughter and granddaughter. You three girls are my "why." To Buddy, my best friend. Our walks through the woods have always brought me peace. Finally, to Em and New Book Authors Publishing for your professionalism and attention to detail in bringing my words to the reader.

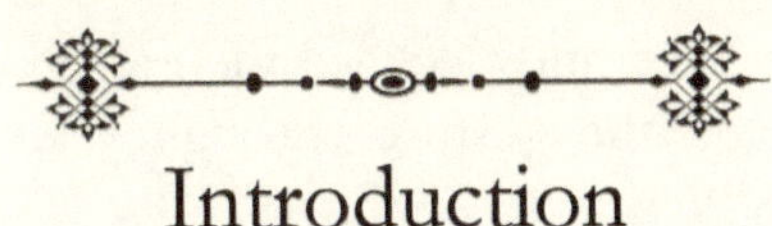

Introduction

The black Mercedes pulls up to the front of the restaurant in Lincoln Park. It is just one of many navigating the streets of Chicago near the lake. The naked affluence sharply contrasts with the homeless who recline against the occasional darkened building. There is no middle class in this area. Either you are rich and powerful or poor and powerless. Neither socioeconomic class takes notice of the other. As soon as it is clear for him to open his door, the uniformed driver steps around the car and opens the rear passenger door with a slight bow.

He opens an umbrella to shield his passenger from the cool drizzle that falls steadily from the black sky and stands expectantly. The man who emerges from the rear compartment exits the car slowly as if the act of standing from the leather seats is the last thing in the world he wants to do. The passenger looks around and then proceeds to the entrance of the restaurant with the driver keeping pace, an umbrella in perfect position above the man's head. As they reach the entrance, the man looks at the driver and speaks loud enough to be heard above the traffic passing on the street, "I don't know how long this will take. Wait here. I have a flight to catch immediately after."

The driver nods curtly and says, "Of course sir."

He then opens the door of the restaurant allowing the man to enter before walking back to the car to wait.

The Maître d looks at the middle aged, overweight man in the expensive suit, large mustache and tired eyes and gives his best impression of welcoming an old friend to the restaurant for the hundredth time this evening. The man's arrival in the Mercedes did not escape his attention.

"Welcome to Cochon Ivre. Do you have a reservation Monsieur?"

The man looks at the Maître d with an expression bordering on contempt as he says, "Quispe. General Alejandro Quispe. Reservation for two."

The Maître d studies his computer and finds the reservation with a wave of his hand. "Of course, General. Your table is ready. May I take your coat?"

Quispe shakes his head and declines the gesture with a wave of his hand, having perfected the gesture through years of practice. "Just show me to my table."

The Maître d guides General Quispe through the crowded restaurant to a table by the windows at the front with a view of the traffic and the lake. Once Quispe is seated, the Maître d asks, "May I start the General with a cocktail perhaps?"

Quispe doesn't look up. "Chateau Margaux."

"Excellent choice Monsieur. Your waiter will be with you in a moment."

He finally looks up from the gleaming silverware on the table. "Don't bother. We won't be dining this evening."

With a slight raise of his eyebrows the Maître d replies, "Of course sir, as you wish."

General Alejandro Quispe, descendant of royalty, one of the Belgian upper class and newest member of the advisory group to the World Health Organization's Influenza Vaccine Selection Committee sits at his table and observes the diners who surround him and their façade of opulence thinking, "These peasants have no idea what true wealth is."

The restaurant touts itself as home to Chicago's elite. White tablecloths and linen napkins adorn every table. The furnishings are made of fine cherry which complements the dark wood motif. Everything in the restaurant is top of the line, crystal glassware, fine silver and uniformed staff. General Quispe is unimpressed.

He has always hated coming to Chicago. In his opinion, it is a slum from one dreadful end to the other. He is also angered by the fact that he is being treated like nothing more than an errand boy. He arranges the silverware on the table and thinks, "This whole journey into the dark recesses of hell to meet with little more than a trained animal. It is simply beneath me."

He misses New York and plans to fly back right after this meeting and never return to this Midwestern shithole again. He is startled from these dark thoughts by the Maître d arriving at his right shoulder. "General, I am so very sorry. Please forgive my lack of memory. I did not realize that your favorite table was in the back of the dining room. I'm having the table prepared now. Whatever you order this evening will be taken care of by Cochon Ivre."

General Quispe looks up startled and then around the restaurant.

His eyes stop on a man in a nondescript gray suit standing by a table in the back. The man is smiling at him with the look a wolf might give an eviscerated jack rabbit. Quispe gives the Maître d a look of resignation and says curtly, "Of course. Thank you for accommodating me."

The Maître d replies as he leads the general to his new table, "Thank you for being so understanding sir."

As they arrive at the table, Horace MacGill puts out his hand and displays a perfect smile. Quispe notices the large incisors as he takes the hand he doesn't want to shake. Inside the hand is a flash drive. Quispe withdraws his hand and places the drive in his pocket as he looks at MacGill thinking, "Mercenaries. They come in all shapes and sizes with one thing in common. They are nothing more than animals working for the highest bidder."

Quispe has the overwhelming urge to wash his hands. After the two take their seats, the Maître d makes his exit. MacGill is already holding a tumbler of bourbon in front of him. Quispe looks at MacGill and says in a low tense voice, "Why the theatrics? What was wrong with the other table?"

MacGill smiles and says with a confident tone, "All about controlling my environment General. If we work together long enough, you'll learn that about me. I always control the environment."

Quispe raises his eyebrows and leans forward. "How many candidates on the drive?"

MacGill smiles a cagey smile. "Just one, General."

Quispe looks like he is going to jump out of his seat. "One. Just one? What if we don't like him?"

MacGill leans back in his chair. "It doesn't matter what you like General. He's the one they've picked. Trust me. He's the one. All the metrics say so. Now relax and have some supper."

MacGill leans forward and chuckles as he says, "It's on the house."

General Alejandro Quispe looks across the table at a ghost in human form and realizes that there is power easily seen and then there is power which is only felt.

Chapter One

The automated flagger assistance device stands like a sentinel at the edge of the construction zone on Fruitridge Avenue. So far, Konrad Pearce has watched the gates raise and lower four times allowing five vehicles at a time to enter the zone and exit. All the while, the construction crew stands by the white pickup truck with the flashing yellow lights consuming their morning coffee.

He feels a bead of sweat beginning its laborious journey from his temple to his neck where it will soak into his necktie, already feeling too tight. The air conditioning in his Subaru wagon is barely compensating for the sweltering Indiana heat. Konrad looks at the street department crew and wonders which idiot decided to block the street on a weekday at 8:00 am. He shakes his head and mutters under his breath, "Today of all days. Why did it have to be today?"

He looks in the rearview mirror at his reflection and the unusual three-day stubble that he didn't have the energy to get rid of this morning thinking, "What does it matter anyway."

Konrad looks at the watch Jennifer had given him on his birthday only a month ago. An Omega Speed Master which she spent too much on. Now he would die before parting with it. It was her last gift to him. As he looks at the watch his eyes blur with emotion, causing him to forget for a microsecond that he is going to be profoundly late for his first day back to work.

"Fuck. I've got to get a handle on this. People are depending on me."

With each rise and fall of the gate, his vehicle inches closer to the construction zone. Finally, it is his turn to move through the area. He looks at the red eye of the traffic arm, flashing in a rhythmic pattern. It is almost as if this thing is a living being, imposing its will on the line of traffic. Konrad wonders as he passes if the red eye is taunting him. He steps on the gas and moves through along with his group of five cars. As he moves past the laughing workers he thinks, "Assholes."

Then, he's on the other side and moving through the bumpy streets of Green River, Indiana toward Highway 43 and Emmer Pharmaceutical.

Once he turns onto the highway his mind wanders to Jennifer and Chloe. He'd been hired at Emmer right after graduating from Indiana University upon obtaining his bachelor's degree in neuroscience and met Jennifer shortly after. Marrying Jennifer just seemed like the next right choice. It wasn't long before Chloe was born and Konrad's life seemed to be heading toward perfect. Jennifer had held his hand as he fought his way through a doctorate program while working full time. Now, it seems it was for nothing. Konrad thinks, "Sixteen years. Sixteen years and now it's all gone. Jennifer's gone. Chloe's gone. My life is gone."

He thinks how some described their death as a senseless, random tragedy. Konrad doesn't believe in random. There is an order to the universe which he can only describe as an immense spider web with countless intersections and angles. In a microsecond he was bounced through those angles straight into hell. There was nothing random about the truck driver speeding down I-70 and running over his wife's car, killing Jennifer and Chloe. It was the simple fact that the truck driver had chosen to stay behind the wheel too many hours and that fact was the causative factor in their deaths. That driver made a conscious choice and there is nothing random in that. Konrad thinks of what his life was prior to meeting Jennifer. She had brought order to his life which he had always craved. Now all he has left is his research, the familiar order of science.

He snaps from his thoughts as his brain registers the gray metal cooling towers which are the pharmaceutical plant. Konrad decelerates at the last minute causing the driver of the white ford pickup following him too closely on the highway to blow his horn and quickly change lanes. The Subaru winds down the short drive to the fence and guard shack. An overweight guard steps out of the shack with a clipboard he shifts from his left hand to his right as he hitches his pants up. The guard looks at Konrad and smiles. "Hey Doc, glad to see you back."

The guard's expression becomes serious as he says, "Sorry for your loss Doc. Anything I can do, you let me know."

This is what Konrad has been dreading since the funeral. Countless expressions of sympathy that only make the hole in his chest widen. He looks at Harry with red rimmed eyes and replies, "Thanks Harry. I appreciate the sentiment."

Harry nods and steps back inside the shack where he presses a button and the large chain linked gate slides open. Konrad moves through the gate and finds his parking space near the entrance to his labs. He takes a deep breath and lets it out slowly thinking, "Okay. This is only day one. Just make it through this first day."

He checks his watch one more time before punching in his four-digit code and entering the research and development area. It is a short elevator ride to his team's offices on the second floor. The elevator doors open with a groan and Konrad gladly steps onto safe ground as he scans this place of familiarity. These people are like a second family to him and he is glad to be back and away from the tomb like quiet of his home. He looks to his right and sees Annie Rowan sitting at her desk intently staring at her computer screen. As the elevator doors close, she looks up. "Dr. Pearce, we weren't expecting you back so soon. Can I get you anything?"

Konrad just smiles and says, "No thank you Annie."

She stands hesitantly and then walks up to him giving a quick, awkward embrace. "We've missed you."

Then she quickly returns to her desk. Konrad has always liked Annie. She joined the team three years ago with a bachelor's degree from Indiana State University in biology. He'd recognized her intelligence from the first few minutes in the interview for the lab assistant position. Not something one would assume from this petite woman with her signature strawberry blonde ponytail and lab coat. When the interview was complete, he knew Annie was a diamond whose shine was hidden behind a natural shyness. She had been a member of the college swim team and had obtained her degree on a full athletic scholarship. Konrad walks the last few yards to his office at the end of the cubicles, unlocks the door and sinks into his leather chair thinking, "Okay, just take a minute and then see what's going on in the lab."

He closes his eyes. When he opens them, he finds Candace Swanson standing in the doorway looking at him with a concerned look. "We weren't expecting you back for at least another week. Konrad, are you sure you want to be here?"

A tall, athletic woman with midnight black hair, Candace came to the team seven years ago with a master's degree in virology from Colorado State University. Her passion for science had won her the coveted job at Emmer as his associate. He realizes that somewhere along the way, they have become friends.

"I can't stay in that empty house any longer. I'm going to drive myself crazy."

She moves into the office and closes the door, looking at him with tears in her eyes. "We're all heartbroken Konrad. Jennifer and Chloe were like family to us."

He looks down at the floor and replies, his voice thick, "Thank you Candace. I know they felt the same about you too."

He stands and looks around the office realizing how it lacks any personality. Jennifer always said that a man's office reflects his personality. Konrad judges himself in that moment to be strictly analytical, almost cold. It is a place befitting his position as the Director of Flu Vaccine Research and Development, Emmer Pharmaceuticals but he would trade it all for just a few more minutes with his wife and daughter. Candace moves forward and embraces Konrad, the sweet smell of lilac filling his nostrils. He is immediately embarrassed and asks, "How have things been going with UFV-39?"

Candace steps back slightly and replies, "I wish I could say it was good news but we're at least narrowing things down. We've stumbled on to something that might be an opportunity. Why don't you come and have a look?"

Konrad follows Candace from behind the desk and out of his office. Right before he exits the office, he thinks, "I should bring some pictures from home for the desk."

After a short walk down a nondescript corridor, they find themselves in front of the secure door leading to the laboratories. Both scan their key cards which not only allow access to the area but also automatically logs exactly who is entering the area. As they scan the cards, a two-tone chime announces the successful unlocking of the door. As Konrad pulls the door open, a robotic voice says, "Dr. Pearce and Research Associate Swanson verified."

On the other side of the door is a sterile anteroom painted glaringly white. The walls are white along with the benches and lockers. There are two porcelain sinks and an eyewash station directly across from the lockers. Two showers are positioned at the back of the room. At the end of the row of lockers stands a shelf. Protective smocks are neatly folded on the shelf and are replenished each day. Near the shelf is a large covered linen bin to hold used smocks before researchers leave the lab. Konrad looks at the area with new eyes and thinks, "It is an orderly system. Predictable. If only everything else in life were as orderly and predictable."

They quickly don the sterile smocks and step into the main laboratory. The large steel door shuts with a hissing sound and locks. The laboratory is not expansive, necessitating the prudent use of every available inch. To the right, several rows of shelving hold various forms of testing equipment and supplies all neatly arranged and labeled. To the left stands a secure chamber with a large viewing window and more research equipment. On the outside of the chamber right in front of the large window sits a desk with several computer monitors connected to the cameras and microscope inside the chamber. Konrad walks toward the desk and says to the slightly overweight kid in his wrinkled smock and shock of disheveled brown hair, "Jacob, how are things progressing?"

Startled, the young man swivels in his chair. "Doctor Pearce. We weren't expecting you back." Jacob clears several sheets of paper from the desk and one comic book. He looks back at Konrad with a sheepish expression.

Jacob Smith started at Emmer Pharmaceuticals as a laboratory assistant three years ago. Despite his appearance, Jacob is extremely methodical. Konrad thinks as he waits for Jacob to answer, "He'll probably be my boss one of these days."

Jacob looks at Candace. "We're setting the next set of dishes up now Ms. Swanson."

He turns to Konrad. "Things are going well sir. You're going to be very interested in what we've sort of stumbled on."

He then presses the microphone button and says, "Ben, the Doc and Ms. Swanson are here. How much time before we're ready?"

Ben Kotter looks up from his work at the window and waves. "Glad to have you back Doctor Pearce. We weren't expecting you."

Konrad presses the button. "Yes, I've gathered that. Are you ready for us to have a look?"

Ben Kotter joined the team at the same time as Jacob. A quiet young man with an almost introverted demeanor. His work is impeccable as far as Konrad is concerned. Ben is tall and athletic with a blonde crew cut and creases in his trousers. Ben and Jacob are as different in appearance as night and day. Their skills in the lab mirror each other's. As he watches his lab assistants prepare the experiment, he thinks, "I couldn't have put together a better team."

Candace steps up to the desk and presses the button, "Okay Ben, when you're ready, go ahead and start the first dish."

She looks at Konrad and says, "Emmer received the standard flu strains for this season's vaccine production while you were away. The usual H1N1 and H3N2. We also received a strain they're seeing in Austria that we've seen since 2021. We looked at these and found them to be quite unremarkable. Exposure to thermal sterilization simply made them inert. What was interesting is when we looked at the strain coming out of Phuket, Thailand. While high heat does disable this strain's ability to multiply, at temperatures ranging from 98.4 to 104 degrees Fahrenheit the virus seems to thrive. Totally out of the ordinary."

Konrad looks at the monitor attached to the microscope and says, "Okay Ben, introduce the specimen when you're ready."

As the trio watches the cellular display, the flu virus antigen attaches to the red blood cell in the Petri dish and begins the process of replication. Candace looks at Jacob. "Okay Jacob, turn up the thermostat."

Konrad watches as the temperature begins to rise in the room. As the temperature rises above 100 degrees, the activity in the dish begins to speed up. The virus replicates faster than any army of immune cells could keep pace with. The B and T cell lymphocytes are quickly over run and then they simply begin to ignore the infected blood cells. Konrad steps up and says, "Wait. What just happened? It can't have mutated that quickly."

Candace looks at Konrad and replies, "Take a close look at the protein spikes on the replicated virus. They're completely different. It's the heat. It shouldn't be acting like that, but it is. It's almost as if it's intelligent."

Konrad presses the microphone button. "Ben, run it again please."

They run the test twice more with the same results. Konrad has a sick feeling in his stomach. He thinks, "These samples are kept on ice until they get here. There's no way they could have known what they were sending us."

Candace sees the look on Konrad's face and says, "I know what you're thinking Konrad so hear me out. This is the perfect specimen for our universal flu vaccine research. If we can beat this one, it will put us years ahead. If you notify the CDC, they'll take the project away from us and send it to one of the big labs."

Konrad looks at Candace in disbelief and replies, "You're not suggesting we sit on this?"

Candace touches Konrad on the shoulder. "Let's go to your office so we can talk."

Konrad looks at Jacob. "Send me the numbers from what we just did and clean up. I want to look at this more closely." Jacob nods his head and says, "Okay Doc. It'll be in your mailbox before you can get to your office."

Konrad and Candace leave the lab together without speaking. They remove the smocks in the anteroom and then head to his office.

Konrad is in deep thought as they make their way down the short hallway. "As aggressive as the antigen drift is on this virus, if it starts to spread, it could kill millions. A fever is a normal reaction to a virus. It's what the body uses to fight the infection but with this strain, a fever will only make the infection worse. What is she thinking?"

They both enter Konrad's office in silence. Konrad walks around his desk and sits down with a heavy sigh. In truth, he knows Candace is right about the research being taken away from him. He has published a few papers in obscure scientific journals regarding the feasibility of a universal flu vaccine, but a project like this would most assuredly go to a larger company. Someone with the resources and personnel to tackle the project, and more importantly, someone famous enough to sell the idea to the public. He thinks about the last ten years of his life. He's devoted so much time to developing this vaccine. So many hours away from Jennifer and Chloe he'll never get back and can now never make up for. He realizes the research is all he has left. It is the only reason he has to exist. Konrad looks at Candace, his friend, and realizes she is the only one he could trust with a gamble of this magnitude. Candace looks into his eyes, and he knows she sees the indecision.

Candace, sitting on the arm of the loveseat shrugs her shoulders and says, "Konrad, we've worked too hard just to have this taken away without even trying."

Konrad looks up from the floor. "Candace, right now this strain is spreading in Thailand. We don't even know what the infection rate is. This could be a brush fire in the making. Don't you see that this rises above professional misconduct? We must notify the CDC of what we've got."

She stands and walks toward the desk. "And then what Konrad? You and I have been neck deep in this research for seven years together. I've put any personal life I might have had on hold. How many hours did you sacrifice at the expense of your family? Just to have it taken away? For someone else to step in and piggyback on our work? Jennifer once told me that you were the most driven man she had ever met. This research was an obsession. Where is that man now? I'm sorry but I think this is worth the gamble."

Konrad follows her with his eyes as she moves around the desk and puts her hand on his shoulder, saying in a softer tone, "Konrad, you are one of my dearest friends and I know this is a lot to swallow with what you're going through but, we can actually make a difference here. Ask yourself, what would Jennifer want you to do?"

Konrad stares at Candace and says, his voice tight, "What would

Jennifer have me do? What would she have me do? She wouldn't have me do anything."

His voice breaks. "Jennifer is dead. She was killed by some asshole that's lucky he died in the accident as well. Don't fucking bring Jennifer into this?"

Candace walks back around the desk and toward the door. She stops in the doorway and says without turning, "Just sleep on it Konrad. Twenty-four hours isn't going to make a difference. We can at least determine what makes this particular virus tick and then go to the CDC with a full report."

She turns and looks at Konrad quizzically. "Have you heard any reports from anyone in the scientific community about massive deaths or infections in Thailand?"

Konrad remains silent. Candace says as she turns to leave, "I haven't either."

Konrad arrives at work the next day to find Harry standing his post at the gate. He opens the gate as Konrad approaches, waving as he drives through. After a long night in a house that ceased to be his home the second he'd lost his family, Konrad is anxious to get back to his work in the lab. Although he hasn't slept, he feels energized at the prospect of tackling this new challenge the flu virus has dropped in his lap. He thinks as he steps off the elevator, "There is nothing random. I'm meant to do this. It's all about angles and intersections."

He'd spent the night with a bottle of white wine, Jennifer's favorite, as he searched his soul for the right thing to do. In the end, he'd bargained with himself into thinking a delay in the reporting was justified for the science, his science. After ten years and thirty-eight attempts with nothing to show for it but thirty-eight failures, he can't quit now. The mental strain of always getting close but never achieving sterile immunity because the damn virus mutates so effectively has taken a toll. This new sample may hold the key to beating them all and that is why he must at least look at it thoroughly.

He walks past the empty cubicles and sees Candace in her office. "Where is everyone?"

Candace comes around from behind her desk with a smile and stops in the doorway to her office, folding her arms as she leans against the frame. "They're in the lab. What have you decided?"

Konrad motions with his head as he says, "Let's head back. I want to speak with everyone at the same time."

They walk down the hallway without speaking. As they enter the lab,

Ben, Annie and Jacob look up from the paperwork they're studying as they stand around the desk. As Konrad and Candace move toward the desk, he can see the question in all of their eyes. "I've decided we're going to single out this strain for a small, limited rodent study. I want to start with the UFV-39 vaccine. I also want to find out everything we can regarding the method of action, right down to the genome and what exactly we're looking at. Let's map it and see what we can come up with. We'll give it thirty days. That's all. I'd like to know what everyone thinks. We're a team so with this, everyone can express their opinion."

They all nod and are smiling. Jacob says, "We're with you Doc."

Konrad looks at all of them, one after the other. "Okay. Everything we're doing from this point forward doesn't leave the lab. I guess that I don't need to say it but what we're getting ready to do is filled with potential liability, for all of us. Does everyone understand?"

Konrad rubs his hands together, "Okay, let's get things going. The clock is ticking."

The lab assistants move away from the desk to set up the process for obtaining the genetic instructions for the virus strain. Konrad looks at Candace and says quietly, "Let's head back up front. There are some things we need to discuss."

Back in Konrad's office, Candace assumes her usual place on the loveseat and Konrad stands in front of his desk. She looks up at him, eyebrows raised in a question. "What did you want to discuss?"

Konrad crosses his arms and says, "I want you to get in touch with the hospitals in Phuket. Identify yourself and say that your inquiry is just routine monitoring of the flu strains we're vaccinating against this year. Ask them to contact you if there's a spike in cases. If it looks like this thing is spreading rapidly, I'm going to pull the plug."

Candace sighs deeply. "Okay Konrad. I'll keep you updated. Anything else?"

Konrad replies, "No, I guess that's it for now. Hopefully, we can make some kind of progress."

Candace rises and leaves him to his thoughts. Konrad looks around his office and thinks, "What am I doing? There's a good chance this is all going to blow up in our faces."

He wonders what his wife would say about all this. Konrad misses her counsel and her level head. She was the counterweight that kept him on an even keel. Without her, he's a crippled boat limping along in unfriendly seas. He thinks about life and death as he mutters under his breath, "It's all so inevitable."

Chapter Two

Warren Densin sits at the bar in his downtown Atlanta condominium and looks at the calendar on his telephone. When he'd been promoted into the position of Mid-Atlantic Pharmaceutical Communications Liaison for the CDC, he hadn't realized what a never-ending treadmill he would be running on. Days filled with telephone call after endless telephone call, tracking down answers that he doesn't understand half the time for scientists who look on him as just another mid-level errand boy.

In truth, he has as much contempt for them as they for him. Maybe more. Whatever he has to put up with from these egomaniacs in white lab coats, it's worth it. His paycheck isn't anything to brag about, but the position has proven to open the doors for side opportunities. Even if the people offering those opportunities, whoever they are, scare the shit out of him. He thinks, "Better to eat the carrot than feel the stick."

He looks at his watch and jumps up from the barstool partially spilling the bowl of soggy cereal that sits in front of him as he says, "Shit, I can't be late again. I'll clean it up when I get home."

He grabs his suit jacket still in plastic and heads for the door. He stops and takes one more look in the mirror located in his exercise area before heading through the door and locking it behind him. Warren isn't an athlete by any means. At one hundred and forty pounds, his five-foot six-inch frame wasn't meant to impress at the beach. The round glasses and mousse laden hair are more suited to pick up women at the library looking for the sensitive type. Warren doesn't have much luck at the library either. Being shallow doesn't allow one to be too sensitive. A short elevator ride later and he's in his black Prius navigating the downtown traffic of Atlanta Georgia. He'll never understand why they put the CDC here of all places. The traffic is a nightmare.

A brutal thirty-minute drive in the Georgia heat and Warren pulls under the building into the cool darkness of the employee parking. He pulls into his numbered parking space, jumps from his car and runs for the elevator thinking, "Made it again. Warren, you are a stud."

As the elevator rises from sub-level two to the second floor where his cubicle is located, Warren hums along with the elevator music, butchering the song completely. As he steps out on the second floor into an expansive room of slightly larger than normal cubicles, he sees Sandra, his office crush sitting at her desk with her high heels neatly positioned next to the leg of the desk and her bare feet tapping the carpeted floor. Warren hooks his thumb under the hangar, his jacket is draped over and swings it over his shoulder like he's seen the models in men's fashion magazines do. After he's sure the proper image is being presented, Warren walks over to her cubicle thinking, "I wonder what color panties she's wearing today."

Sandra looks up as he arrives at her desk with his gleaming smile and says, "Hey Sandra, want to grab some lunch or something in a little while?"

She smiles a weary smile and replies, "Warren, the answer hasn't changed from the last dozen times you've asked me. I'm seeing someone. He's tall, athletic and he outweighs you by fifty pounds. Are you suicidal or something?"

Warren shrugs off the rebuff and leans in whispering, "Relationships are just like Vegas blackjack Sandra. If you're careful, you can cheat at both."

Sandra just shakes her head in response. Warren finally taking the hint, at least for today, smiles and says whimsically as he turns to walk away, "Think about it. You don't know what you're missing."

He arrives at his cubicle to the ringing of the telephone on his desk. Hanging his jacket on a hook by the door, Warren picks up the phone saying, "CDC Atlanta, Communications Liaison Office, this is Warren."

The voice on the other end of the line oozes from the receiver like warm honey as Warren feels a loosening in his bladder. "Good morning, Warren. You were almost late again. Tsk, tsk my young friend."

Warren sits down in his chair nervously and looks around before replying in a whisper, "Um, good morning. How can I help you?"

The voice chuckles as it replies, "That's the spirit Warren. Have you received any messages from our friends at Emmer?"

Warren begins looking through the stack of messages on his desk. "I don't see anything."

The voice replies, "Good Warren. Good. You'll make sure and call the number I gave you if you do, right Warren?"

He unconsciously nods into the receiver trying to find his voice. "Oh yes. Yes, I will. You can count on me."

As he looks at the receiver his mind tries to decipher the eerie silence as his bladder spasms. Finally, the voice replies, "Oh, I know I can count on you Warren. That's why I chose you. I just want you to remember that when you accepted the money, you bought a ticket for the whole ride. I need you in your current position, so straighten up Warren. Get to work on time and Warren, leave Sandra alone. We wouldn't want her to become a liability now would we, Warren?"

The line disconnects but Warren's mind doesn't immediately register the termination of the connection. When he puts the telephone back in its cradle, his hand is trembling, and he has the sudden urgent need to urinate. He heads to the bathroom, steps into a stall and vomits the cereal he'd eaten for breakfast in the toilet. Warren is sweating profusely and realizes he is having a panic attack. He thinks as he uses the deep breathing exercises his therapist taught him, "Calm down. Relax. Breath and for God's sake don't pass out."

He exits the stall and steps to a urinal on shaky legs. When he's finished, he steps to the sink and splashes cold water on to his face, looking into the mirror thinking for the hundredth time, "Who is this guy?"

As he steps from the restroom and heads back down the hall toward his cubicle, he passes Sandra going toward the restrooms. She smiles and pointing says, "You forgot something Warren."

He looks down and mumbles, "Oh. Thank you."

Warren doesn't look back up as he zips his fly and steps past her, not noticing the look of puzzlement on her face. He reaches his cubicle and sits down in his chair, exhausted, thinking back to the unpleasant memory of meeting the man that the voice belonged too.

It was six months ago, and Warren was out having a drink to celebrate his new promotion. The bar was quiet, which was not unusual for a Wednesday night. He was having his usual drink, an expresso martini with extra coffee beans on top. It was his fourth and last. Warren figured he shouldn't overdo the lonely celebration with a fifth. He finished his drink, wiped the frothy mustache from his upper lip, paid for his tab and then headed for the bathroom to urinate before leaving. While he was standing in front of the urinal, a man in a gray suit stepped up to the urinal next to him. As the man unzipped his fly he said, "Good evening, Warren. I have a proposition for you."

Startled, Warren looked over at the man and what he saw made the hair on the back of his neck stand up. The man's voice almost hissed like a snake with honey on its tongue. His eyes were reptilian with the coldness of a gravestone. His face was unremarkable, lacking any distinguishable characteristics. Warren found his voice and said, "I don't know who you are, but I don't fly that way. Not interested."

Warren zipped his fly and turned to walk past the man as the man turned and stepped in front of him. This caused Warren to size the man up and what he saw put him on the losing end of a physical confrontation. There was something in the way the man stood and looked at him. It was the look a hyena might give a dying antelope. The man was wearing a slight grin but like the hyena, there was no mercy in it. Warren looked up at the man and said, his voice quivering, "You'll need to find another date, now can I get past?"

The man snickered as he said, "Warren I'm not looking for a date. You're going to help me with something much more fun. Now before you run off, I want you to look at your phone and tell me what's in the download file. Go ahead, I'll wait."

The man's self-assurance scared Warren causing him to involuntarily reach for his cell phone. What he found on his telephone were hundreds of pictures of naked children. Warren gasped and managed to sputter, "I didn't, I, what the fuck! Who are you?"

The man smiled and looked at Warren with those cold eyes. "Who I am doesn't matter Warren. Now that you know what I'm capable of, let's go out and have a nice quiet conversation. I'll buy you another martini to calm your nerves."

Warren followed the man to a table in the back of the bar and sat down tensely as his tormentor motioned to the waitress. As the man sat down, Warren leaned forward and started to speak but the man put his finger up and smiled signaling Warren to wait. The waitress walked over to the table and the man ordered, "I'll have bourbon as it comes. My friend here will have an expresso martini, extra beans."

Then the man looked at Warren as the waitress left and smiled. "Okay Warren, you must have a thousand questions rolling around underneath that meticulously styled hair of yours, but I want you to squash all of that curiosity. I'll talk and you listen."

That's when Warren got angry and had risen to leave. That is when he realized what his position in the conversation was. Warren said as he rose, "No, I think I'll just walk and by the way, fuck you."

The man just smiled and grabbed Warren's forearm in a vise like grip. "Sit down you little pedophile."

Warren broke in, "I'm no pedophile. You did that somehow. I didn't download that crap."

The man told him to calm down and had threatened to tell the FBI what was on his telephone. He'd even guaranteed that they would get a copy of Warren's phone records. That is when Warren sat back in the chair and listened as the man had outlined what he would have no choice in doing. The drinks arrived and the man smiled his snake like smile as he said, "Warren, we're interested in any communications from Emmer Pharmaceuticals to the CDC. All you must do is notify us if they contact you. We'll decide if you forward the message to your supervisors, or we may alter the message a little bit before you forward it. Either way, you contact us first before you do anything. In return, you'll start getting an envelope each week with adequate compensation for your help. Do it not and I guarantee you they'll pull a train on your ass every night in the federal penitentiary you sick little pervert."

With the last statement, the man chuckled. He'd given Warren a plain white business card with a telephone number. As the man rose from his seat, he looked down at Warren. "We'll be watching Warren. Enjoy your martini."

With that the man moved toward the door like a wisp of smoke, without anyone even noticing as he passed.

Now as Warren sits at his desk he chews on the cuticle of his thumb and wonders what he's been dragged into. Whatever it is, he knows it's not good. He feels like a mouse trapped in a maze in which his route is controlled by electric shocks. He knows the only thing he can do for now is go the opposite direction of the pain. For the rest of the day Warren goes about his regular duties tracking down answers for the pharmaceutical companies under his area of responsibility. By the end of the day, he's feeling much better and even manages to plan where he'll eat supper. He thinks, "Maybe I'll have Italian tonight."

He looks at his computer screen and sees that it is quarter past five so he notates where he is on his to do lists and shuts the monitor down. As Warren stands from his desk, he fleetingly thinks of asking Sandra out to dinner but dismisses the thought almost immediately. Something in the way the voice had said, "liability" won't allow Warren to approach her again. After all, he's not a total asshole.

He grabs his jacket and makes his way through the cubicles toward the elevator. As he passes Sandra's cube, he hears her call after him, "Have a nice evening, Warren."

He half turns and keeps walking as he says, "Yeah, you too."

When Warren reaches the lower parking level, he looks around the garage before exiting the elevator. He's being watched and he knows it.

This makes him picture the mouse in the maze again. He has so many questions. "Why did they pick him and what is going on at Emmer Pharmaceutical that interests whoever 'they' are?"

Warren isn't a fool and would never actually ask the questions. Somehow, he thinks that would end badly for him. "They" are people he doesn't want to anger. He climbs into the Prius and backs out of his parking spot to begin the trip home through the insane traffic. As he pulls into his parking spot at the condo, he breathes a sigh of relief, exits the car and makes his way to the elevator. He decides to order in tonight and have it delivered. Today was just too stressful. Warren scrolls through the contacts on his telephone and settles on The Pasta Palace and orders an Italian sub with pasta and a cannoli. He sits down on the couch, grabs the television remote and says to no one in particular, "Now, what to watch while I wait on my food."

In less than thirty minutes, Warren hears a knock at his door.

He smiles, moves to the door and opens it to find a Palace bag sitting on the floor with no delivery person in sight. He closes the door and places the bag on the counter, removing the contents. There is a small envelope included with his meal. Warren looks around the room and then opens the envelope. Inside there are five coffee beans.

Chapter Three

Horace MacGill sits at the empty conference table in the basement of the Arlington high rise known as Trojan 34. This is one of the few places that he knows beyond a doubt, it is safe enough for him to close his eyes and he does so gratefully. The organization with its many tentacles has hundreds of these places of safety across the country for men just like him. The shepherds who move the masses of sheep to the places where the real owners of the earth want them to be, doing what they're supposed to do.

He relaxes his shoulders and enjoys the cool blackness of oblivion which is only enhanced by the darkened room surrounding him. The table is mahogany with a deep wood grain you can almost feel with your eyes. It is much larger than it needs to be but to the providers of the furnishings, excess is a way of life. Horace is positioned at the head of the table facing a video uplink, encrypted a thousand times when activated. His chair is soft Italian leather which wraps itself around him like a high dollar call girl. The room is secured with a steel door deep underground. This worldwide meeting will be completely and utterly private.

As his mind drifts, Horace thinks back to thousands of moments which brought him to this exact place at this exact time. He was an idealist as a young man and had joined the Marine Corps as soon as he was old enough to sign the papers. He had learned early on that he was forgettable. This would be an asset in later years but at the time, it proved to be a painful awakening. When he'd told his parents that he'd joined, they didn't seem to notice or care. As tenured professors at Georgetown University, they were educated and refined. Horace was a dull emotionless child who did not fit into their world of intellectual snobbery. In truth, they'd forgotten him the day he was born. Then came the six combat tours all over the sandbox as a reconnaissance sniper which led him and his special skills to more lucrative assignments with the alphabet agencies. He made a name for himself because of his lack of remorse or mercy. Horace thinks as his consciousness floats, "It was all for the good old USA back then. What a fucking chump I was."

After enough blood was spilled, Horace was called to serve the real masters of the earth. They are the ones who turn the planet from behind a veil so thickened with layers they'll never be caught holding the knife. He chuckles and says to no one in particular, "Neither will I."

Horace knows the secret now. This is something that can never be taken back. Countries, borders, flags are all just holding pens for the masses. They are someplace for the sheep to feel comfortable in their self-identification. What he fought and bled for all those years was a myth, but his eyes have been opened now and he sees the blinding light of truth. The masses of the world are just sheep to be herded and used for the landowner's discretion. Some were born to be used for profit and some for the slaughterhouse. That's the cold hard truth.

He has been working on his part of this particular project for two years. Horace thinks, "Two long years of putting every chess piece into place and then replacing some when they forgot that the carrot was just a gift, and the stick was always there. Liabilities can never be tolerated."

The video feed hums to life pulling Horace from his thoughts. He hears someone clear their throat and knows that the meeting has started. "I suppose ladies and gentlemen that we should have a roll call to make sure everyone is in attendance. I'll start. Horace MacGill.

The voices begin to follow, "North American Region."

"South American Region."

"North Africa."

"South Africa."

"Asia Major."

"Asia Minor."

"Atlanto-Antarctica."

"Pacifico-Antarctica."

"Australia."

"Europe."

Horace clears his throat and says, "Good. That appears to be all ten regions of the globe. Thank you all for attending. I've prepared an operational briefing outlining our progress thus far. As you all know, preparatory work for the launch has been painstakingly cached for each stage of the operation. Launch for phase one of the operation was initiated two weeks ago."

Horace looks down at the desk as if in deep thought. "Unforeseen events necessitated a slight alteration in the plan, but we're back on track."

A female voice belonging to the North American Regent says with a heavy northern accent, "Unforeseen events? It has been my experience that those do not exist in your operations, Mr. MacGill."

Horace shifts in his seat slightly and replies, "Madam, plans are made for all contingencies but the principal's family dying suddenly can be termed as unforeseen. I was going to use them as a coercive tool, but I have already pivoted in that strategy."

The North American Regent continues to press MacGill. "Would you like to share this new strategy Mr. MacGill?"

Horace smiles slightly, "That strategy is developing at the present with several variables, all mapped. I assure you, I have everything under control. May I continue?"

The silence gives him his answer. Horace continues, "I have pawns at information choke points with the CDC and the World Health Organization as well as inside the principal's research operation. More pawns are being developed for future stages to cover all angles."

An Australian accented voice interrupts, "Shouldn't you have had those assets in place already?"

Horace feels his ears warm and thinks, "Keep your head man. These entitled assholes have no idea what it takes to put something as elegant as this is together."

He takes a deep breath and replies, "Sir, as the Australian Regent is fully aware, every operation, especially one of this magnitude is extremely fluid and requires ongoing development."

The male voice replies with a "Humph."

Horace begins again, "The sample is in play and with the release of the proper catalyst our principal's response should follow the predicted path to a positive outcome."

A sultry female voice belonging to the Regent from Asia Minor interrupts, "Horace, what if the principal proves to be unpredictable?"

Horace looks into the camera and says, "Those variables have been planned for. I feel the need to remind everyone that the target package I prepared and presented at our last meeting contained the psychological aspects of this man and predicted behaviors. He'll follow the script one way or the other. I guarantee it. I was under the impression from our last meeting that everyone was in agreement on the choice. Was I mistaken?"

His inquiry is met with silence. The sultry voice continues, "Does your plan include significant collateral damage Horace?"

Horace shakes his head, "Madam, at the present I don't see a plus in that although that option is not off the table. The primary goal in each stage of the operation is designed to achieve the greatest results with the lowest profile and exposure thereby obtaining the requested outcome. Mass collateral damage would only complicate things."

The Regent from Asia Minor replies, "I see. As usual Horace, you seem to have thought of everything."

Horace concludes his presentation. "Phase two begins in two weeks. I have the next set of assets ready to move into place at that time. Are there any other questions?"

His question is met with only silence. "Well, ladies and gentlemen, I'll bid you good evening. Again, I want to assure you that you've placed your trust in the right man."

With that, the video feed terminates. Horace sits back in the chair and relaxes into the leather one more time. His is a Spartan life where creature comforts are few. The few are enjoyed to full measure. He closes his eyes once more and considers the condescending manner in which the regents had spoken to him. This consideration evokes the memory of his parents when he was growing up. Horace had never quite measured up to their expectations. It was just easier for them to simply ignore the fact that he existed. Enlisting had been his final "fuck you" to them and their so-called superiority. He briefly wonders what they would think of him now and then just as quickly thinks, "Who gives a shit. Neither one of them thinks anything anymore. Death has a way of evening those things out."

He stands wearily from the chair and moves to a fireproof safe in the corner of the room where he expertly turns the combination and opens the drawer marked pending. Horace instinctively looks around the room and deposits the current brief in the drawer, closes it and spins the lock. He steps to the door, taking one more look around the room before exiting, closes it and punches the ten-digit code into the keypad hearing the large mechanical deadbolts move into place. Outside the safe zone, Horace is again in the world and therefore, hostile territory.

He moves down the darkened corridor, his footfalls a whisper as he passes the mechanical equipment in the bowels of the building. As he reaches the service elevator, he takes one quick look around and enters the elevator, punching the button for the second floor. As Horace exits on the second floor, he casually scans left and right then turns left and proceeds to the public elevator and pushes the button for the main floor of the building.

As the elevator begins to descend Horace realizes something is gnawing at his psyche. The regents had come close to unbalancing him. Had they deliberately tried to attack his efforts so far as a test or was it their natural tendency to be assholes? Horace thinks as he exits on the main floor, "Never forget Horace, you are expendable."

As he reaches his BMW, Horace pulls an encrypted satellite telephone from the glove compartment and dials a local number. The call is picked up in three rings by a man with a Pakistani accent. "Hello?"

Horace answers, "Hello Balil. Do you know who this is?"

Balil hesitates and then replies, "Yes. Yes, I do."

Horace smiles, "Good Balil. It's been a while. How is your mother? Is she still enjoying her home in Karachi?"

Balil's breath catches in his throat then he regains his voice and answers in a whisper, "My mother is very well, thank you. I am very thankful for your generosity. What can I do for you?"

Horace knows that this fish is still firmly on the hook, but it never hurts to remind an asset of both the carrot and the stick. "Balil, you'll be receiving a telephone call in approximately one week from an old friend of yours. You'll remember her when she calls. I want you to have a suitcase packed Balil and to be ready to leave at a moment's notice when you get the call. There is going to be a need for your special skills and the special things that you've developed. I believe you might have shared this secret with a certain someone at a conference you recently attended in Chicago."

Balil thinks back to the conference he'd attended in Chicago a month ago on the future of biological engineering. It was just one night but he'd felt so safe and comfortable with her. She was a friend from college. Someone to reconnect those days to the present and the sex was amazing. Before he knew what he was doing, he'd shared his secret, to impress her or maybe just simply to share it. Now, he really doesn't know why but once the words went forth, they couldn't be taken back. She was the only person he'd shared the breakthrough with. There were still experiments to be completed and papers to write, patents to be obtained and his fortune to be made.

By the time he'd returned to Arlington, the voice on the telephone was waiting for him with a simple choice. Provide a favor at some point in the near future and his mother would live comfortably in her new home in Karachi or be motherless. It was a choice that wasn't a choice at all. He breaks from his thoughts to the sound of the man's voice. "Balil? Are you listening to me? Do you have the special bots that I requested?"

Balil answers slowly, "Yes."

He can almost hear the man's smile over the telephone. "Good Balil. You'll let me know when she calls. Don't let me down Balil, your mother is depending on you."

Balil is silent for a full ten seconds then replies in a whisper, "Of course. I will do as you say. I'll be ready."

Horace disconnects the call and starts his BMW, immediately backing the vehicle out of the parking space and heading for the street. He accelerates into traffic, traversing the roads he knows like the back of his hand on the way to his agency apartment on Randolph Street. Arlington is his base of operations, but Horace never sets down roots in any one place. That's the nature of his existence. He thinks as he drives, "I can be gone in thirty seconds if I need to be."

He shakes his head as he pulls into the apartment complex parking area and thinks, "The glamorous life of a spook."

Horace sits in the driver's seat for a minute and visualizes the next set of angles. He'll need a small leak to get the news media involved but an insulated one. It has to be something subtle but with enough shine to catch the eye of the buzzards in the mainstream media. A scoop which looks hidden but really isn't. He knows just the pawn to cast the fly into the water. He reaches into the glove box and retrieves the satellite telephone, exits his vehicle and heads for his apartment on the tenth floor.

Horace enters through the front and takes the stairs to the third floor. Once there, he walks to the elevator and rides the rest of the way to the tenth. Exiting the elevator, he turns left and walks straight to his apartment, entering without turning the lights on. It is his practice to string a piece of dental floss across the entry hall and the hall to the bedroom at ankle height. Horace checks that these are still in place and knows that there have been no unwanted visitors in his absence. He pours himself a glass of bourbon and sits down on the couch with a sigh, pulls the telephone from his pocket and dials.

The call is answered after two rings by a meek male voice, "Hello?"

Horace smiles, saying, "Warren, do you know who this is?"

The sounds of laughter and clinking glasses can be heard in the background. Warren says, "Yes, I know who this is."

As Warren answers, he feels the familiar feeling of his bladder beginning to spasm. Horace replies, "Warren, I need a favor, and I need you to focus. How many expresso martinis have you had and don't lie, I'll know."

Warren answers, his voice tight, "Two. I swear just two."

Horace grins into the telephone. "I believe you Warren. Now, will you do me that favor?"

The reply is swift, almost pleading. "Yes, of course. I'll do whatever you need."

Horace nods his head and says, "Good Warren. I knew I could count on you. I need you to pretend you're an unidentified source in the CDC for the media. Can you do that Warren? Just leak a little information to someone you know who reports the news?"

Warren looks at his cell phone in disbelief as he stammers, "I don't know anyone in the news media. I mean, please believe me I really will do whatever you say but I don't know how I can do this."

Horace responds softly, "Now Warren, tsk, tsk. What about your friend who has the social media channel? Doesn't he like to report the news?"

Warren chuckles and then coughs. "Who? Leonard? He's just an internet hack. I mean, he has a respectable following but he's not WSV News."

Horace intentionally allows a pause before he answers, "Warren, you're either an asset or you're a liability to me. Which are you, Warren?"

Warren answers quickly, "I'm an asset. No question."

Horace replies, "Good Warren. Invite Leonard out for a martini. Tell him unofficially that the CDC has been tracking a virulent influenza virus in Thailand, and it won't be long before we see it in the United States. Tell him the CDC is gearing up for a big flu season and brainstorming on how to get everyone to take the flu vaccine this year. Make sure you emphasize how hot this information is. He must let you remain anonymous. That's it Warren. That's the whole favor. I'll add something extra for you in your envelope this month and you'll have proven yourself an asset. Goodbye Warren. Don't let me down."

Horace disconnects the call and takes a swig of the bourbon. He looks out the balcony window and thinks, "Now, if that little pedophile does what he's supposed too, stage two will start without any effort on my part at all."

Any direct contact with the news media is out of the question for Horace. He strokes his chin and stairs off into space thinking, "News people are too unpredictable. You get the wrong crusader and then you start piling up bodies. That doesn't help anyone. No, this way is better. More insulation and a social media hack will be easy to eliminate if he doesn't follow the program. Warren had better be convincing."

Chapter Four

Warren sits at his desk in the all too familiar cubicle that has become his prison. He stares at the telephone, willing it to ring because he needs more than anything for it to ring. He'd called earlier in the day and left his friend, Leonard Weinzcuff a message inviting him out for a drink this evening. Hopefully his friend will return the call otherwise Warren runs the risk of moving from the asset column to the liability column in the ledger of what he knows to be his survival. Every time he thinks about the telephone calls from the number, his bladder spasms like he's some little girl who can't hold her water. Warren looks at his watch and sees that it is 4:00 p.m. He stares at the telephone, the constant office chatter just a murmur in the background. His armpits are moist, and he knows for sure, the sweat stains on his white cotton dress shirt are going to be noticeable.

Through his mental fog, Warren comes to the realization that someone is standing in his cubicle doorway. He turns to see Sandra standing with her arms folded and one beautiful hip leaning against the cubicle partition. She's wearing his favorite dress. It is dark blue; form fitting and accentuates the curve of her perfect breasts. She's so close that he can smell her perfume. Usually, this would cause a rise but today his mind is consumed with other things besides the beautiful Sandra. She smiles and says, "Wow, what are you so focused on Warren? I said your name twice and you didn't even flinch."

Warren looks at the telephone and then back at Sandra. "I've just got a lot on my plate right now. I'm kind of stressed. What can I do for you Sandra?"

Sandra raises an eyebrow and smiles saying, "You haven't stopped by my cube for a few days. Did you know that my boyfriend and I are quits? I thought maybe you'd like to take me to dinner this evening."

Warren stares at her incredulously. Of all the times for her to warm the cold shoulder she's been clubbing him with for the last six months. He thinks, "I truly have sunk into the depths of hell."

He looks at her with an apologetic look. "Sandra, I've got something really important going on tonight. You have no idea how much I hate to say no but, I really can't get out of this. Can I have a rain check?"

She raises her eyebrows and purses her lips while shrugging her shoulders. "Sure. Stop by anytime. You know where I am."

With that she walks away. Warren looks back down at the telephone and thinks, "Fuck, fuck, fuck! Ring you bastard."

When it does Warren almost falls backward in his chair. He lunges for his cell phone, picking it up off his desk like a short stop scooping a grounder off the grass. "Leonard, where have you been man?"

Leonard Weinzcuff laughs into the telephone as he says, "Warren, what are you doing? You're breathing like you're on a treadmill or something. Take a breath, little man, I just got your message."

Warren leans back in his chair and closes his eyes trying to calm himself. "Listen amigo, I need a drink and someone to talk too. Are you free tonight?"

Leonard replies, "Hmmm, yeah. For you I'm always free Warren. Hey, how's Sandra looking today?"

Warren looks toward Sandra's cubicle and thinks, "Nothing like pouring salt into a wound Leonard."

He turns his back to the cubicle opening and whispers, "Delicious. Now where do you want to meet?"

Leonard laughs and says, "Man, you do sound like you need a drink. How about the Rusty Horseshoe over in Buckhorn at seven?"

Warren nods his head and says, "Okay, see you then."

The call disconnects and Warren puts the telephone down on his desk. He holds his hand up in front of his face. It is shaking. He has a sudden urge to urinate and heads into the bathroom. Once finished, Warren splashes cold water on his face and looks into the mirror saying quietly, "It will be okay. It's just a little lie. What harm can come from a little lie to my friend? I have no choice. No choice at all."

He wipes the water from his face with a paper towel and heads back to his desk to finish up for the day. Once he gets to a stopping point, Warren logs off his computer and leaves without slowing at Sandra's cubicle. Before the elevator doors open, she is standing beside him. They enter the elevator together and as the doors close, she moves closer to him. Her perfume is intoxicating. He's never been this close to her before. She turns to face him, her breasts rising and falling directly in front of his chin. "Warren, I think I'd like to try it with you. I'm tired of the guys I've been dating. Gym rats can be so shallow. I know you can't make it tonight but let's do something soon. You won't regret it."

Then she bends down and kisses him on the mouth. It is a long, lingering kiss full of promise. Warren feels lightheaded but manages to sputter, "Yes, I'd like that."

The doors open and she walks toward her car as he watches her from his place just outside the elevator. She looks over her shoulder once giving him a smile that melts flesh and bone.

Warren watches her drive out of the garage and then makes his way through the Atlanta traffic to his condominium. He rushes in, takes a quick shower then once dressed runs back out the door and heads across town to Buckhorn and The Rusty Horseshoe. He makes it to the bar fifteen minutes early and enters through a heavy wooden door with a metal horseshoe nailed at eye level.

The horseshoe is upside down which strikes Warren as being unlucky. As he enters, the smell of cigar smoke mingled with the heavy odor of hard liquor strikes his nostrils. He waits by the door as his eyes adjust to the dim lighting. Once his eyes have adjusted, he sees the heavy wooden bar with its red vinyl padded rail and scarred stools worn down from thousands of patrons sitting in them over the years. There are a few early birds sitting at the bar and a few people sitting in the booths to his right sucking on barbecue chicken wings and ribs.

The waitress is already busy and doesn't notice him as she moves to the booths to provide more drinks. Warren moves through the tables and chairs and takes a seat at the end of the bar closest to the back wall of the room. As he takes his seat the bartender, an overweight man with an apron around his waist and a cigar hanging from the corner of a mouth, permanently frozen in a mocking sneer gives him a nod. Warren looks around and then says, too loudly, "Can I get an expresso martini with extra beans?"

The bartender chuckles and shakes his head, motioning to a board with several drinks written on it. "Just what you see on the menu 'Mr. Bond'. Would you like that shaken or stirred?"

Then he laughs and continues wiping down the bar. Warren feels the heat rush to his face and then says, "Okay, I'd like a screwdriver."

The bartender stops wiping the bar and says, "Of course you would."

Chuckling, he begins making the drink. Warren looks toward the door and sees Leonard enter, dragging his loafers across the floor so they make an audible scuffing sound. Leonard looks toward the bar and says, "Hey Mike, I'll take a white Russian, extra on the commie."

Mike the bartender waves at Leonard as he moves toward Warren. Seeing this, Mike asks, "Hey Lennie, that your date?"

Leonard raises his middle finger and says, "Don't be an asshole, Mike."

The bartender just chuckles. Leonard reaches Warren and sits down heavily on the stool next to him. Mike serves up the drinks and places a small umbrella in Warren's screwdriver then walks away chuckling. Leonard says loud enough to be heard, "You're an asshole Mike."

Leonard looks over at Warren and says, "Okay amigo, how's it going? You sounded like you were wrapped pretty tight over the telephone."

Warren takes a sip of the screwdriver through the little plastic stirring straw. The umbrella bumps his nose. Leonard grabs Warrens drink before he can set it down and removes the umbrella, saying as he does this, "Oh hell Warren."

Warren looks around then says, "Leonard, you're not going to believe the day I had. It was the worst, best day of my life."

Leonard looks sideways at Warren. "Okay my friend, spill it."

Warren smiles, "You remember Sandra, right? Well, she wants to hook up with me. She kissed me on the elevator after work."

Leonard claps Warren on the back. "Oh yeah, the lovely, delicious Sandra. See, I told you perseverance pays off. Good for you, man."

Warren takes another drink of his screwdriver. "The funny part is, I started ignoring her and that's when she warmed up."

Leonard chuckles and says, "That's women for ya man. They are fickle. So, with all this good shit goin' on what's got you so stressed?"

Warren looks around and says, "I saw some shit at work that I don't think I should have seen and I'm not sure what to do about it. It was in an interoffice memo."

Now Leonard sits straight up on his stool. "What exactly did you see Warren?"

Warren leans toward Leonard. "The CDC Influenza Monitoring Section is brainstorming on how to get everyone to take the flu vaccine this year. Something about a virulent strain coming toward us from Thailand. I guess it's a bad bug. They're trying to hide it or something."

Leonard looks around the bar. No one is listening to the pair. "You know Warren, if you don't spill the beans, you're just as guilty. My ratings are down so I could use a scoop. What do you say brother? Be my unnamed source."

Warren can't believe it's actually working. He almost smiles and thinks, "Okay, just stay cool. I hafta play hard to get."

He looks down at the bar. "I don't know Leonard. If they ever found out I told, it would be my ass."

Leonard shakes his head and puts his hand on Warren's shoulder. "Don't you trust me buddy? We're amigos, right? I'm a journalist. That's as good as saying I'm a priest at confession. Did you happen to save the memo?"

Warren shakes his head. "Hell no, I shredded the damn thing. I don't want them to ever know I saw it, but if this thing's headed our way people need to know so they can prepare."

Leonard smiles a fatherly smile. "Leave it to me brother. I'm your knight in shining armor. Now tell me everything you remember about the memo."

Leonard looks down the bar. "Mike, set us up another round."

The next day, Jacob Smith and Ben Carter are sitting at the kitchen table of the apartment they share in Green River. The apartment, located above the detached garage of a small house on Sixth Avenue, is anything but spacious and the neighborhood happens to be the dividing line between the not so bad and the really bad areas of Green River, Indiana. Known as the "Avenues" by the local inhabitants, it is a neutral zone where the affluent rarely visit and the police patrol regularly. The Avenues serve as an unwritten agreement between the criminal element and law enforcement. "You can conduct your business as long as you stay on your side of the line."

The tiny apartment isn't much with a small kitchen, two small bedrooms which could serve as closets and a living room with one small bath but, the price is right for a tight budget. Ben smiles at Jacob and says, "Checkmate! I whipped your ass again my friend. What's wrong with you this evening? You're usually giving me a run for my money at least."

Jacob shakes his head and replies, "I didn't sleep real well last night."

Ben laughs, "Well pay up amigo."

Jacob slides a dollar bill across the table. Ben raises his eyebrows and asks, "So, are you going to tell me what kept you up? Something from that 'deep dark web' you're always surfing?"

Jacob looks at Ben, eyebrows raised and replies, "As a matter of fact, I did, and it scared the shit out of me. Here, let me show you."

He goes into his small bedroom and returns with a laptop computer. With a few keystrokes Jacob pulls up Leonard Weinzcuff's webcast. They both watch as Leonard describes an extremely virulent strain of influenza originating in Thailand and the CDC's efforts to cover up its existence. At the completion of the webcast, Jacob closes the laptop and looks at Ben with a worried look. "If this guy is legit and I think he is, he's talking about our sample. This is too much of a coincidence for it not to be."

Ben shakes his head and replies, "Okay, let's say you're right, why would the CDC cover it up?"

Jacob stands and says, "I don't know but my gut is telling me we've stumbled onto something we shouldn't have. If the government is trying to hide something, people start getting disappeared when they're involved with it."

Ben strokes his chin and asks, "Do you think we should tell the boss?"

Jacob puts his hand on Ben's shoulder. "Pardon me for asking this, but are you nuts? Doc Pearce and Miss Swanson have already made up their minds. You and I are just along to take care of the lab rats, but I can tell you this, if things look like they're going sideways, I'm headed back to Alaska where the government can't find me. If you're smart, you'll do the same."

Ben laughs and replies, "You gonna hide out in the woods or something?"

Jacob nods as he says, "Laugh if you want to amigo, but I have a cabin in Banik my parents own and you're welcome anytime. If this Weinzcuff is right, a shit storm is headed our way, and the government wants it to happen."

Ben looks at his friend with a wry smile, "Well I appreciate the offer 'Mountain Man'. Now, how about you sit down and let me beat you at another game before you and I get 'disappeared'."

Jacob cocks his head to the side and replies, "Sure, why not. Let me put this computer away."

He moves toward his bedroom thinking about the storm that might be approaching. One in which no one is prepared for.

Three days later Ruth Evans, Deputy Chief Public Information Officer, is sitting at her desk sifting through a stack of proposed additions to the CDC's internet information page when her office telephone rings. She answers it not knowing her day is about to get much worse. "Hello, CDC Public Information Office, this is Ruth."

On the other end of the line is her boss, Joel Smith. "Ruth, have you seen the news this morning? I've received calls from all the major news outlets wanting a comment on some internet broadcast by some unknown hack who says he's got a source here at the CDC. Can you come down here to my office? I want to show you something."

Ruth stands from her desk and walks down the glass walled corridor to Joel's much larger office, knocks on the door and then enters in response to the wave of his hand. He is a small, round man with a chronic bead of sweat on his forehead. It is all Ruth can do not to grab a towel and dry his balding head with it. She is picturing that very thing in her mind when he hangs up the telephone and begins to rant. "That was another one. Have a seat."

Ruth does as Joel commands. "What is wrong Joel? You're not making any sense. What internet thing are you talking about?"

Joel paces around the desk and turns his laptop around. He punches a few keys and then turns to face Ruth. "Just watch it for yourself. Who the fuck is this guy? He's stirred up a hornet's nest."

Ruth focuses on the laptop screen as a seedy looking man at a desk with a microphone begins to talk into the camera. "Good evening. This is the Weinzcuff Report. I'm your host, Leonard Weinzcuff. Tonight, I've got something of special interest to all of my followers out there in the great void we know as social media. Everyone remembers the last pandemic. The fear and chaos it created will not soon be forgotten. Well, once again, I'm here to speak the truth no matter where it might lead. I'm not going to make you wait, well maybe for just sixty seconds while I recognize my sponsor, Big Daddy's Night Crawler Farm right here in the big ATL. Before you drop that line in the water, stop by Big Daddy's. They're a jumpin'. Okay, welcome back. Yours truly has a secret. A secret I've just learned from an unnamed source deep inside the CDC. I reached out to the CDC for comment but they have as yet refused to respond. What does that tell you folks? Seems pretty fishy to me, how about you? It seems an internal memo disclosed that a superbug is on its way here. That's right folks, a nasty ol' flu bug. They want everyone and I mean everyone to get the flu vaccination this year. What I want to know is what else they're not telling us about this bug. I wish I could have actually seen the memo but, wouldn't you know it, it has disappeared from the face of the earth."

At that Joel slams the laptop closed. "He goes on for a solid hour like that. Have you heard anything at all? What's he talking about?"

Ruth watches as a bead of sweat runs down Joel's temple and says, "I have no clue, Joel. Is there a flu bug headed this way? I mean, do you know if it even exists? You know how these guys on the internet are. They're just looking for hits on their sites. He's probably full of shit."

Joel looks at Ruth. "Well even if it does exist, it doesn't until upstairs tells us it does. In the meantime, I'm not getting my ass in the ringer by asking questions above my pay grade. Call the major news outlets and schedule a news conference. Issue a denial and don't take any questions. We're going to get ahead of this."

Ruth sighs and says, "Alright Joel, I'll take care of it first thing tomorrow. Is there anything else?"

Joel takes a handkerchief from his back pocket and wipes the sweat from his head. "No. I don't think so. I'm sorry I came at you like I did. It's just that it doesn't take much to panic these yokels."

Ruth raises her eyebrows and smiles slightly. "You mean the taxpayers who pay our salary?"

Joel walks back around the desk. "Don't get all self-righteous on me. You know as well as I do, they're always looking for a reason to start a riot around here."

Ruth stands and says, "Alright Joel, I have some calls to make."

The next evening, Horace MacGill is sitting in his leather easy chair in front of the television sipping from a glass of bourbon in the dark as he watches the nightly news. He smiles as he watches the Deputy Chief Public Information Officer for the CDC step to a podium located in an annex building to the Centers for Disease Control. "I'm glad you all could all make it. I'm going to make a quick statement but unfortunately won't have time to take questions at this point. I think we've all seen Mr. Weinzcuff's video and the allegations he's made. I can tell you that his claims are categorically false. The CDC is very forthcoming regarding potential threats to public health and safety as demonstrated on our public website. Although his claims are outlandish, we do agree that it is always a good idea to get an influenza vaccination yearly. Thank you. Please make sure and visit our website for future updates."

With that Ruth Evans steps away from the podium and walks out the door as the reporters scream questions. Horace looks at the television and begins to chuckle. He takes a long swig of the bourbon and says, "Beautiful Warren. Absolutely beautiful."

Horace reaches over to the end table and picks up his laptop. With a few keystrokes, he sends the target package via secure link thinking, "Now, time to kick the hornet's nest."

He punches in the numbers on the satellite telephone, and the call is answered immediately by a monotone voice, "Hello, Verification please."

Horace replies, "Papa Alpha Whiskey 337. I just sent you a target package."

The voice asks, "Timeline?"

Horace replies, "Immediate."

The voice asks, "Preference?"

Horace replies, "Something elegant but slightly suspicious."

The voice asks, "Disposition?"

Horace replies, "Termination."

The voice replies, "Accepted. Expect outcome within twenty-four hours."

The call disconnects.

Chapter Five

Leonard Weinzcuff looks up at the clear blue Atlanta sky as he walks past outdoor seating areas in front of the restaurants and shops in Buckhorn Village. He feels good and his steps are light as he carries his grocery bag toward his upstairs apartment. Leonard loves living in this part of Atlanta with its proximity to the downtown center, yet it is an area with a slower pace. It doesn't hurt that he lives right around the corner from his favorite bar, The Rusty Horseshoe.

The sidewalks are fairly busy as the shoppers and occasional tourist meander through enjoying the quieter side of Atlanta. His broadcast has created quite a stir as one news outlet followed by another played it safe and ran his story so as not to miss out on the scoop completely. And the denial by the CDC was tantamount to an admission. It was, in a word, beautiful. Leonard thinks as he walks, "My little buddy Warren has given me a one-way ticket to the big time."

As Leonard turns the corner putting him on the street where his apartment is located, he sees a middle-aged woman walking a long-haired dachshund. The dog is well groomed and seems to bounce as it makes its way up the street toward him. Leonard is in such a good mood; he decides to pet the dog as the woman and her furry companion meet him on the quiet street. As Leonard reaches down, the woman says something in German. He stops and only has time for a brief glimpse of the woman's face before the dog attacks his left leg in a frenzy of biting and barking. Leonard immediately yells, "What the fuck! Get it off me! Get it off me!"

The woman screams, "Oh my God! I'm so sorry."

She bends down and grabs the dog by the collar trying to make it let release Leonard's leg while he shakes it trying to dislodge the canine. Leonard doesn't see the woman remove the insulin auto-injector from the pocket of her jacket as she crouches in front of him, nor does he feel the fine needle pierce the flesh of his right calf or the full load of insulin enter his leg. His focus is completely on the dog and the adrenaline spike. The woman yells in German, the dog stops the attack, and the woman stands up with the dog in her right arm as she apologizes emphatically. Warren, still shaking pulls his pant leg up and seeing that the dog's teeth didn't break the skin says, "It's okay. I shouldn't have tried to touch your dog. No harm done."

The woman thanks Leonard and hurries on down the street, whispering into the dog's ear. The excitement concluded, the few witnesses go back to their meandering, the tiny dog attack just another meaningless happening in their day. Leonard begins to walk the last half block to his apartment building. As he reaches the steps to his apartment, his body feels as if it is being deflated. He feels dizzy and his vision begins to blur. The last conscious thought Leonard Weinzcuff has on this earth is the fact that he is famished. Leonard collapses on the street, seizing violently.

Many hours later, Warren stands outside Leonard's hospital room in the Intensive Care Unit speaking with a neurosurgeon. He looks into Leonard's room through the window and barely recognizes his friend who is completely covered in black bruises. The life support machine hisses rhythmically inflating and deflating Leonard's chest. It is the only thing keeping his friend from the abyss. The doctor says, "Mr. Densin, I know this is a lot to take in and I'm sorry you're here under these circumstances but, Mr. Weinzcuff doesn't have any family and has listed you as his medical power of attorney."

Warren looks away from his friend quickly and stares at the doctor. "What are you saying? You're not saying that I have to make the decision whether to turn him off or not? No, no, no, no way. That's crazy!"

The doctor puts his hand on Warrens arm and says, "I take it that you didn't know?"

Warren replies tightly, "No Doc. I had no idea. Why would that fucker put this on me? I thought he was my friend."

The doctor looks directly at Warren. "He is your friend and must think a lot of you. He knows you'll make the right decision. I can't tell you what to do but I can advise you. Your friend suffered what is called a grand mal seizure due to a sudden drop in blood sugar. The ambulance crews were very busy, and his emergency was cued at dispatch for almost five minutes. By the time EMS finally arrived, Leonard had been seizing for eight minutes. Five usually results in brain damage. Leonard seized for ten. I assure you, your friend is never going to wake up. There is no brain activity."

Warren chokes back a sob and says, "You're saying he's brain dead?"

The doctor just nods his head gravely. Warren looks at Leonard then back at the doctor and says, "Doc, I know he wouldn't want to just lay in that bed forever. He was such a funny guy."

Warren's eyes fill with tears. "Man, if you could've only met him, you'd know."

Warren walks into Leonard's room and holds his friend's hand. "Go ahead and unplug him Doc. I'm sorry Leonard. You were my only friend."

The paperwork is signed, the machines are unplugged and all the lights that are Leonard Weinzcuff simply go out. Warren begins to sob.

After the procedure is completed, Warren walks out of the hospital into the Georgia night like a man beaten. He finds his car and begins driving the streets of Atlanta aimlessly. It is almost midnight when he finds himself in the parking lot of Sandra's apartment building. He walks up the stairs and then stands in front of the door he has thought about knocking on a thousand times. Tonight, he raises his hand and knocks. In a few minutes, he hears movement on the other side of the door and then it opens. Sandra standing with a smile that quickly turns to concern. She ushers him into the apartment. "Warren, what's wrong. You look terrible?"

Warren recounts the night's events as she sits next to him on the couch, holding him as he cries. After he is through, she kisses his tear-stained cheeks, takes him by the hand and leads him to the bedroom. She stops at the door and embraces him, her long brown hair brushing his face as she whispers into his ear, "I'll do anything you want Warren. Anything."

They step into the bedroom and close the door.

The next day, Warren is sitting in his cubicle thinking about the night before. He still can't believe how such a nightmare of a day could end so pleasurably. He looks in the direction of Sandra's desk and feels a familiar stir. He knows beyond a doubt that he is in love and maybe he has been for a long time. Last night sealed the deal. This morning had been easy. There were no awkward moments before he'd left her apartment early this morning. A quick trip to his condo to shower and change and he was on the road to work. She was already at her desk this morning when he'd arrived and had smiled and winked when he'd passed her desk. Last night took the sting out of Leonard's death, at least for now. He thinks, "Love has the power to do that."

Meanwhile eight floors above Warren, Ruth Evans sits at her desk watching the morning news as a reporter stands in front of a quaint building in Buckhorn. Ruth turns the sound up and listens to the reporter. "Yesterday a social media sensation died on the steps you see behind me. Leonard Weinzcuff who recently broke the story of a possible attempt to cover up a virulent flu virus by the CDC collapsed and never regained consciousness. Information is limited at this time pending an autopsy. Sources inside the Atlanta Police Department who wish to remain anonymous have indicated that Mr. Weinzcuff's death seems unusual and foul play has not been ruled out as yet. We'll have more on this story as it develops."

Ruth turns the television off and tosses the remote onto her desk saying, "Dammit. Does this crap never end?"

She purses her lips and rolls her eyes as her telephone begins to ring. She answers, "Public Information Office CDC, this is Ruth."

Joel Smith's voice booms through the phone, "Ruth, did you see the news? This shit just keeps getting worse."

Ruth finds herself getting angry. "Joel, you're the one who ordered the press briefing. I wanted to ignore this son of a bitch. The minute we made that statement, we put him all over the news. We gave him the credibility. Now the conspiracy nuts will probably think we killed the guy. I'm going to say this once and that's it. Wait until the autopsy before we comment. Are you hearing me? I'll do whatever you want on this, but my advice is to wait."

Joel is silent for a moment, then replies, "Sure, we'll wait Ruth but this is on your desk. You had better have a plan when these buzzards in the media start circling the carcass. It's not my ass on the line, it's yours."

The call disconnects, Ruth takes the telephone away from her ear and stares at the receiver thinking, "You sweaty little fat head son of a bitch."

Ruth pictures herself running down to Joel's office and strangling him with a towel. She says under her breath, "You caused this you prick. Now you're putting the whole thing on me? We'll see about that."

Chapter Six

Five hundred miles from Atlanta, Georgia Candace Swanson stands at her desk in Green River, Indiana listening to a doctor from Thailand on speakerphone inform her that all the data she is requesting is regularly sent to the CDC in America and he doesn't have time to dredge the numbers up twice. "Ms. Swanson, you should call your CDC in Atlanta for this information."

This call like the last six has revealed nothing. Candace thinks, "The doctors in Phuket are certainly being tight lipped."

She looks around the office at what has been her home for the past seven years and thinks about all the work. The late hours full of experiments and all of the disappointments. So far, the team has thrown everything they can think of at this strain from Phuket but the damn thing folds and mutates faster than antibodies can be manufactured. The key is to stop the mutation, but how?"

They are close. Candace can feel it in her soul. They are so close, but they are running out of time. She is afraid. Afraid, Konrad will lose his nerve and pull the plug on the tests before they find the answer. "It's here, right in front of our noses but we can't see it."

She knows if she can just buy a little more time, they'll crack the code. "I must get ahead of Konrad on this. He's still grieving and isn't thinking straight. I can't let him pull the plug. He's not taking this away from me. I've worked too damn hard. I've sacrificed so much."

She looks at the ceiling and thinks, "And Konrad. He's stopped shaving and started sleeping in his office. He hasn't combed his hair in a week. He looks like some mad scientist."

Candace asks herself, "What am I going to do? We are so fucked."

As Candace ponders these unanswerable questions, Annie Rowan sits at her desk located in the outer offices of the R&D Labs and watches Candace as she paces the floor in her office talking to herself. It is obvious that she is distraught. Annie had dialed the number on the card last night and had told the man of all the failures and how Dr. Pearce seemed to be losing his mind. She was given the instructions to make the introduction. The man had decided that it would be Candace who should be the one to speak with Balil first. It was Annie's task to make that happen.

She thinks back to when she met the man for the first time. It was when she had gone to Chicago to attend the conference on the future of biological engineering. Annie was standing in line at a specialty coffee shop near the hotel where the conference was being held. As she began to pay for her chai tea latte, the man, who was behind her in line, reached around and placed the money for her drink on the counter. He'd smiled and said, "Here Annie, let me get that for you."

Startled, she'd asked, "Thank you, but do I know you."

The man smiled a disarming smile. She took notice of the large canine teeth. "You're at the conference, right?"

She smiled and let down her guard ever so slightly. "Yes, I don't remember seeing you there."

The man chuckled, "Well, I'm very forgettable."

He collected his drink from the barista and said, "Do you have a minute to chat? Let's get that table over there."

That is when he had started talking about her family in an easy, almost hypnotic voice. He knew about her brother and the leukemia. The massive amount owed to the hospital and his only chance at long term survival being the continued medical treatments. He even knew about her father who was self-employed with no medical insurance and the pending foreclosure of their home. He seemed to know everything. She had just sat and listened, dumbstruck. That is when he'd made the offer, if that's what you want to call it. "Annie, I represent some very powerful people who are connected beyond your wildest dreams. People who can help you with these challenges. Would you like help Annie?"

Her eyes filled with tears, and she'd nodded. "Annie dear, don't cry. I'm here to help. The people I represent have purchased the debt on your parent's home. Now I'm going to make a quick call and then I want you to call your parents and have them check the balance on your brother's hospital bill. Would that be, okay?"

The man had made a telephone call and said into the phone, "We're confirmed. Make the payment."

Annie had called her parents and had them check the balance. Over a million dollars had been paid. The balance was zero. She remembers the predatory smile with no kindness in sad eyes. Annie had asked, "Who are you?"

That is when the man had said, "It doesn't matter who I am Annie.

What matters is what I can do. Annie, I need a favor. Something easy that's well worth the gift I've given to you and your family. If you do me this favor, Kenny's medical bills will forever be taken care of. Would you like that, Annie?"

As she sits at her desk, Annie realizes that her answer had been her deal with the devil. She had again nodded her head. He'd continued, "Now Annie, I know you work for Dr. Pearce at Emmer Pharmaceuticals. At some point soon, things will start to fall apart in the lab. Things will go awry."

The man had handed her a card with a telephone number. "I want you to call me when that happens."

She remembers how the man smiled at her as she'd said, "Okay."

It was the smile a wolf gives a cornered rabbit. "Now, there are a couple more things Annie. One of your old classmates from ISU is here at the conference. His name is Balil Zaidi. Do you remember him?"

Annie had nodded again, her eyes wide. "Annie, I believe Balil has created something wonderful. I want you to gain his confidence Annie. He'll be going back to Arlington after the conference, so you won't have much time. You'll have to be very persuasive. I also want to know everything that goes on in Dr. Pearce's lab. You'll call me regularly with reports. How does that sound Annie?"

She'd known something was very wrong and had started to object but the man had put his finger up and moved it slowly back and forth as he looked at her. Everything in the world disappeared except for the man's face. It had changed and she now saw the coldness of death in his eyes. "Annie, I can stop the payment just as easily as I sent it. Your parents' home will foreclose and they'll be homeless. Your brother will die without treatment all because of you. Do you want that? If not, you'll do as I ask."

She'd found Balil the next day and had slept with him that night. It sickened her but she knew the man was telling the truth and without the treatments, her brother would most assuredly die, and her parents would be financially ruined. She'd found the answers the man wanted and had reported to him ever since.

Now as she sits at her desk, she knows this may be her only chance to catch Candace alone because Annie knows time is running out too. She stands and walks back to Candace's office. Her legs feel weak as she knocks lightly on the door frame. Candace is sitting at her desk looking at the computer monitor. As Annie knocks, she looks up and attempts to smile. "What can I do for you Annie?"

Annie steps inside and looks back toward the cubicles before closing the door. "Candace, I need to speak to you about something you said in the lab today."

Candace sighs, "Sure Annie, what's on your mind?"

Annie clears her throat and tries to swallow the dryness. She knows that she'll only have one chance to make her case and also knows her brother's life depends on how well she does. "As we were watching the virus mutate, do you remember saying that we might have a chance if we could put something in the cell to physically stop the mutation?"

Candace sits forward in her chair and says, "Yes. I remember. What about it?"

Annie takes a deep breath. "What if I knew someone who has developed something like that?"

Candace rubs her eyes and laughs. "Annie. Honey. Nothing like that exists."

Annie sits down on the loveseat and leans forward. "It does Candace. I know the nano-scientist who created it. It's not public yet but I know he'll help us if I ask."

Candace gives Annie a sympathetic look. "Nano-scientist? As in nanobots? Those haven't been developed to a scale that would help us, Annie."

Annie nods her head and looks directly at Candace. "They have. We had a 'thing' at the biological engineering conference. He showed me his research on his computer. I saw the videos. They work. They're programmable. He works at a government lab in Arlington. I could call him. Please, just at least talk to him about what we need."

Candace throws up her hands in exasperation. "Sure. Why the hell not. We're all out of ideas anyway and according to the news, we needed an answer yesterday. I'll talk to Dr. Pearce about it and let you know."

Annie stands and walks toward the door. Before opening it, she turns and says, "You know that I respect Dr. Pearce, but are you sure he's well enough to make a decision like this?"

Candace just looks at Annie. "Dr. Pearce is fine. Like I said, I'll let you know Annie."

Annie opens the door and says, "Of course Candace. Thank you."

She returns to her desk, looks around and dials the number on the card. In two rings, the man's voice answers, "Yes Annie? Good news I hope."

Annie says, her voice a shaking whisper, "I tried, and I think Candace is interested but she is going to check with Dr. Pearce and he's had some kind of mental breakdown. I don't think he'll be receptive."

Horace is silent for a second. This new angle will pose some challenges. A shuffling of the deck is in order. "It's alright Annie. Keep calling me with updates."

Then the line goes dead.

Candace sits back in her desk chair and closes her eyes thinking, "Has it really come to this? Fucking fairytales? I can't believe I'm actually entertaining nanobots of all things. I must be desperate or crazy."

She looks around the small office decorated in chrome and leather and realizes she had made a mistake in pushing Konrad to wait in notifying the CDC of the virus strain. She whispers to herself, "He made his own decisions, but I knew what buttons to push."

Now Konrad is at the very least suffering from depression. She also knows that she has contributed to his condition. She's angry. Angry at Konrad, at herself and most of all, angry because she has devoted so much to something that is now going to destroy her and the ones she cares about. Candace stands up from her chair and says with quiet resolve, "Fuck Konrad. I won't let it happen. Nobody's pulling the damn plug on anything."

Candace walks out of her office and sees that she has caught the attention of Ben, Jacob and Annie. They watch her as she walks over to Konrad's office and enters without knocking. As she enters, she sees Konrad asleep on the loveseat. He is clutching a small, framed picture. "Konrad. Get up, we need to talk."

Konrad rises groggily into a sitting position. "Candace? What is it?"

Candace stands with her arms folded and says, "Konrad, look at yourself. You should go home and get some rest. You're not doing yourself or anyone else any good here. Go home and get a shower, shave and take a few days off. We'll take care of things here."

Konrad looks at Candace as if she's just slapped him in the face. "I'm fine. I'm perfectly capable of doing my job."

Candace moves toward Konrad facing him, her tone softer. "I know you're capable of running this place, but you shouldn't be here. Not like this. The others are starting to notice. You're exhausted and frankly, you look like shit Konrad."

He stares at her. "What about the tests? We're running out of time. I'll have to report what we have to the CDC with nothing to show for the delay. We'll all be done. They'll at the very least reprimand all of us. Do you want that on your resume'?"

Candace grabs Konrad's hands and says imploringly, "Just take two days. You've been going non-stop. Take two days and we'll keep going. If we make any breakthroughs at all, I'll call you."

Konrad looks around the office. "But what about?"

Candace cuts him off. "Go home Konrad."

Konrad sits back down on the couch and stares at his bare feet then begins to put his shoes on. He stands and she hugs him tightly, whispering in his ear, "It will be alright. Get some rest."

Konrad walks out of the office and enters the elevator without looking back. Candace steps out of the office and says, "Alright everyone, let's get busy. Annie, make that call."

Chapter Seven

The room is cool, dark and familiar. It is a rare place of refuge for men like him. Horace sits in the leather chair with only a hint of light from his computer screen, waiting for the secure video uplink to initiate. He had requested a meeting with the North American Regent because as much as Horace hates to admit it, he needs assistance. This is a rarity to say the least. He thinks as he waits, "That fucking doctor. His family was everything to him and I misjudged their place in relation to his work. Fate is a fickle bitch."

Horace sighs and says to no one, "Well, I'll adapt and overcome. That's what I do."

The video feed hums to life and Horace knows the meeting has started. "Thank you, Madam, for agreeing to meet with me."

A woman's voice responds, "This is highly unusual Mr. MacGill. Considering your reputation, I'm going to trust the need for this meeting is warranted."

Horace can feel his ears starting to turn red. What he is about to say almost causes him physical pain. "Madam, due to an unforeseen development, I'm going to need your assistance with a challenge which will require an extra level of insulation."

There is a moment of silence and then the female voice says, "An unforeseen development? I was under the impression from our last meeting that all contingencies had been planned for. Those were your words, were they not?"

Horace's eye twitches. "They were Madam but I'm afraid the principal, while still serving his ultimate purpose will have to be taken out of play for a period of time to facilitate the initiation of phase two."

The North American Regent sighs, "Alright Mr. MacGill, what is your plan and how can I be of assistance?"

Horace answers as vaguely as possible. "Madam, the principal's replacement is a motivated subordinate. I just need a third party to push her in the right direction. I have identified the third party and the motivation for him to act. To put it bluntly, I'm going to need intervention on a scale above just a target package."

The female voice chuckles, "And what exactly are you asking for?"

Horace's eye twitches again. "Madam, first, I need for approximately thirty percent of Emmer Pharmaceutical stock to be devalued on the New York Stock Exchange."

The female voice exclaims, "My word! Are you trying to destroy the company?"

Horace moves his head from side to side fighting the tension building in his neck. "No Madam. I'm just creating a need. Secondly, I need a deciding official from the Health and Human Services Office to offer Emmer Pharmaceutical the exclusive contract for influenza vaccine supply and distribution."

Horace can almost hear the Regent's head slowly nod. "My, my Horace. You never fail to live up to your reputation. Very Machiavellian of you to say the least. Consider it done."

Horace nods and says, "Thank you Madam Regent. Your assistance is appreciated."

The Regent replies slowly, "Undoubtedly Horace. Undoubtedly."

The video feed stops and Horace sighs thinking, "Back on track. I'm almost there."

The next day, Reginald Emmer sits at his oversized teakwood desk located six hundred and seventy miles west of Arlington in Green River, Indiana. The office is spacious with a level of opulence distinctly out of place for the surrounding community. Reginald's ability to enjoy his good fortune, though dulled long ago by an air of entitlement, is completely beyond his mental capacity at this moment as he watches the stock prices of Emmer Pharmaceutical plummet. His head screams and his stomach roils as he grabs for the telephone and dials his portfolio manager. The call is forwarded to voicemail. "Dick! This is Reginald Emmer! What the fuck is happening to my stock! You better call me back you son of a bitch!"

Reginald slams the telephone back onto the cradle and sits back into the massive desk chair with built in shiatsu massage. He looks at the stock exchange read out as his stock continues to fall and chews on the cuticle of his left pinky finger. He is reaching for the telephone when it begins to ring. "Hey Reginald, this is Dick."

Reginald grips the receiver, "Dick, what's going on with Emmer stock? It's down twenty and still falling."

Dick sighs, "First Reggie, take a deep breath."

Reginald jumps out of his chair. "Don't tell me to take a deep breath you condescending asshole! Answer the question and don't call me Reggie."

"Okay, just know that I got you buddy. I'm not going to lie, this is a hit but personally, you're good. It looks like everyone decided to unload Emmer stock all at the same time. Could be a hostile takeover or it could be fate. At any rate, it looks like it's evening out now. Let's just watch it and see. It might be that one entity bought it up. You're still the major stockholder so you're not going to lose the company. I'll try to figure out what happened and let you know before the next board meeting."

Reginald looks at the receiver then says, "I'm going to need some answers fast Dick. I'm not fucking around."

He disconnects the call and thinks, "I'm fucked at the next board meeting. Simply fucked."

Meanwhile down in the Research and Development Department, Candace Swanson sits in her office with Balil Zaidi. Candace looks over Balil's shoulder as he watches a video of the Phuket virus replicating and mutating. "So, you can see by the rate of antigen drift, we can't get ahead of it. We need something to stop or at least slow the mutation."

Balil looks at Annie who is sitting on the sofa and smiles. "May I watch the videos a few more times?"

Candace looks from Balil to Annie and smiles despite herself thinking, "That must have been quite a 'thing'."

She says to Balil, "Of course. Watch it as many times as you want."

Balil watches the video two more times in deep concentration as Candace and Annie look on. "Please forgive me Ms. Swanson. I have a degree in biology, but I am no virologist. From what I'm seeing and what you've shared with me, I am assuming that you're trying to create a vaccine to address an unlimited number of flu virus mutations, correct?"

Candace replies, "Yes Balil, that's about the size of it and please call me Candace."

Balil chuckles, "I'm very sorry, but that is quite impossible."

Candace raises her eyebrows and says, "That's not the answer I was hoping for. I'm sorry to have brought you here if it was a waste of your time."

Balil smiles and shakes his head. "Oh no Candace. Quite the contrary. Let me explain. My bots are nothing more than protein molecules which can be programmed for a certain task inside the cell. As you know, protein molecules do everything inside the cell to include assisting in DNA replication. My nanobots are intelligent. They make more of their kind so they can reproduce exponentially once introduced. They never go away. Once in the body, they are there for the life of the host and never stop working."

Annie stands up and walks over to Balil. "That's all well and good Balil but we need something to stop the mutations, and you said that it wasn't possible."

Balil looks at Annie, interest in his eyes. "Yes, in the sense that a bot can recognize every variable and attack it like a vaccine, but, what if you already have the vaccine to stop every kind of influenza?"

Candace looks at Annie and laughs. "That's sort of what we're trying to develop. We don't have it. That's why you're here Balil."

Balil turns in his seat to face Candace. "You're looking at the problem like someone without nanobots. You now have bots. Listen, every flu virus has an initial strand of DNA then the mutations start farther up the chain. What if I can design a bot to recognize the base DNA of every mutation and then continually cut every mutation out making every strain of influenza the same. You will then only have to vaccinate for one strain of flu. No matter what the strain is, once it enters the host, the bots will change it to the desired strain. Your vaccine will create the strain it is vaccinating against. No more guessing every year because you will know that the only flu strain is the target strain. You'll have eradicated influenza."

Candace has focused every bit of her attention on Balil as she asks, "Your nanobots can do that?"

Balil smiles triumphantly and says, "Yes and much more. My breakthrough will cure a great many diseases. We can start with influenza first."

Annie puts her hand on Balil's arm. "How long would it take to make the nanobots?"

Balil looks at the ceiling then at Annie. "For you Annie, a week. Give me one week and I'll be back with the bots. I just need to know which flu strain you'd like the bots to turn all the other strains into."

Candace replies, "Type C Balil. Let's go with Mississippi/80. It's the least deadly of all of them. I'll print you the profile."

Balil looks at Annie and says, "That will be fine. I'll fly back to Arlington tomorrow and be back within the week with the bots. Annie, it has been a long time since I was in Green River. Do you know of a good place to get supper?"

Annie looks at Candace and then at Balil. Sure Balil, I know a place near your hotel."

Candace steps back around her desk. "Take the rest of the day Annie. I'll see you tomorrow. And Balil, thank you."

She hands Balil the printed sheet on Mississippi/80 and he and Annie leave.

Candace sits down at her desk and rubs her eyes. The stress of the last few weeks has left in her a deep fatigue. She thinks about calling Konrad but dismisses the idea. She thinks, "No. Not yet. Konrad doesn't need to know until I have solid results. He's not reliable right now."

She stares at the computer screen and the virus it depicts saying under her breath, "Alright you bastard, give me a week and I'm going to kick your ass."

Back in the labs, Ben and Jacob work with the laboratory rats. They feed them, weigh them and do assessments on each of the rodents to ascertain whether they are healthy, making entries for each rodent. Jacob looks around the lab instinctively and then at Ben, whispering, "The government killed that guy."

Ben looks up from the tablet he is typing on and with eyebrows raised asks, "What? What guy?"

Jacob looks incredulous. "What do you mean, what guy. The guy from the internet. Weinzcuff, they killed him as sure as I'm standing here."

Ben stops typing and asks, "He's dead? How?"

Jacob throws up his hands and leans in toward Jacob. "Man, you are dense. Do you know that? The dude had a seizure on his front steps. It's all over the internet. They're saying he was foaming at the mouth and everything. EMS took their sweet time getting there too. I'm telling you man, there's a coverup going on."

Ben shakes his head and chuckles, "Or, he just had a seizure."

Jacob puts a rat in its cage after rubbing its ears. "Doesn't it seem odd to you that right after blowing the lid off this story, the dude up and dies. I mean, they don't even care how it looks anymore."

Ben asks, "Are you listening to yourself? Do you really believe there's some evil boogey man running around for big brother, killing people? You've been watching too many movies my friend."

Jacob brings another rat over to the table. "I'm just saying it's possible. I'm going to say it again, if things start to get weird around here, I'm heading for the woods. You're welcome to come. That's all I'm saying."

Ben smiles and nods his head as he replies, "I appreciate the offer, but things would have to get pretty weird for me to go running off into the woods with a psycho like you."

He lightly punches Jacob in the shoulder almost making him lose his grip on the rat.

Chapter Eight

The home is a brick two story with a big yard suitable for a family. It is located in one of the more affluent subdivisions of Green River. The yard usually neatly trimmed is uncharacteristically overgrown. There are several small plastic bags hanging from the mailbox which contain warnings from the homeowner's association about the appearance of the yard. All the shades and curtains are drawn making the home look abandoned. The only sign of occupancy, the car parked haphazardly in front of the double garage doors. Inside, the home is dark.

Empty food cans line the kitchen counters and several bags of trash stand in the kitchen like silent witnesses to the slow agony of grief. Konrad Pearce sits in the living room, alone and feels every second of the silence in his once happy home. He sits in his recliner, all his senses dulled. Partly due to the grief and partly to the tumbler of whiskey he balances on his thigh. As he stares at the blackened television screen, memories of his wife and daughter play out in a movie that only he can see.

It has been eight days since he'd walked out of the laboratories at Emmer Pharmaceutical. His laboratories. He takes a sip of the whiskey. "Who does Candace think she is? That bitch practically threw me out of my own lab. And not a fucking word from any of them on what's going on. I bet they're all in on it. "Fucking et tu, Brute", Konrad says to himself as he looks at the blank television screen, "I'm going back to work tomorrow. She's not getting away with this. I'm going in and I'm going to fire that conniving bitch."

He stands unsteadily from the recliner and throws the whiskey tumbler against the fireplace wall creating a shower of Jim Beam and shattered glass then goes upstairs. Konrad sets the alarm on his watch and falls into bed wearing the same sweats he's been wearing since arriving home.

Across town, Reginald Emmer paces his office, brooding over the decline in his company's stock prices. He stops at his desk and looks at the computer monitor showing the stock exchange ticker tape and the bad news going round and round and round. Each time 'EMR' shows up on the screen and goes slowly past, Reginald says, "Shit!"

The price of the stock fluctuates slightly but never rises. Reginald thinks, "Why hasn't Dick, that little prick, called me with an answer?"

Just as Reginald is about to start another round of the office in his constant pacing, a female voice comes over the intercom, "Mr. Emmer?"

Reginald presses the button and says, "Yes Norma, what is it?"

Norma replies in her nasally voice, "Harry is calling from the gate and says that a Lynn Smith from the Department of Health and Human Services is there requesting to speak with you. I've checked your calendar and haven't found an appointment. Would you like to speak with her?"

Reginald's breath catches in his throat as he thinks, "Has Norma lost her mind?"

He sputters, "Yes for heaven's sake. Send an escort to meet her at the door and bring her in."

Reginald tries to smooth the wrinkles on the front of his polo shirt, checks that his belt is straight and instinctively checks that his fly is zipped. In a few minutes, Norma opens his office door and ushers in a woman dressed in a blouse, skirt and high heels with a leather briefcase. She has short black hair and is obviously all business. "Mr. Emmer, my name is Lynn Smith with DHHS, you can call me Lynn. Thank you for seeing me on such short notice."

Reginald moves across the office and shakes her hand with a moist palm. "Absolutely Lynn, the pleasure is all mine. How can I help you?"

Reginald looks at Norma who is still standing at the door. "Mr. Emmer, would you like coffee?

He looks at Lynn and says, 'Oh yes, would you like coffee?"

Lynn chuckles and says, "No thank you. It's very nice of you to offer though."

Reginald doesn't take his eyes from Lynn and says, "That'll be all Norma. Hold all my calls."

Then to Lynn, "So, what do I owe the pleasure?"

Lynn takes a seat on the small sofa. "Reginald, may I call you Reginald?"

Reginald answers quickly as he turns one of the chairs in front of the desk around to face his guest, "Oh yes. Of course. Please."

Lynn pretends not to notice Reginald's fleeting glance at her legs and says, "I promise not to take up too much of your time Reginald. I'm here as an emissary for the lack of a better word. What progress have you made in manufacturing this year's influenza vaccine? I mean, are you on schedule?"

Reginald realizes that he hasn't really been keeping track but hasn't heard anything to the contrary. He thinks, "As they say, no news is good news."

He says quickly, "Oh yes. We're right on track. My R&D folks are an outstanding group."

Lynn smiles, "That's wonderful news. I would like to discuss a contract with you off the record of course."

Reginald leans in and nods his head and says, "Of course, totally off the record."

Lynn crosses her legs and daintily adjusts her skirt at the knee. This action is like a magnet for Reginald's gaze which amuses her. She smiles and says, "We would like to expand your contract for this year's influenza vaccine production and distribution a bit above just the Mid-Atlantic Region. Could your company handle such an increase?"

Reginald is almost giddy. "Emmer is not a pharmaceutical giant, but we have excellent production facilities. What kind of increase are we talking about?"

Lynn leans back into the plush sofa. "We'd like you to supply the United States and partnering nations. We'd like for you to be the sole supplier."

Reginald's hands begin to tremble imperceptibly as he thinks, "Billions. She's offering me billions."

He takes a deep breath and says, "I'm sure we could handle that. I do what I can for my country."

Lynn smiles a knowing smile, "Well, I appreciate your patriotism, and it doesn't hurt that this will surely fix your stock market challenges."

The color drains from Reginald's face as he replies, "That's just a hiccup. I assure you. My company is as strong as ever."

Lynn smiles a disarming smile, "Of course Reginald. We are fully confident in your abilities to serve your country. Now at this stage, all of this is purely informal and off the record, in fact, I was never here but I'm sure that there would be no 'hiccups' in getting you the contract as long as nothing has delayed the production of the vaccine on schedule and Reginald, I do mean on schedule. No delays."

Reginald stares at her for a second, not comprehending and then it hits him. "Of course, Lynn. I can assure you with moral certainty that there will be zero delays from my R&D labs. Zero."

Lynn nods her head and stands, "Oh and Reginald, there's one other tiny thing. I want you to replace Dr. Pearce as director of the labs. Not a dismissal, more like an extended hiatus."

Reginald looks at her in surprise. "Konrad? But I don't have anyone else to run it."

Lynn raises her eyebrows and smiles saying, "Oh Reginald, of course you do. I would go down there and give her the good news if I were you. The Department of Health and Human Services is excited to work with you."

With that, Lynn stands and walks out of Reginald's office leaving him sitting in the chair dumbfounded.

The next morning Konrad Pearce's watch begins chiming at six. He rolls over in bed and groans as he grabs his forehead. As he sits up, his head swims and a jolt of nausea hits him full force. Konrad barely makes it to the bathroom before his body fully rejects the remaining contents of his stomach. As he hugs the commode, he thinks, "What was I thinking? I'm never drinking that much again."

Then he begins to laugh at the absurdity, saying under his breath, "Everyone says the same damn thing."

He gets to his feet and wipes his mouth on his sweatshirt sleeve then looks in the mirror at a face he does not recognize as he says to the reflection, "You look like shit old man."

He showers, shaves and dresses in a white dress shirt and trousers without enthusiasm. He can't bear the thought of putting a tie on and decides that this will have to do. He says into the vanity mirror, "I'm not going to dress up to fire that traitorous bitch anyway."

Konrad gets into his Subaru wagon and heads off on the drive to Emmer Pharmaceuticals. Traffic is light and he makes good time, pulling onto the drive and rolling up to the gate and the familiar face of Harry Smith. "Hey Doc."

Konrad smiles and says, "Hello Harry. How have you been?"

The smile fades from Harry's face as he says, "It'll be just a minute Doc. I gotta make a call."

Konrad sits at the closed gate and begins to get an uneasy feeling in his stomach.

Up in Reginald Emmer's office the intercom rings. He presses the button and is rewarded with Norma's voice saying, "Mr. Emmer, Harry is calling from the gate. Doctor Pearce has just arrived."

Reginald instinctively raises his hand to his mouth to chew on his cuticle then says, "Norma, have security send an officer to the gate and escort Doctor Pearce to my office. Make sure they know that he is not to go to the labs. Is that understood?"

Norma replies, "Yes Mr. Emmer. I'll take care of it."

In a few moments, Konrad opens the door to Reginald's office and barges in followed by Norma's nasally protests and a very large, bald-headed man in an Emmer Pharmaceutical security uniform. Konrad stands in the middle of Reginald's office and says, "What the fuck Reginald? I come back to work, and I'm met by this uniformed goon. Are you trying to tell me something, friend?"

Reginald looks over Konrad's shoulder at the security guard and says, "Thanks Carl. Just wait outside please."

As the door closes Reginald yells, "Norma, hold my calls!"

Reginald stands behind his desk and raises his hands in a conciliatory gesture. "Please just calm down and take a seat Konrad."

Konrad takes a step toward the desk and Reginald steps behind his large executive chair. "Don't tell me to calm down Reginald. Tell me what's going on or I swear that ape outside the door won't be fast enough."

Reginald raises his hands again. "Okay, okay. Just fucking, relax will ya. Let's talk this out like civilized men."

Konrad takes three steps back and sits on the sofa. Reginald comes around the desk and sits on the corner of the teakwood monstrosity. He takes a deep breath and says, "Konrad, I'm putting you on a paid leave of absence for six months."

Konrad quickly stands from the couch. "The fuck you are!"

Reginald leans back a little and puts his hands back up before saying, "I have to Konrad. You need time to grieve, and I need to get this year's flu vaccine produced. I need someone who has their head in the game. It's for the best. Six months and you can come back with a fresh start. Just six months and it's with pay."

Konrad sits back down, clenching his fists and leans forward on the couch. "I'm not going anywhere. Those are my labs and I'm going to run them. Send Candace on a hiatus."

Reginald leans forward and says in a low tone, "No Konrad, those are my labs. This is my company. We're friends and that is why I'm extending this courtesy to you but make no mistake, you're my employee."

Konrad says tightly, "Please Reginald, this work is all I have left."

Reginald softens and says, "I'm sorry Konrad but the decision has been made. You can go fishing or to the beach. A cruise maybe or Carl can escort you off property with a severance check. I'm sorry."

Konrad puts his face in his hands and says, "You have no idea what's going on in your own labs. If you did, you'd fire that bitch in a second, you schmuck."

Now it's Reginald's turn to lean forward. "What did you say? What's going on in the labs?"

Konrad leans back on the couch and looks out the window. "Trust me. You don't want to know, but I can tell you one thing, we're fucked. You won't be able to produce an effective vaccine this year because there is a dumpster fire headed our way."

Reginald feels a cold bead of sweat begin to make its way down his temple. He says in a low, tight voice, "What are you talking about Konrad? What have you done?"

Konrad looks at Reginald quickly and replies, "I haven't done anything but try to solve the problem. We couldn't figure it out. It was a latent mutation in the sample from Thailand. It was perfect for the universal flu vaccine research we've been doing but it's too aggressive. We can't get ahead of the mutations. Millions are going to die this year, and I couldn't stop it."

Konrad puts his face in his hands for a second time and weeps.

Reginald walks over and puts his hand on Konrad's shoulder. "You're not making any sense. Anything like that should have been reported to the CDC as soon as you identified it. It would be all over the news."

Konrad just looks at Reginald with moist eyes as Reginald says in a flat tone, "Konrad, let me guess, you narcissistic prick, you didn't fucking report it?"

Konrad shakes his head and says, "It was our research. My research! I wasn't about to let some asshole from the CDC take my research away without at least trying. You don't get it, do you? This is my life's work!"

Reginald stares at Konrad with a cold stare and yells, "Carl!"

Carl steps through the door instantly looking left then right before focusing on Konrad. Reginald sighs and says tightly, "Carl, escort Doctor Pearce off property. Make sure you get his credentials before he leaves."

Then to Konrad, he says, "You're on vacation with pay until I notify you differently. Don't try to come back before then. You can thank our friendship that you still have a job. Now get the fuck out of my sight."

Carl steps over to the sofa, his presence sending a clear message. Konrad stands up and walks with Carl through the door without looking back.

Reginald waits five minutes then steps through the door and tells Norma on his way out, "Clear my schedule for the rest of the day. I'm going to R&D."

As he walks across the facility, Reginald's mind is spinning as he tries to think of a way out of this mess that doesn't lose him a fortune. He arrives at the entrance to Research and Development and punches in his access code. The elevator ride is a short one and as the doors open, he sees that everyone is gathered in Candace Swanson's office at the end of the cubicles along with another man he doesn't know. Reginald steps off the elevator and walks directly to Candace's office without anyone in the group noticing his arrival.

They are all intently focused on her computer screen. He stands in her office doorway for several seconds before clearing his throat. Candace is the first to look up, her eyes growing wide as she realizes who she is looking at. She stammers, "Mr. Emmer, I had no idea you would be stopping by today."

Reginald takes little notice of the others in the room as his gaze is completely directed at Candace. "Ms. Swanson, I think you and I should have a talk. Don't you agree?"

Candace feels a weakness begin to creep up her legs and quickly enveloping her whole body. She turns pale. "Of course, Sir."

The others start to leave but Reginald stops them by putting his hand up. "All of you can remain. Candace and I will use Dr. Pearce's office."

Candace steps around the desk and walks through the office door followed by Reginald. As he turns to leave, he says, "Don't anyone go anywhere. We'll be right back."

They enter Konrad's office and Reginald closes the door behind them. He looks at Candace with a stony stare and says, "Candace, I suppose congratulations are in order. I am putting you in charge of Research and Development while Dr. Pearce is away."

Candace's eyes widen as she asks, "Away for how long? Is Konrad alright?"

Reginald cocks his head to the side. "I think you know what Konrad's condition is. He and I had quite a conversation a little while ago. Quite a conversation. As the new Director of Research and Development, you need to be made aware of the position your little stunt has put me in."

Candace looks at Reginald innocently and asks, "What stunt?"

Reginald puts his hand up. "Don't! I know about the side research and the failures to report the hidden mutation so don't play innocent with me. You and that asshole have caused me a major problem and now you and I are going to figure a way out of it. Do you have any idea what you've done? You have single handedly destroyed my company. Single fucking handedly. I ought to have you arrested. And by the way, who is the guest?"

Candace holds her hands out in a conciliatory gesture and says, "Mr. Emmer, please let me explain. Konrad and I have been working on a universal influenza vaccine for years. This sample holds all the characteristics of multiple flu strains due to the aggressive mutation. It was the perfect one to study and try to beat. We felt it was worth the gamble."

Reginald takes a step forward and says, his voice tight, "You thought! You thought! Who the hell are you to take a gamble like this without consulting me first? This gamble will cost me billions unless we can figure a way out of this. That's billions with a 'B'. Make no mistake, it will cost me, but it will also cost you."

Candace sits down on the couch and looks at the floor. "We've done it."

Reginald looks at Candace. "Oh, I know you've done it. Now the question is, how do we undo it?"

Candace looks up at Reginald, a slight smile on her face and says, "No Mr. Emmer, we've done it. We've beaten the mutation. That's what we were looking at when you came in. We've beaten influenza completely."

Reginald looks at her incredulously and replies quickly, "What did you say?"

Candace stands and walks around the room rubbing her hands together. "The guest in my office is Balil Zaidi. He's a nano-scientist and has designed a protein molecule that can be programmed to perform complex tasks inside the cell. A microscopic robot if you will. His 'robots' are able to change any flu mutation into a single target mutation."

Reginald looks at Candace with a blank look and says, "Maybe you'd better dumb it down a little Candace. I'm not a virologist."

Candace smiles and says, "It'll be easier if I show you. I can pull the video of our latest try on Konrad's computer. What you'll be looking at is UFV 40."

Candace walks around the desk and brings the video up, turning the monitor around so Reginald can see it. The video starts with an extremely magnified view of the virus attaching itself to the host cell. Candace begins a narrative of what is transpiring. "As you can see, the virus is taking over the cell. As the virus takes control of the cell, the nano-proteins go to work, reconfiguring the DNA before replication can begin. The resulting copy of the virus is the target strain. In essence, the vaccine is creating the strain it is designed to vaccinate against."

He unconsciously chews the cuticle of his ring finger then realizes what he is doing and quickly stops. "That's absolutely brilliant Candace."

Reginald is thinking of riches beyond his wildest dreams. Candace smiles and says, "I can't take all the credit. Balil knew exactly what his bots could accomplish. It was a team effort. I plan to write the literature to present this to the FDA for authorization to begin animal studies. If that goes well, I expect small human trials to start by the end of the year. By next flu season, we should have FDA approval."

He walks around the desk and sits in Konrad's chair. Staring off into space Reginald thinks about his deal with DHHS. He thinks about the delays this will cause, and he thinks about his fortune lost. He thinks, "I'm not going to trade a fortune now for a shared fortune later. No, I'm going to get rich now and richer later."

He looks at Candace, studying her like one might study a dog that might bite. "Candace there are some things in motion that you are not aware of. I want to trust you as a confidante. Can I trust you, Candace?"

Candace nods her head. "Yes Mr. Emmer, I'm very devoted to this company and my work."

Reginald walks around the desk and sits next to Candace on the sofa, taking her hand in his. "Candace, are you a patriot? I mean do you love this country and the people in it?"

Candace replies slowly, "Of course Mr. Emmer."

Reginald moves closer and says, "The government has approached me to be the sole supplier of flu vaccines to the nation. I told them that Emmer Pharmaceutical was willing to do whatever it took to help this great nation, but I needed you as the head of my labs. They were resistant at first because of your experience but I fought tooth and nail to get you this promotion."

Candace looks directly into Reginald's eyes and says, "Thank you sir."

Reginald looks around the room and then back at Candace. "They've entrusted us to get the flu vaccine out on time. You've undoubtedly seen the news regarding the strain that you've been working to defeat, well, they've taken notice too. They trust me Candace to save thousands and I trust you. This is your baby and these are your labs."

Reginald sees that he has her full attention now, like a cobra mesmerizing its victim before striking. "Candace we're going to save thousands, maybe millions of Americans. I'll give you a week to do a small animal trial but then it's business as usual. You'll design the vaccine for production with UFV 40. No one will be the wiser and next year we'll approach the FDA as if we've just discovered it. Then we'll jump through all the hoops and bureaucratic red tape. In the meantime, this flu season will result in the least lives lost in history."

Candace looks at Reginald with surprise. "Mr. Emmer, that's crazy. This is all experimental. What you're talking about is a crime."

Reginald replies quickly, "My dear, our forefathers committed a crime when they first declared their independence from England. What this situation calls for is a pioneer. Someone with the guts to do what's right in the eyes of God. There's the law and then there's the spirit of the law. I'm for saving the country, what about you?"

Candace's mind is spinning. She is fatigued and knows this is just one more step down a deep rabbit hole. "I don't know sir. If it ever came out, nobody would care how many lives we saved."

Reginald sighs in exasperation and says, "Well, not only would we be saving lives Candace, but you personally stand to become wealthy beyond your wildest dreams. Millions Candace, millions."

Candace stands and walks across the room, her back to Reginald. "Maybe we could get an emergency waiver from the FDA to speed up the testing process."

There is a long silence then Reginald replies, "No Candace. There can be absolutely no delays, none, period. Look Candace, we're making history here. You and me. The question you must ask yourself is what side of history do you want to be on. The side who writes it or the poor bastards left in obscurity. I know where I want to be?"

Candace's shoulders slump and that is the moment Reginald knows he has broken her. He walks over and puts his arm around her shoulders. "It will be okay, I promise. Ultimately, if anything goes awry, this is my company and the buck stops with me, but our country is depending on us."

With that, Reginald gives her a slight hug and walks toward the door. "Remember Candace, not a word of this leaves this office. Patriots must stick together, or they hang together. Candace walks back across the office and sits on the couch, speechless. She wants to cry and almost does but regains control of herself. She knows what a rabbit in a trap feels like and looks around the office for a way to escape but sees none. She composes herself and walks back to her office where everyone is still waiting and says, "We're moving on to a small animal study. We have one week. I need everyone to remember that not a word of this can be shared with anyone. Our experiments have always fallen under trade secrets but that is especially the case now."

The lab assistants head back to the labs to prepare the animals for the trials, leaving Candace and Balil alone in the office. Balil looks at Candace and says, "Why so glum Candace? We have eradicated influenza. You should be jumping for joy."

Candace moves around behind her desk and sits down in her chair with a sigh. She rubs her eyes tiredly and says, "I'm happy Balil. I just think everything is catching up with me."

Balil chuckles and says, "Not to worry Candace, things will get much easier now. God is always on the side of the righteous. I think it is time for me to return to Arlington. I would appreciate updates on your progress and don't hesitate to contact me if you need me. I'm always here for you and Annie."

Candace walks around the desk and hugs Balil which surprises him. As they embrace Candace says into his ear, "Thank you Balil, but I'm not so sure that I'm very righteous."

The embrace is short lived and the two part. Balil laughs and says, "You might surprise yourself Candace. Tell Annie that I'll look forward to seeing her again."

With those words, he picks up his briefcase and leaves the office.

Candace sits in the silence and thinks, "I wonder what God is thinking about me right now."

Across the plant, Reginald sits down in his oversized office chair and smiles to himself thinking, "In another year, I could be a multibillionaire. I love the sound of that. As for Candace Swanson, she's made her bed and now she can lay in it. If this ever comes out, she'll take the fall. No one can prove I knew anything about it. There's true power in culpable deniability."

Reginald feels like a king. He leans back in his chair and yells, "Norma, get me some coffee and a sandwich!"

Chapter Nine

Konrad lays on the couch in his darkened home and snores loudly. His is the deep sleep of a man teetering on the abyss. Since returning home six days ago, his world has been a series of blurred awakenings and merciful passing's into oblivion thanks to a good supply of Kentucky bourbon. He forgot his promise to 'never drink that much again' at about the time he drove out of the gate at Emmer Pharmaceuticals. Konrad had a fleeting glimpse of Harry waving as he drove past the guard shack at a high rate of speed. He did not return the wave.

He smiles slightly as he dreams of feeding Chloe pieces of dry cereal while she sits in her highchair. She is only a year old and smiles each time he puts a piece into her tiny fingers. Jennifer stands behind him and laughs as she watches her daughter clumsily find her mouth with untrained hands. Chloe is learning to feed herself and doing very well. Konrad feels his heart swell with the love only a father can feel for his beloved daughter.

His dreams are interrupted by a faraway pounding and the ringing of his doorbell. He jerks awake with a start and looks around the unfamiliar surroundings of the now empty house before rolling off the couch and landing flat on his back on the floor. Konrad grabs his forehead, attempting to ease the stabbing pain he feels there. He raises himself off the floor and goes to the door on wobbly legs, realizing with the first step that he is only wearing one sock. He thinks, "Who gives a fuck."

He reaches the front door and opens it just as David Smith, Jennifer's father, is drawing his fist back for another round of pounding. Gloria, his wife is looking on from behind with worry in her eyes. David jumps back in surprise as the door opens. "For heaven's sake Konrad, we've been out here pounding for nearly twenty minutes. I was getting ready to call the police."

Konrad looks at the two, his eyes reacting slowly as his gaze shifts and says sleepily, "I'm alright. I'm just, I'm alright."

David moves forward and brushes past Konrad as he says, "The hell you are. We're coming in."

Konrad stumbles back and leans against the open door shaking his head and chuckling as he silently invites Gloria in with a wave of his hand saying, "Same old David. It's always been his way or the highway."

Gloria looks at Konrad nervously as she passes in pursuit of her husband, saying as she passes, "We were just worried Konrad."

Konrad closes the door and sighs as he slowly turns toward the interior of his home. He hears David's voice from the living room exclaim, "This place is a wreck! What the hell have you been doing Konrad? Jesus Christ!"

Konrad slowly walks toward the living room. As he enters, he sees David picking up various empty bourbon bottles from the floor and depositing them into the trash can he carries. He points at two half empty bottles on the coffee table and says, "Gloria, pour those down the sink."

Konrad leans against the living room door frame with his hands in the pockets of his sweatpants and says calmly, "Gloria, if you touch those bottles, I will take them from you and pour them over your head."

Both David and Gloria stop moving and look at Konrad with wide eyes. David asks, "What did you just say to my wife?"

Konrad stands up straight and walks over to the couch, sitting down heavily. "You heard me. Put the trash can down David and take a seat, or you can leave, but what I'm not going to put up with is the overbearing attitude I endured the whole time Jennifer, and I were together, so, take a fucking seat."

David starts to sputter a reply but Gloria steps over and puts her hand on his arm. "C'mon David, let's sit down and visit with Konrad."

David looks at his wife and then relents, sitting in the easy chair that sits facing the couch. Gloria says, "Konrad, we've been worried about you. We haven't seen you since the funeral and when we called your work, they said you were on vacation. Honey, we just want to know if you're alright. That's all."

Konrad looks at Gloria with half lidded eyes and says, "I'm just peachy Gloria. What would make you think otherwise?"

David looks around the room. "Well, if you want the truth, this."

Konrad laughs out loud. "You were always good with spitting the truth out David. I'll give you that."

Gloria stands next to David's chair and puts her hand on his shoulder, squeezing. "Konrad, please let us help you through this. Would it help if I came and stayed with you for a few days?"

Konrad lays his head back on the couch and sighs, "Look, I'm not trying to be an asshole. Really, I appreciate what you're both doing. I just need to work through this on my own. Seriously, it looks bad but I'm fine. I just need a couple more days then I'll be right as rain. Okay?"

Gloria looks down at David who is staring at Konrad tightlipped. She takes a deep breath and forces a smile saying, "Well, can I at least make you some food so that you don't starve to death over here? How about some eggs and bacon or something?"

Konrad softens a bit and says, "That would be nice Gloria. I'm not sure what I have in the house but I would appreciate a home cooked meal."

Gloria moves to the kitchen quickly, relieved that she now has a mission and can be away from the awkward atmosphere in the living room. David stares at Konrad and Konrad stares back. Both men refusing to break the gaze then something in David's eyes change. He looks like he is seeing something familiar. There is a soft recognition that is barely noticeable. Konrad catches it because he is looking intently at the man.

David begins to speak, at first in just a low whisper. He looks down at his lap and then back at Konrad. "You know, when I first decided to call the military quits, I was a wreck. I was in Special Forces. Did you know that Konrad? We operated all over the world, on and off the books. I spent most of my time in the jungle. To this day I can still smell the stench of it on some nights. The first man I ever killed was on a jungle trail down in Panama under heavy canopy. We just happened to walk around a bend in the trail at the same time. He was as surprised as I was. I was just slightly faster on the trigger and nearly cut him in half with my twelve gauge. I was only nineteen years old. When I got back to the states, I did just what you're doing Konrad."

Konrad finally breaks his gaze and turns his head as a tear escapes. He quickly wipes his eyes with the sleeve of his sweatshirt.

David continues, "I've been down the road you're traveling on son and let me tell you, it's a dead end. I had Gloria to help me through it but in the end, I had to be the one to decide to either get on with life or not."

Konrad looks at David now, tears in his eyes as he asks quietly, "How?"

David looks through Konrad and shakes his head slightly before his eyes focus again. "You just move forward one inch at a time. But you have to decide. Gloria and I are here for you, but we can't drag you out of this. You have to decide to walk out. That's it."

Gloria calls from the kitchen, "It's ready!"

David stands and starts toward her voice. Konrad looks on the floor, finds his other sock and follows the older man toward his first home cooked meal in what seems like a lifetime.

Across town, Candace Swanson stares at her computer screen reviewing the data of the small animal trial. The mortality rate in the control group for the Phuket strain is, in a word, catastrophic. Conversely, in all of the UFV 40 testing groups, no matter the strain of virus introduced, test subjects totally recover with only mild symptoms. There is no arguing with the scientific data, UFV 40 has total efficacy.

As Candace moves the cursor up and down the screen, a war is being waged inside her mind. She knows in her heart that the right thing to do is to use UFV 40 as this year's vaccine, but she also knows that what is perpetrated in the dark always comes to light. For the past six days, she hasn't slept more than three hours a night with the prospect of what she is doing haunting her every thought. As she looks at the screen, she thinks, "Mr. Emmer thinks I'm an idiot. If this ever comes out, I'll be the one wearing orange. That prick is so transparent. The only two things he cares about in the world are himself and his money."

She stands suddenly and walks around the desk, grabbing the remote for the small flat screen television mounted on the wall in her office. She turns it on, and the screen comes to life in the middle of a news report. The female reporter is standing in front of what appears to be a makeshift memorial with flowers and stuffed animals hanging on a picket fence in a picturesque shopping district. Several people are in the background waving at the camera. Candace turns the volume up to listen to the reporter. "That's right Michael. I'm standing in front of the former residence of the social media sensation Leonard Weinzcuff. If you recall, Mr. Weinzcuff collapsed without regaining consciousness on the sidewalk behind me several weeks ago. As you can see, admirers have created this memorial to honor the fallen hero who broke the story of a possible cover-up by the CDC. Mr. Weinzcuff died shortly after breaking the story. This morning the Atlanta Police Department announced they will be closing the investigation into his death. As you recall, his death was ruled undetermined."

The picture switches to an anchorman in the studio. "Allison, what are the local residents saying?"

The reporter replies, "They aren't too happy about the investigation being closed. I have a local resident right here who's agreed to talk to us. Sir, could you give us your name and thoughts on this case?"

A man in his sixty's steps in front of the camera and says, "Uh, my name's Harry Underback. I own the purse store over there."

The reporter looks back and forth between Harry and the camera. "What do you think about the investigation being closed so quickly?"

Harry takes a deep breath and says, "Well, if ya ask me, I think it's a bunch of bull. Seems awful fishy that boy just droppin' dead right after he made that accusation against the CDC and all. It's mighty fishy indeed."

The reporter tries to pull the microphone away from Harry but he grabs it and leans in facing the camera. "Just a minute, I want to say hello to my granddaughter. Hey Martina, papaw's on television!"

Harry releases his grip on the microphone and begins waving at the camera. The camera moves to Allison, the reporter who says, "This is Allison Reston reporting from Buckhorn. Back to you Michael."

Candace turns the television off and walks toward the door of her office whispering, "Does it ever end? I can't get away from it."

At the same time as Candace is having these thoughts, Ruth Evans is walking to her car in the underground parking area at the Center for Disease Control in Atlanta. She is mentally drained from the constant tightrope she must walk in dealing with her boss, Joel Smith. She thinks as she walks, "It never ends. The news media has latched onto this David Weinzcuff thing, and they won't let it go. The guy was a hack, and they've made him into some kind of hero." As she reaches her vehicle, a man and woman step from the fire stairs and quickly approach her from behind. Ruth hears the footfalls and quickly turns to see a news crew with a microphone and camera ready. As she turns, the woman says breathlessly, "Ruth Evans? Sandy Smithers, WKTT News Atlanta. I'd like to ask you a few questions."

Ruth puts her hand up and says, "No comment. You get questions answered at our regular briefings."

As she turns around to leave, Sandy says, "Bernie, turn off the camera."

Then to Ruth, "Ruth, listen, just hear me out."

Ruth sighs and turns around to face Sandy with a look of resignation. Sandy asks, "Aren't you tired of this guy? I know I am, but my producer keeps sending me out on this story. I want to put this creep to bed once and for all. Help me out. There's no strain from Thailand, right? I mean you guys would know. Just give me a statement and this Leonard Weinzcuff can rest in peace as far as I'm concerned. What do you say?"

Ruth looks at the ceiling of the garage, then at Sandy. "Okay, but no camera."

Sandy smiles and says, "Okay, no camera."

She searches in her bag and finds a pad and pen signaling that she is ready. Ruth puts her briefcase on the trunk of her car and says, "First of all, our hearts go out to Mr. Weinzcuff's family regarding his untimely but natural death. I can tell you that we are not monitoring any especially virulent strain of flu anywhere. Not only Thailand but in the world. However, the CDC always recommends that everyone receive a flu vaccination each year and it is always important to follow that guidance. I know some won't believe what I'm saying and to those individuals, I say, if you're worried about the flu then get vaccinated. That's the only sure way of remaining healthy during flu season."

Sandy is writing feverishly as Ruth speaks. At the conclusion Sandy says, "Thank you so much Ruth for going on the record and clearing things up. Be sure and watch my report tomorrow."

She then motions with her head and she and Bernie hurry away. Ruth gets in her car and sits behind the wheel mentally tallying the number of days before she can retire. The total is too many. She thinks, "I am so tired of this shit."

She leans her head back and sighs so deeply, Ruth feels it in her soul then puts her car into drive and starts the long drive home.

Back in Green River, Indiana, Reginald Emmer is putting on his sport coat in preparation of leaving the plant for the day when Norma Wheeler's nasally voice comes over the intercom, "Mr. Emmer, Candace Swanson is on line one."

Reginald rolls his eyes, presses the button saying, "Send it through."

As he answers the telephone, Reginald hopes for good news and answers in a jovial tone. "Candace, I've been thinking about you. How are things going?"

Candace answers without enthusiasm. "Mr. Emmer, we've completed the animal trial with excellent results. UFV 40 has shown very good efficacy. I think we're ready to send it to the Production Department. Are you still intent on following this course of action?"

Reginald smiles a cagey smile and says, "I'm sure whatever you've prepared Candace is of the highest quality and extremely safe. If you say it's ready, then it's ready."

Candace remains silent for a moment then says, "I can finalize things here on my own. I'd like to give my lab assistants a month off with pay. They're not needed for this final step and shouldn't be involved."

Reginald thinks for a minute then says, "I think that is an excellent idea, Candace. You all have been working very hard down there. In fact, I think once production starts, you should take some time off too. Say, three months with pay. When your lab assistants return, I'll put them on records finalization until you get back. Take a vacation and put it on your corporate card. It'll be my treat."

She answers in the same flat tone, "Thank you Sir. That's very generous of you."

Reginald laughs, "It's only the beginning Candace. Only the beginning my dear. Now if there's nothing else, I was heading out for the day."

Candace answers, "Of course Mr. Emmer. Have a nice evening."

The line goes dead. Reginald sighs and puts his jacket back on the chair, yelling, "Norma, call production and have Zwerger report to my office before he leaves."

Norma answers over the intercom, "Yes Mr. Emmer."

Reginald thinks, "We're twenty feet apart with an open door between us and she still insists on using the intercom. It might do that up tight bitch some good to yell now and then."

Fifteen minutes later, David Zwerger, Director of Production, walks through Reginald's office door. Reginald puts on his best smile and says, "David, it's been a while. How have you been? Have a seat, we need to talk."

David moves his six foot two, lanky frame to the love seat and sits down. Reginald moves around the desk and says, "David, we've got some big things coming our way and I know you're going to be up for the challenge. You are the one man in this place that I can trust if I can trust anyone."

David raises his eyebrows in a look of surprise. "Thank you, Mr. Emmer. I'm glad you feel that way."

Reginald smiles a sideways grin and asks, "How many injectable med lines have you got running right now?"

David looks at the ceiling as he does the math and then says, "Eighteen if you count the two insulin lines. Why?"

Reginald frowns at the question from his employee but keeps going. "What would it take to convert all of them to influenza vaccine production?"

The other man looks incredulous. "Well, I suppose the refitting and sterilization could be completed in two or three weeks but you're talking about taking a lot of needed medications into a shortfall. The insulin lines alone will cause a shortage in a matter of months."

Reginald huffs and says, "Well, another company will have to pick up that load. I'm going to need every line to manufacture influenza vaccine. Can you do that?"

David runs his hand through salt and pepper hair saying, "I can do it but that's going to be a lot of flu vaccine for just the Mid-Atlantic Region. Are you sure boss?"

Reginald answers impatiently, "Yes, I'm sure. If I wasn't, I wouldn't be asking David. Double the shifts on the maintenance side and get the lines ready. You said two or three weeks. I need it done and ready to go in two. No later than that, understand?"

David looks at Reginald and clasps his hands together. "I'll take care of it Mr. Emmer."

Reginald smiles and claps the bigger man on the back saying, "Thank you David. I knew I could count on you. Have a nice evening. Say hello to Cynthia for me."

David nods and says, "Its Claudia sir. My wife's name is Claudia."

Reginald waves his hand in the air saying, "Of course. Say hello to Claudia."

David stands and makes his way out of the office. Reginald sighs with relief, puts his jacket on and walks out of the office, waving to Norma over his shoulder as he leaves without a word.

Chapter Ten

Ruth Evans stands in front of her desk, morning cup of coffee in hand as she watches the morning news from WKTT in Atlanta. Dale Sprock, anchor and iconic face of WKTT faces the camera and smiles a toothy smile. "Good morning and welcome to the news. Today we start with a special report from our very own investigative reporter, Sandy Smithers, who is in the studio with us today. Sandy, I hear you have something very special for our viewers this morning."

The camera cuts to Sandy sitting at a smaller desk. She flashes a disarming smile as she shuffles several sheets of paper, her long blonde hair draped over her right shoulder. "Yes Dale. I conducted an exclusive interview with Ruth Evans, Deputy Public Relations Officer for the CDC yesterday afternoon. I went into the interview with the intent of asking the tough questions everyone is asking, and I was not disappointed. Ms. Evans was very frank with me but insisted on speaking off camera. She expressed sympathy for Leonard Weinzcuff's family. If you'll recall, Mr. Weinzcuff was a social media icon who recently broke the story of a cover-up at the CDC. His recent death, in Ms. Evans words was untimely but of natural causes. This caused me to ponder how she would know this since the coroner's report ruled the death 'undetermined' in nature. I decided to dig deeper into the accusations made by Mr. Weinzcuff."

Dale cuts in saying, "That is interesting Sandy. Were you able to find out how Ms. Evans knew the death of Mr. Weinzcuff was due to natural causes?"

Sandy shakes her head. "No Dale, Ms. Evans would not elaborate. She did emphatically state that the CDC is not currently monitoring a virulent strain of flu, however, she did not deny that one existed. What struck me as interesting is that she once again stated that the only way people will be safe this flu season is to receive the vaccination."

The camera cuts back to Dale. "That sounds ominous Sandy. Thank you for the report and we'll be looking forward to updates as you continue to follow this story.

Sandy's face appears for a brief moment as she says, "Thank you Dale."

Dale's smiling face once again comes on the screen as he says, "Well, I guess if it's the only way we'll be safe, we should all follow that advice and get a flu shot this year. Now let's check in on the weather with Buck Helix."

Ruth turns the television off and throws the remote at the wall screaming, "That Bitch!"

Five hundred miles away in Green River, Indiana, Candace Swanson enters the R&D Labs at Emmer Pharmaceutical and immediately sees Annie and Jacob standing behind the desk located in front of the testing chamber. Inside the chamber, Ben is suited up and preparing the trays of UFV 40 for transfer to the Production Division. The only step left is to blend the vaccine. The actual production will be completed by David Zwerger's personnel. Candace moves up next to Annie and pushes the intercom button. "Ben, would you step out here please."

Ben looks up and then nods before leaving the chamber. Candace looks at the three for a brief moment before speaking, "I want to say thank you for all of your hard work on this project. I hope you all know that you are like a family to me so please take what I am about to say as me looking out for your best interests. I'm sure all of you know the historical significance of what we've accomplished but the last step in the process, I'll complete on my own."

Annie begins to object but Candace puts her hand up as she shakes her head. "No Annie. Up to this point, what we've done is verifiable research. Going further, well, you all know what that is. I don't have to say it and I won't have any of you involved. Mr. Emmer has authorized a thirty-day vacation with pay. When you return, you'll be assigned to document finalization until I return in ninety days. You're still bound by the non-disclosure agreements that we all signed, and trade secret laws so don't breathe a word of this to anyone."

Ben looks at Candace with his trademark schoolboy grin and asks, "Candace, we're already up to our neck in this, why not let us finish?"

The other two nod in agreement. Candace looks at Ben with a sad smile and replies, "Not as far as the law is concerned Ben. All of you can go home and enjoy the time off. I'll finish up here and then I'm leaving. I'll see you all in three months."

Annie, Ben and Jacob look at Candace for a moment and then walk out of the lab leaving Candace alone. Once in the outer offices, Jacob empties a box of copier paper and uses the box to clean out his desk.

No one questions what he is doing because it is obvious, he does not plan on returning. Annie stands in her cubicle and begins to weep as Jacob walks toward the elevator. Before reaching the end of the room, he stops and turns. "Listen guys, you have my number. I'm heading back to my cabin in Alaska. You're both welcome there anytime. Something bad is coming our way, I can feel it and I don't plan on being around for it. Just call me if you need anything. It's a safe place up there."

With that, he turns and walks into the elevator. Once the elevator door shuts, Annie says through her tears, "That's just like Jacob."

Ben walks over to Annie's cubicle and wraps her in a crushing hug saying, "I'm not coming back Annie and if you're smart, you won't either. I got a bad feeling about this whole thing too. I have since the start. Don't be a stranger sis."

With that, Ben releases her and walks toward the elevator. Annie asks, "What about your stuff?"

Ben turns and says, "Funny thing about it is, I got nothing here I care about except the people and the work. It seems to me; I'm not going to be able to take either one with me."

He walks into the elevator, leaving Annie alone. She stares down at her desk through her tears for a moment and then pulls the card from her purse. After wiping her eyes, she picks up her cell phone and dials the number. The man's voice answers in that poisonous honey tone. "Yes Annie, more good news I hope?"

Annie begins to speak quickly saying, "No! No, it's not good news. Everything has fallen completely apart. Dr. Pearce is on permanent leave of absence. Candace is sending all of us on vacation. Ben and Jacob are quitting, and I think I might too. Candace is in the...."

Horace rolls his eyes and cutting her off says, "Annie, Annie, get a hold of yourself. This is what I want you to do. Picture what you want to say, number each thing in your head and tell me each thing one at a time."

Annie takes a few deep breaths then says, "Candace is in the lab doing the final mixture all by herself, then she's going to release the vaccine for production on her own. Mr. Emmer had her in the office the other day and when she came out, she looked like she'd seen death. She's sent us all home. Something bad is going on. Everyone is quitting and I am too."

Horace stays very quiet for a few seconds then asks, "Annie, do you know for sure that she is combining UFV 40?"

Annie gets a sick feeling in her stomach as she says, "No. How could I? She's kicked us out of the lab. I mean, why wouldn't she?"

Horace takes an audible breath and says very slowly, "Annie, you must find a way back into the labs. I need eyes on verification that the vaccine is being mixed as planned."

Now it's Annie's turn to be silent before asking, "How am I supposed to get back into the lab and why are you so interested in the vaccine?"

Horace stares out of the sliding glass doors of his apartment, the anger building in his chest. "Your job isn't to ask questions Annie. Your job is to make sure your brother and parents are taken care of, so, do your job and find a way to help Ms. Swanson. I'll expect a full report by the end of the day."

The line goes dead as Annie stares at the elevator. She has the fleeting vision of running for the door and never looking back but then sees the picture of her family on the desk and the vision turns into a wisp of smoke evaporating before her eyes. Annie puts her telephone back into her purse and walks toward the lab entry doors. She dons her smock and enters the labs to see Candace in the chamber working over the trays of UFV 40.

Candace doesn't notice her until she actually opens the door to the chamber and walks in. At first, she is unable to make out what Candace is saying due to the negative pressure blower that kicks on each time the door is opened but once the door is closed, she can hear Candace ask her why she has come back. Annie looks directly at Candace and says, "Balil was my idea, Candace. I'm partly responsible for where you are now. I'm not leaving until you do. Either we both walk out now, or we both stay until we're finished. I won't take no for an answer."

Candace's eyes fill with tears as she moves toward Annie, hugging her. "Thank you, Annie. It's silly but I've never felt so alone in these labs. Thank you for coming back."

They work together, mixing UFV 40. In the end, they are looking at a tray cart with hundreds of vials neatly packaged and ready for production. Candace picks up the telephone and calls David Zwerger. The phone is answered in two rings. "Zwerger, can I help you?"

Candace hesitates but then says, "Mr. Zwerger this is Candace Swanson in R&D. I have the influenza vials ready for your department."

Annie watches as Candace makes the call and sees that her hands are shaking. David replies, "Good. I'll send someone over to pick them up."

They do not have to wait long before two men in production

smocks arrive to take the cart. As the elevator door closes behind them, Candace looks at Annie and says, "Go home Annie. I'm going to finalize the paperwork and then I'm leaving as well. Thank you for staying with me. It means more than you'll ever know." They hug briefly then Annie with tears in her eyes turns and walks toward the elevator. She stops briefly at her cubicle and retrieves the picture of her family then she is gone. Candace looks around the office that has been a home away from home for so many years and feels a deep sadness which reaches to her soul. She brings the progress notes up on the computer and makes the final entries for this day's events making sure to leave no mention of the nanobots. She thinks, "Next year, if I survive, I'll present UFV 40 to the world."

She doesn't have high hopes that she will. She thinks about Konrad and wonders how he is doing, briefly considering paying him a visit but dismisses the thought. She knows that as painful as the thought is, his friendship is lost forever. She looks around her office and thinks, "It may be time to disappear."

Candace has always been good at that. She thinks back to the days before Colorado State University and her time in Fort Collins. Candace thinks of Mary Beth Willows and wonders how she is doing. It has been years since she has laid eyes on the woman who had saved her from the streets and a lifetime of running. A lifetime of hiding. It was Mary Beth who had put her on the right track and suddenly, Candace misses Mary Beth's soft voice, gently guiding her in what to do next. She shuts her computer down and heads for the elevator. As Candace walks down through the silent cubicles, a sob escapes. She stands at the door and turns the lights out, taking one more look around before getting on the elevator, not knowing whether she will ever return.

Annie Rowan sits in her car at Emmer Pharmaceuticals and finally breaks down in response to the stress and hurt this day has brought. When she is done shedding the tears that had to come, she dials the number on the card. It is answered immediately by the man and his syrupy voice. "Annie, good news I hope."

Her voice tight, she says, "We packaged UFV 40 and it is at the Production Department. I helped with it myself."

Horace replies, "Annie, you sound like you've been crying dear. There's no need for tears. You did an excellent job. Think of all the good you've done for your family. Cheer up, your work is completed for now. Enjoy your vacation and never breathe a word of this to anyone. Your family is counting on you Annie. Oh, and Annie, may I give you some sage advice for the future? There's a reason for the saying 'curiosity killed the cat.' Never, ever question me again."

The line goes dead. Annie stares at her telephone, her conscience gnawing at her and contemplates an idea. She thinks, "They can't be watching me all the time. Nobody is that big. He didn't know what was going on in the lab until I told him. Whoever he thinks he is, he doesn't see everything."

Annie hesitates for another moment looking at her telephone then dials Konrad Pearce's number. It rings five, six, seven times and she is about to hang up when Konrad's sleepy voice comes on the line. "Hello?"

Her eyes widen as she realizes the chance she is taking and can barely find her voice. She replies in a whisper, "Dr. Pearce? This is Annie Rowan. How are you?"

When she says her name, it is like a bolt of electricity runs through Konrad, jolting him into alertness. "Annie, I'm fine. Is everything at the lab alright?"

Annie hesitates again then answers. As she does so, she looks around for anyone who might be watching her. "No Doctor. Everything is not alright. We sent the vials to Production just a little while ago. I'm scared, Dr. Pearce. There's something in the vaccine. I don't want to talk over the telephone. Can you meet me tomorrow?"

Konrad stammers, "Yes Annie. What are you afraid of? What's in the vaccine? Are you talking about the mutation?"

Annie replies on the verge of tears again, "Not now. I don't want to say anything over the telephone. I think I'm being watched. Meet me at Green River Park at the first pavilion by the lake around eleven. Can you do that?"

Konrad replies, "Of course Annie. Green River Park at eleven. I'll be there."

Annie says, "Thank you Doctor."

Then she hangs up. Annie starts her car and begins the short drive to her home on the North side of Green River.

Five hundred miles away in Arlington, Virginia Horace MacGill's telephone rings. He presses the connect button and listens to the soft tone as the satellite thousands of miles above the earth completes the connection. "Hello?"

Horace listens as the asset gives him the report. "Sir, Annie Rowan just contacted Dr. Konrad Pearce and has set a meet at eleven tomorrow at a local city park. We have a recording of the call if you'd like it."

Horace replies, "Yes. Send it."

The asset replies, "On the way sir."

Horace ends the call and sets the phone on the coffee table thinking, "Annie, Annie, what are you up too?"

In a few minutes, Horace's computer dings. He opens the recording and shakes his head, thinking, "Unfortunate. I was going to let her just live her life. It's too bad really but, I can't let a liability put the operation in jeopardy. Loose ends tend to pop up where you least expect them."

His eyes become cold and black as death as he finds the target package and sends it via burst transmission. He picks up the satellite telephone and dials. It is answered on the first ring. "Hello?"

Horace says, "I just sent you a target package."

The voice replies, "Verification?"

Horace repeats the code as he has so many times before, "Papa Alpha Whiskey 337."

The voice asks, "Priority?"

Horace answers, "Expedite. Before ten hundred hours tomorrow."

The voice asks, "Outcome?"

Horace replies, "Termination."

The voice asks, "Preference?"

Horace replies, "Something relatively painless."

The voice replies, "Package accepted. Expect outcome within requested timeframe."

The line goes dead and Horace sighs as he sits back on the couch. He looks out of the sliding glass doors and thinks, "I've got to hand it to her, that little girl surprised me. It doesn't happen often."

The next morning, Annie Rowan's alarm begins chiming at six. She rises from her bed quietly, dresses in a pair of sweats and grabs her swimming bag on her way out of the house. She was on the swim team in college and has always used the pool to relieve stress. She turns the key to her old Volkswagen Jetta and it rumbles to life, spitting blue smoke from the tail pipe.

As she backs out of her family's drive she is looking forward to the water. The sun is just peeking over the rooftops when she arrives at the exit from her subdivision and pulls out on the four-lane headed toward The Riverside Gym and its heated swimming pool. As she pulls into the mostly empty parking lot, she smiles and thinks, "The world doesn't seem as scary now that I've had a full night's rest."

She gets out of her car and enters the gym, scanning her key fob causing the entry scanner to ding and turn green. There are just a couple other dedicated souls in the gym, walking on the treadmills. They take no notice of her arrival because they are fully absorbed in whatever is playing on the ever-present ear phones. Her heart is light as she enters the lady's locker room, changes into her swimsuit and finds the pool empty except for one other swimmer. Annie Rowan steps into the water to begin her morning workout. As she swims up and down the pool, the water cascades over her body, cleansing her soul of the angst she felt yesterday. She swims and, in the act, realizes, she is happy.

Just as Annie is entering the water, another patron walks through the front entrance to the gym. She is of medium height and petite with shoulder length blonde hair. She is wearing a stylish, yet plain sweat suit and carries a gym bag. Her appearance is one of just another dedicated exercise enthusiast. No one notices that she doesn't scan a key fob, but instead, strolls right past the unmanned reception area and heads straight for the women's locker room.

As she enters, she nonchalantly scans the room for anyone else and finding no one, walks the row of lockers looking for Annie's clothes. She finds the locker and defeats the cheap combination lock in seconds with practiced precision. The woman opens a locker close to Annie's and places her sweat jacket inside, then sits down on the bench and removes a small battery-operated hair dryer from her bag. She goes to the sink and wets her hair slightly then returns to the bench pulling Annie's canvas tennis shoes from the locker. The woman reaches into her bag once more and produces a pair of rubber gloves and a small syringe with an atomizer tip. She mists the inside of each shoe with the entire contents of the syringe and uses the hair dryer to dry the shoes then places them back in the locker. The woman carefully removes the gloves and places them inside a heavy sandwich bag along with the syringe, then places it back into her bag. All of this takes less than five minutes. She re-locks Annie's locker and sits back down on the bench to wait.

As Annie and the other swimmer step into the locker room from the pool side, the woman picks up the dryer and begins drying her slightly moist hair. As Annie steps in front of her locker, she smiles and nods to the woman who nods back and then stands and moves down the bench, sitting in front of the locker her jacket is in saying, "Oh, I'm sorry."

They both laugh as Annie says, "That's okay. No big deal. Did you enjoy your workout?"

The woman smiles and replies in a monotone voice, "Oh yes, I love coming here. It's a great stress reliever."

Annie puts out her hand and says, "I'm Annie."

The woman looks at the outstretched hand for a brief moment then takes it and replies, "Delores. Nice to meet you, Annie."

Annie replies, Nice to meet you, Delores. I've got to get a shower, or I'll be late for an appointment but, maybe I'll see you here sometime and we can work out together."

Delores says, "Yes, maybe."

Annie grabs her towel and steps to the shower. When she returns, Delores is still there drying her hair. Annie smiles and dresses quickly, putting her moist bare feet into the canvas tennis shoes. She waves and awkwardly says, "Well bye."

Then Annie is outside and walking toward her car and the fentanyl begins to do its work. It starts as a mild weakness in Annie's legs. Her feet start to go numb as she thinks, "Wow, my electrolytes must really be depleted."

She gets to her car and sits in the driver's seat, a feeling of deep nausea taking hold of her stomach. She fumbles the key into the ignition but can't seem to remember which way to turn it. Annie looks in the rearview mirror and takes a deep breath trying to clear her head thinking, "Why are my lips blue? That's so odd."

She reaches for her gym bag on the passenger seat and searches for a packet of sports drink thinking, "I must have really over done it."

No one is in the parking lot to notice as Annie slumps over the seats of her car except Delores sitting in a car across the lot and she does not move to help. Annie moans slightly as her breathing becomes shallower with each breath until the rise and fall of her chest just simply stops.

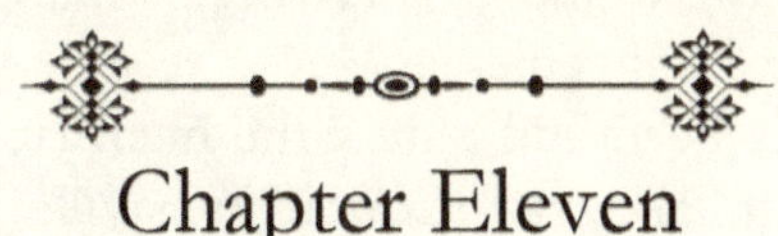

Chapter Eleven

Konrad negotiates the traffic through town toward the pharmacy. The news of Annie's death two weeks ago had hit him exceptionally hard, and he'd slipped back into the bourbon haze Gloria and David had so gently helped him crawl out of. It was they, who had found him lying in the back yard, so drunk he couldn't even hold his head up. The morning after they'd found him, Gloria had nursed him through the alcohol withdrawals while David held his tongue until Konrad was lucid, at least on the surface.

As they were leaving Konrad's house, David had turned to him and in a low, serious tone had said, "I'll not believe my daughter devoted herself to a coward and I'll not have my wife being a nurse maid to a weakling."

For the first time since he'd known David, he saw in the man's eyes what that enemy soldier had seen before his life ended. David put his finger in Konrad's chest. "You're depressed and that's a shame, but you need to unfuck yourself. Like I said before, you have to be the one to move forward. The next time we find you like this, I'll have you put in St. Mary's Rehab under an emergency commitment order. You're going to straighten up one way or the other Konrad."

As David had said this, he had pushed his finger into the meat of Konrad's chest for emphasis. As Konrad looked closely at the man, he realized David could be a very violent man if provoked. David had walked out of the door without looking back. It was Gloria who had returned and given him the doctor's name on the torn slip of paper saying, "He's an excellent practitioner. I've been seeing him for years."

Konrad had made the appointment the next day and had been officially diagnosed with clinical depression. He looks over at the prescription sitting on the passenger seat and thinks, "Xanax. How did I get to the place where I need Xanax?"

He pulls the Subaru into the parking lot of Baller Family Drugs and notices several people standing outside near the door. The place looks crowded. Konrad parks and walks across the lot to the front door with his prescription in hand. As he gets to the door, he notices a large handwritten sign on the window. "Flu vaccine unavailable for at least a month. Sorry for the inconvenience."

Konrad shakes his head and enters the pharmacy to find the lobby full of people. The pharmacist, Connie Westville looks up from the counter with a worried look on her face as she says, "Konrad, what can I get for you?"

Konrad looks around the room and raises his eyebrows. "I can wait. Aren't these folks ahead of me?"

She shakes her head and Konrad steps through the crowd. A man in the back says, "You gotta have some flu vaccine left over from last year. I'll take that. Nobody here believes you don't have something."

The crowd mumbles their agreement as Konrad hands Connie his prescription. He looks around the room and sees that some of the crowd appear to be agitated and thinks, "If they'll riot over toilet paper why not vaccine?"

He turns from the counter and says, "It doesn't work like that. We produce a different vaccine every year. If Connie says she doesn't have it, then she doesn't."

He turns back around and hears the man in the back say, "We? You work out there at Emmer?"

David looks over his shoulder and says, "I am, or was the lead scientist out there, so yeah, I worked at Emmer."

The man in back asks, "Well you must know something about this bad flu headed our way or are you part of the cover up too?"

Now Konrad turns back around and fixes his stare on the man in the back. "I know enough to know that you can vaccinate yourself every day for the next year and it won't make a fucking difference asshole. Now if she says she doesn't have anything then she doesn't. You people need to leave."

The man begins to stammer a reply as the rest of the crowd stares at Konrad. They all move forward talking at once and Konrad backs a step toward the counter and says over his shoulder loudly enough for everyone to hear, "Connie, call the police. Once you asked these people to leave and they didn't, you can charge them with trespass."

Connie picks up the telephone and the crowd stops their slow advance and then starts to trickle through the exit. The man in back says, "You better have something soon. I'm not dying of some oriental flu just because you can't run your business."

Konrad turns back around as the last of the mob leaves. Connie looks at him quizzically and says, "Thank you Konrad. I was getting worried but, what do you mean it won't make any difference?"

He looks at her and replies, "Just forget I said anything Connie. Take the vaccine because it will help but, you and your husband should stay away from crowds once the season starts and wear a mask when you're in here. I'm afraid this flu season is not going to be pretty."

She looks at Konrad with a worried look and then steps to the back to fill his prescription. Konrad leans on the counter and thinks as he waits, "They have no idea. God help us."

On the drive home Konrad listens to the local news on his radio which serves as something to focus on other than his own problems. The newscaster says with flair, "And now for the local news. Unemployment rates are expected to drop sharply in the Green River area according to city leaders due to the recent announcement that our very own Emmer Pharmaceutical has been awarded the sole distribution contract for the entire nation in providing this year's influenza vaccine. When contacted Reginald Emmer, Owner and CEO stated, "We're very grateful here at Emmer that the Department of Health and Human Services has entrusted us to serve this great nation by providing the vaccine."

The newscaster smiles at a man to his left. "Well Skip, what do you have in sports?"

Skip Dunkin replies, "Alot Dwayne, but first, I'd like to say that Reginald Emmer is a true patriot."

Konrad reaches quickly and turns the radio off. He grips the steering wheel as if it were Reginald's throat making his arms shake with exertion as he thinks, "That sneaky son of a bitch. I wonder if Candace was in on it. Of course he's going to put that worthless vaccine into production. It's worth billions."

Konrad pulls into a gas station parking lot and dials Candace's cell number. The call goes straight to voicemail just as it has since he'd been put on "vacation." He ends the call without leaving a message. Konrad calls Reginald's office next and the call is answered immediately by his secretary Norma, who says in her nasal voice, "Mr. Emmer's office, how may I help you?"

Konrad says a little too loudly, "Norma this is Konrad, put him on."

Norma responds, "Doctor Pearce, I'm very sorry but Mr. Emmer has left for the day. Would you like to leave a message?"

Konrad almost screams into the telephone, "Yeah! You tell that prick he'll have to face me sooner or later! I know he's probably standing right there, and I know what he's up too. You tell him that!"

He ends the call and puts the car in gear thinking, "I'll just wait at his house. He'll have to come home at some point."

Konrad drives through Green River Indiana toward the east and Yorkshire Subdivision where no home is valued at less than several million dollars. It is the home of Green River's elite. Konrad has visited Reginald there many times when the two were on better terms. He thinks, "Hopefully that prick forgot to tell the security guard about me."

His intuition is correct, and the guard waves him through the gate and into a different world. The minute the Subaru's tires hit the subdivisions network of smoothly paved roads; Konrad can feel the difference. Immaculately maintained hedge rows line every street. It's as if the grass is truly greener here. Small speed limit signs are visible at various points along the drive to Reginald's house, but they aren't needed as Konrad instinctively controls his speed to take in the beauty. The sheer grandeur of the community makes him hate Reginald even more. He pulls into the circle drive in front of the home which, to the ordinary folk of Green River is a mansion and sees Reginald's Mercedes-Benz sitting at the front door. Konrad thinks, "I got you now, you little prick."

He gets out of the car and makes it a little over halfway to the door when Reginald appears in the doorway with his hand held up, a smug grin on his face. "Konrad don't take another step. The police are already on their way. You, my friend, are trespassing in a place where the city leaders take that very seriously. If I were you, I'd get back in my car and return to the normal folk."

Reginald chuckles as he says the last part. Konrad's blood boils. "Normal folk? You arrogant asshole! You're not going to get away with this shit. Did you have something to do with Annie's death? Was that you?"

Reginald raises his eyebrows and shrugs his shoulders in a dismissive gesture. "Annie, poor thing. I was heartbroken to hear about it. To think that you had a heroin addict working in your labs. You really weren't on the ball at all, were you, old friend?"

Konrad starts to move forward saying, "She was no more of an addict than you are, you son of a bitch!"

Before he can move four steps, two police cruisers and a supervisor's vehicle pull into the circle drive. A policeman jumps out of the lead vehicle and screams at Konrad, "Freeze asshole! Do not take another step!"

The police officers, hands on their holstered side arms move up quickly and grab Konrad by the arms, leading him back to his car and bending him over the hood. He is handcuffed and roughly searched. The supervisor turns to Reginald who is still standing in the door and asks, "He doesn't have anything on him Mr. Emmer. Do you want to press charges?"

Reginald looks down at the ground, sighs and then looks at Konrad. "No, he's an old friend who's having some psychological issues. No, just escort him off the premises please."

One of the police officers' steps up to the supervisor and hands him the bottle of Xanax. "Saw these through the window Sarge. Went ahead and searched the vehicle. Nothing but the pills."

The sergeant nods and turns to Konrad. "Doctor Pearce, why do you have a script for Xanax?"

Konrad looks at the ground and says, his lip trembling, "I'm depressed alright. I'm fucking depressed but that has nothing to do with why I'm here. That asshole is breaking the law. He's producing a worthless vaccine."

The sergeant looks at Konrad and says in a calm voice, "Look Mr. Pearce, you seem like an okay guy. Mr. Emmer isn't going to press charges. He's an upstanding member of the community so I doubt very seriously, anything he's doing is illegal. My advice is to go home. Just go home and don't come back. If you do, it won't be up to Mr. Emmer if you go to jail. Catch my drift?"

Konrad, realizing that he is beaten nods his head. He looks at the sergeant's name tag and thinks, "Jamison. I'll remember that."

The sergeant nods his head at one of the officers and the handcuffs are removed. As Konrad walks to his car, the sergeant says, "Remember what I said, we'll follow you out of the community."

The sergeant walks up to Reginald and hands him a card. "Anything else we can do for you Sir?"

Reginald replies with a grin, "I'd like a copy of the report if you don't mind."

The sergeant nods his head. "Call me tomorrow at the number on the card Sir and I'll give you the report number so that you can request a copy.

As Konrad pulls out of the drive, two patrol cars following, he looks at Reginald standing in the door and catches a trace of the smug grin before hearing faintly, "Thank you officer for taking care of my misguided friend."

On the drive home, Konrad keeps his mind occupied by thinking of all the ways that he would like to kill Reginald Emmer. There are many. He arrives home and steps into the dark house without turning the lights on. His mood is one in which the ambient light from the afternoon sun coming through the windows is still too much and he wishes for nightfall. He feels beaten. Beaten by a man he considers inferior and that is the thing that hurts the most. To be outmaneuvered so completely by that wealthy asshole. He goes to the kitchen and looks at the pictures of Jennifer and Chloe on the refrigerator door. He thinks, "They were my whole life. How do you move on from everything?"

No answer comes. He reaches in and pulls a package of bologna out, stands at the counter and eats the meat straight from the package, thinking, "What is most important to that asshole and how can I fuck him royally?"

He looks at the dwindling packet of meat as he chews without tasting. The thought occurs to him that he should have started with a couple slices of bread. Then the answer hits him. He says to no one, "I should have reported the variation to the CDC when we found it. I can still do that. It's not too late."

Konrad leaves the bologna on the counter and goes into his study, finding his small book of contacts. He pulls his telephone from his pocket and dials the number. It is answered in two rings. "Centers for Disease Control and Prevention, Warren Densin, may I help you?"

Konrad takes a deep breath and prays that this Densin guy is not just some flunky but will actually do his job. "My name is Doctor Konrad Pearce. I am the lead scientist at Emmer Pharmaceuticals and I have identified a mutation in one of the samples from Phuket Thailand. You are the point of contact for my region, are you not?"

Warren sits straight up in his chair, almost spilling his cup of coffee. "Uh, yes Doctor. How can I help you?"

Konrad rolls his eyes and says, "I just told you how you can help me. Connect me with someone regarding influenza research."

Warren remembers the instructions from the man who had given him the card. This is the call he has been waiting for. His bladder spasms. "I'm sorry Doctor. They are all unavailable, can I take a message?"

Konrad pulls the telephone away from his ear and looks at it before asking, "All of them? They're all unavailable? Are you shitting me?"

Warren takes a deep breath praying that this asshole will believe the ruse as he answers flatly, "Yes sir. It's some kind of retreat. They have them all the time down here. You know how the government is."

Konrad sighs a heavy sigh and says, "Listen, I need you to write all of this down. I'll speak slowly. There is a mutation in one of the influenza samples that makes it extremely virulent."

Warren breaks in, "I'm sorry sir, did you say violent?"

Konrad rolls his eyes and says, "No! Virulent. V.I.R.U.L.E.N.T. Virulent. The flu vaccine has already gone to production at Emmer, and it is going to be totally ineffective against this strain. I need someone to contact me immediately. Do you understand?"

Warren smiles and says, "Of course Doctor. I've got it all written down and I'll pass it along. Is there anything else I can help you with?"

Konrad looks at the telephone again thinking, "This asshole's an idiot."

He asks in an exasperated tone, "When are they due back from this retreat?"

Warren feels the balance of power has shifted and leans back in his seat. "Oh, I don't know Doctor. You know how these scientists are. It could be a week or so. I'll be sure and get them the message as soon as they return."

Konrad grits his teeth and says tightly, "A week! Is there anyone else that I can talk to?"

Warren smiles a smug grin and says, "Not at this time. I'm your point of contact Doctor. I'm sure if you just give me your contact information I can."

Konrad ends the call, cutting Warren off. He paces the floor and runs his hand through his hair thinking, "That fucker was either incompetent or stonewalling me. Either way, something isn't right. The CDC doesn't close down their entire influenza research lab for a retreat. That's ludicrous, but then again, it is the government."

He continues to pace the floor, tapping his left fist again and again into the palm of his right hand, saying to no one, "Think Konrad. There must be some way to get the word out about what Emmer is doing. That fucker isn't getting away with this."

Then it hits him like a punch to the gut. "That reporter down in Atlanta. Yeah, someone in their own back yard. What was her name? Sandy something. Smithers. Sandy Smithers, WKTT."

Konrad finds the number on the internet and dials his telephone.

Five hundred miles away Horace MacGill's satellite telephone chirps. He picks it up and sees from the identification number, it is Warren. He smiles a knowing smile and hits the button to connect the call. "Warren, so nice of you to call. Good news I hope."

Warren clears his throat and says, "The guy from Emmer Pharmaceuticals just called. He said that there was a virulent mutation and that the vaccine they're producing is no good. He made me write it down. What do you want me to do with the message?"

Horace rolls his eyes and thinks, "Sometimes a pawn can be amusing."

He asks after a moment of silence, "What do you think you should do with it Warren?"

Warren feels his bladder spasm and asks, "Pass it on?"

Horace is starting to enjoy his game with Warren and chuckles before replying, "No Warren. Any idiot could do that. That's why I picked you. You're much smarter than that. Try again."

Warren swallows the lump in his throat and says, "I should shred it."

Horace chuckles again and says with exuberance, "That's my boy! Yes Warren, shred it."

Warren feels almost lightheaded in what he is about to ask, but can't help himself. "Is it true?"

Horace stands from the couch and is silent for a long moment before replying, "Warren, did you just ask me a question? A better question might be, how's the lovely Sandra? Are you two still an item?"

Warren feels the heat rise to his face. "Don't bring her into this. You had me pass that story to my friend and now, magically he's dead. I just want to know if I'm responsible for that."

Horace sighs into the telephone and says, "Warren, you're the one who brought her into this. I told you to stay away from her. Alas, now your futures are intertwined. If you become a liability, I'm afraid she does too. You know your friend died of natural causes or haven't you seen the news? So, no more questions. Ignorance my little friend is bliss. I'm sending you a picture. Enjoy."

The line goes dead, and Warren pulls the telephone from his ear just as it dings with a message. The picture is of Sandra entering her apartment. The photographer must have been standing only twenty feet away. The message is loud and clear as Warren stands and hurries toward the bathroom.

Horace sits back down on the couch and scowls thinking, "I'd terminate that little prick, but I need him in that spot for a little while longer. It's too late in the game to put another pawn in place. His number will come up though. Yes, it will."

He looks out of the sliding glass doors at the waning light and thinks, "It's time. One more phone call. I hope you've been watching the news, Alejandro."

Horace dials the number and waits as the telephone rings five times before being answered by an exasperated voice. "General Quispe."

With a wolfish smile Horace says, "Good Evening General. How is the weather in New York?"

There is silence on the line for several seconds before General Quispe asks flatly, "What do you want?"

Horace can feel the vehemence coming through the telephone as he says, "Why General, you don't sound glad to hear from me."

Quispe answers quickly, "Why should I be glad to hear from you. From what I can tell, your whole operation is floundering. Have you seen the news? People are lining up outside pharmacies looking for vaccine that won't be available for at least six weeks all because some internet hack leaked a story. Questions are being asked, and I don't have the answers. No, I'm not glad to hear from you."

Horace smirks and says, "Everything is going as planned General. All of the pieces are just where I want them to be, in fact, it's playing out better than I planned. In any case, it's time for you to make your announcement. Have a good evening, Alejandro."

Quispe does not reply, and Horace ends the call. He steps into the kitchen and pours a tumbler of bourbon, then sits back down on the couch and thinks, "Time to knock the top off of the ant hill."

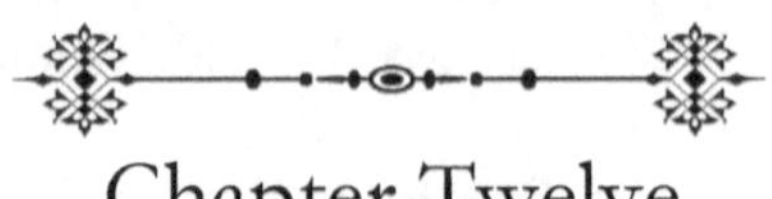

Chapter Twelve

Connie Westville stands in her kitchen drinking her morning cup of coffee and watching the morning news on the small television sitting on the counter. The anchorman, Dan Kingman looks at the camera with his trademark serious look and says, "And now with the national news, General Alejandro Quispe of the World Health Organization's Flu Advisory Committee spoke from New York yesterday, answering growing rumors that the nation will be facing an especially virulent strain of influenza this year. General Quispe stated that The World Health Organization regularly monitors worldwide flu activity and hasn't noticed any uptick in flu cases above normal. General Quispe did pointedly state that it was especially important this year as it is every year for everyone to receive the influenza vaccine."

She turns the television off and rubs her forehead. She'd been dealing with a growing number of customers demanding the flu shot, of which she had absolutely none. She thinks, "What is wrong with these people? I can't just make it magically appear."

Connie looks down at the counter and reads the letter from the school one more time thinking, "And now this. Tommy telling all the kids in his class that his mother, 'The Pharmacist' said that the flu shot wasn't going to do any good."

She says under her breath, "Talk about taking something out of context."

She'd been telling Ike about what Konrad had said when Tommy had walked in. Ike has been a great husband and partner for their whole marriage and is someone she can vent to when needed. The Konrad thing was just too creepy, and she wanted to bounce it off of him. Tommy wasn't meant to hear it. She shakes her head as she thinks. "Now, Miss Hunsley has asked me to speak to Tommy's class. Doesn't she understand that I have a business to run?"

She takes the last drink of her coffee and steps into the living room. "Okay kiddo, turn off the television so we can get you to school."

Tommy huffs and turns the television off, dramatically dropping the remote on the couch cushion, then he stands and grabbing his book bag walks out the front door. Connie taps him on the rear with her hand and says, "Cheer up kid. I hear you've got a celebrity coming to speak to your class this morning."

He looks over his shoulder at her as he sulks down the sidewalk and says, "Yeah, right mom."

The drive is a short one even though traffic at this hour of the morning is heavy because of the elementary school. They pull into the visitor's parking and walk into Miss Hunsley's class together. As they enter, Miss Hunsley, stands and welcomes Connie with a firm handshake saying, "Thank you so much for coming. Your son has quite the following. I'd say he'd have a very successful career in politics if he chose to pursue it."

Connie rolls her eyes and says, "I'm sorry for the trouble. It shouldn't take long to clear up."

Miss Hunsley claps her hands and tells the students to take their seats. She clasps her hands and smiles at the class saying, "Good morning, everyone. We have a special treat this morning. Mrs. Westville has agreed to come and speak to us this morning about the influenza vaccine."

Connie smiles and nods to the class from her seat at the front. Miss Hunsley turns and says, "Well, I guess I'll turn them over to you."

Connie stands and clears her throat, "Good morning class. My name is Connie Westville. I'm the pharmacist at Baller Family Drugs and I want to talk to you about influenza and the important role you play in fighting it. Does everyone know what influenza is?"

The children nod their heads. Connie continues, "Good. It's a virus and we must do everything we can to fight it off so that we stay healthy for ourselves and our families. Can anyone tell me what we do to fight a virus?"

A little girl on the left raises her hand and says, "Wash our hands?"

Connie smiles and says, "Yes, washing our hands is important but there's something else that we do each year that's very important."

A little boy in the front raises his hand and Connie nods toward him. The boy stands smiling and says, "We get a shot."

Connie clasps her hands in front of her and smiles saying, "Yes. The vaccination is a shot that prepares our bodies to fight the virus and it's very important that you get the vaccination. So, I'm going to ask all of you for your help. I need you to be my messengers. Okay? I need you to spread the word that everyone needs the flu shot this year. Will you help me?"

The children nod their heads. A little girl in the back stands up and says, "But Tommy said that you said it wouldn't work this year."

Connie smiles and looks back at Miss Hunsley before answering, "Well, Tommy misunderstood something he overheard me telling his father. The vaccine is tested by our government and will be very effective at helping you fight off the virus. I guarantee it, but you must get the vaccination for it to work. So, will you all help me and get the flu shot this year?"

The children again nod their heads. Miss Hunsley stands and says to the class, "Let's give Mrs. Westville a round of applause to thank her for coming in today."

The children clap their hands. Connie smiles and says, "Wow! Thank you."

Miss Hunsley walks Connie to the door and says, "Thank you for taking the time to speak to the children. I think you made an impression."

Connie replies as they shake hands, "I hope so. It is really very important."

She turns and leaves, hoping that what she said was the truth.

Just as Connie is leaving the school on her way to work, Sandy Smithers is storming toward her editor's office at WKTT in Atlanta. As an investigative reporter who has her sights on an anchor chair, Sandy isn't very good at taking no for an answer and that is just what she has received in her email from Kyle Bruin. She walks through the newsroom to the sound of a hundred keyboards being tapped furiously to produce the daily news but seems not to notice as she walks. She reaches his office door and taps on the glass twice before entering without being invited.

Kyle looks up briefly with an annoyed expression and then returns to staring intently at his computer monitor. He says without looking up, "The answer is the same whether you're standing in my office or sitting at your desk Sandy, and don't try to change my mind with that smile either. It's not going to work."

If he had bothered to look, Kyle would have noticed that Sandy wasn't smiling. "Kyle, I've been chasing this story all over Atlanta for weeks and now, I've finally gotten a break and you're telling me no. I'm telling you; this guy is legit and he wants to talk."

Kyle looks at her over his thin wire glasses and says, "One out of ten sources are legit Sandy. What makes this one worth a drive to nowhere Indiana? I already told you; I can't spare the camera crew. We had three homicides just last night alone that need to make the evening edition."

Sandy sits in the overstuffed chair in the corner of the office and says, "I'm telling you; I have a good feeling about this one. He says he's the lead research scientist for Emmer Pharmaceuticals and he wants to spill the beans. He says Weinzcuff was telling the truth. He's willing to go on the record Kyle."

Kyle stops reading, takes his glasses off and rubs his eyes. He looks at Sandy and smiles a tired smile saying, "Look, I've got a budget and there just isn't money in it for you to run all the way up there on a wild goose chase. There's plenty of news right here in Atlanta. I'll make a deal with you. Close this Weinzcuff thing out and I'll put you on this Buckhead murder. There could be some ties to the cartels. It's full of dangerous stuff. I know you like that."

Sandy stands up putting her hands on her hips. "I'm not going to put a story to bed unless I'm finished with it, and I'm not finished with this one. There's something going on and I intend to blow it wide open, with or without your help."

Kyle looks at her with an exasperated look and says, "Dammit Sandy. One of these days, you're going to learn when enough is enough."

He throws up his hands in surrender and says, "Fine. You can go. I said you and you alone but you're driving your own vehicle. No flight, no camera crew, just you and a laptop. I'll cover the cost of lodging for two nights then you're bringing your ass back here and covering the local news. Understood?"

Sandy walks around the desk and kisses Kyle on the forehead, ignoring his halfhearted protests. "Thank you, Kyle, you're a sweetheart."

He goes back to his computer screen and says with a glance in her direction, "Get out of here, will ya. I've got work to do."

The next morning, Sandy throws her suitcase and laptop in her Miata and plots the route to Green River, Indiana on her telephone. She takes a deep breath and thinks, "Eight hours and fifty-six minutes. I hope this guy is legit."

She puts the car in gear and begins the long drive north.

In Arlington Virginia, Balil Zaidi walks into the main entrance of Bionan labs as he has done for the past four years and approaches the security turnstile. He slides his badge through the reader and a red-light flashes three times. Balil tries it again with the same results. His difficulties have not escaped the attention of the contract security guard. With a nervous laugh, Balil steps over to the guard's desk and says, "I'm sorry, my card seems to be malfunctioning. Can you help me?"

The guard looks at Balil with an annoyed look and holds his hand out for the card. Balil hands him the card and the guard punches his information into the computer. He looks at Balil with suspicion and says, "It looks like your access has been pulled sir. You should have received some sort of notification. Would you like for me to call Human Resources?"

Balil's hands begin to shake as he slightly bows and says, "No thank you, I must have missed it. I receive hundreds of e-mails a day. I'll go back home and get it straightened out."

He takes his card and leaves the building without looking back, knowing the guard is watching him. Balil grew up in Pakistan and knows what happens to someone who knows too much. Visits in the middle of the night were common, in which people who went to bed in their homes were missing in the morning, never to be heard from again. Since finding out about Annie's death from her father when he'd called her, Balil has been afraid of this. His heart aches for her and her family. He is sweating by the time he reaches his car, his mind races as he tries to figure out what to do.

He knows that to blindly run means certain death. As surely as he knows this, he also knows, his days are numbered. He reaches his vehicle and holds his breath. As he is about to turn the key, his cell phone rings, making him jump. He is breathing rapidly with his hands covering his face as the telephone continues to ring. Balil pulls it from his pocket and answers, "Hello?"

Horace says, "Balil, so good of you to answer. How has your morning been so far?"

Balil replies without emotion, "Challenging. My access to Bionan has been revoked."

Horace chuckles slightly and says, "I'm afraid that while your service has been admirable, your usefulness has come to an end, Balil. The State Department has discontinued your work visa. I'm afraid that it is time for you to return to Pakistan. Do you understand Balil?"

Balil swallows hard and replies, "Yes. I have been expecting this since I heard about Annie. Is my fate to be the same?"

Horace chuckles, "I will leave that up to you Balil. Bionan Labs has graciously agreed to purchase your wonderful discovery but, as I said, your services are no longer needed. There is a package on your kitchen table Balil and a flight leaving Dulles at midnight tonight for Karachi. Be on it. Remember, your mother is counting on you."

The call is disconnected, and Balil breathes a shuddering sigh of relief. He pulls the car out into traffic for the drive to his apartment to pack a bag. When he arrives, he enters his apartment slowly, expecting death to come at any moment. His youth trained him to accept death and so he has, but if the man gives him the option, he will certainly live. He packs a small duffle with just a few things and opens the package on the table to find ten thousand dollars in cash, a first-class ticket and a simple sheet of paper with an off shore account number. Balil doesn't bother to check the balance of the account.

At this point, he considers each breath to be a gift. He puts the cash in a sock and shoves it in the duffle, then walks out of his apartment for the last time, knowing he will never return. He parks his car in long term parking and makes his way to the departure gate, his dream of being an American citizen completely vanished. He boards the big jet on schedule, finds his seat and waits, still not expecting to see the sunrise. The airliner rumbles down the runway and when the wheels finally leave the ground, Balil dares to think of the future again.

Chapter Thirteen

Reginald storms into his office. As he passes Norma's desk, he says with a sideways glance, "Get Zwerger on the phone and get me a cup of coffee."

Norma looks up, with a look of surprise on her face. "Good morning, Mr. Emmer. Your coffee is already on your desk. I'll contact Mr. Zwerger for you."

Reginald stops in the doorway, his shoulders droop as he says without turning around, "Thank you Norma."

He continues into the office and shuts the door behind him. Reginald paces the floor, unable to sit in the overly expensive office chair designed to ease the stress of the elite executive. As he stops in front of the massive teakwood desk, chewing on the cuticle of his finger, he looks at the telephone, willing it to ring. His focus is so complete that when it does finally ring, he takes a quick step back as if it is a rattlesnake ready to strike. He answers quickly, "Emmer."

The voice is yelling over loud machinery in the background. "Mr. Emmer, this is David."

Reginald doesn't bother with formalities but gets straight to the point saying, "David, where are we at on production?"

David yells, "We're at full production. I've authorized overtime to run seven days a week for two shifts. Cancelled all vacations and trying to hire more line personnel. I should be able to add another shift within a couple of weeks."

Reginald's lips become a thin line separating his chin and nose. "What's our daily unit output?"

David replies, "Roughly a hundred thousand doses between all the lines, more or less."

Reginald looks at the ceiling and sighs, "Have you started shipments yet?"

He thinks, "This is like pulling fucking teeth. Why can't he just give me a full report?"

David replies, "Not yet. We're filling the trucks and staging them to go out at the same time to the distribution centers."

Reginald feels a bead of sweat working its way down his spine. "No David. That's not what I want. I want trucks leaving here non-stop with full loads. People are starting to line up outside pharmacies all over because of this supposed super flu. Hell, I heard they just about had a riot at Baller Drugs. We need vaccinations on trucks and out of here. Do you understand me? I want it done yesterday."

David is silent for a moment then asks, "Is there a super flu, Mr. Emmer?"

Reginald looks at the telephone for a moment then says, "How the hell should I know David. The point is, there are a lot of people who think so and they're starting to get desperate for this shot already, so get your ass in gear."

David replies, "Will do boss."

The line goes dead, and Reginald looks at the telephone in disbelief. "That prick just hung up on me."

He decides that the affront isn't something he'll address in the near future. He thinks, "Thankfully David probably doesn't know it, but he's the only one who can save my ass right now."

Across town Sandy Smithers stands in front of the mirror in her room at the Carriage Inn. The hotel isn't top of the line by her standards, but then again nothing is top of the line in Green River as far as she can tell. The drive was a long one and when she'd made it into town, she'd stopped at the first place she saw for a room. She looks at herself appraisingly thinking, "Doctor Pearce is going to pour his heart out when he sees you, Sandy."

The form fitting skirt accentuates the curves of her body and the light blue blouse goes perfectly with her long blonde hair in a look that is professional yet flirty. Her beauty has opened many doors that were closed to other reporters. Sandy isn't ashamed to use it when the situation calls for it. One last look and she moves to the door and her Miata parked right outside the room.

Climbing in, she puts Konrad's address into her telephone and the directions pop up almost instantly. She thinks, "Twenty-four minutes and I start the interview that may get me that anchor's spot. She smiles to herself, puts the car in reverse and pulls out onto the four lane which serves as the main thoroughfare for Green River. Traffic seems heavy for the small town, everyone driving at a snail's pace. She is used to Atlanta where drivers make quick decisions and stick with them. There is none of that here. Sandy drives under an old railway trestle and passes a huge graveyard as she thinks, "What a shame to die in a place like this."

The entrance to the subdivision is nothing special. No gates or anything really to mark it as a separate community from the rest of the town. As she looks for Konrad's home, she thinks, "This place was probably a big deal back in the seventies."

Most of the homes are well kept but have that bi-level architecture so popular back then. She shakes her head. As she pulls into the drive at the end of the cul-de-sac, she sees a man pushing a wheelbarrow through the front yard. He is middle-aged, tall and moves like an athlete. She thinks, "He rides a road bike or maybe a runner. Something tame that helps him to unwind."

Sandy puts the car in park, opens the door and stands with practiced grace. "Doctor Pearce?"

Her arrival hasn't escaped his attention, and Konrad sets the wheelbarrow full of mulch down, removes his gloves and slowly walks toward her. "That's right and you are Ms. Smithers. I recognize you from your news reports. He puts his hand out and shakes her hand, noticing that her grip is firm and full of confidence. He realizes she has completed this ritual thousands of times before. Konrad motions with his head for her to follow him toward the house and says, "Why don't you come inside, and we can talk."

His home is dark and cool giving it a sharp contrast to the late summer heat. Konrad barely uses lights anymore, the darkness matching his mood. As they enter the living room, Sandy senses the sadness in this place. "Doctor, I really appreciate your call and your willingness to speak with me."

She thinks, "I'll have to be careful with this one. Something has broken him."

Konrad says, "I hope I'm doing the right thing by having you here. Please call me Konrad. We have a lot to talk about."

Sandy motions with her hand and asks, "Mind if I look around? I like to get to know who I'm speaking with."

Konrad sits down on the couch and with a lazy wave of his hand says, "Sure, go ahead. Make yourself at home."

As she walks around the room, Konrad notices the way she moves. There is a certain graceful strength in her movement. Then he remembers Jennifer and feels ashamed of himself averting his gaze.

Sandy can feel him watching her as she moves around the room looking at the framed photos on the wall and mantle. She turns and asks, "Your family?"

Konrad strokes his goatee and says, "Yes, my wife Jennifer and my daughter Chloe."

She smiles and replies, "I would like to meet them. Are they here?"

Konrad smiles with a tinge of sadness and says, "I'd like to think they are but no, you can't meet them. They were killed in a traffic accident a while back."

Sandy walks over to the easy chair facing Konrad, sits down and says, "I'm sorry Konrad."

She thinks as she says this, "So that's what's broken him."

Konrad sits back on the couch and rubs his face with both hands. "Not your fault. It was just a truck driver who made a poor decision. Can I get you something to drink? I have coffee, tea, I think and water."

Sandy smiles and says, "Maybe a bottle of water if you have it."

She doesn't trust this man yet. Konrad goes into the kitchen and gets a cold bottle of water out of the fridge and hands it to her with a knowing smile thinking, "Smart girl. I wouldn't trust me either."

Konrad sits back down on the couch and leans forward, rubbing his hands together. "I feel that I should be totally honest with you up front Sandy. Is it alright if I call you Sandy?"

Sandy smiles and nods thinking, "Take your time Sandy. Build the rapport."

He puts his hands on his knees and leans back taking a deep breath saying, "What I'm about to tell you, I can't take back. I'm pretty sure that this goes much farther up the ladder than Reginald Emmer. My lab associate, Candace Swanson has, as far as I can tell, dropped off the face of the earth. One of my lab assistants died of a fentanyl overdose. She was no addict, and you already know about the Weinzcuff guy. It's dangerous to know what I know. Understand?"

Sandy pulls a small audio recorder from her purse and says softly, "Why don't you start with your name and tell me your story."

Konrad continues, "My name is Doctor Konrad Pearce. I am the lead research scientist at Emmer Pharmaceuticals. I've been or was working on a universal flu vaccine at Emmer for the past seven years, give or take. When my family was killed, I took some time off. When I returned, Candace showed me a mutation in one of the samples from Thailand which in a word is catastrophic. I won't go into the science."

Sandy interjects, "No, please do Konrad."

Konrad sits forward and rubs his hands together collecting his thoughts. "Okay. Well basically, the human body has several mechanisms for combating a virus. One of the main mechanisms is a fever. Viruses have a tough time replicating in a warm environment above, say one hundred degrees. This mutation contradicts that. It thrives between one hundred and one hundred and four. Another aspect of this mutation is that it mutates fast. I mean incredibly fast. You can see the implications. Mass deaths on the scale of the Spanish Flu. Anyway, I should have notified the CDC but, I wanted to study it and possibly use it to perfect the universal flu vaccine that we were working on."

Konrad rubs his forehead and whispers, "Stupid. So fucking stupid. It was my pride. I wanted to beat it but, I've failed. Failed on so many levels."

Sandy looks at the broken, guilt-ridden man and realizes she'll have to gently guide him back on track. "I'm confused Konrad, you're saying that you didn't notify the CDC?"

Konrad shakes his head and looks at the floor. Sandy leans forward and asks, "How about Weinzcuff? Did you have any contact with him? Were you, his source?"

He looks up quickly. "No. I tried to contact the CDC right before I contacted you, but they stonewalled me. I was never able to make a report."

Sandy leans her head to the side, her blonde hair falling from her shoulder. "So where did Weinzcuff get his information? If what you're saying is true and I have no reason to doubt you, there is a super flu and Weinzcuff was telling the truth, so, someone in the CDC already knows and they're keeping it a secret."

Konrad's eyes widen as he says, "Reginald has put the vaccine into production, and he has the contract to supply everyone. It will be fairly effective against normal flu variants, but this mutation has it beat out of the gate. Why are they hiding it?"

Sandy sits back in the chair. "How bad do you think it will get Doctor?"

Konrad shakes his head and says, "There's no way to tell. It depends on how contagious it is. I had Candace trying to monitor the cases in Thailand, but she wasn't having much luck."

Sandy looks at Konrad inquisitively and asks, "Isn't all of that data reported to the CDC? I mean, if there is a super flu, surely, they would know, right? Yet both the CDC and The World Health Organization have made statements to the contrary. What do you make of that?"

Konrad shakes his head and replies, "That is the problem, I don't have enough data to make anything of it. Reginald and I had a falling out and he's put me on extended leave of absence. I might as well be on the dark side of the moon. The one thing that I do know is, that bug is real. I saw it."

Sandy gives Konrad her signature smile and leans in. "So, tell me about the universal flu vaccine. Are you close to developing it?"

He replies softly, "Not even. I haven't been able to develop a way to stay ahead of antigen drift. Mutations, they're what's kicking my ass. It doesn't matter anyway. My career is finished."

She looks down at the floor then back at Konrad. "Why are you on leave of absence Konrad?"

His shoulders slump as he replies, "I don't know why he initially put me on extended 'vacation' but I gave him cause just a few days ago. I haven't handled myself very well since my family's death and then Annie dying the way she did. I snapped and went after Emmer. There's a police report and it's not good."

Sandy looks away for a moment and replies, "I see. Do you think he'll talk to me?"

Konrad looks at Sandy with an appraising look and says, "Knowing Reginald, he'll be waiting at the gate for you himself.

Sandy blushes despite herself and says, "Well, we'll see. I think I'll pay Mr. Emmer a visit. You wouldn't happen to have his personal cell number?"

She stands as does Konrad and they shake hands. Konrad gives her the number and stands with his hands in his pockets waiting as Sandy says, "As of right now Konrad, you're a protected source. I won't use your identity unless you allow me too. I'm going to try and verify as much of what you've told me as possible. Thank you for this Konrad. I'll be in touch."

As she is heading out the front door, Konrad calls her name. She stops for a second and looks back as he says, "Remember what I said. Be careful."

Then she is gone and the loneliness of the house envelopes him once again.

When Sandy reaches her car, she pulls her cell phone out and dials Reginald's personal phone. The call is answered after several rings by an impatient male voice, "Reginald."

Sandy answers in a slightly sultry tone, "Mr. Emmer, this is Sandy Smithers from WKTT News Atlanta. I've heard so much about you and have been looking forward to speaking with you. Do you have a few moments? I'm in town and can buzz right over."

There is silence on the line for a few seconds and then Reginald says, "I've seen you on the recent news stories regarding this Weinzcuff character. You have a very commanding screen presence Miss Smithers, although I fear you're on the wrong track. It is 'miss' isn't it?"

Sandy smiles and thinks, "Game, set and match."

She says, her smile oozing through the telephone, "Yes Reginald, it is. I'm still working on that story and wanted to get your opinion, you being the sole distributor of the influenza vaccine. Can we meet? I'm really trying to put a few things to bed."

Reginald's breathing quickens slightly, "I'm at your service Sandy. I'll have an escort at the gate when you arrive. How do you like your coffee?"

Sandy smiles and says, "Surprise me Reginald."

Thirty minutes later she pulls the Miata up to the gate and revs the engine. A very large, bald headed security guard is standing near a golf cart on the other side, with the look all security guards have. Harry steps out and checks Sandy's driver's license then pushes a button sending the large chain link gate on its lumbering journey to the side. She pulls through, parks in the visitor's parking adjacent to the gate and walks over to Carl and the waiting golf cart.

As she walks over, Sandy notices that although Carl unashamedly watches her approach, it is not the look she is used to getting from men. She can tell that this one is all business and not susceptible to her feminine charm. She tries to make small talk saying, "This is such a big facility. I bet you stay pretty busy providing the security here. I bet you see all sorts of things."

Carl stares straight ahead as he drives toward the administrative building saying, "If you say so."

Sandy smiles to herself thinking, "I wish I had time to interview you. I bet it would be all sorts of fun."

She has always liked a challenge. As they pull up to the building, Carl parks the cart, sets the brake and steps out in one fluid motion saying, "Please follow me."

He doesn't look back to see if she does. A short elevator ride and they enter Reginald's outer office. It contrasts sharply to the manufacturing environment that she has just ridden through. Everything is made of heavy wood that actually looks expensive. Sandy thinks, "This creep had to have had a decorator. There is no way he chose this himself."

This causes her to think briefly about where one would find a decorator in Green River, Indiana. The wooden nameplate with the highly shined brass front identifies the plain middle-aged woman sitting at the desk as 'Norma'. She looks at Carl and says in a nasally voice, "I can handle it from here Carl. Thank you."

Carl replies, "Just contact dispatch when you're ready for me to escort the lady out Mrs. Wheeler."

Then he is gone. At that moment, Reginald opens the door to his office and smiling, moves toward Sandy with his hand outstretched. Although it makes her skin crawl, Sandy accepts his handshake, noticing the dampness of his palm. She must mentally force herself not to wipe her palm on her skirt after he releases her hand. He turns to Norma and says, "Norma, would you make us some of that Cuban select I had imported?"

Norma raises an eyebrow and nods her head. "Of course, Mr. Emmer."

She thinks as she says this, "Not a snowball's chance in hell Reginald. It'll take a lot more than fancy coffee with this one."

Reginald and Sandy go into his office and Norma gets up from her chair shaking her head.

After entering the office, Sandy finds a seat on the small sofa, quickly pulling her notebook and recorder out and sitting it beside her, successfully blocking Reginald's attempt to join her. He looks around the office as if he is lost for a moment then walks behind his desk and sits in the oversized executive chair with an air of superiority saying, "So, Sandy, how can I help you?"

Sandy picks up her notebook and thinks, "I'll have to let him be the one in charge. He likes the power."

She puts on a demure smile and says, "Well, I really just wanted to interview the man who has led his company into being the sole provider for the influenza vaccine to the nation. Tell me, how you accomplished such a feat?"

Reginald leans back in his chair and says, "You know, the common man doesn't realize it Sandy, but our government loves a winner. They may posture and spout about the contest not being relevant. You know, everyone getting a prize at the end of the race, but in the end, Uncle Sam loves a winner and that's what I am, a winner."

Sandy looks down at her notes feigning nervousness. "Was there some kind of application process to obtain the distribution contract?"

Reginald laughs smugly saying, "Oh usually, but honestly, they practically begged me to take the job. Do you know why Sandy? I'll tell you, because they knew that Emmer Pharmaceutical was the logical choice if they wanted it done right."

Sandy slowly tightens the hypothetical leash around Reginald's neck. "Have you started production yet? I mean, you're talking at least five billion doses. That has to be a daunting task, even for a man like you."

Reginald stands and walks to the window, looking out over the facility. "It would be for most men Sandy, but I'm built of some pretty tough stock. I won't lie to you, the crown gets heavy at times, but yes, production is underway, and units are already arriving at various pharmacies around the nation. I made a promise to my country, and I intend to keep it."

Sandy looks at Reginald, standing like a king surveying his empire and thinks, "What a small, little man. Time to close the trap."

She asks, "Even if keeping that promise means the vaccine won't be very effective?"

It's as if Reginald is struck by lightning. He spins to face her and blusters, "What? What did you say?"

Sandy looks at Reginald innocently and says, "Well, with this super flu I don't see how the vaccine will be very effective. Or have you developed something to combat it?"

The color drains from Reginald's face as he asks, "Who have you been talking to?"

Sandy smiles as she slowly shifts the control of the interview. "I have a source, Reginald. This individual tells me that the super flu does exist, and that the vaccine won't help."

The color returns to Reginald's face as he grins malevolently. "Yeah, I bet you do have a 'source'. A source with good reason to try and wreck my company because I fired him for incompetence. A man with emotional problems who showed up at my home and tried to attack me. You should vet your sources better Sandy. There is no super flu young lady. I think it's time for you to leave."

Sandy keeps her cool demeanor, leaning back on the sofa. "So, to confirm, the minute we start talking about a possible super flu, you're going to throw me out. Am I correct?"

Reginald walks to the door, opens it and tells Norma, "Call Carl, Miss Smithers is ready to leave."

Sandy looks at Reginald with a cagey smile and says, "C'mon Reginald, I would really like to get your side of this. It will play so much better than reporting that you refused to comment. How about at least providing the paperwork on your testing processes."

Reginald looks at Sandy, his smug demeanor having returned and replies, "Like I said Sandy, there is no super flu. It doesn't exist. The World Health Organization and the CDC will back me up on that, furthermore, I'm a hero and patriot so write whatever the fuck you want. If you want the testing documentation, put a request into the FDA. Have a nice trip back to Atlanta."

Carl walks into the office and stands by the sofa looking at Sandy. She methodically puts her notebook and recorder back into her bag then stands and straightens her skirt before turning toward Carl saying, "Follow me."

She walks out of the office, not looking back to see if Carl does.

Two days later, Sandy is sitting in the co-anchor's chair next to Dale Sprock thinking, "I'm getting closer to your chair Dale. Soon, very soon."

She'd driven all the way back to Atlanta right after the meeting with Reginald, the anger fueling her desire to get back and make this report. She thinks about Reginald Emmer and what a smug little prick the man is. She is jarred from her thoughts by Dale saying, "Well Sandy, what developments do you have for us?"

Instinctually, the beaming smile appears as she faces the camera, "Well Dale, I've been able to uncover a lot. I spoke with a confidential source inside Emmer Pharmaceuticals who insists there is a super flu and that they have seen it. I'm sure you'll all remember that Emmer is the sole supplier for the influenza vaccine this year. My source claims that they attempted to contact the CDC regarding the alleged super flu but were unable to make a report. I was also very fortunate in interviewing Reginald Emmer, Owner and CEO of Emmer Pharmaceuticals. The interview was, for the most part, pleasant however, when the subject of the super flu came up, Mr. Emmer ended the interview with a simple denial. His responses mimicked the denials we have already seen from W.H.O. and the CDC. Mr. Emmer declined to comment on the efficacy of the vaccine that he is producing and refused to provide the literature on any testing prior to distribution. He was uncooperative, so, as of this point, there seems to be more questions than answers."

Dale turns to face the camera. "That's interesting Sandy, I for one hope that the vaccine is effective. I'm not ashamed to say, I received my shot yesterday and would encourage everyone to follow the advice of the CDC and get vaccinated."

Sandy looks at Dale with a guarded look then smiles and says, "That is my hope too Dale. I'll continue to follow with more updates."

The Camera cuts to a full facial shot of Dale, smiling as he says, "Thanks Sandy, now on to the weather in the beautiful city of Atlanta."

Sandy walks off the set thinking, "That was totally weird. What is wrong with him? No clarifying questions? Nothing to lead the viewer into interest in future reports? He just follows up with a canned statement to get the vaccine? Hell, he might as well be working for the CDC. That was definitely not Dale."

Sandy leaves the studios and walks the room full of cubicles to her desk. She drops her news copy on her desk and sits down in the chair thinking, "I'm always moving up hill. It's all so tiring and what in the hell is up with Dale?"

Her thoughts are interrupted by her desk telephone ringing. She picks up and says, "WKTT, this is Sandy Smithers."

A female voice responds, "Miss Smithers, I just watched your report on this year's influenza vaccine. I have information if you're willing to travel."

Sandy sits straight in her chair and grabs a pen and paper. "You could just tell me over the phone. I mean, if you're legit."

The woman replies, "Oh, I'm legit but we can't speak over the telephone."

Sandy's lips tighten into a line as she says, "Look, I'm all out of company money so you're going to have to convince me or we're through talking."

The woman replies flatly, "My name is Candace Swanson and you really need to hear what I have to say."

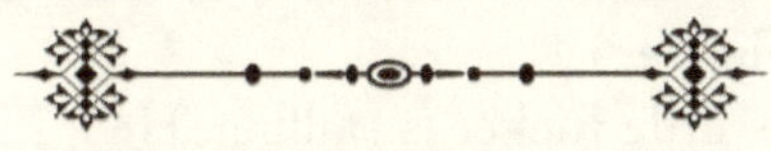

Chapter Fourteen

Ruth Evans stands in her supervisor's office and waits patiently for him to stop pacing back and forth. Since arriving at work this morning, she has had the unwanted privilege of listening to him rant about last night's WKTT news report on the 'so called' super flu. Early on in his diatribe, his hand ringing had become one monotone syllable after another which she has ceased to pay attention to. He turns to her quickly, jarring her from her thoughts and says, "Well, have you?"

Ruth looks at Joel and asks, "Have I what?"

He gives her an exasperated look and says, "Have you been in touch with the Mid-Atlantic Liaison to see if anyone from Emmer has contacted them? This 'source' claims to have tried to make a report. Am I speaking too quickly for you Ruth?"

Ruth replies stonily, "No Joel, I haven't. I've been in your office for the last hour listening to you so, no, I haven't. Would you like me to?"

Joel replies through clenched teeth, "Yes, I suppose that would be amazing of you Ruth. Please do that."

Ruth turns to leave, and Joel sits down in his chair with a huff. On her way to her office, Ruth mutters under her breath, "That little bald-headed fucker. I hate him, I hate him, I hate him."

She looks up the extension and dials. It is answered by a cheerful voice, "Mid-Atlantic Liaison, CDC, this is Warren Densin. How may I help you?"

Ruth rolls her eyes and says, "Mr. Densin, this is Ruth Evans, Deputy Chief Public Information Officer, do you have a minute?"

Warren sits up in his chair and focuses on the telephone. "Yes Ms. Evans. What can I do for you?"

Ruth takes a deep breath. "Mr. Densin, has anyone from Emmer Pharmaceuticals in Green River, Indiana contacted you in regard to filing any type of report?"

Warren begins to sweat. All calls to the internal extensions are logged, someplace. That's how the government works. If he lies,

Warren knows that it will catch up with him if any official inquiries are started. He decides to take the ambiguous route. "Green River? Not to the best of my knowledge."

Ruth thinks, "This little fucker is stalling. Hell, I invented 'not to the best of my knowledge."

Ruth speaks slowly and quietly, "Warren, tell me the truth. Did someone from Emmer contact you? Be honest."

Warren feels the violent need to urinate. He crosses his legs and closes his eyes. "No, I swear. I haven't talked to anyone."

Her chest rises and falls with a deep breath. "Alright Warren, please let me know if anyone does try to contact us, won't you?"

Warren replies through clenched teeth, "Yes ma'am, I will."

The line goes dead and Warren rushes to the bathroom. Ruth stands and looks at the telephone. She sighs and thinks, "I'm going to have to address this at the next press briefing. As of right now, I can retire in thirty days and I'm none the wiser. If I check the telephone records, I am right back in the middle of a shit storm. Joel thought he was going to lay all this crap on my head, well, I think I'll leave this little problem for him to handle after I'm gone."

Warren returns to his desk and pulls the card from his drawer. He dials the telephone, and the call is answered in two rings. "Hello Warren, good news I hope."

Warren stammers, "No, I don't think it is. I'm sorry but Ruth Evans, the Deputy PIO just called me and asked if I had been contacted by Emmer. I lied and told her no, but she can check. I'm going to get caught. I'm so fucked."

Horace looks at the ceiling of his apartment and sighs. "Warren, settle down. You need to find something to relax you, my young friend. I would've thought the lovely Sandra would have been just the thing but obviously not. I see that she's joined you at your condo. Congratulations. Now, obviously you've forgotten who I am. That call was scrubbed from the records as soon as you called me. Remember, I'm here to help you, Warren. As long as you're on my team, you're safe. Understand?"

Warren nods his head, staring out the window. Horace continues in his smooth hissing voice, "I need you to say that you understand Warren."

Warren jumps in his chair and replies, "Yes, yes, I understand. Thank you."

Horace smiles his reptilian smile and replies, "Good Warren. I'm counting on you and so is Sandra."

The line goes dead and Warren exhales.

Horace MacGill walks into his kitchen and pours a tumbler of bourbon. The chirp of his computer calls him back to the living room. The chirping of his computer is almost always bad news. Another angle to traverse, another challenge to overcome. His satellite telephone rings, and he answers it immediately. "Hello?"

The asset replies, "Sir, we've monitored a telephone call on Sandy Smithers' office telephone. Origination is Key West, Florida. I took the liberty of sending you the recording. It appears Candace Swanson has resurfaced on the grid. We have a location, what are your instructions?"

Horace thinks, "This isn't good. No, not good at all."

After a moment's silence, Horace says, "Continue to monitor. I want daily reports."

The asset replies, "10-4 sir."

The line goes dead, and Horace takes a seat on the couch thinking, "A target package is out of the question for this situation. A reporter who's a crusader can't be eliminated quietly and Swanson, now that she's made contact, is definitely off limits. Talk about a dog after a bone. There would be no stopping Smithers. No, this is going to require some finesse."

Just outside of Atlanta, Sandy Smithers settles in for a long drive, the Miata purring under her like a large feline. Sandy loved the machine from the first minute she sat behind the wheel. The leather seat feels comfortable and familiar, wrapping itself around her as she lightly grasps the wheel. Most of her stories have been written in her head while driving the car, long before putting them down on paper. Traffic is, as usual, heavy on 75 south. Sandy stays in the left lane, passing vacationers and less committed drivers without a second glance. She has someplace that she needs to be, and she needs to be there without delay. Sandy has a destination, a mission.

The departure from WKTT this morning was messy. The kind of messy you just don't come back from. After Sandy had concluded her telephone call with Candace, she had an address in Key West, Florida, a short amount of time to make a long drive and a huge problem. She knew before even walking into Kyle's office that he wouldn't authorize the trip. She thinks as she weaves in and out of traffic, "That prick wanted this story dead a long time ago."

Now, she wonders if there isn't another angle that he's playing. Have the folks at the CDC gotten to Kyle? Sandy doesn't know for sure. She thinks back to her exit from WKTT and cringes. She'd put on the smile that had won so many men over in the past and had confidently walked into Kyle's office to ask about going to Florida. It had turned nasty almost immediately. Kyle had taken his glasses off and rubbed his eyes saying, "I thought I was clear on this Sandy, no more time wasted on this wild goose chase. You're on the homicide in Buckhead."

As always, she'd decided well before going into the office that she had to win. There was something to this story, she could feel it. This was her anchor's spot. It was her ticket to the big time. Sandy had replied, "There are plenty of people here capable of handling a homicide in Atlanta. For fuck's sake Kyle, it's like covering a traffic accident on the freeway. I could almost cut and paste from the last one. No, I'm covering this story, not Buckhead."

She'd realized then that she hadn't closed his office door after she'd entered. She turned to see everyone in the newsroom looking in her direction. It was an irreversible mistake. Kyle had looked at her with a stony glare. That's the moment she realized, there could be no concession. No private negotiation. This would be an all too public war of their wills. He had said resolutely, "I need reporters to cover Atlanta news Sandy. You need to decide right now whether you want to do that or cover conspiracy theories. I'll expect something on Buckhead by the end of the day."

Sandy looks back now and realizes she'd painted both of them into a corner. She'd huffed and said, "Sorry Kyle, I'll be in Florida."

She'd walked out of the office and Kyle had followed her out into the cubes. He'd never done that before. He had yelled, "Sandy, if you walk out that door, you can take your crap with you because you're fired!"

A scene played out plenty of times before. Kyle had fired her many times as she'd left his office, always to change his mind after they'd made up. She would bring in the big scoop and he would hire her back. All nice and private with no pride lost. This was different. Sandy had turned and said, "Good! I'll let you know where to send my things."

She'd stormed out and headed straight home to pack a bag. Now she finds herself on the highway, driving to a meeting with a woman she knows nothing about, chasing a convoluted story which may be nothing but a dead end. There is a certain freedom in being unemployed. There is also terror because the bills will continue to keep coming and her savings account balance is nothing to be proud of. Sandy shakes her head and thinks, "Hopefully Kyle will call in a bit and tell me I'm rehired."

She doesn't believe he will this time. The public display they'd made was irreversible for both of them. She can only hope that this story will pan out, and quickly. The miles pass under the humming tires of the Miata and Sandy fills those miles with these dark thoughts. She sees the large green sign for a rest area and decides to stop for a break. As she pulls onto the exit, her phone begins to ring. She smiles and thinks, "I knew you couldn't stay angry at me forever."

Sandy answers with a cheerful 'hello', expecting Kyle's voice. Instead, a man says, "Sandy? This is Cal Hendley."

She recognizes the name immediately. Cal Hendley is the producer of three major news shows in New York. He is a career maker. She finds her voice and says, "Hello Mr. Hendley. Good morning, what can I do for you?"

Cal replies, "Sandy, I've been trying to track you down all morning. I called WKTT and they told me you'd gone on to other opportunities. Is that true?"

Sandy replies slowly, "Well, I've moved on, that is true. As for other opportunities, I'm considering several directions."

Cal laughs and says, "Well, I've been watching your work, Sandy. I've been following it very closely actually and I like what I see. I'd like to propose an opportunity for you to consider. I'd like you to fly up here to New York and speak with me about a co-anchor's spot on the Times Square Morning Report with Blake Peters. Are you familiar with the show?"

Sandy can't believe what she's hearing. This is her lifelong dream being handed to her in a rest area on I-75. A lump forms in her throat. She stammers, "I, I don't know what to say. Of course. Yes, of course. When do you want to meet?"

Cal chuckles again, "Wonderful Sandy. It'll have to be tomorrow morning. This is time sensitive. The opening has just become available. Jenine Gomez has abruptly decided to devote herself to her family and has resigned so I must fill it quickly to guarantee continuity in production. There's a first-class ticket waiting at the Southwest terminal in Atlanta for you. You leave in eight hours."

Sandy almost becomes dizzy at the thought. She thinks, "It's almost too much. Here it is Sandy. All you have to do is grab it."

She thinks about this story and Candace who is waiting for her at this moment and replies, "Cal, I'm on the road. Can I call you back in fifteen minutes?"

Cal is silent for a moment then says, "Sure Sandy, I realize this is a whirlwind. Fifteen minutes but then I'll need an answer and Sandy, opportunities come few and far between in this life. This one won't come again. Make the right decision."

The line goes dead, and Sandy just looks at her telephone as she exhales a long slow breath. Then the tears come. Long quiet sobs of relief. She thinks about all the years of sleepless nights and deadlines culminating in this moment. She thinks about the story she has gambled her future on and realizes it will die unless she pursues it. Sandy feels a deep sadness as she realizes that for all her haughty aspirations, she will not be the one to save the world. In the end, she is just like everyone else. Sandy Smithers, investigative crusader is a myth. She dries her eyes and dials the telephone. It is answered immediately, "This is Cal."

She smiles slightly and says, "Cal, this is Sandy, I'll see you tomorrow morning."

Cal laughs, "Excellent Sandy. I've booked you a room at the Excelsior. A car will be waiting at the airport for you, and they'll also pick you up tomorrow to bring you to the studios. Come prepared to do some preliminary shooting. Congratulations Sandy."

Sandy looks in the rear-view mirror of the Miata and notices a tinge of sadness in the eyes as she says, "Thank you so much for the opportunity, Cal. It means a great deal to me."

Cal chuckles one final time and says, "The pleasure is mine Sandy. See you tomorrow."

He hangs up and Sandy sets the telephone on the passenger seat. She thinks about the long drive she'll be replacing with a short flight, the packing she still must accomplish and her future in New York as she puts the car in gear and merges into traffic in search of the next exit to turn around and head back to Atlanta.

Chapter Fifteen

Candace sits at a table just inside the Java Hut in Key West, Florida. Her position gives her a good view of the street without being too exposed. She looks up and down the street, focusing on each vehicle and person thinking, "Old habits die hard."

Candace doesn't believe she is being paranoid. The secret she carries is explosive enough to be a death sentence and she knows it. Her life is worth nothing compared to the billions at stake. It is a cold hard reality, and she is very familiar with the coldness of reality, having never lost the instincts honed as an orphan in the 'system'. Candace was living on her own by the age of fifteen and learned the skill of disappearing through necessity.

As a foster, she learned the meaning of the saying, "Spare the rod and spoil the child." She was never spoiled. After running away for the last time, she had hitchhiked to Colorado from Baton Rouge, working at various low paying jobs for cash along the way. She'd been a waitress for a while and a hotel maid. She'd learned the value of cash and how it made you invisible to those searching for you.

Mary Beth Willows had been the one who had turned her life around. She was a waitress in the small diner in Ft. Collins where Candace had been hired to wait tables. Mary Beth was the one who had taken her in and given her the confidence to get her GED. She'd helped her get the financial help needed to go to Colorado State. Mary Beth is, as far as Candace is concerned, the mother she had lost so many years ago. Memories of Mary Beth have always been a well of strength for Candace when things in her life got hard. Things are extremely hard now as she sits and waits for Sandy Smithers to show up. She is already very late, and Candace is getting the feeling that she isn't going to show. It is an intuition which has saved her more than once.

She'd had the same feeling on the last day in the lab. The feeling that told her to disappear. To run and hide like the old days. She had gone straight to the bank and withdrawn most of her funds. Then she'd driven straight home, packed an overnight bag and left, leaving her cell phone and credit cards behind. On her way out of town, Candace had stopped at a kiosk and bought a burner phone then she was on the road to Key West. It was a place where everyone had a past and kept it to themselves.

It was easy to disappear in a place such as this. Candace looks around once more and that is when she notices the gray panel van sitting across the street and half a block up. The man behind the wheel looks over his shoulder and says something. There is someone in the back. The fine hairs on the back of her neck stand up and her pulse quickens. The little voice inside of her is screaming, "Run Candace!"

She knows better. To run is to let whoever it is know that she has seen them. Candace looks around the tiny coffee shop nonchalantly and studies each of the other patrons. Most of them are reading or conversing, but there is one man in the back corner just sitting and staring at his coffee cup. She realizes that he has been there for a while. He is athletic with short, cropped hair. She looks away and then slowly looks back at him and sees that he is now looking at her. A smile is exchanged as she gets a good look at him.

He is wearing a t-shirt and swim trunks, as most of the patrons are but this man is wearing running shoes. Not the flip flops so common in Key West. She takes a sip of her latte and dabs her mouth with a napkin then stands and steps to the counter, leaning across and asking the tanned teenager in a whisper where the back door is. He looks at her quizzically and says, "Its back that way, toward the bathrooms lady but it's for employees only."

Candace smiles and laughs saying, "Oh, I'm sorry, so, where are the bathrooms?"

The kid shakes his head and points. Candace heads down a short hallway in the direction of the bathrooms but doesn't turn into the bathroom. Instead, she hits the bar on the back door without slowing. It slams open and an alarm sounds but she is already through the door. She slams it shut, finding herself in an alley behind the shops. She looks left and right realizing that the alley angles back to the street at both ends. She is breathing hard as she thinks, "I have to create some angles."

She looks left and sees an old upright freezer next to the door. Candace gets behind it and shoves with all her might. The freezer topples over, blocking the door from opening. She turns around and sees a six-foot privacy fence. Running the short distance to the fence,

Candace climbs on an overturned milk crate and gets over the fence, the rough wood scraping her stomach. As she drops down behind the fence, she hears the door alarm again. Finding herself in a small backyard, Candace crouches just on the other side of the fence for a moment, catching her breath.

There is a barking dog roped to a doghouse trying its best to get loose. She puts her finger to her lips in a feeble attempt to get the dog to quiet down. Her efforts are met with more insane barking. She gets to her feet and barely dodges the dog as it lunges at her. She runs through a gate to the front of the house and out on to a quiet street where she hears several screams and then a yelp. Candace runs across the tiny street diagonally and then through another back yard.

When she hits the alley on the other side, Candace runs. She runs as fast as she can to her tiny apartment three blocks away. The apartment isn't much. Just one room above a bait shop but it is just the kind of place one lives in when they don't want to draw attention. She puts a sun hat on and packs quickly before getting into her car, looking around once more. A turn of the key and the engine roars to life. She calmly backs out of the rear parking and into the alley thinking, "That bitch set me up."

Candace has been here before and knows she only has minutes to get away. She heads North with no destination in mind other than away. Her thoughts are whirling in her head as she thinks, "Why did she do it? I was trying to help her."

A thousand miles to the North, a satellite telephone begins to ring and the man standing in his kitchen lets out an audible sigh. Horace thinks, "What now?"

He moves to the living room and picks the telephone up from the coffee table, answering with his usual ambiguous greeting, "Hello?"

The asset begins his report, "Sir, things have gone south on us in Florida. Our subject spooked and dumped our surveillance. I'm afraid the team didn't see it coming and she was gone before they knew that they had been made. Sorry sir."

Horace's eyes narrow and his jaw flexes. "She dumped your surveillance? Now how in the fuck did a scientist, of all people, evade your team for Christ's sake? Did you at least have someone at the bridge?"

The asset stammers, "I thought it best to deploy our assets in a rotating tail. The other team had just switched and was out of place. The eyes on asset reports that he thought she was just going up to the counter for a refill, but it looks like she exited through the back door.

He pursued but lost her. We're patching his leg up now. Dog bite. She got ahead of us. My sincere apologies Sir."

Horace takes a deep breath and says in a low tone, "Your 'sincere' apologies? That makes me feel much better. What countermeasures have you taken?"

The asset is silent for a moment then says, "I've sent one team North on the highway to see if we can catch her. Second team is still here in Key West in case she's still in the area."

Horace sees the logistics in his mind's eye and says, "No, not good. Call the team pursuing her back. The last thing we need is a Florida trooper pulling them over for speeding. That'll get messy. Just stand by in Key West and await further instructions and need I say it, keep your fucking eyes open."

Horace ends the call before the asset can reply. He thinks, "Candace, there is more to you than meets the eye."

He goes to his computer and pulls the investigative file up on Candace Swanson and begins to read. He mutters under his breath, "Surprises, surprises, I've missed something about you Candace my dear and when I find it, I'll find you."

He sets the computer down and goes to the kitchen, pouring himself a tumbler of bourbon. He returns to the couch and puts his feet up as he begins to read.

Two hundred and thirty miles North of Horace and his tumbler of bourbon, General Alejandro Quispe sits in the back seat of the black Mercedes looking out of the tinted windows. The car slowly makes its way up 45th Street in bumper-to-bumper traffic. Alejandro looks out the window at the filthy masses and thinks, "Vermin. Millions of filthy human beings, breeding like rats in a cage. The Regents are right. There are simply too many of them."

He scowls as he looks at them, wandering through their pitiful lives contributing absolutely nothing. As they pull to a stop at a traffic light, Alejandro sees something out of the ordinary amidst the human mass bumping and shoving their way up and down the sidewalk. He realizes that this is not the first block he's seen this anomaly. He rings the bell, and the driver lowers the privacy screen. "Can I do something for you General?"

The driver is a stocky man with black hair and a body builder's physique. He also doubles as a bodyguard for his clients. Alejandro asks, "Yes, you can. Do you see that line of people wrapped around the building over there?"

Alejandro points and the driver looks in that direction. He nods his head once. Alejandro says, "It's not a food kitchen. Most of them are well dressed. What are they doing? I've seen the same thing every three or four blocks."

The driver says blandly, "Pharmacies General. Everyone is trying to get the flu vaccine. That super flu has everyone scared to death. I got mine yesterday. The pharmacies keep running out."

Alejandro raises his eyebrows and says, "Is that so? How long did you wait in line to get vaccinated?"

The driver smiles, "I stood in line for two hours. That's quick from what I'm hearing. Hey, aren't you with the World Health Organization?"

Alejandro settles back in his seat thinking, "This is why I don't have conversations with the help."

He answers nonchalantly, "Yes I am."

The driver looks over his shoulder and asks, "So, how bad is this stuff? The virus, I mean?"

Alejandro assumes his usual demeanor and says curtly, "The vaccine will be effective, but without it, I'll just say it will be catastrophic. Now, close the screen, I have a call to make."

The driver is surprised at first but then resumes his stoic demeanor, nods and closes the screen. Alejandro thinks, "That filthy mercenary just might pull this off after all."

A week later, Sandy Smithers sits in her dressing room at the Morning Report's Manhattan studios. The past few days have been a whirlwind of filming test shots, signing contracts and a quick trip back to Atlanta to tie up all the loose ends of a sudden move. She is tired but her first day as co-anchor of The Morning Report is enough to keep her energized. Her meeting with Cal had gone well but it wasn't long before she'd seen both sides of the man. He had been professional with a magnetic charisma that was, to say the least, persuasive but when she'd mentioned the story that she was working on in Atlanta, his serious side came out.

"Look Sandy, I'm going to stop you there. You're not in Atlanta anymore. This is the big time. I've got plenty of news for you to cover. In fact, your first piece will be on how people around the country are reacting to the rumors of this flu bug, but, no more conspiracy theories. Our take is that the vaccine is going to do just fine. Understand? Our job is to educate the public and convince them to take the vaccine, period. Telling them that the vaccine might not be good enough will just cause panic. That story is dead Sandy."

Sandy remembers the look in his eyes when she'd said, "I thought the news was supposed to be the truth."

Cal had looked at her, his mouth a thin line and said, "The truth is what I tell you it is Sandy. You read what's on the teleprompter. That's your job now, if you don't want it, say the word. There are plenty of journalists who would kill to have your spot right now."

She looks in the mirror and can still feel the sick feeling she'd felt when she'd replied, "Of course Cal, whatever you say."

His charming smile had returned in an instant as if the exchange had never occurred. "That's my girl. We're a team around here. You're going to kill it tomorrow. I can feel it."

Now Sandy looks in the mirror and thinks, "Be smart Sandy. Let someone else save the world this time."

Her thoughts are interrupted by a knock on the door. "You're needed in makeup Ms. Smithers."

She looks into the eyes of the reflection and knows that she has betrayed herself as she thinks, "No makeup artist will ever be able to cover up what I see."

As she bargains with herself, her telephone rings. She answers it and hears a familiar voice on the other end of the line. "Sandy, I haven't heard from you. Now I know why. Your old boss told me about your fancy new job in New York. Congratulations."

She stammers, "Konrad, I really can't talk right now. I'm about to go on air in a bit. Can we talk later?"

Konrad is silent for a moment then says blandly, "Sure. What is it they say for luck in show business? Break a leg? I'll be watching."

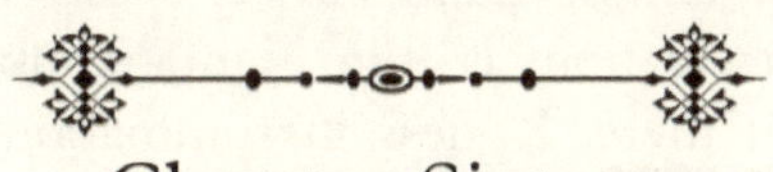

Chapter Sixteen

Konrad sits at his kitchen table looking at his computer screen and the news streaming service he's logged into. He types in the search, "Times Square Morning Report" and chooses the show as soon as it pops up. He has watched the show in the past, usually to get the news on Wall Street. He looks at his cell phone sitting next to the computer and feels tightness in his gut thinking, "She sold out. I just know it."

The show begins with Blake Peters and Sandy sitting at a glass news desk with a picture of the New York skyline covering the wall behind them. Both are smiling. Blake starts by welcoming Sandy to the show. There is some lighthearted banter. Konrad gets the sense that Sandy is ill at ease. He notices that she has a pen in her right hand which she unconsciously twirls through her fingers. He thinks, "Something's definitely off about her."

Blake looks over at Sandy and says lightheartedly, "Well Sandy, I guess we're starting off with a story that's near and dear to your heart. I know you've done a lot of research regarding this year's flu vaccine. From all reports, people are flocking to get the shot all over the country. What's your take on it?"

Sandy looks at the camera, then at Blake and says, "That's right Blake, but first, I would like to thank everyone for welcoming me so warmly. I already feel like I'm part of the family."

They both laugh then Sandy continues, "As you know, I was working on a similar story in Atlanta and let me tell you, the amount of information is so extensive. It has been an eye-opening experience."

Blake nods his head. "I just love stories like that. You can really sink your teeth into them."

Sandy smiles a beaming smile and says, "Exactly and believe me, that's just what I did."

They both laugh and Sandy continues, "I researched the vaccine extensively and although I'm not an expert, I spoke to the experts, and they all say."

Sandy looks down at her paperwork then looks back at the camera. Konrad can see just a hint of sadness in her eyes. "They all say that this year's influenza vaccination is the right combination to handle everything that's out there. I guess in summation, I'd like to say to everyone standing in line to receive your flu shot, you're on the right track. It really is the only way to truly be safe this flu season."

Sandy takes a deep breath and smiles at the camera saying, "So Blake, what do you have for us this morning?"

Blake swivels in his chair and says, "The market Sandy. The market is up, and I'll explain it all after this short commercial break."

Konrad slams his laptop closed and stands up. He looks around the room, trying to find something to focus on besides the rage that fills his entire being. He says to the empty room through gritted teeth, "I knew it. Is there no one I can count on? There's just no way to win."

He looks at the ceiling saying, "Oh Jennifer, I'm going to lose. I can't win this. Honey, why did you leave me?"

Konrad looks around the room once again and thinks that he ought to have some breakfast, but he has no appetite and dismisses the thought. He grabs the Xanax bottle from the counter and takes one, washing it down with a drink of the cold coffee he'd made early this morning. He thinks as he walks toward the stairs, "What's the point."

He climbs the stairs to the bedroom he shared with his wife and climbs into the unmade bed. With nothing in the waking world to hold him there, he finds sleep and in so doing, relief.

As Konrad descends into nothingness, he finds himself at the bottom of a well. The darkness envelopes him as he clings to the slimy stones in the chest deep water. He looks up at the small patch of sunlight far above his head and locks his jaw in a scowl thinking, "I've got to climb, or I'll die down here."

Slowly he begins the ascent, grasping at the small stones jutting from the sides. His arms and legs ache from the effort as the numbing cold makes his limbs heavy. He reaches a point just high enough to see over the lip of the well. He is almost out but his body is so heavy that he can't pull himself over. Then he sees her. It is Jennifer and she is sitting a few feet from the well, in the grass. She looks at him sternly and says, "You must pull Konrad. You can't quit. They want you in that well my darling. Don't you see? They need you trapped in the darkness."

Konrad replies, "Jen, I can't. I'm so tired."

Then her face is suddenly inches from his as she screams, "Fight back Konrad!"

He awakens with a start and immediately looks around the room for Jennifer, but she has dissolved with the dream. He sits up on the side of the bed and rubs his face with his hands. He is ashamed and angry with himself as he looks in the dressing mirror and says, "Enough of this shit."

Konrad stands and goes downstairs to the kitchen where he finds the bottle of medication. He pours the pills down the disposal and slams the bottle into the trash, saying again, "Enough of this shit!"

There is seething rage in Konrad as he runs back upstairs and finding his telephone, dials Sandy's number. The call goes straight to voicemail. At the beep Konrad says, "That was quite a show. You're one hell of an actress. Well, I'm not going away and neither is my story. You can fucking bet on that."

He changes into some biking shorts and a long-sleeved jersey, then puts his cycling sneakers on and goes to the garage where his road bike is hanging on the wall, awaiting him like an old friend. Konrad had spent many hours peddling the titanium bike through the streets of Green River as the stress of his job melted away. He gets the bike down and airs the tires up thinking, "It's been too long my old friend."

Konrad puts the bike outside and leans it up against the garage. He goes back into the kitchen, grabs a bottle of water and then he is peddling toward the entrance to his subdivision. The wind feels good and his legs protest as he peddles furiously with no destination in mind. He tightens his helmet strap and hits the main drag heading west toward the city center. Konrad bikes up every street, traversing Green River over and over.

It is miles that he needs to eradicate this weakness from his mind and body. It is only miles that will calm the rage. As he passes Baller Family Drug, he sees a line of people extending out of the door and down the sidewalk. He also sees Jennie Green, one of the pharmacy technicians arguing with a man at the door. Konrad rolls into the parking lot and hears the man say as he motions with his hand to the woman and three children standing behind him, "I've got babies. We shouldn't have to wait in line."

Jennie tells the man, "Sir, everyone has to wait in line. That's just the rules, now please, just go get in line and we'll be with you as soon as possible."

The man is dressed in blue jeans, a work shirt and work boots. The embroidered patch on the front of his shirt identifies him as "Mike." He makes no move to leave the door but just glares at Jennie. Unable to help himself Konrad says, "Hey Mike, why don't you just go stand in line like everyone else?"

Mike spins on Konrad and says, "Why don't you peddle your bicycle down the road and mind your own fucking business?"

Another man steps up from the line and says to Mike, "I don't know who you think you are buddy, but you're not cutting in front of me, kids or no kids. There are plenty of families waiting."

Mike steps up to the man and replies, "You think you can talk to me like that in front of my wife and kids. I'll kick your ass."

The two men start to scuffle and trip as they both vie for the upper hand. They fall into Konrad, knocking him off his bike and onto his back, all three sprawling onto the concrete parking lot. Konrad leaps to his feet and straddles Mike, grabbing him by the shirt yelling, "Stop it! Just stop! You're fighting over nothing you idiot! The vaccine is no good! It won't help you!"

Then Konrad looks at the rest of the crowd that has gathered. "Did you all hear me? The vaccine is useless!"

Mike, the fight gone out of him now asks as he lies on his back, "What the fuck did you just say?"

Before Konrad can answer, two patrol cars screech into the parking lot. All three men stand up as the police officers start herding the crowd back onto the sidewalk. Konrad brushes tiny pieces of gravel from his knees as the police interview Jennie. He hears her say, "No, the one on the bike was just trying to help."

The officer walks over to Konrad, Connie close behind and says, "Hey Doc. I was one of the officers at Emmer's place. You doin' okay?"

Konrad looks at the officer and the sergeant insignia on his collar. "Yeah, Jamison, right? I'm fine. Just getting some exercise when I saw Jennie having some trouble."

Jamison smiles and says, "Well, you're free to go Doctor, unless you want to press charges."

Konrad shakes his head and blows a deep breath out. "No, I don't think that's necessary."

Connie steps around the police officer and asks, "Konrad, do you want a band-aid or something? Your knee is bleeding."

Konrad shakes his head and replies, "No. Sorry for the trouble. I was trying to help."

This time, Connie shakes her head and says, "You didn't cause it Konrad. This is the third time today that the police have been here. People are getting absolutely stupid about this vaccine."

Konrad looks around and says, "That doesn't surprise me. It's happening all over. I don't know what's wrong with people. Fear makes them do strange things."

He gets on his bike and says, "Well, I'd better head home. I'll see you Connie and officer, thanks."

Jamison holds his hand up as if to stop Konrad and leaning in says, "Just some advice Doc. I'd quit with saying the vaccine is useless."

Konrad looks at him and says, "I can exercise my rights, can't I? Free speech and all that."

Jamison just smiles and replies, "Just some advice Doc. We don't want to cause a panic, that's all. Have a nice evening."

He turns and walks away. Connie touches Konrad's arm and then follows. The ride home seems much longer mainly due to Konrad's knee. The fall had caused some minor damage, making his knee twinge each time he peddles the bike. Konrad arrives home just as the sun is setting, feeling exhausted and energized at the same time. He puts the bike in the garage and goes into the kitchen for a much-needed meal. He hasn't been to the grocery store for a while so the choices are limited.

After some searching, Konrad settles on a frozen pizza. He puts it in the oven then jogs up the stairs for a shower. The water feels good and as it hits him; it cleanses his soul as well as his body. After the shower, he throws on some sweats and goes back downstairs for supper. As he cuts the pizza, he looks at the picture of Jennifer and Chloe taped to the fridge door and says, "Thank you sweetheart."

Seven hundred miles to the southeast, Candace sits in a dark motel room eating a chicken sandwich and sipping from a bottle of water. The place smells of stale linen and roach spray. Not the Ritz by any stretch of the imagination, but they took cash and that is what she needed. From the looks of the vehicles in the lot, this is a place for construction workers and weekend partiers. With this type of clientele, come the narcotics and prostitutes. She's stayed in worse places and smiles slightly as she thinks, "At least the door locks."

Candace had driven straight from Key West to Raleigh, North Carolina, only stopping for gas and food. As she eats, she stares at the window from her place at the table and thinks, "How did they find me? It had to be the call to Sandy. She either told them or they've tapped her phone. Either way, I can't make that mistake again. These people, whoever they are, obviously have the resources to do all sorts of things. I'll have to be careful and create more angles. I'll have to outthink them."

Her thoughts are interrupted by people passing her room. There is a man singing and he is obviously drunk. She can only guess because the curtains are drawn. She stops chewing and waits for what seems like an eternity while the group passes then she finishes the bite held frozen in her mouth. Candace's thoughts go back to when she was just a girl, hiding from the police and social services. Hiding, always hiding and now she has come full circle, hiding once again. She thinks as she chews, "Think Candace. You know how to do this and you're good at it."

Candace takes a quick shower and gets dressed in some fresh clothes, repacks her bag and lays down on the bed, hoping for a full night's sleep. The luxury of relaxing anyplace is a thing of the past and she knows it. She knows she has already been in this place too long and to be ready to move at a moment's notice is the only way to stay ahead of the hounds.

The next morning Candace quickly rises in bed, rubbing her tired eyes as the sun peeks through a small gap in the curtains. She finds her telephone and stares at it for a long moment, deciding if the gamble she is contemplating will work. She looks around the room and thinks, "I've got to throw the hounds off. They'll catch me sooner or later if I don't create some angles. It's all about angles now. If they're listening in, I'll buy myself some time by using that against them."

She decides the gamble is worth it and dials the phone. It is answered after five rings by a sleepy male voice, "Hello?"

Candace takes a deep breath and says, "Konrad, this is Candace, please don't hang up."

There is silence on the line for a moment and then Konrad replies, "Hello Candace, what do you want?"

She knows that she only has minutes to make her case. "Konrad, I'm on the run. People are chasing me. I'm scared."

Now Konrad sits up straight, his attention focused. "Who's chasing you? What are you talking about? Where are you?"

Candace replies quickly, "They were watching me Konrad. They're probably watching you too. I got away but I don't know for how long."

He looks around the room and runs his hand through his hair, trying to clear the sleep from his mind. Konrad says more forcefully, "Who Candace? Who is after you?"

Candace says, "I don't know. There were men in Key West watching me. I tried to meet with Sandy Smithers to tell her what I know. I think that's how they found me."

Konrad's face reddens as he says, "That traitorous bitch already knows about the mutation Candace. I told her and she's chosen to ignore it."

Candace says quickly, "No Konrad, there's more. There's something in the vaccine. We put something in it. I have to get off the phone Konrad. I'm going to Baton Rouge. I have friends there who run a bed and breakfast called Charmante Maison. I can hide there."

Konrad puts his hand on his forehead. "What do you mean you put something in the vaccine? Candace, what the fuck did you do? Was Annie involved in this?"

Candace stammers, "Yes, she helped me prepare the vials for production. Reginald forced me to do it Konrad. He was going to destroy us all. Where is Annie? Is she okay? Have you spoken to her?"

Konrad is silent for a moment. "Annie's dead Candace. She contacted me and wanted to meet. She was scared. The morning we were supposed to meet, she died of a fentanyl overdose. I think she was murdered. That kid was no more of an addict than I am."

Candace voice breaks, "Murdered? Oh Konrad, it's my fault, oh my God."

Konrad answers in a stern tone, "What did you put in the vaccine? What was it?"

Candace realizes she has already been on the telephone too long. "Not now Konrad. I'll contact you when I reach Baton Rouge."

Konrad says quickly, "Candace? Candace? Don't hang up!"

It is too late. Candace ends the call and stares at the phone thinking, "Alright you assholes. Have fun in Louisiana."

She breaks the telephone in half and puts the pieces in the water tank on the back of the toilet. She stands and watches them sink, then replaces the lid, grabs her bag and walks out the door.

Two hundred and seventy miles away Horace holds the telephone, willing it to ring. Candace Swanson is turning into quite a liability. Horace dislikes liabilities. He gazes at the wall, unseeingly and thinks, "Candace, if you weren't such an important part of the puzzle, I would kill you myself."

In answer to Horace's thought, the telephone rings. Horace answers it immediately, "Hello, good news I hope."

The asset replies, "We just got a hit from Doctor Pearce's phone. Candace Swanson contacted him. It looks like we have a destination for her. I sent you the recording."

As if on cue, Horace's computer chimes. He listens to the recording and smiling his cold reptilian smile, dials the telephone. The call is answered immediately, "Hello?"

Horace says, "Baton Rouge, Louisiana. A B&B called Charmonte Maison. She's headed there now. I want you there ahead of her so get your asses to the airport. I'll have a plane waiting. When you get eyes on her, try not to get made this time. I'm on my way. I'm going to handle this myself."

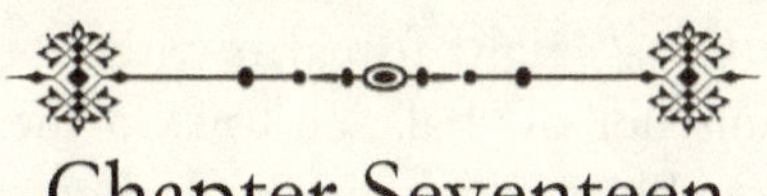

Chapter Seventeen

Cora Mendez stands on the 34th Street and Herald Square subway platform waiting on her train as she has every afternoon for the past ten years. She is a middle-aged woman accustomed to hard work and her looks tell the tale. Cora has been riding the same train to the same office building, doing the same job since starting with the cleaning service a decade ago and the prospects of doing anything else for the next decade are slim. Cora is just another resident of New York who has accepted her life of servitude where every day's train ride is just about surviving. Other people have the finer things in life. That's just how it is and will always be for Cora Mendez.

She stands patiently by the stone pillar, her purse and lunch bag hanging from her arm, her eyes staring at nothing. The only difference in this afternoon from another is the soreness she feels in her left arm from receiving this year's influenza vaccination. She'd waited all morning in line for it, but the way people were flocking to get the damn thing, Cora wasn't about to chance being without it. She has to stay healthy so that she can work. She stands, surrounded by a hundred other people crammed onto the platform, all of them together, yet alone.

The cool temperature of the underground station does nothing to offset the usual smells of body odor and urine. Cora is just one of a mass of people, neither standing out nor being invisible. As usual, in addition to the riders, there is always the one crazy that patrols the platform like an erratic sentinel from a universe only they can see. Cora tries to ignore the man as he passes by whispering to himself. As bad as the platform smells, this man smells worse. He circles around so that he is standing in front of Cora and says, "You got any change for me? The Reaper's always on my shoulder."

Cora puts her hand to her nose and shakes her head from side to side. She looks around but no one is paying attention to the interaction. To get involved is to invite the attention of the crazy upon yourself. It is an unwritten rule. The lunatic's eyes grow wide as he screams, "Well, if you got no change for me, then you can use it to pay the ferryman, bitch!"

The lunatic grabs Cora's right forearm with both of his hands in a vice like grip and pulls her off balance toward the tracks. She tries to resist but he is incredibly strong and hurls her onto the tracks, the contents of her bags spilling out as she falls. Cora lands on her feet but falls forward striking her face on the hardened steel of the rail bed. Bolts of pain shoot through her entire body. Cora can hear screaming in the distance but more importantly, above the screaming, she hears someone yelling, "The train! Oh my God, the train!"

She gets to her feet, standing in the rail bed. As she turns toward the platform, she can see the train coming. She also sees the men laying at the edge of the platform with arms outstretched toward her. They are screaming something at her but she can't make it out over the ringing in her ears. She looks back toward the train, barreling at her, unstoppable, a force with only one ending. This is when Cora realizes that unless she moves toward the platform, she will die. Her mind screams, "Move!"

Her body does not comply. It's as if the two are disconnected somehow as she stands and faces the train, accepting her fate. In the microsecond, before eighty tons of screaming steel hits Cora, the engineer's face appears in perfect clarity. His look of shock and dread surprises her as she thinks in her last second on earth, "My babies. My poor, poor babies."

Cora's body evaporates in a crimson mist to the sound of screams that are not her own.

Back in Green River, Indiana, Konrad sits on the couch in his living room in the dark holding an ice pack on his swollen knee as he thinks, "How fucking stupid. Why did I even get involved?"

The altercation at the pharmacy could have ended badly. He makes himself a promise not to get involved again. Konrad flexes his knee and thinks about the call from Candace. "What had she meant when she'd said she was being watched? Watched by whom?"

He throws the ice pack to the side and stands, limping into the kitchen for a cup of coffee, thinking, "And who's chasing her. She said they might be watching me too. What has she gotten herself into? What has she gotten me into?"

His jaw tightens as he asks himself, "Candace, what did you do?"

Konrad moves to the kitchen sink and pulls the curtains covering the window ever so slightly to the side to look out at the darkening backyard seeing nothing out of the ordinary. He then limps into the living room and looks out of the picture window at the front yard. "Nothing here either."

Konrad shakes his head and smiles, "Now I'm acting as paranoid as Candace sounded."

He turns to return to the kitchen and is startled by the ringing of his telephone. He picks it up off the couch and answers it. A female voice begins, "Doctor Pearce? My name is Darci Mitchell and I'd like a few moments of your time."

Konrad's eyes narrow as he says, "I'm not in the market for anything."

He begins to disconnect the call when Darci says quickly, "I'm not selling anything Doctor. I believe you have something that I could use."

This peaks Konrad's interest. "Darci, what do you think I have?"

She replies quickly, "I'd like to share a short story with you, Doctor Pearce. I have a friend who happens to be a police officer. We were at a restaurant having a cup of coffee yesterday evening and he was telling me about a former employee of Emmer Pharmaceutical telling everyone who would listen that this year's influenza vaccine is worthless. Not just any employee Doctor, but a research scientist. Sound familiar?"

Konrad goes back to the window and looks out into the blackness. "Exactly who are you, Darci?"

Darci feels Konrad's interest over the telephone and smiles. "I'm an investigative reporter for the Green River Morning News, Doctor and I would really like to hear what you have to say."

Konrad chuckles, "My time was already wasted by Sandy Smithers. She used that same line, Darci."

Darci replies, "Oh yes, Sandy Smithers. I was following her CDC story. Seems she's changed her position on the super flu since she's made the big time. I find it kind of interesting. Don't you? Well Doctor, I'm not Sandy and I hope you'll give me the opportunity to prove it."

There is a moment of silence and then Konrad replies, "Alright Darci, why not. I'm sure your police friend has already provided you with my address and my calendar appears to be empty at the moment. When would you like to come over?"

Darci chuckles and says, "Wonderful, I'll see you in a minute. I'm actually parked just down the street."

It's Konrad's turn to smile as the line goes dead. "How did I not see that coming?"

In a few minutes, the doorbell rings and when Konrad answers it, he is surprised. Darci is the exact opposite of Sandy Smithers. Where Sandy was voluptuous, almost glamorous, Darci is petite with short brown hair and glasses. Konrad thinks as he looks at her, "She looks like a teenager. This must be a joke."

She stands halfway inside the door and puts out her hand, "Doctor Pearce, I'm Darci. I really appreciate your time. Konrad realizes that he is staring at her and quickly puts out his hand, receiving a firm handshake. "Come in Darci. It's nice to meet you. Would you like something to drink?"

Darci shakes her head. "I just had something Doctor, thanks."

They walk into the living room and sit on the couch. Darci takes a deep breath and then says, "I'm interested in your story Doctor."

Konrad waves his hand and replies, "Please call me Konrad."

She smiles and says, "Okay Konrad, tell me why the vaccine is worthless. I mean according to my friend, he's heard you say that twice. Is that correct? It's worthless?"

Konrad sighs and then begins telling Darci the same story he'd told Sandy when they'd met in this very room. When he finishes, Darci, eyes wide whistles and says, "That's quite a tale Konrad. So, this super flu from Thailand is actually real?"

He nods his head. "I've seen it. If it gets started in the US, it will be brutal."

Darci looks down at her notes. "So, help me out here, why would the CDC want to cover something like this up?"

Konrad shakes his head. "That I can't figure out. All I know is that I tried to report it and was stonewalled by some low-level clerk. Sandy suddenly had a change of heart in following the story and it pretty much ended there. Reginald Emmer knows about this and is still touting the vaccine as effective against this year's strains. There's no way to prove him wrong because he's covered all his bases."

Darci looks at Konrad directly. "And you have no hard proof of any of this, correct?"

Konrad leans forward shaking his head. "No. Not a shred. It's all in the lab and I'm barred from the facility.

Darci replies evenly, "Whenever I start on a story Konrad, I always answer one very important question. If I can't answer the 'why', then I won't put it in print. There is always a 'why'. So, what you're describing is a conspiracy. First and foremost, why are the CDC and WHO ignoring the existence of this super flu? Secondly, why are they pushing everyone to get this vaccine if it's ineffective?"

He looks at the young girl who obviously has maturity beyond her years and says, "I don't have an answer for either question."

Darci just nods her head and replies, "I'm going to try and chase this down Konrad. I won't promise you anything except, I'm good at what I do and if the answer's out there, I'll find it."

Konrad looks at Darci and says, "There's one other thing, I suspect two people have died because of this. I just want you to be careful."

Darci laughs and says as she stands, "That's part of the job Konrad. I spent twelve months in the Middle East as a combat reporter. I'll be okay."

Konrad walks Darci to the door. They say goodbye, she shakes his hand and pausing in the doorway says, "You should probably put some ice on that knee."

Then she walks out into the night.

The next morning, Reginald Emmer stands in his office at Emmer Pharmaceuticals looking at the New York Stock Exchange on his computer. To say that he is elated would be an understatement. His company's stocks had gone through the roof once it was released that Emmer was the sole provider of flu vaccine for the nation. Reginald gazes at the screen and thinks, "I've come farther than dear old granddad ever dreamed of going. I'm already a billionaire."

Reginald's revelry is interrupted by Norma's nasally voice as she walks in and says, "Don't forget about the lunch and learn at the Green River House at eleven Mr. Emmer."

He looks up from the computer screen and rolls his eyes. "Tell me again why I have to go to this thing."

Norma gives him the look one might receive from a mother explaining something to a child for the tenth time. "It is good public relations sir. People want to meet the man who put Green River on the map, so, you must go and answer questions about your operations here, your amazing success, etc. etc. There will be several news agencies there and the Mayor's Office will be sending a representative."

Reginald takes one more look at the computer screen then says, "Okay but clear my calendar for the rest of the day. I'm going to the golf course after. I need to relax."

Norma, one eyebrow raised replies, "Yes sir. If you leave now, you'll get a good parking space. You know how bad the parking is downtown."

Reginald looks at Norma appreciatively and says, "You're right. I don't know what I would do without you Norma."

Norma just smiles and nods as she walks out of the office thinking, "It'll be nice to have a day without that needy little asshole in the office."

Reginald sighs as he turns his computer off and walks out of the office. It is a short drive to the Green River House. Parking is indeed atrocious and as Reginald pulls into the small parking area in back, he thinks, "You'd think with all the taxes I pay, they could at least provide me with valet parking."

He steps out of his Mercedes, locks it and walks around to the front of the building where he is met at the door by an attractive redhead. She smiles and puts out her hand. "Mr. Emmer, I'm Janet Cohen with the mayor's office. I'm so glad you could come."

Reginald smiles and replies, "Call me Reginald."

He follows her into the building thinking, "This day is looking better and better by the minute."

The food is laid out on several tables with white linen tablecloths. It is all buffet style finger food consisting of quartered sandwiches, fruits and vegetables with an assortment of dips. Food designed to be consumed by a person as they mingle. After all, that's the point of the whole get together. It's just an avenue for the business leaders of Green River to get face time with the newly richest man in the community. Reginald Emmer has become simply, the biggest fish in the investor pond. In addition to the Green River elite, two news agencies have shown up to record the event for posterity. Darci Mitchell from the Green River Morning News and Danny Rosetti from WSV. A nationally syndicated news agency. After today, the whole nation will know if Reginald Emmer can balance a plate of food and work a room at the same time.

Darci looks across the room as her prey moves from one group of people to the other, seeking yet another pat on the back or handshake. Her eyes narrow as she formulates her plan of attack thinking, "I'm going to see just how cool you really are, Reginald."

Danny Rosetti steps up near Darci and tugs on her sleeve. "What's up Darci? You have that look in your eye."

Darci quickly looks at Danny then says, "Just formulating some questions for our guest of honor."

Danny laughs, "I might just tag along when you get started if you don't mind. Did you know this guy's company was sinking right before he got the contract for the flu vaccine? Kind of fishy."

She looks over her shoulder at Danny, eyebrows raised. "I'd forgotten about that."

As the plates empty, the attendees begin to gravitate to the seats arranged in rows in front of a table at the front of the room. Sunlight streams through the large windows of the conference room turned into a buffet, furthering the cheerful atmosphere. Janet guides Reginald to the table at the front of the room where a microphone is located. As he sits, he sees the camera crews getting ready. Janet stands at the front and says loud enough to be heard above the murmur, "Ladies and gentlemen, please take your seats. Mr. Emmer will now answer a few questions from the media. I trust everyone was able to meet Mr. Emmer and speak with him."

As everyone takes their seats, Janet walks to the back of the room and says to Darci and Danny, "Okay, your turn. I think to be fair; you should take turns. One for one. Is that agreeable?"

They both smile and nod. Danny says with a slight bow, "Ladies first Darci."

She takes a deep breath and signals the camera crew, then says, "Mr. Emmer, Darci Mitchell from the Green River Morning News. Thank you for taking time out of your busy schedule to answer some questions. How does it feel to be the man supplying the nation with the influenza vaccine?"

Reginald nods and replies, "Well Darci, great question. I must admit, at times, quite daunting, but I'm a patriot and when my country calls, I accept the task and hope I'll prove myself worthy."

Danny follows up. "Danny Rosetti, WSV News. As I understand it, people around the nation are standing in long lines to get your vaccine. Can you describe the process in getting the doses out in significant numbers to handle the demand?"

Reginald smiles and thinks, "This is going to be a piece of cake."

He folds his hands on the table and replies, "My people are working seven days a week, twenty-four hours a day to fill the demand. Each and every one of them, are heroes in my eyes."

Danny nods and makes a note in his notebook as Darci asks, "Referencing the lines Mr. Emmer, it seems that a rumor has caused this great demand. Any comment on the supposed super flu?"

A bead of sweat appears on Reginald's temple. "I really couldn't comment on that. My research and development section developed a very safe and effective vaccine to address all flu variants that the CDC and WHO felt were a threat this year. Being vaccinated is the only way to ensure your safety."

Danny follows up quickly, "Have you been vaccinated sir?"

Reginald jumps as if he has been slapped. "What did you ask me?"

Danny repeats the question. "Have you been vaccinated? I mean, if it's the only way to be safe and your vaccine is going to address all the recognized threats, have you taken it personally?"

Reginald stammers, "Well, I have been working long hours and haven't had a chance to get it but, I intend to."

Darci smiles and looks at Danny. The attendees are looking at the reporters as well. "Mr. Emmer, you mentioned your research and development section. Didn't Doctor Konrad Pearce head that section up until just recently?"

Reginald sees what is happening but it is too late. He has been trapped by the two reporters who are obviously working together. He stammers, "I really don't see what Konrad Pearce has to do with anything. He is a former employee, yes but."

Darci cuts Reginald off with a quick follow up question, "Dr. Pearce has been critical of the vaccine, was recently separated from your company and now we find that you yourself haven't been vaccinated. Are these things related sir?"

The attendees begin to whisper, and Reginald feels like he wants to vomit. I'm not going to comment on that. I stick by my earlier statement that the vaccine is safe and completely effective."

To Darci's surprise, Danny is the one who puts the nail in Reginald's coffin. "Mr. Emmer, I believe any unfounded rumors or criticism of your fine company could easily be put to rest. Would you be willing to receive the vaccine on camera from a vial picked by me from your own assembly line?"

The room goes silent, everyone waiting on Reginald's answer to the obvious challenge. Reginald looks at Janet who in turn looks at Darci and Danny with hate in her eyes. Reginald looks at Danny with a smug look and raises his chin with an attitude of superiority. "Yes. Yes, you can come to Emmer Pharmaceutical tomorrow and pick any damn vial you want from any of the lines. I stand behind my product. I'll have someone give me the shot and you can film it but be there early, I have a lot of work to do."

With that, Reginald gets up and walks toward the door with Janet close behind as she says, Mr. Emmer, I'm so sorry about that. I had no idea that they were going to do that."

Reginald quickly spins to face her, almost losing his balance. There are tears in his eyes as he says, teeth gritted, "You tell the fucking mayor, I'm going to destroy this town for this. I'll move my company out of this nothing community. Then see what happens to your tax base."

He gets in his car and speeds out of the parking lot, tires spinning. Janet goes back inside and steps up to Darci and Danny who look at her innocently as the attendees are leaving. She puts her hands on her hips and says, "You two think you're pretty smart. What was that? Do you realize how much revenue this town receives from Emmer's company? I'll be calling your producer, Darci. Jessi Markham and I go way back, and you just fucked yourself young lady."

The next morning Konrad stands at the kitchen counter and watches the coffee slowly drip into the carafe. The rich smell of it awakening his taste buds in anticipation of the first cup of the day. When the carafe is finally filled, he thankfully pours a cup and takes a sip, closing his eyes in appreciation. Walking into the living room, he turns on the television and sits on the couch to watch the Green River Morning News. He smiles as he watches the report of the luncheon and takes pleasure in the obvious discomfort Reginald appears to be in. Konrad takes another sip and thinks, "Serves you right, you sneaky bastard."

He isn't thrilled that Darci had used his name but the mention of it seemed to throw Reginald off. He says to the empty house, "Your sins will always haunt you, Reggie."

Konrad must admit, Darci is obviously true to her word. She seems to be chasing the story down. It is much more than Sandy accomplished. He just hopes that she is cautious. Annie's death still bothers Konrad immensely. He wonders out loud, "What were you going to tell me Annie?"

He realizes that he will probably never know. Konrad walks back into the kitchen, his knee feeling much better and throws the filter full of coffee grounds into the trash. The bag is almost full, so he pulls the bag from the trash and carries it out the back door to the cans at the corner of the garage, depositing the bag and tightly closing the lid. As he turns around, he sees that the back door is ajar. "Had he closed it behind him?"

Konrad tries to remember. He heads back inside and as he closes the door; he smells the slightest hint of lilac. Without turning Konrad says, "Hello Candace."

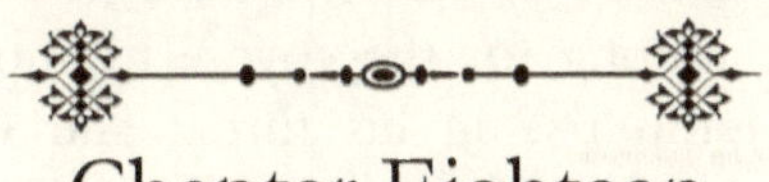

Chapter Eighteen

Marsha Kelly walks into the bedroom she has shared with her husband Jim for 12 years and approaches the bed. She reaches down gently and lightly rubs her husband's arm. She is the only person on earth who can accomplish this feat without risking injury. Jim is and has been a Federal Correctional Officer at the United States Penitentiary, Green River, Indiana for the last ten years and he doesn't sleep peacefully. She whispers, "Jim honey, it's time for you to get up if you're going to be on time for your shift."

Jim rolls over and raises up in the bed, looking around and orienting himself, quickly realizing he is at home. He looks at Marsha with bleary eyes and replies sleepily, "I'm not going in today. I called the joint last night before I laid down. I don't feel right."

His voice cracks as he says the last part. Marsha sits on the side of the bed and looks at her husband with concern. He is, without a doubt, the toughest man she has ever met. The admission is uncharacteristic of the man she knows. "Jim, this will make three days in a row you've called in. They're going to want a doctor's note. What's going on honey? Please tell me."

He shakes his head then turns his face away from her. "Can't talk about it. I'll get the fucking note if they ask for it. Fuck'm."

She puts her hand on his arm again and replies, "Alright Jim, but I'm here. I'm right here. Whatever is going on, we can face it together. Please don't shut me out."

She stands and starts to walk out of the room. He calls after her, "I'm alright honey. Just having some troubles. It'll be okay. Penitentiary stuff."

She turns slightly and looking at him says softly, "Okay."

Then she walks out of the room, leaving him alone in the early morning darkness. Jim sits up on the side of the bed and works his ankles in a circle, flexing his feet. After ten years of standing on reinforced concrete all day, they hurt every morning. He looks toward the bedroom vanity and the mirror containing his reflection and starts to face the fact that he may have lost his nerve. He analyzes his reflection noticing a change in the once hardened eyes. They are now the eyes of a rabbit waiting for the coyote to show up. Hunted and scared. He feels a lump rise in his throat and wonders where the correctional officer who could work any cell house without fear or hesitation has gone. He is a member of the prison special operations team and a solid hack.

Jim thinks of Marsha and his son Jacob and feels ashamed of himself. "Oh God, what is the matter with me?"

He scratches his head and closes his eyes. For a microsecond, the image of a revolver in his mouth is crystal clear. His eyes snap open, the butterflies in his stomach resuming their crippling dance and thinks, "No!"

He thinks back to when the feelings had started. It was four days ago. He remembers because he'd received the flu vaccination that morning. The bureau mandated it so there wasn't a choice in the matter. The only exceptions were religious and health. Jim wasn't a church goer, and he was in perfect health. They'd set up in the front lobby to vaccinate staff on their way in. Get the shot and you can go to work. That was the mandate. He had thought at the time, "No big deal. It's just a flu shot."

Even though, at the time, he'd wondered why the big push for everyone to get it. He'd walked in, set his lunchbox down and given them his arm, then he'd gone to work as usual. The "butterflies" had started a few hours into his shift. He couldn't explain what he was feeling and brushed it off. Now he knows it was fear. An emotion totally foreign to him. Jim stares at the wall, seeing nothing and remembers. The inmates though, society's predators, had smelled it on him almost immediately. Gone was the hardnosed hack they were used too and replacing him was pudding nailed to the wall.

Jim found that he couldn't bring himself to order an inmate to do anything. Dirty cells, he let slide. He tried to order an inmate to submit to a pat down during noon mainline and the inmate had told him to go fuck himself. Jim just let the inmate walk right past him into the block. Word got around quick, as it always does in a pen. Toward the end of his shift, six outlaw bikers surrounded him at the end of the range and threatened him. The leader of the group telling him, "Officer, you better get into your office and stay before you get hurt."

Jim had looked in the eyes of the leader and had been unable to muster the courage to respond. He'd just walked to his office and closed the door. The cell block ran itself for the rest of his shift. He thinks back to it now and the shame is almost unbearable. He once again looks in the mirror, tears filling his eyes and wonders, "How can I tell Marsha that her husband has turned into a coward?"

Across town, inside the secure perimeter of USP Green River, Lieutenant Clay Dorfman stands in the Associate Warden of Custody's office. Associate Warden Niler is an old hack himself and understands the mechanics of operating a maximum-security prison. Dorfman likes Niler and the feeling is mutual. The office, not overly extravagant, is decorated in dark wood and chrome. The desk is highly shined, and the walls are adorned with the many awards AW Niler has accumulated over the years. Dorfman looks at AW Niler and says, "I think we may have a problem, Sir and I don't know what to do about it."

Niler looks at Dorfman from behind the desk and raises his eyebrows in surprise. "I don't think I've ever heard you say that, Clay. Must be a damn sizeable problem."

Dorfman nods his head with a concerned look. "Something's going on with the officers on my shift and I can't get any of them to talk to me about it. They're not policing their units or enforcing rules. It's like they've laid down. I caught a guy in his office with the door locked when I was making rounds yesterday. He wouldn't even walk the cell block with me when I made my tour of the unit. The guy is usually a motivated hack. When I asked him what was going on, he just said he couldn't explain it."

Niler leans forward in his chair. "Are you telling me, all of the officers on your shift aren't doing their job?"

Clay shakes his head, "Not all of them. The towers are doing okay. Mostly old timers out there but inside, we've got a problem."

AW Niler stands and looks at Dorfman. "What did you do about the officer you caught in his office with the door locked, Lieutenant?"

Dorfman shifts his weight and replies, "I sent him to the towers and brought an old timer in to run his block. I mean, I could've sent him home but, I gotta staff the posts. We're already shorthanded as it is."

The AW leans back in his chair and replies with a sardonic smile, "Sounds to me like it might be a lack of leadership in the Lieutenant's Office. You all should be spending more time out and about. I'm sure the officers will follow your example. Get out and show them how it's done. On another note, I heard that you have refused to be vaccinated. Is that true?"

Dorfman straightens his shoulders slightly and replies, "That's correct, Sir. I won't be receiving the flu shot."

The AW raises his eyebrows and asks, "May I ask why?"

Dorfman replies slowly, "My religious beliefs don't allow me to receive vaccines. We believe God provides everything we need to combat illness. I'm not the only one."

AW Niler shakes his head and says, "You see, that's what I'm talking about. You're not setting a good example for your troops. I'd tighten that up if I were you, Lieutenant."

Dorfman's mouth becomes a thin line. "No disrespect Sir, but how about you?"

Niler looks at Dorfman directly. "What about me?

Dorfman returns the stare making the AW look away. "Have you been vaccinated?"

AW Niler looks at the floor and nods, "Of course. I received mine on the first day. Why do you ask?"

Dorfman takes a step toward the desk and replies, "Because, Sir, a vaccination is unimportant when you start talking about losing control of a maximum-security penitentiary and that's what is getting ready to happen if the officers don't do their jobs."

AW Niler raises his hand to his mouth in an attempt to cover a sad smile. "Clay, I'm sure it'll be alright. Sometimes I wonder if we've ever been the ones in control of this place anyway."

Clay Dorfman can't believe his ears and can think of no polite way to reply so he simply turns and walks out of the office without another word.

Seven hundred and seventy miles away from the impending disaster at USP Green River, Horace MacGill lies on the bed, staring at the ceiling in the honeymoon suite at the Charmonte' Maison Bed and Breakfast. He looks around at the deep red motif and his upper lip rises in a half snarl. The room is immaculate, and the accommodations have been more than adequate since he arrived a week ago, but the décor of the room designed for romance started to grate on him about seven hours into his vigil. Horace looks around the room and thinks, "I had no idea that there was so much whore house red in the world."

The room is furnished with heavy wooden furniture from a time long forgotten. Deep cherry and mahogany with a queen-sized bed topped with a mattress so thick Horace has to hop up to sit on it. Old style bed springs remove any chance of an undisturbed night's sleep as they announce to everyone in the place the occupant's every move.

Horace lies there on the mattress and wonders if putting the springs on the bed was some kind of sick joke perpetrated by the proprietors.

The smell of roses permeates his nostrils as he ponders this question. The daily delivery of the flowers is just one more unwanted interruption. He stands and moves to the dresser where a bottle of bourbon waits like a sentinel to his vigil. Horace thinks as he pours a water glass full of the liquid, "Candace, where are you? You're not coming, are you, you sneaky little bitch."

He takes a drink and looks at the ceiling, stretching his neck as the fiery liquid makes the journey down his throat. That is when Horace notices the chipping paint above the bed and wonders how many young women had also noticed the paint as their new husbands clumsily had their way with them. The bed springs creaking in time to the act of consummation.

The vision that these thoughts conjure up almost makes Horace smile, but it does nothing to alleviate his sour mood. It only serves to validate his opinion that the human race as a whole is little more than pathetic. He walks to the window and moves the curtain slightly to look out thinking, "What a waste of time the act of fucking is."

Horace is no stranger to the pleasures of a woman's body, but his tastes have always been specific and unique. He stands at the window and thinks about the many women who were willing, all well compensated for their participation of course. It was their willingness that always amazed him. The pain he inflicted was never in itself satisfying, but the power over another human was what flipped Horace's switch. He mutters under his breath as he stares out the window, "Even that got boring after a while."

Horace sighs heavily, accepting the hard, cold truth, turns and moves back to the dresser, retrieving his telephone. He dials the number as he finishes the bourbon. The call is answered immediately, and Horace says, "Pack it up, she isn't coming."

Back in Green River, Indiana, Konrad stands in line at the First Central Bank and Trust. There is a long line of patrons in front of him. An old man in a long-sleeved shirt and blue jeans who keeps pulling his worn leather wallet out and looking at the paperwork it contains. There is a young woman holding a baby with a toddler continually pulling on the hem of her blouse. The businessman who keeps looking at his watch. Twenty other normal people who dare not step outside the velvet rope which guides them in an orderly manner to the next available teller. Konrad half smiles as the image of livestock moving through a chute leaps into his mind. He thinks, "We are nothing more."

The past week had been a tense one. He'd allowed Candace to hide out in his home because as much as he resented how she had treated him; it appeared that their fates were intertwined. That, and the fact that in his heart, she was still a friend. She certainly acted like she was being hunted. He'd pressed her for more details about what she and Annie had put into the vaccine, but she refused to elaborate unless he helped her.

This Candace was much different than the friend he had known and worked with. This Candace was street smart and tough. It dawns on Konrad that this is really who Candace always was. The other Candace was an act. She'd driven from Raleigh, North Carolina to Green River and parked her car at the truck stop on highway 46. Its presence there would not raise any suspicion. Then she'd simply walked three miles to his house in the dark and hid in the lawn mower shed in his back yard until he'd taken the trash out.

As he thinks about it, Konrad cannot help but admire the economical effectiveness of her planning. The irrefutable fact was that Candace was on the run. Who she was running from Konrad couldn't guess, but he had seen enough to know that she was good at it. She was working the angles, and she was working him.

Konrad almost wishes that she had come to him as the old friend, but her motive was much more basic. She had explained in a matter-of-fact way that she couldn't get near her bank accounts. "They would be watching."

Whoever they are. The one oversight Reginald had made was that he hadn't dropped either one of them from the payroll. Candace made an electronic transfer of funds the night before to Konrad's account. In exchange for the full story, he simply had to make the five thousand dollar withdraw and she would be gone. Maybe it was simply the scientist in Konrad or maybe he just wanted to know what she had gotten him into. Whatever it was, he was going along with the plan to finally know the answer that had haunted him for some time. Konrad's thoughts are interrupted as he finds himself next in line. A teller is waving him forward as she says, "Next!"

She is a middle-aged woman with brown hair and a plump figure squeezed into a green skirt and blouse. Her hair is pulled back into a bun. As he approaches, she smiles and asks, "What can I help you with?"

Konrad looks around then says, "I'd like to make a withdrawal."

He passes the withdrawal slip under the small glass window along with his driver's license, looking around the bank again. As he does so, Konrad notices a man at the back of the line in blue jeans and a windbreaker looking at him. The man looks down at his paperwork. The hairs on the back of Konrads neck rise as the teller asks, "Wow Dr. Pearce, going on vacation?"

He has no time for small talk and the nosiness of most of the town's inhabitants has begun to grate on Konrad. He smiles and says, "No. It's for hookers and booze."

The teller looks up quickly and says in an exasperated tone, "Well, you could have just told me it was none of my business."

She counts the bills out quickly and says, "Sign here please."

Konrad picks up the pen and looks around the bank again. The man is still in exactly the same place in line as before. Konrad signs the slip and takes the cash, turning abruptly and walking out of the bank. The teller says loud enough for Konrad to hear as he walks away, "Well, you have a good day too."

Konrad exits the bank and makes it to his car, stopping to look around before getting in and starting the ignition. He sees no one following him. He looks in the mirror and thinks, "You're acting like an idiot. There's no boogeyman."

The drive home is uneventful. He follows Candace's instructions and circles back on at least two city blocks along the way to see if he has a tail. Of course, Konrad doesn't believe there is anyone following him, but he does it because he had promised her he would. As he pulls into the drive, he sees the shades are all still drawn closed. Konrad gets out and walks around back, entering through the back door, where he finds Candace sitting at the kitchen table in the dark. She is wearing blue jeans and a t-shirt with "Key West" embroidered on the front. He notices that she is also wearing running shoes. Konrad drops the envelope full of bills on the table and says, "Okay, now it's time for your part of the bargain. Tell me."

Five hundred miles away, Ruth Evans stands in Joel Smith's office and watches the ever-present bead of sweat work its way from the top of his head to his eyebrows. She smiles as she realizes that this is her last day at this place. He looks at her in surprise. "Ruth, you can't be serious. We're right in the middle of this super flu mess and you're telling me you're leaving?"

She moves to the sofa in front of his desk and sits. "I've got the sick leave on the books Joel. I'm going to use it and retire. I guess this 'mess' as you call it will be on your desk instead of mine."

Joel's face reddens as he remembers the threat he'd made. "C'mon Ruth, let's not be rash. I admit, I'm a hot head sometimes. I'd never throw you to the wolves. There was nothing to that doctor's claim anyway. I mean, you checked it out, right? No attempted report."

Ruth sits back on the couch and smiles, enjoying the unusual upper hand. "You know Joel, you should have been nicer to me when you had the chance. I went downstairs and asked that little weasel, Densin if he'd received any calls and he denied it but, I'm pretty sure he was lying to me. Of course, I'm retiring so that's not my problem now."

Joel leaps out of his chair. "Didn't you check the phone logs?"

Ruth slowly shakes her head as she stares at Joel. Now there are several beads of sweat as he says through clenched teeth, "You bitch. Get out of my office. In fact, you can start your retirement this instant. Get out of my sight."

Ruth smiles a confident smile, pulls a tissue from the box on the end table and stands. She throws it on Joel's desk and says, "Wipe that sweat off your head, it's disgusting."

Before he can think of a reply, Ruth walks out without looking back. Joel sits back down at his desk and considers the shit storm he now finds himself in. If it is true that this Densin character had stonewalled a scientist trying to report an irregularity in a vaccine, all hell would break loose. Joel wipes the sweat from his forehead and thinks, "I could let it go and hope it never comes out but, that means I look over my shoulder from now on. No, I've got to get ahead of this. We're too far into the distribution of the vaccine. People everywhere are clamoring for it. Hell, I've taken it myself. No, I've got to completely control this Densin character. I need him under my thumb."

He brings up the agency telephone directory on his computer, finds Warren Densin's number and dials. The phone is answered almost immediately, "CDC Mid-Atlantic Liaison, this is Warren, how may I help you?"

Joel replies in his friendliest voice, "Mr. Densin, this is Joel Smith, Chief Public Information Officer. I'd like to speak with you in my office."

He hears Warren's breathing quicken. "Well sir, I could come up to your office, I guess. What did you want to talk about?"

Joel thinks, "You know damn well what I want to talk about."

He replies, "Just a friendly conversation, in my office."

Warren's voice begins to crack, "When would you like to see me sir?"

Joel sighs, "Now Mr. Densin. I would like to see you now."

Warren replies, "I'll be right up."

It sounded to Joel as if Warren might have been beginning to hyperventilate. In a few moments, a winded Warren Densin knocks on Joel Smith's office door. Joel looks up from the papers on his desk and says with a smile, "Mr. Densin, please come in and shut the door."

Warren looks down the hall before entering the office and sees Ruth Evans carrying a box toward the elevators. She is smiling at him. His heart sinks as he walks into Joel's office and closes the door. Joel stands and tells Warren, "Have a seat young man. We have an important matter to discuss."

Warren sits in the same seat Ruth had occupied less than an hour before with his hands folded in his lap, waiting like a man at the gallows. Joel stands silently taking in the view of all that is Warren Densin and he is sorely unimpressed by the weakling who sits before him. Warren refuses to meet his gaze and his knee slightly bounces up and down. Joel thinks, "You're nervous and you should be."

Warren looks up as if he's about to say something but then looks away again. Joel's plan is a simple one, as old as time itself. Keep your enemies close and under your thumb. As Joel looks at Warren, he thinks, "This is going to be a piece of cake. I could break this little piss ant like dry kindling but we're too far down the rabbit hole now. No, Warren Densin will not be the one to end my career."

Joel walks around the desk and puts his hand on Warren's shoulder. "Mr. Densin, let me make one thing perfectly clear, I know that you did receive a call from one of the scientists at Emmer Pharmaceuticals."

Warren starts to stammer an objection, but Joel puts slightly more pressure on Warren's shoulder saying, "No Warren. I know you did so don't try to deny it."

Warren looks up at Joel, then down at the floor. Joel continues with the sales pitch. "Warren, I want to thank you."

At this, Warren looks up in surprise. "What?"

Joel smiles a cagey grin and says, "I want to thank you Warren, for protecting this agency's reputation and not allowing some crack pot to interfere with the nation's vaccination program. Do you love your country, Warren?"

Now Warren is looking at Joel's face, eyes wide. "Yes sir. I love my country."

Joel starts pacing the floor behind Warren. "I want to think your reasoning behind stopping that doctor from getting his crazy ideas heard was because you knew the ramifications and, as a patriot, were not going to stand for it. I respect that. Isn't that why you did what you did?"

Warren looks over his shoulder at Joel and nods slowly. Joel nods curtly and continues. "Warren, not every employee of this agency loves our country like you and me. In fact, some would want you fired for your bravery but, I hold the view that what's best for the country justifies any means. Do you agree?"

Warren looks at Joel wide eyed and says, "I've always felt that way too."

Joel smiles in a half grin as he walks around behind his desk and sits down. He sighs and says, "I need your help, Warren. My Deputy Chief just walked out, and I need someone I trust to replace her. Someone who loves their country and the agency. Someone who'll have my back. It would be an acting position at first, selected by me until we can go through all the formal hoops but, I want you in the position. Are you interested?"

Warren leans forward and says almost too quickly, "Yes, of course."

Joel leans back in his chair and replies, "Good Warren. You won't have to do any press releases. I'll take over those duties. Your role will be more behind the scenes. Researching and writing. How does that sound?"

Warren replies, "That sounds fine. Thank you, sir. Really, thank you."

Joel waves his hand and says, "No thanks are needed. Give me a week to make the proper notifications then we'll move you up to your new office down the hall."

Warren, sensing the meeting is over stands and starts to turn toward the door when Joel stops him. "Warren, I probably don't need to tell you that word of what you did for the agency must never be uttered to anyone. Do you understand?"

Warren nods his head, turns and walks out of the office. As soon as Warren makes it back to his desk, he pulls the card from its place in the drawer and dials the number. The call is answered in three rings by a silky-smooth hiss. "Warren, it has been a while since I've heard from you. Good news I hope."

Warren feels his bladder constrict as he replies, "Yes. I think it may be good news, but I wanted to ask you first."

Horace smiles his reptilian smile and says, "Why, Warren, that is very thoughtful of you. Please, tell me your news."

Warren stammers then blurts out every detail of what transpired in Joel Smith's office. Horace is silent for a moment then says slowly, "So what you're telling me is, is that they know about the call you received and want to promote you. Is that correct?"

Warren nods his head and replies, "Yes. Can you believe it?"

Horace chuckles and says, "Yes Warren. I can indeed, believe it."

He leans back into the plush seat of the private jet and takes a sip of bourbon, thinking, "The survival instinct of every government employee is almost like the sun setting, completely and utterly predictable."

Horace can hear Warren breathing over the telephone as he says, "I like it, Warren. You'll be of much greater use to me in that position. Congratulations. I'll be in contact Warren. Be ready."

Horace looks out the window of the jet at the countryside passing far below and thinks, "I like Joel Smith. I would've made the same move."

Chapter Nineteen

onrad stands from the couch and runs his hand through his hair as he shakes his head saying, "I don't believe it Candace. What you're talking about just doesn't exist. Programmable protein molecules of that size? Do you know how crazy you sound?"

Candace looks up at Konrad from her chair and replies, "I know what it sounds like Konrad, but I'm telling you, I've seen them and they work. They completely alter any flu virus at the base DNA level to become one single virus. I watched them alter the Thailand specimen before it could mutate. We've done it. We've beaten influenza."

Konrad walks toward the kitchen, talking as he goes. "I don't know where to start. I think you've been duped, Candace. This nano-scientist, Balil, what was his last name?"

Candace takes a deep breath and looks down at the floor. "Zaidi. His name is Zaidi."

Konrad continues, "Right. Zaidi. He comes to you with this discovery, and you add it to the vaccine without any trials? Are you out of your mind?"

Candace stands quickly and walks to the kitchen, holding out her hands in a pleading gesture. "I told you Konrad. I did it for us, all of us. Reginald was going to destroy us if I didn't play along. He wouldn't wait for the trials. His exact words were 'no delays'. My back was against the wall. I did it for everyone. You said it yourself Konrad, millions were going to die if the Thailand strain broke out. I just thought that saving millions was justification enough to break the rules."

Konrad looks at his coffee cup as if contemplating the weight of the world. "If you're telling me the truth and the vaccine is harmful in the slightest, you'll be used as a scapegoat. They'll hang both of us out to dry for this. I'm talking about criminal prosecution. They will have no mercy. Where is this Balil now?"

She shakes her head and says in a thick voice, "I don't know. I tried to contact him on his cell but the number is out of service. I'm scared Konrad."

Konrad's mouth tightens into a line. "You should be, in fact, we all should be terrified. Millions of people have already taken the vaccine Candace. Damn you for this. I have to see these proteins for myself. I suppose it would be wishful thinking to think that you may have saved the video files onto a flash drive. Did you?"

Candace shakes her head. "Everything was on my computer in the lab. As far as I know, my credentials are still in my apartment, but I can't go near the place and even if I could, I don't know if they would let me past the gate at Emmer."

Konrad stands at the sink, looking out the window to the back yard and says, "We may not have to go to Emmer. I've known Reginald for years. He didn't trust the onsite data backup. You documented the experiments on company equipment? The lab cameras?"

Candace raises her eyebrows in surprise and answers, "Of course. How else?"

Konrad nods his head. "Then the files are at Reginald's in a remote backup. We just have to convince him to let us take a look.

Meanwhile in Arlington, Virginia, Horace MacGill pulls his BMW into the parking lot of his apartment thinking, "It's good to be home if home is what this place is."

He exits his vehicle and shouldering his bag, walks around the building, entering from the other side. He takes the stairs to the second floor and then the elevator for the last eight floors to his apartment. Horace turns the key in the lock slowly and enters, setting his bag down on the floor just inside the door.

He moves slowly through the darkened apartment, finding the dental floss across the hallway intact, exhaling, he relaxes. He returns to the door, retrieving the bag and no sooner sits it on the bed when he hears the ringing of his satellite telephone from the kitchen. A half second later, his laptop chimes. Horace moves to the kitchen thinking, "That is never good."

He answers the telephone in his usual manner and immediately hears the apprehensive voice of one of the assets assigned to monitor various strands of the massive web Horace is managing. "Sir, I'm afraid there may be an acute situation. We've monitored bank activity for Candace Swanson in the form of a transfer of funds."

Horace smiles and replies, "Good, she just fucked up. When did it occur?"

The asset hesitates and then replies, "Yesterday."

Horace's pulse quickens. "Yesterday, and you just caught it?"

The asset says quickly, "We caught it via our daily review of accounts for all subjects being surveilled."

Horace takes a deep breath and asks, "Nature of the transfer?"

The asset clears his throat and replies, "Five thousand dollars to Konrad Pearce."

Horace pushes the telephone to his ear and says slowly, "Hmm, Konrad Pearce, interesting."

The asset replies quickly, "I'm afraid there's more sir. Our team on the ground monitored Dr. Pearce at the bank this morning making a sizeable withdrawal."

Horace has the sudden urge to throw the telephone. Instead, he takes a deep breath and says, "I'm confident that you are monitoring Dr. Pearce appropriately. I want eyes on him every second. Candace Swanson has made contact and more than likely is in Green River. He'll lead us to her and when he does, I want her taken into custody. Alive, is that understood?"

Horace can almost hear the asset's head nodding over the telephone as he replies, "Yes sir. We've got it under control."

He thinks as he hears this, "I sure as hell hope so otherwise, we might have a target package on all of us."

Horace stares at the wall and visualizes the angles thinking, "You are a pain in my ass Candace. How in the world did I not see you coming? Your fun is coming to an end though because you're out of cash and the only way for you to get what Konrad Pearce has is to come out of the shadows. When you do that, you're mine."

Back in Green River, Konrad sits at the kitchen table across from Candace and says, "So that's the plan. I'm going to call Reginald and see if I can talk him into letting us look at the data backup for your experiments with the Thai strain. I'm hoping he's cooled off enough that he might agree if you're with me."

Candace shakes her head. "You can't call him from here Konrad. I'm almost positive that your phones are tapped. When I called and told you that I was going to Baton Rouge, I was counting on the people who were chasing me to go there. If they find out I'm here, I don't know what will happen, but it won't be good."

He looks at her for a long moment, then stroking his chin says, "Okay Candace, let's test your theory. I'm going to run out to my car and take off in a hurry. You watch from the upstairs window and see if anyone scrambles to follow me."

Candace nods and Konrad grabs his keys. "When I get back, I'm going to pull into the garage. I've got to figure out how to smuggle you out of this house. Go upstairs and I'll count to twenty, then I go."

Candace stands and walks out of the kitchen, pausing to look back at Konrad for a moment before exiting. Konrad begins to count. At twenty, he moves to the door, keys in hand. At the door, Konrad pauses for half a second as he takes a deep breath, then he throws the door open and steps out quickly closing and locking it behind him before sprinting for his car.

Candace watches from above as Konrad backs out of the drive and then drives down the street at a high rate of speed. Through a small opening in the curtains, she sees a dark blue Chevy Caprice pull away from the curb and follow in the direction Konrad had taken. She says quietly, "They're here."

The vindication she feels at being correct is little consolation to the fact that the people who are pursuing her have either tracked her here or they are also watching Konrad. Both scenarios are bad.

Konrad makes good time as he maneuvers the Subaru through the streets of Green River on his way to the truck stop on 46. He enters the parking lot, barely slowing until he pulls up in front and parks. Jumping out of the car Konrad looks around and walks briskly inside. He looks to his left and asks the girl at the fuel desk, "Where are your payphones?"

She points to the back and replies, "Back there but you have to buy a phone card."

Konrad rolls his eyes and retrieves a pre-paid telephone card from the display, pays for it then turns and heads for the bank of telephones in the hallway near the showers. He picks up the receiver and dials Reginald's number. The call is answered after five rings by a barely familiar voice. It is Reginald's but he sounds like he has been crying and is on the edge of panic. "Hello?"

Konrad speaks quickly, "Reginald, its Konrad, please don't hang up."

There is silence for a moment then Reginald replies in a desperate tone, "Konrad? Oh, thank God! Konrad, you have to come over and tell me what's wrong with me."

Konrad stares at the wall. "I'm no doctor, Reginald."

Reginald sobs, "Yeah but you're the scientist who developed this vaccine and I've been getting steadily worse since I took it! I can't concentrate. I can't make a decision. My head is killing me. Something's terribly wrong. I can't bear the thought of leaving my house. You have to come over and look at me, you son of a bitch! To top it off, those fuckers from the DHHS took everything."

Konrad holds the receiver close to his ear. "What are you talking about? What did DHHS take?"

Reginald begins to sob as he says, "They came in and made me sign my company over to them. Oh Konrad, what have I done?"

Konrad takes a deep breath and replies, "Stay where you are Reginald. We'll be there as soon as we can."

He doesn't wait for a reply, pulls the card from the phone and walks through the truck stop to the exit. His mind is reeling as he walks, thinking, "What did Reginald mean? Why in heaven's name would he sign his company over to the government? It sounded crazy."

His thoughts are interrupted as he bumps into a man coming in as he is going out. He looks up, apologizes and keeps going. It isn't until he reaches his car that Konrad realizes the man, he collided with was the same man from the bank. He looks around once more, gets into his car and starts the short drive home. As Konrad turns on to his street and the house comes into view, he pushes the garage door opener, and the door starts rising in its familiar journey to the top.

Konrad doesn't have to wait and pulls into the garage, closing the door before exiting his vehicle. He kills the engine and sits in the Subaru listening. The house is dead quiet. He enters the house and finds Candace waiting by the staircase with eyebrows raised in the unspoken question. Konrad looks at her and says, "He wants me to come over. He sounds pretty messed up and said something about the government taking his company from him. We need to get over there but how are we going to get out of here without being seen?"

Candace smiles slightly, "The same way I got in. I don't think they're watching the back Konrad. Are you up for a walk?"

Konrad nods, "To the truck stop?"

Candace says, "Yes. It'll be dark soon. We'll walk to the truck stop using the same route I used to get here. From there we'll call a taxi."

Konrad replies quizzically, "Why not just use your car?"

Shaking her head, Candace says, "You were followed Konrad. My car stays where it is in the back lot of the truck stop. Too many things could go wrong by using it. A collision or traffic stop. Anything involving the police and I'm afraid I might end up like Annie. I just know too much. The people who are following me have resources Konrad. We can't afford to take the chance."

They don't have to wait long before darkness begins to drape the back yard in shadow. Candace stands and pulls on a dark hoodie, much too big for her lithe frame. She starts toward the door, but Konrad stops her as he picks up the money. "We should take this."

Candace nods in agreement as Konrad looks around the kitchen, finally finding the waist pack he wore while riding his bike. He looks inside and pulls out a few carbohydrate gel packs and a pack of chewing gum. Once the pack is empty, he opens it and puts the money inside. He fastens it around his waist and nods toward the door. They step quietly from the back door and then through the back gate into the alleyway behind Konrad's home.

They move straight across the alley and through the gate of the home directly behind Konrad's. It is a chain link fence and the hinges squeak as the gate opens. Both wince at the unwanted noise. They move quietly toward the front, staying close to the large shrubs which border this yard from the next, carefully avoiding the many children's toys strewn everywhere. As they reach the front and go through the gate, Konrad hears a noise from the front of the house and pulls Candace into the shrubs. He whispers almost silently, his lips close to her ear, "Its Dan Taylor. He owns this place."

They hear Dan say to his young daughter, "It's not out here on the porch honey. Let's go back and look in the house."

Konrad feels a bead of sweat make the slow journey down his spine. His jaw is clenched. He hears the front door open, then close. Konrad nods at Candace and they step from the shrubs, hurrying toward the street. The neighborhood is quiet, and they do not encounter anyone as they walk. It is still early in the evening in this neighborhood full of families with children. Dinners are being enjoyed. Television is being watched. No one is aware of the drama which is unfolding right in their midst. Candace takes the lead as they walk quickly around the large pond at the entrance of the subdivision and toward the main road. They walk in silence, each absorbed in their own thoughts. The only sound is of distant traffic and the much closer bull frogs who call this pond their home. They turn right after exiting the subdivision and begin the walk to the truck stop three miles away.

Forty-five minutes later, they ascend the final hill and are greeted by garish flood lights and the sound of diesel motors. The bright lights and noise are a stark contrast to the quiet of their walk. They cross the large parking lot, avoiding the many cars pulling in and out of the gas pumps and enter through the front as Konrad had earlier in the day.

Just inside the door, Candace stops and grabs Konrad by the forearm. "Let's wait here and watch for a second to see if we were followed."

They stand to the side of the door and watch for five minutes, seeing nothing unusual. No one inside takes exceptional interest in the couple as they wait. Konrad finally turns, walking in and purchasing a telephone card. They both walk to the back where the showers and phones are located, passing several truck drivers who do take obvious interest in Candace. She avoids eye contact, following closely behind Konrad. He calls the Green River Taxi Company and speaks with the lone raspy voiced dispatcher who promises a taxi within twenty minutes. Candace leans into Konrad and whispers, "Tell them to come to the back entrance. We should leave by a different door. In the meantime, we should try to blend in."

Konrad can't help but smile as he hangs the phone up and looks in her eyes asking, "How does one do that?"

Candace looks away self-consciously and says, "You know, act like we're shopping. Walk through the aisles. Blend Konrad."

Konrad grins slightly and motions with his hand. "After you."

They walk up and down the aisles looking at truck deodorizers, Candace holding different scents up to Konrad's nose for him to sample. To anyone watching, they might have looked like a happy couple on vacation. Every so often, one of them would glance at the rear door. In almost exactly twenty minutes, a beat-up green minivan stenciled with "Green River Taxi" pulls up to the doors and honks twice.

Konrad and Candace look at each other then head for the door. The cabbie is an overweight man with a beard and a mustard stain on his shirt. This does nothing to draw attention away from the perspiration stains. They climb in the back and Konrad gives the driver Reginald's address. The cabbie looks in the rearview mirror at Konrad and says with a shrug, "That's a nice neighborhood mister. I'm not trying to get into your business but, are you sure you wanna take her home. I know a couple of nice hotels that take cash and aren't too far from here."

The insinuation is clear, and Konrad can feel the heat rise into his face. "You're right. It's none of your business, just drive."

The cabbie chuckles, his whole mid-section rising and falling with the raspy laugh. "Okay pal, whatever you say."

No words are exchanged as the cabbie maneuvers the minivan through the familiar streets of Green River to Reginald's home. As they pull into the circular drive and stop, the cabbie looks into the rearview mirror and says, "Eighteen-fifty, mister."

Konrad hands him a twenty-dollar bill and then hesitates before leaving the cab. He pulls a fifty from his wallet and tears it in half, giving the cabbie one of the halves. "I don't want you to wait here but don't go too far. This shouldn't take long."

The cabbie chuckles, handing Konrad a business card with a handwritten number on it. He leans toward the passenger door and says, "That's my personal cell number. The name's Arnold. Give me a call when you and the young lady are finished. I'll be down at the sandwich shop across from the entrance to this place."

Arnold chuckles once more then drives away as Konrad and Candace walk around the house to the rear entrance. Konrad knocks on the door and yells, "Reginald! It's Konrad, open up!"

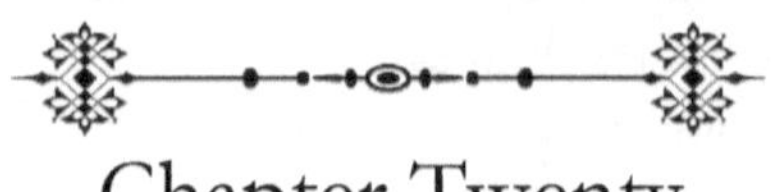

Chapter Twenty

Horace MacGill sits in the leather chair positioned in front of the video uplink located in Trojan 34 waiting for the meeting with the Regents to begin. He closes his eyes and lets his mind wander, soaking up the dark coolness in the room. It is late in the evening and the constant maneuvering is catching up with him. He knows that he needs sleep.

The interior of this room is his only place of total safety and the only place where he can fully relax. The outside world is entirely enemy territory. Horace never lets himself forget this. He thinks about Candace Swanson and her uncanny ability to outmaneuver him which almost makes his blood boil. Horace isn't used to playing catch up and that is exactly what he's been doing since she slipped his team in Key West.

She was just a scientist, not worthy of closer inspection. Had he been on his game, he would have recognized, as a runaway living on the street, Candace would have developed a skill set for just the challenge she is facing now. His jaw tenses as he thinks, "She's obviously good at it, but her luck won't hold out forever. I'm close. Very, very close."

It occurs to him that a review of the surveillance procedures for Konrad Pearce will have to be completed immediately after this meeting. Something is bothering Horace. A loose end that he can't quite identify. There is no room for loose ends, especially where it comes to catching Candace and putting her on ice until things pass the point of no return. Then, what she knows will mean nothing. His thoughts are interrupted by the appearance of a blue light on the video equipment which means the meeting is beginning.

As before, Horace conducts a brief roll call. At the conclusion, the North American Regent begins to speak, "I would like to commend you Mr. MacGill on what seems to be a success in the making. Our projections indicate greater than ninety-five percent compliance in receiving the flu vaccine, worldwide by October."

Horace nods and the Regent continues, "As you can imagine, demand of this magnitude has created a challenge in supply. It was my decision, of which I'm informing the body at this point, to informally nationalize the pharmaceutical industry in what is currently known as the United States via the Department of Health and Human Services. All very legal of course, national security and whatnot. I felt it necessary to ensure the supply of the vaccine and destroy any evidence regarding development."

Several of the Regents can be heard huffing, one cough and Horace begins to feel his face flush. The Regent from Asia Minor finally speaks in her sultry voice, "Of course, the Regent from North America has full authority to take such an action in her sector however would it not have been wise to have a discussion regarding these actions prior? I'm sure the body would be interested in hearing how you took such a drastic step informally."

The North American Regent huffs, "Conversation? I see no need for such things. It is my sector and my decision. The circumstances surrounding the development of this vaccine would have certainly come to light eventually. My goal is full compliance before that occurs. Mr. MacGill has already demonstrated through his request for my intervention in securing Emmer Pharmaceutical as the sole supplier, the need for my continued intervention. The DHHS simply convinced the owners of the pharmaceutical companies to sign over their companies to the government. Those that resisted the opportunity were removed."

Horace feels his anger rising. "If I may interject Madam Regent, there was no need for anyone to be 'removed'. I already have a 'scapegoat' if you will, in place. All blame for the introduction of the vaccine in its current formulation will rest solely on her shoulders when events do come to light. I make it a practice to keep 'removals' to a minimum in my operations."

The North American Regent laughs, "Oh yes, I've heard about your 'scapegoat' Horace. Tell me, have you found her yet?"

The question feels to Horace as if he has just been slapped in the face as he becomes instantly aware that he has a mole in his organization. "Not at the present Madam."

Horace's anger gets the best of him. "As the Regent is probably unaware through lack of real-world experience, clandestine operations are fluid and never run exactly according to plan. That is why you have me. To handle the unexpected."

It is stupid and he realizes his error as soon as he makes the statement. There is dead silence on the call for a microsecond before the regent responds. "You would do well to watch your tone Horace and instead spend your energies finding your 'scapegoat'. You were selected for this position due to your expertise. Please do not give us cause to reevaluate our choice. Now, I have many matters to attend to. Do you have an updated progress report?"

Totally subdued, Horace replies, "Considering the numbers regarding compliance, we should start seeing indications that the next phase has begun. The chaff should begin to separate from the wheat fairly quickly at this point. In my estimation, the project is completely on schedule. Please accept my apologies for my earlier errant comments Madam."

The words burn in Horace's throat as he assumes the demeanor of a lowly servant. The Regent does not reply but ends the connection leaving Horace completely alone in the darkened room. He feels the seething anger in his gut thinking, "There is a traitor in my midst. I'll have to watch my every move. Candace, you bitch, where the fuck, are you?"

He sits in the chair for a long time, staring into nothingness. The room doesn't feel as safe as it had when he'd first entered. For the first time in a long time, Horace realizes just how vulnerable he really is, and he doesn't like it. He wonders who the Regents really are and how they came to be. He asks himself, just mouthing the words, "How does one amass such great power?"

The glaring realization hits him that he may not live long enough to know the answer. Horace follows his usual routine in leaving the building and heads for the non-descript BMW. As he reaches his car, his satellite phone begins to ring. He answers the call immediately, "Hello. Good news I hope."

The asset answers in a hopeful tone, "We've monitored a telephone call from Doctor Pearce to Reginald Emmer via the tap on Emmer's line. It originates from the truck stop on Highway 46 near Pearce's home. I sent you the recording. Awaiting instructions."

Horace replies, "I'll get back to you."

He opens his laptop and pulls up the file. As he listens, he thinks, "So that's what you were doing at the truck stop. You know I'm listening. That's interesting."

Horace sits straight up in his seat as he listens to the recording. He listens to the call again and then, clawing for his telephone says, "Aw, fuck me!"

Horace dials the telephone quickly and the asset answers almost immediately. Horace asks in an urgent tone, "Are you on site at Pearce's home?"

The asset responds quizzically, "Yes. We've had a team on site 24/7 just as you instructed, sir. Is there a problem?"

Horace grips the telephone. "You've got three sixty coverage on the residence? No gaps?"

The asset exhales audibly and responds, "We were instructed to be ghosts. There was no way to cover the back of the house in that capacity. Just no cover. We're watching the front which has been sufficient. The target is unaware of our presence."

Horace is unable to contain his composure any longer. "You imbecile. He's got help. This fucking scientist knows you're there. Did you listen to the call? He said 'we'. 'We'll be there as soon as we can'. Doctor Pearce has help and I'm betting its Candace Swanson. She's in the fucking house with him. I need you to make an entry now! Low and slow. Snatch and grab. This situation gets contained immediately. They are not to be allowed to make contact with Emmer. Do you understand? We'll hold them at the safe house on Dallas Drive."

The asset responds in a voice riddled with tension, "On it Sir. I'll instruct the onsite team to make entry."

Horace responds in a low, dangerous tone, "Get this done. I'm on my way."

He disconnects the call, then hesitates and dials. The call is answered by a sleepy voice. Horace says, "Get the jet ready. I'm going to Green River, Indiana."

The sleepy voice instantly becomes alert. "Departure time Sir?"

Horace grimaces, "Within the hour."

He sits in his car and feels each second as it passes, opening his computer, Horace has one more task to complete before he heads to the airport. He pulls up the file on Reginald Emmer and sends it via a massive web of hijacked servers thinking, "I wasn't planning on this for a while but that bitch poking her nose into my operation has thrown my timeline off. Regent or no, she has no idea what she's doing."

He dials and the call is answered immediately, "Verification?"

"Papa Alpha Whiskey 337"

"Outcome?"

"Termination with prejudice."

"Preferred method?"

"Botched robbery. Additionally, secure all electronic equipment. Computers, phone, etc."

"Timeline?"

"Immediate."

"We have a team in the area. Expect outcome within three hours."

The call disconnects signaling the impending demise of Reginald Emmer. Horace seethes as he thinks, "Emmer was controllable. The DHHS is not. It's a wild card that I wasn't expecting, caused by a pretentious bitch filled with self-importance."

Horace's hate for the Regents grows every time he interacts with them. They never fail to remind him of his lowly standing in their world. They are untouchable, but he is very touchable. He says to himself, "You're expendable Horace. Never forget that."

Because he knows this truth, it is an angle to be played like any other. As he looks past the light cast by the overhead lights of the parking lot, into the blackness of the night, Horace says under his breath, "Control is all about angles."

Horace throws the car into gear and heads for the airport. There will be no time to stop at his apartment and pack. The drive seems much too long and Horace exhales audibly as he exits 395 toward the airport. He enters through the rear cargo gate and pulls up to the private hangar. The smell of jet fuel is heavy in the air as he exits his car to find the small jet idling outside the hangar. The co-pilot meets him at the stairs and asks, "Any bags Sir?"

Horace looks at the young man with barely disguised contempt and says pointing at the laptop case hanging from his shoulder, "Just this. Let's get going, I'm in a hurry."

The co-pilot nods and steps into the jet followed closely by Horace. As he gets inside Horace yells to the pilot, "Get us up. I need to be in Green River yesterday."

They are aloft for only a few minutes when Horace's telephone begins to chime. He answers the call immediately, not wanting to hear the report but needing the information. The asset doesn't wait for Horace to ask the question but begins speaking quickly, "The house is empty. They must have left through the back door. They're on foot so they can't be far, but we're blown. We were heading back to the van and some old geezer who said he was with the neighborhood watch started asking us what we thought we were doing. He had his cell phone out and threatened to call the police. We had to leave. What would you like us to do?"

Horace doesn't hear the question because as he looks out the window of the plane, he sees phase three of his operation going up in smoke. If they are at Emmer's house when the cleaning team gets there, Pearce and Swanson are dead as well. Rules are rules and one of the cardinal rules in being a cleaner is absolutely no loose ends. Horace thinks briefly about trying to call them off but realizes another one of the rules is no cancellations once the order is given. He thinks, "I am so fucked."

The asset repeats the question and Horace replies tiredly, "Return to the safe house and wait. Make sure a car is waiting for me at the airport. I'll let you know what our next move is when I get there."

He walks up the aisle to the cockpit and asks, "What is our ETA?"

The pilot turns and says, "Thirty minutes give or take. Can we get you anything Sir?"

Horace doesn't respond but just turns and walks back to his seat. He sits down and resumes looking out of the window and thinks about angles.

As Horace is contemplating these things, Konrad and Candace stand in Reginald Emmer's living room and contemplate the physical and emotional wreckage sitting on the couch in front of them. Reginald leans over a small trash can filled with blood-soaked paper towels. He is disheveled with dark circles under his eyes, and he is visibly shaking. His hands are blood stained well above the wrists. He looks up at Konrad with pleading eyes and says in a nasally voice around the paper towel he holds to his nose, "You've got to help me Konrad. I've been sick since I took that damn shot. This is your vaccine. You've got to figure out what's wrong with me."

Konrad shakes his head and looks straight at Reginald. "No buddy. You need a real doctor. You've got to get that bleeding stopped or you could die. That's the simple truth. Let me call you an ambulance."

Reginald stands shakily; his eyes glassy. "No! Fuck you, no! I took that vaccine on national television. My reputation is on the line. You've got to fix this. Undo it. You're a scientist so make me an antidote."

Candace interjects, "There is no antidote you asshole. That's what he's trying to tell you. If you keep bleeding like that, you'll go into shock. You need to go to the hospital. Don't you get it? You're bleeding out. How long has this been going on?"

Reginald sits back down heavily and tosses the bloody paper towel missing the trash can. He unrolls another one and holds it to his nose. "All fucking day. At first it was just a trickle, but it keeps getting worse."

Candace sees the opportunity and seizes it saying as she looks hard at Reginald, "He might be able to help you, but he wasn't there for the introduction of the nano-bots. He hasn't seen how the vaccine acts. There must be some way we can access the video files of the initial experiments."

Reginald leans back shaking his head then quickly leans forward. "How are you going to do that? Those fuckers from DHHS took my company. The military is guarding Emmer Pharma. Even I can't get back in the labs."

Konrad looks at Reginald in disgust. "How did they take your company from you Reginald? How could you let that happen?"

Reginald almost sobs as he says, "That bitch from DHHS just waltzed into my office with the papers and told me to sign. I knew it was wrong but I couldn't stop myself. She gave the order, and I followed it. I can't explain it. I'd love to get my hands around that bitch's throat."

He leans in toward Reginald. "You've got a remote backup Reginald, don't deny it because I know you do. Where is it and what's the password?"

Reginald snorts, spewing blood on the floor. "I'm not giving you the password to my files. You're crazy."

Konrad leans back quickly, avoiding the blood. "Fine, bleed out. You asked for my help asshole. To do that, I need to see the films from the lab, and you better decide quickly because the clock is ticking for you, my friend."

Reginald looks from Candace to Konrad with blood shot eyes then says through the paper towel, "The backup is in my study."

He looks down at the floor in defeat as Konrad asks, "The password?"

Reginald spews more blood as he says, "Fuck! Fuck, fuck, fuck! It's Norma. The password is Norma."

Konrad almost laughs. "Your secretary? You're pathetic."

Reginald looks up and quickly replies with a gurgle in his voice, "It's not like that you bastard."

Konrad just nods his head slowly, grinning as he points to the study door and tells Candace, "That's the study. Go ahead and pull up the films."

Then to Reginald, "Change your paper towel Reggie."

Reginald glares at Konrad as he tears another paper towel off of the roll. After a few minutes, Candace says, "Got it, come and see."

Konrad turns from Reginald and goes into the library where Candace sits behind a large mahogany desk. The light from the computer illuminates her facial features, causing Konrad to stop in the doorway and take in her beauty. It would not be the first time. Candace looks up from the computer and asks quizzically, "What?"

She reaches up and runs her fingers through her midnight black hair self-consciously as Konrad, breaking his stare, moves quickly around the desk. As he leans down, looking over her shoulder, she starts the film showing the initial experiments. Konrad can't believe his eyes as he watches the birth of his universal flu vaccine. His mind warring between the marvel on the screen and the hypnotic scent of lilac in his nostrils.

Candace senses his presence, his cheek almost touching hers. She turns her head, their faces inches apart and kisses him on the mouth. Konrad returns the kiss, gently. They linger like this, neither one wanting the moment to end but fate and Reginald Emmer intervene. Konrad has completely forgotten the film when he hears the sound of something heavy hitting the living room floor.

Their lips part, the moment abruptly ended. Konrad notices a flash drive on the desk as he quickly heads toward the study door. He points at it and says, "Copy those files."

Candace, still unfocused from what has just transpired between the two looks at Konrad quizzically and asks, "Why?"

Konrad answers with one word as he strides from the room, "Proof."

As he exits the study, Konrad sees Reginald lying on the floor face down. There is an ever-widening pool of blood, the source of which appears to be Reginald's nose and mouth. Konrad quickly moves to Reginald's side and checks for a carotid pulse. Finding none, he rolls Reginald to his back and begins CPR. Candace appears in the doorway of the study with the flash drive in her hand. She asks tensely, "What happened?"

Konrad slides Reginald's phone to her with one hand and continues chest compressions, quickly answering, "I don't know. I think he bled out. Call for an ambulance."

Candace picks up the bloody telephone and looks at it before looking at Konrad who is feverishly pumping on Reginald's chest. With each compression a fresh geyser of blood exits Reginald's mouth and nose. Candace, her face a mask of stoniness says, "No Konrad. No ambulance. These people will find us."

Konrad starts to protest but the flash of headlights illuminating the stained-glass windows at the front of the house as someone pulls into the circular drive causes both of them to fall silent. Konrad stops his efforts to revive Reginald and moves to the windows along with Candace. As they peek out of the window next to the door, a small middle aged blonde female exits a non-descript gray van. Two large men come around from behind the van to join her. They are all wearing black coveralls, gloves and disposable shoe coverings. Konrad looks at Candace, his mouth a thin line. "They've found us."

Candace is the one to react first as she pulls Konrad by the arm and whispers, "We have to go Konrad. We must go right now."

He doesn't resist as she pulls him through the living room and down the hall to the back door. They don't slow down as they exit the house, running for the shrubbery at the back corner of the yard. As they enter the thick foliage, small branches drag at their clothing and whip their faces. They lie down and stay motionless, praying that they won't be seen. The only sound is their breathing which they both try to control. Candace slowly reaches down to her pocket and feels the outline of the flash drive, only then realizing that she still has the bloody phone clutched in her grasp. She also feels Konrad's chest rise and fall against her side. As they watch, the three from the van step gingerly around the corner of the house and stand motionless at the back door which was left open during their flight.

Each of the three reaches into their coveralls and produce large semi-automatic pistols with silencers attached. As Konrad and Candace watch, frozen on the ground, the three from the van crouch and move through the door with practiced grace. Konrad feels a sick feeling in his stomach as he realizes that the people who are pursuing them are professionals and that they are obviously not interested in talking. He feels Candace squeeze his upper arm in an unspoken, "Get ready."

As soon as the three from the van get into the house and out of sight Candace begins to slowly inch deeper into the foliage. Konrad follows, staying as low to the ground as possible. Within minutes they make it to the road, both exhaling in relief. Konrad whispers, "If we go right, up this road there is a walking path through the woods which takes us down along the main highway. It'll be dark but I know the way."

He can barely make out Candace nodding her head in the darkness as they stand and make their way toward the path, their soft footfalls and breathing the only sounds in the darkness. Before long, they come to a slight bend in the road. Konrad gently grabs Candace's elbow and guides her to a barely noticeable opening in the tree line. What awaits them is a walking path made much darker by the forest. Konrad feels his way along the mulched path, guiding Candace who moves as if she is blind with one arm outstretched into black nothingness. After about a mile, Konrad stops to Candace's relief and whispers, "Give me Reginald's phone. I'm going to have Arnold pick us up on the road. It's just up ahead."

Exhausted, Candace does not object, but instead hands Konrad the telephone. He uses the light from the phone display to read the number on the card and dials, hoping Arnold is still waiting. The call is answered in three rings. "Yeah."

Konrad breathes a sigh of relief and responds, "This is the guy who has the other half of your fifty."

Arnold chuckles, "Well, you've taken longer than I figured. I was beginning to wonder. Do you need me to come pick the lady up?"

Konrad replies, "No. Pick us up a quarter mile west of where you said you were going to wait. We'll be waiting."

Arnold is silent for a moment then chuckles and replies, "Okay Mr. Bond. See you in a few minutes."

The line goes dead as the call disconnects. Arnold puts his half-eaten sandwich on the passenger seat, wipes watered down mayonnaise from his lips and puts the minivan in gear saying under his breath, "Something hokey about this whole deal but fifty bucks is fifty bucks."

Konrad feels the light touch of Candace's hand on his arm as she whispers, "Break it. Break it and throw it away."

He does as she says, breaking the telephone in half and tossing the pieces into the darkness before leading Candace the last fifty yards to the road. They manage to wander into a blackberry thicket in the dark, the thorns ripping at their flesh as they cross. By the time they make it to the road, they are bleeding from a hundred tiny cuts. Konrad stops just inside the tree line and waits.

In a few minutes, he sees the green minivan approaching slowly. He looks left then right then steps out onto the side of the road with his hand raised. Arnold speeds up and immediately pulls to a stop in front of the two. The sliding door opens and Candace collapses into the car, followed quickly by Konrad. Arnold looks at his passengers and chuckles, his torso keeping time with the laugh. "You really know how to show a girl a good time buddy."

Konrad doesn't have the energy to reply, but just hands Arnold the other half of the fifty and says, "Just please drive."

They speed down the road in silence until Arnold says, "Well, where to big spender?"

Konrad racks his brain for the answer. They can't go back to his house, and they can't drive around all night. "How about one of those motels you mentioned. Someplace that takes cash."

Arnold looks in the rearview mirror and smiles saying, "Yeah buddy, I can hook you up. The way you two look, I was going to suggest the emergency room but you're better off staying away from that place anyway."

Konrad leans forward in the seat. "What's going on at the hospital?"

Arnold half turns in his seat. "It's been all over the news this evening. They're busting at the seams down there. They're telling people to stay away if they can. It seems a whole bunch of folks dying from, get this, fucking nose bleeds."

It's as if Konrad has been punched in the gut by an ice-cold fist. Candace does not react to the news but just stares blankly ahead. They pull into the parking lot of a seedy looking motel which proudly displays the hourly rates on the office window. Arnold looks in the mirror at Konrad. "Will this do buddy?"

Konrad looks at Candace, then at Arnold and replies, "Perfect."

They exit the taxi but before the side door closes, Konrad ducks his head back in and hands Arnold a hundred-dollar bill. "Look, you seem like a nice guy. Do yourself a favor and forget this ride tonight. Don't talk about it with anyone. You just dropped us off at the big house and that's the last you saw of us. Trust me, you don't want to get involved in this. Understand?"

Arnold laughs and says, "Sure big spender. We were never here, but, if you need another ride that doesn't exist, give me a call. I can use the cash."

Arnold turns away as the passenger door slides shut. The taxi drives off and Konrad puts his arm around Candace's waist, guiding her toward the office window. As they reach the window, Konrad notices the steel bars. He rings the buzzer and a pale, twenty-year-old with acne and dark circles under his eyes appears almost immediately. The night manager smiles a smile filled with discolored teeth. "Can I help you folks?"

Konrad says, "We need a room for the night. Do you have anything?"

The kid smiles and looks at his computer. "We've got a couple. The Cabana suite and the Sahara suite. That'll be one hundred for the night. You can take your pick."

Konrad looks at Candace who seems to be more lucid. She rolls her eyes and says, "The Sahara will be fine."

Konrad puts the money in the tray as the night manager smiles and says, "I'll get you some clean sheets and towels. Those are an extra ten but I'd strongly recommend them."

Konrad puts the money in the tray and the manager returns with the linens and a key. "It'll be number forty-three. It's up the stairs and to your left. Have a nice time."

The manager smiles and shakes his head as he walks away. Konrad looks at Candace and asks with the hint of a grin, "Shall we dear?"

She doesn't respond but just begins walking toward the stairs. Konrad follows carrying the linen, his mind racing as a plan begins to take shape.

Chapter Twenty-One

Marcie Faunier holds the steering wheel of her minivan in a white knuckled grip as it idles at the Margaret Avenue railroad crossing in Green River, Indiana. It is almost midnight, and she is exhausted from her three to eleven shift as a certified nursing assistant at the County Home for the Elderly. It is a place of abandonment for the geriatric population with no insurance and little personal possessions available for the county to seize to pay for their care. It is a place Marcie has come to think of as "hell on earth."

Green River is known for several things like the college that seems to own half the town and the prison which provides half of the town's revenue. There's the pharmaceutical plant which recently became the town's lead employer and the railway hub which gridlocks traffic on every major thoroughfare.

As she sits in her vehicle staring at the red flashing lights of the railroad crossing and the flashers of the vehicle in front of her, she thinks about her ex-husband, Ray and the way he left her high and dry in Green River with two sons and a home on the verge of foreclosure. The knot in her stomach grows as she falls into the mental spiral which always comes if she has too much time to think.

The only thing that she is certain of in this moment is that she hates Ray almost as much as this train which is blocking the crossing and keeping her from her boys. She'd left them at home alone in the government assisted housing because, on a CNA's pay, a babysitter is out of the question. The train lumbers back and forth as the railroad workers uncouple and re-couple railcars. She grits her teeth and thinks, "How can people put up with this? Every fucking night I have to wait on a train somewhere. I'm going to go crazy in this place."

Marcie thinks about poor Mrs. Anderson and how she passed away tonight. She'd been abandoned by her family and had died badly, begging for water. Her constant thirst was just a figment of her imagination and the dementia that had ravaged this sweet lady in the end. When she first landed the job, Marcie had come close to driving herself mad, constantly bringing Mrs. Anderson cups of water throughout her shift in an attempt to keep up with the constant pleading.

In the end, she had become numb to the old woman's constant cries as had the other staff members on the floor. The guilt of this fact has weighed on her all evening and now, this train. Marcie seethes as she thinks of her life and how everyone but her seems to have complete control over it. Tears blur her vision as she fights back a sob and thinks, "I couldn't even say no to a shot. How could I afford to say no when they threatened to fire me if I didn't get it. Those fuckers, they didn't care one little bit about me or my boys. Just get it, or else."

Marci feels her pulse quicken and instinctively places two fingers on her wrist. Fifteen seconds later she thinks, "One forty. Way too fast. I'm going to have a panic attack if I sit here any longer. Finally, she can take it no longer and claws for the door handle. Her breathing is quick and heavy as she steps out of the car and bending slightly, screams with all her might. Several other drivers exit their vehicles. Some of them are her coworkers. Marcie screams again, yelling, "How can you people stand this! How can you stand it?"

Marcie sinks to her knees and sobs. She feels the wetness on her upper lip, but it doesn't register at first. Not until it begins to stream down her face in rivulets. She puts her fingers to her nose and, as she brings her hand away, realizes that the wetness is blood. Copious amounts of blood coming from her. She is surprised, then confused, not comprehending the sheer volume of blood leaving her body in pulsing waves.

She looks down and realizes that she is covered in blood. An ocean of her blood. Marcie hears shouts and the crunch of gravel beside her as other drivers come to her aid, the bouncing light of flashlights playing on the ground. Then the pain hits her, instantly excruciating. Her neck and the side of her head feel like they are on fire. Starbursts cloud her vision as she chokes, then vomits a frothy red fountain. Marcie hears a woman's voice scream, "Someone call an ambulance, she's choking."

She thinks of her boys, at home by themselves in that dirty government housing which has always had the underlying smell of roach spray and feels a deep sadness. With unseeing eyes, she reaches blindly and finds someone's hand to hold as the blurry light of the world becomes a pinpoint and then, like a candle flame extinguished, it simply goes dark.

About the same time as Marcie Faunier is choking to death on her own blood, Horace sits in the passenger seat of the dark blue Chevy Caprice and mulls over the current situation. His mood is not helped by the sour smell of body odor and two-day old fast food coming from the upholstery of the vehicle. The vehicle is clean to the eye, but it is apparent this team of operators could use some sharpening. He thinks, "It's no wonder she got past them. No fucking discipline."

Horace's mind goes back to his days as a tactical operator, contracting in every hot spot imaginable. He would be a ghost, making insertion and exfil without leaving trace. He thinks, "Hell, I even shit in a plastic bag and carried that out. These young shitheads have no idea. They're sloppy and sloppy gets you dead."

Every so often, the young driver glances at him furtively. Horace smiles thinking how the driver utterly fails in hiding his nervousness. He also enjoys the sense of power he holds over the young asset. The feeling helps lessen the sting of Horace's latest meeting with the Regents. His revelry is interrupted by the ringing of his telephone. It is from a number solely meant to be dialed and never to receive a call from. It is from the cleaners. "Yes?"

A monotone female voice speaks quickly, "I have vital information."

Horace replies, "Your breaking protocol. I challenge Spartan."

The female replies, "Shield."

Horace's mouth tightens into a thin line as he thinks, "This cannot be good."

He says slowly in his serpent like hiss, "Well, I'm waiting."

The female begins speaking in a bland tone, "Our team has departed the target area with all requested materials. The subject was deceased prior to our arrival. There were signs of additional people on site immediately prior to our arrival. The target appeared to have expired from some medical condition. I put a round into the back of his head to make it appear as if it was a botched robbery as requested. It appears someone was viewing a film on the target's computer. There was a whole bank of data storage at the residence. I've transmitted the film to you. We'll stay on station in the area pending further requests."

The call abruptly disconnects and Horace's body tenses as he thinks, "This is very bad indeed."

In short order, the Caprice turns on to a wooded lane and then into a heavily wooded drive which curves around a large hill. The natural landscape completely obscures the house from the road. There is a metal shed separated from the house by a small yard, lush with high grass.

The house itself is a two-story vinyl sided home that was probably once a very nice place. Now it is overgrown with hints of green mold edging the vinyl siding. Horace looks at the house in the garish light of the vehicle headlights and thinks, as he has many times before, of the cruelness of nature. The driver pushes a remote and the garage door rises on squeaking tracks. The car pulls forward into the garage and the driver closes the door. He looks over at Horace who waits to exit the vehicle until the garage door is completely closed. As he waits, Horace catches the driver's look and exhales resignedly.

He follows the driver through a white door leading into the entryway of the home. To his left is the front door, the windows covered in thick curtains. Directly in front of him is the staircase to the second floor. The house has the musty smell of long inhabitation, and the once white carpet is now a mottled gray. Sounds echo off the bare walls, reminding everyone inside that this is now a place inhabited by ghosts, living and dead. Horace has spent many hours in houses just like this one in every country on the globe. Every one of them being different in appearance but each evoking the same feeling of loss and loneliness.

He follows the driver into what was once the kitchen. The appliances are long gone, and the tile floor is cracked and broken. A lone coffee maker sits on a far counter. Horace scans this room and the adjacent family room where several sleeping bags and personal gear are still lying on the floor. His mouth tightens into a line as he thinks, "Sloppy. They're not ready to bug out if needed. So fucking typical of this generation."

He moves to the kitchen counter and pulls the laptop out of his satchel, situating it so the others in the room can't see the screen. The film sent by the cleaner soon plays after a few keystrokes. It is as bad as Horace had feared. He thinks, "I must assume they've copied this. Candace, what have you done?"

He pulls the satellite phone from his pocket and dials the number. It is answered immediatcly. As he has many times before, Horace recites the secret words that will mean the death of another person. It is just more collateral damage of which Horace always tries to keep to a minimum. "I'm expanding your duties."

The woman on the line is quiet for a brief second and then replies, "This is a break in protocol. I challenge 'Shield'."

Horace's grits his teeth and says tightly, "Spear."

The woman repeats the accusation, "You're breaking protocol."

He grips the telephone tightly and says in a voice low with menace, "I think we're past that, wouldn't you agree?"

The woman clears her throat and asks, "What do you need?"

Horace looks at the ceiling for a moment and then at the men who are watching him intently. "I'll be sending you two target packages. I need their location. They evaded the surveillance team and contacted your last assignment. They were the 'others' on scene. Additionally, they got to your last assignment's location somehow. I'm hoping they used the only taxi company in Green River. Check it. If that is the case, I want that trail to disappear."

The woman asks, "Any preference?"

Horace shakes his head as he replies, "No, use your imagination."

The woman, her voice colder says, "Consider it done. I have some ideas. What would you like us to do when we find the others."

Horace speaks slowly and clearly, "Just keep tabs on them and inform me the second you've found them."

The woman replies, "Understood."

The call disconnects and Horace finally looks up at the five men standing in a semi-circle, looking at him expectantly. "Which one of you was in charge of the surveillance on Konrad Pearce?"

A man in his mid-thirties steps forward. He has short black hair and a muscular physique. His eyes are worried. Horace looks around the room. "Well, what's your name and how long have you been doing this kind of work?"

The man says, "Uh, it's Hanes Sir. I've been contracting for about ten years or so. I know things didn't go exactly as planned, Sir, but, we did the best we could."

Horace holds up his hand silencing the man. "Any of you have less than eight years?"

They all shake their heads, some looking at the floor. Horace nods curtly. "When you signed on, were you informed that this mission would be unlike any you had ever been involved with?"

They all nod. Horace is silent for a moment as he looks at each man individually. "Do you men know who I am?"

They all look at each other, slightly confused. Horace smiles his reptilian smile and says, "You see gentleman, it doesn't matter who I am."

Hanes interrupts, "Sir, can I get you anything?"

Surprised, Horace looks around the room and then back at Hanes. "Yes, I'd like a cup of coffee Hanes. Thank you."

Horace looks back at the rest of the men. "Now where was I?"

Hanes returns with the coffee and holds it out to Horace who looks down at it grinning, his eyes almost luminescent. "Oh yes, I remember now. It doesn't matter who I am, but what I'm capable of."

Without hesitation, Horace sweeps the jacket he is wearing to the side and draws the Walther 380 from his waistband, pulling the trigger only once. The men in the room react immediately diving for cover as the explosive sound of the shot echoes throughout the empty house. A thin film of dust falls from the ceiling. After the dust settles, there is only one man who isn't picking himself up from the floor and dusting himself off. Hanes lies motionless on the floor, staring at the ceiling with sightless eyes.

The round, traveling at nine hundred and sixty feet per second struck him just under the left nostril, destroying any flesh in its path to the brain stem. Once it arrived, the brain was effectively separated from the body and the man was dead before he hit the floor. The smell of gunpowder, blood and feces fills the room as Hanes' blood and brains mix with coffee from the broken cup.

The remaining four men look at Horace in wide eyed horror, none speaking for fear of being the next to be shot. Horace, still holding the pistol moves it back and forth between the remaining assets. "I look around the room and I see sloppiness. Your lack of discipline has cost me dearly gentlemen. Now I have a problem of your making and we're going to solve it together but first, you men are going to get your shit wrapped up and tied off or so help me, none of you survive. Now, two of you take this corpse out to the back of the house and bury it deep. The other two are going to spend some time with me and get this place unfucked. Well, move!"

The men scramble, two of them half carrying, half dragging the body out the front door leaving a trail of crimson on the graying carpet. As they make it to the back of the house, the taller of the two says between heavy breaths, "I'll go get a couple of shovels."

The other, a young looking blonde kid in his late twenties replies, "You're not seriously going to stay after that shit we just witnessed?"

The taller man stops abruptly and turns to look at the younger man. "That's exactly why I'm staying. Do you think for one second that you survive if you run? I mean, after what you just witnessed? These people are connected. Powerful. We're just a small part of this monster and you don't want them sending it after you. It's called compartmentalization. No, the best thing is to follow orders, complete the job, get paid and disappear, man. Whatever they're doing, it's big, mean and hungry. You just better lay low, or you'll get eaten my friend."

The younger man cocks his head to the side and replies, "And you're going to do whatever that maniac says?"

The other man who had already turned to get the shovels looks back over his shoulder with a sardonic grin and replies, "Yeah, I'll do pretty much whatever he wants except get him a cup of coffee."

With that, the man disappears into the darkness, leaving the younger man to relive the final microsecond of Hanes' existence. He looks down at the dark form on the ground and thinks, "I didn't even see the draw. The gun was just in his hand all at once."

He stands, looking at the body as the wind blows and he feels the cold promise of death in the night air.

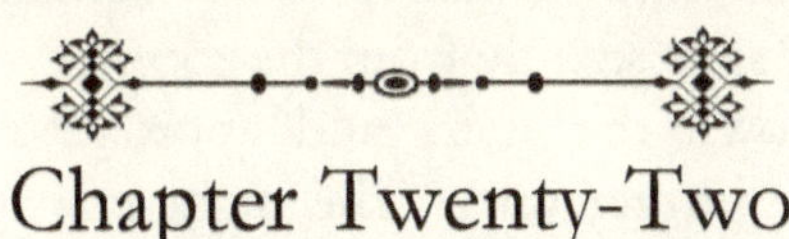

Chapter Twenty-Two

Konrad opens his eyes and feels his heart race as he searches his memory for where he currently is. A drop of perspiration runs from the outside corner of his eye down across his temple and enters his ear. Barely moving his head and looking from side to side, he realizes that he is in the Sahara room at the Romantic Destinations Suites in Green River. He hears the soft purring of Candace's breathing and realizes she is lying next to him.

There is something extremely comforting in her presence and a lump forms in his throat. He thinks of Jennifer and reminds himself that she is gone forever. His eyes fill with tears briefly before he gently shakes his head and the tears away.

He rises slowly, gently sliding from underneath the red satin comforter. As he sits on the side of the bed, Candace stirs slightly. He looks at his watch and sees that it is just a quarter past five. The sun will be rising soon, and he has something to do before that occurs. He stands and turns to look at Candace. She is beautiful. Her hair is still lightly wrapped in towel. She is wearing the cotton robe she'd worn to bed right after showering.

Konrad looks down and realizes that he is still fully dressed in the clothes he'd arrived in. The robe is slightly open, revealing the soft curve of her breast. The thought enters his mind that he wants her. Needs her but now is not the time to think of such things. He shakes his head and mentally chastises himself. They are in trouble, deep trouble. Their pursuers are close, and he has no plan. They need time and that is the one thing they don't seem to have.

Konrad looks around the room at the tapestries on the walls as if the answer might be in one of the ornate designs. The silk curtains hanging from the ceiling around the bed sway softly in time with the ceiling fan's slow rotations. Then, in the dark, the realization strikes him that there is a loose end that needs to be tied. A bread crumb to be swept up before it is found by the people who are chasing them. Konrad finds the waist pack and pulls four one-hundred-dollar bills and two fifties out, putting them in his wallet. He finds the key on the dresser and slips his bare feet into his shoes before looking back at Candace once more and then slips silently from the room.

Konrad walks down the stairs and approaches the motel office window, ringing the buzzer once. The night manager appears on the other side of the bars yawning and scratching a full head of black hair with slender white fingers. He asks through another yawn as he grabs the motel ledger, "Checking out?"

Konrad shakes his head. "No, I want the room for another day. Is it available?"

The manager smiles and looks around as if to find someone to share Konrad's ludicrous question with. "Yeah, it's available."

Konrad leans in and puts a hundred-dollar bill in the tray. "What's your name?"

The night manager looks up startled, "Uh, it's Vincent. Why?"

Konrad replies carefully, "Well Vincent, do you know my name? I mean, I didn't sign the ledger last night."

Vincent chuckles, "Oh hell, that happens all the time 'Mr. Smith'. I took care of it for ya."

Konrad nods his head and thinks, "Okay, now that the temperature check is out of the way."

"Vincent, how would you describe me? I mean, if you were describing."

Vincent grins and looks out from side to side as far as he can see before replying, "Oh, I dunno. Middle aged guy with salt and pepper on his temples. Dark brown hair. Athletic. About six feet. Smokin hot chick on his arm so he's got bread. Why, are you hiding from someone Mr. Smith?"

Konrad smiles thinking, "Now the parlay."

"Let's just say, I'd like to be fat and bald in a cheap suit with a blonde prostitute on my arm. How much would it take for me to look like that?"

He lays a hundred-dollar bill in the tray. Vincent looks at the bill with hungry dark eyes and smiles a knowing smile. "Well, you're definitely fat and bald. Wearing a striped suit a vacuum cleaner salesman would wear but man, your lady is *so* smokin' hot dude. No way she's a blonde prostitute yet."

Konrad's mouth tightens into a line as he drops another hundred into the tray. "How about now?"

Vincent senses the change in demeanor and realizes that he's on the edge of pushing too far. "Okay, yeah, she definitely looks like a blonde slut now. So, Mr. Smith, you never really answered my question. Am I looking out for an angry husband or wife?"

Konrad decides to let Vincent create the lie. "Both Vincent. You're looking out for both. Now Vince, there's more cash where that came from. I'm going to need some things. Can you help me?"

Vincent licks his lips and nods. "I get off at seven. After that, I can get you whatever you need. More chicks, blow, whatever. Just name it."

Konrad shakes his head. "No Vince, me and my girl are just gonna stay in the room and have some alone time. We're gonna need breakfast first and some food to tie us over until tomorrow. Can you do that for me?"

Vincent nods his head as he does the calculations. Konrad smiles and continues, "I'm also going to need a prepaid phone with a shit load of minutes."

Vincent smiles and treading carefully says, "Shit, that's easy. A couple more 'C' notes should take you all the way Mr. Smith."

Konrad hands Vincent one hundred more and says, "One hundred now and another hundred when you get back with my stuff, deal?"

Vincent starts to protest but realizes that Mr. Smith isn't going to stiff him. He's just playing the role of player. Mr. Smith is a normal guy in a tight spot, so Vincent just chuckles, nods and walks away with the cash thinking, "There's more to be made here."

Konrad walks back to the room and enters as quietly as he had exited. As he enters, the sunlight shines in on Candace and she stirs awake, the robe falling open even more exposing more of her breast and abdomen. She doesn't move to close it. "Where were you?"

Konrad looks at her for what seems an eternity and then averts his eyes. "I went down to make a deal with Vincent, the night manager. I got the room for another night. I'm going to take a shower and then I'll tell you all about it."

Candace lies on the bed and listens to the water run until it stops. A few minutes pass before Konrad opens the bathroom door and enters the bedroom with a towel wrapped around his waist. He doesn't look at Candace as he says, "I wish that I had asked Vincent to buy me a change of clothes."

Candace, sensing his hesitation moves to him and loosens the belt on her robe fully, as she embraces him. As their skin touches, warm electricity runs through each of their bodies. Konrad starts to pull away, but Candace tightens her grip and speaks quickly. Breathlessly. "Please Konrad. I know you want to. I need you. I need to feel normal again, if only for a little while." He looks into her eyes and realizes that he has wanted her since she walked back into his life. He reaches inside her robe and two souls fractured by fate become one. As their bodies follow, they gently begin to heal.

After, Candace lies with her head on Konrad's chest. She looks up at him and asks, "How do you feel?"

Konrad moves his head to the side so that he can look into her eyes. "I feel good. Better than I have in a long time. I don't feel alone anymore. Do you know what I mean?"

She nods her head and replies softly, "Yes, me too. So, what do we do now?"

Konrad's facial expression becomes serious. "We've got the proof of what they're doing. We go to the news media. Vincent will be here in a couple hours with breakfast and a telephone. I'm going to contact Darci Mitchell. She wanted proof and now we have it. It's the only way we survive."

Candace shakes her head slightly and replies without looking up, "No. I mean about us."

Konrad gently strokes her hair and replies, "We survive for each other Candace. We survive for each other."

Ten miles away Horace MacGill looks at the men gathered in the kitchen of the safe house on Dallas Drive. The personal gear and bedding in what was once the family room is packed neatly. The hallway carpet has been removed and burned. There is no trace of blood on the kitchen floor. "I want two of you inside Dr. Pearce's home. You'll be staying there but you'll be ghosts. Absolutely no trace, understand? We'll drop you off so that there's no strange vehicle in the area for the neighborhood watch to worry about. Two of you will wait here with me to respond in the event that we locate the good doctor and his traveling companion. If the doctor does make the mistake of returning home, he is not to be harmed, just detained. Is that perfectly clear?"

The men look at each other and then nod. The older man from the burial detail steps forward. "Just for clarity, the doc's traveling companion is also just to be detained?"

Horace looks at the man with a slight smile. His eyes are cold. "Yes. Detain her as well. Since you seem to be someone with some intelligence, I'm putting you in charge of the good doctor's home.

Don't fuck this up. There is no retirement plan. You can take your blonde headed friend with you."

Horace points to one of the remaining men. "Take them and drop them off, then get the fuck back here."

The three men leave without hesitation, glad to be away from Horace. He looks at the remaining man and says, "Now, you and I wait for a telephone call. What's your name?"

The burly man stammers, "Peters Sir."

Horace nods curtly. "Good. Get me a cup of coffee Peters. Black."

Peters moves to the coffee pot and returns a short time later with a cup of steaming coffee. As he hands it to Horace, his hand shakes. Horace laughs a low hissing laugh. "Relax Peters. I still need you."

He sets the coffee cup down on the bar as his telephone rings. He looks at Peters once more with that sinister smile, then answers, "Hello, good news I hope."

The female's voice replies in her usual business-like monotone, "Your instincts were correct. We've identified the only cab driver who was out of pocket during the time frame of our last assignment. It didn't take much to convince the dispatcher to give him up. We're tracking him now. He has a fare, and we have the drop address. We'll wait for him there and take him quietly after he drops the passenger off. Just to confirm that there is no change in your preference or outcome."

Horace replies, "No change. I need him questioned first. I need the location of Doctor Pearce and Candace Swanson."

The female replies without hesitation, "Consider it done."

The call disconnects and Horace smiles his reptilian smile as he looks at the ceiling and stretches. "It won't be long now Peters. Not long at all."

Chapter Twenty-Three

Candace reclines against the oversized pillows set next to the small table sitting on an imitation zebra rug and looks at Vincent as he hands Konrad the greasy fast-food breakfast and the burner telephone. She and Konrad had made love again before Vincent had arrived. It was the first time she had cried in a long time. She'd had just enough time to shower and get dressed before he'd knocked on the door.

Now, as Konrad hands Vincent another one-hundred-dollar bill, the night manager stands and looks at her with a look she has seen many times before, making her skin crawl with disgust. She had known many Vincents while she'd been on the run as a teenager. Like him, they were evil men with only one thing on their sick little minds. Because she recognized the monster, she had always been able to outsmart them, never falling victim to their games.

She looks back at Vincent with a defiant look thinking, "I'm not an easy mark you sick little pervert."

Nevertheless, Vincent's eyes run up and down her body, forming all manner of fantasies in a well-practiced pattern. Konrad notices Vincent's glaring and puts his finger into Vincent's chest forcefully. "Hey! Are you listening to me? I need a change of clothes. So does she. Can you swing that?"

Vincent's eyes blink rapidly as he focuses on Konrad. "Yeah, uh yeah, just give me your sizes and I'll go over to the clothing store around the corner. They got good stuff there. What would you like?"

Konrad's mouth draws into a line as he answers tightly, "Jeans and a sweatshirt."

Vincent looks at Candace with dark eyes. "And the lady? Maybe some fresh lingerie?"

Konrad grabs Vincent by the front of his shirt and drives him up against the wall speaking in a low tone through gritted teeth, "Are you having fun? You think I'm somebody you can fuck with. You've been looking at her the wrong way since you walked through that door.

That's my woman and you'll show some respect, or they'll find you in a trash can motherfucker."

Candace stands quickly. "Konrad!"

Vincent looks at Candace with panic in his eyes as he wraps skinny white fingers around Konrad's clenched fists. "Okay man! Okay. Sorry. You got it, just let me go."

Candace steps forward and pushes Konrad's hands away from Vincent gently. "Just jeans and a sweatshirt for me too."

Konrad steps back and Vincent looks around the room before saying, "It'll cost you three hundred more."

Konrad raises his eyebrows and replies, "Three hundred?"

Vincent raises his chin in defiance. "Yeah, a hundred for the clothes, a hundred for the trip and a hundred for my shirt, man."

Konrad reaches into his wallet and pulls out three hundred dollars, putting it into Vincent's outstretched hand. Candace steps forward and says, "Dark colors, something that doesn't stand out."

Vincent looks at Candace and then quickly at the floor before nodding and replying, "Yes ma'am."

He wastes no time in exiting the room. After Vincent is gone, Konrad looks at Candace and says, "I'm sorry. I overreacted."

He looks in his wallet and then inside the waist pack. "At this rate, the money won't last long."

Candace steps to Konrad and wraps her arms around his waist. "I don't think you overreacted. It was kind of sexy."

They kiss, then Candace steps back saying, "We must get to someplace safe. Someplace where we have a friend, otherwise our money isn't going to last. You're right about that. I think I know of a place but it's quite a drive."

Konrad nods his head and replies, "I've got to get the flash drive to Darci first. Once she has the evidence of what they're doing, we can run, but not before."

They both sit down on the edge of the bed and Candace picks up the remote control, turning the television on. "Speaking of Darci, let's see if we can find the news. I want to know what they're saying about Reginald."

They surf through the channels until landing on the Green River Morning Report. Dan Kingman is already in the midst of reporting. "The recent outbreak of what hospital officials at Saint Anthony General are calling an unprecedented number of fatal aneurisms has caused officials there to extend the emergency room diversion with only extreme emergencies being accepted. Surrounding hospitals seem to be having the same problems and residents are advised to seek care at hospitals in Indianapolis where more resources may be available. In other news, it seems a break may have been made in the case of the Reginald Emmer homicide. If you'll remember, Reginald Emmer was the owner and chief operating officer of Emmer Pharmaceuticals until the pharmaceutical industry was nationalized with the full ratification of all branches of the government due to what some have dubbed the 'Thai Super Flu'.

According to police sources, it was originally believed that Mr. Emmer had been the victim of a robbery gone wrong, however in the latest development, a local taxi driver for Green River Taxi was found deceased in his vehicle with incriminating evidence related to the homicide. Police sources speculate this may have been a dispute over the fare of a prostitute delivered to Mr. Emmer on the night in question. Arnold Jenkins, forty-three of Green River was found with the handgun matching the caliber of the murder weapon and several electronic items belonging to Mr. Emmer in his taxi. The suspected cause of Mr. Jenkins' death has been preliminarily ruled as a heart attack. We'll provide further details as they are made available."

Candace turns the television off and looks at Konrad, noticing that the color has drained from his face. She stands and puts her hand on his shoulder saying, "We have to move Konrad. We've run out of time."

Across town, Horace's telephone rings. He recognizes the number and answers it immediately, "Have you found them?"

The female's voice replies, "Not yet. I'm just giving you an update. We made contact with the taxicab driver and questioned him. They're at a lower end motel near the rail yards. We don't know which one but there aren't that many. It shouldn't take long to track them down."

Horace sighs and asks, "I'm going to assume the taxi driver didn't tell you which motel because he was unable to. What method of interrogation did you use?"

The female is silent for a moment and then answers, "Nothing out of the ordinary. I think his heart gave out. He wasn't in the best of shape but he made us work for the information we were able to obtain. He gave us enough to work with. I'm sure you know how these things go. At any rate, the link between the current targets and our last assignment has been effectively severed."

Horace thinks back to the many interrogations that he has overseen and realizes that under the stress of being questioned a man's heart can quit without warning. It's an inherent hazard. He takes a deep breath and says, "Fine. Keep me informed."

Back at the Romantic Destinations Suites, Vincent knocks on the door of room 43. The door opens immediately and both Konrad and Candace step out. Vincent holds the bags up in surprise and steps back saying, "Whoa! I got your clothes man. What's going on?"

Konrad pushes past Vincent with Candace right behind him. As he looks over his shoulder, he says quickly, "We're checking out Vince and we're going to need a ride to the truck stop."

Vincent follows quickly behind the two saying, "That wasn't in the deal. I mean, I can give you a ride but we gotta talk money."

Konrad stops and turns. "Okay Vincent, how much for a ride?"

Vincent pauses as if deep in thought, then he looks up quickly. "Two hundred?"

Konrad looks at Candace and then at Vincent before replying, "Fine. Two hundred, now let's go."

They find Vincent's Nissan Stanza parked near the motel office and start to get in when someone calls out from the office window, "Hey Vincent. If you're going to hang around here all day, you can just come relieve me early and I'll go home."

Vincent stops long enough to reply, "Go fuck yourself Harold. I'll see you at seven."

He gets in the driver's seat and turns to Konrad. "Money first."

Konrad huffs and pulls out two hundred dollars from his wallet. "Okay, you've been paid now let's get the fuck out of here already."

The old car accelerates, and bucks then rockets out of the motel parking lot, scraping the asphalt as it enters traffic. Vincent looks in the rearview mirror and then at Konrad before asking, "So, who showed up, your wife or her husband?"

Konrad doesn't answer and Vincent takes the hint, concentrating on the drive without speaking again. They pass several pharmacies with the ever-present lines of vaccine seekers outside the doors. There are now police cars in every pharmacy parking lot. As they exit downtown proper, they pass the entrance to Konrad's subdivision and he considers going to his house but realizes instantly that, that would be insane. He accepts the fact that he may never see his home again. Konrad looks over his shoulder at Candace. "Give me the telephone. I'm calling Darci."

Candace reaches in a stolen pillowcase and hands Konrad the telephone. He looks at Vincent and asks, "How many minutes did you get?"

Vincent replies without taking his eyes from the road, "Five hundred. You should be good for a while."

Konrad takes Darci's card from his wallet and dials her number. Her phone rings five, six, seven times and Konrad is about to hang up when a sleepy voice answers, "Hello?"

Konrad answers quickly, "Darci, this is Konrad Pearce. I have the proof you said you needed to run with my story."

Darci replies as if confused, "Wait. What? Who is this?"

Konrad speaks more slowly, "Its Konrad Pearce. You said when we talked that you needed proof. Well, I have it, on film. There are people chasing us. I need to meet you now."

Darci perks up but her voice is still raspy. "Konrad? I'm sorry, I've been sick. Who's chasing you?"

He looks at Vincent who is listening intently. "I don't know who they are, but they aren't friendly. We're ahead of them for now but, I don't know for how long. We need to meet, the sooner the better."

Darci answers quickly, "Hold on Konrad. I'll be right back."

Vincent looks at Konrad with fear in his eyes. "Someone's chasing you? What the fuck have you got me into?"

Konrad replies through gritted teeth, "You got yourself into this, you greedy little shit. Now shut up and drive."

Darci comes back on the line, "There's a mall just north of the prison. I'll meet you at the arcade in an hour."

Konrad replies, "I'll be there."

The call disconnects and Konrad gives the telephone back to Candace.

Vincent starts to slow the car. "You folks can just get out right here. I'm not looking for any trouble, not this kind anyway."

Konrad looks at Vincent menacingly and says, "We're one mile from the truck stop. If you stop this car, you won't like what happens next."

The message is clear, and Vincent continues to drive. They enter the truck stop parking lot and Candace tells Vincent to pull around back. She is relieved to see that her car is still parked where she left it at the back of the lot. Vincent stops the car and Candace gets out immediately. Konrad opens his door then turns to Vincent. "I'm sorry you're in this but it's too late now. Take the money you charged me and take a vacation. These people have already killed at least one man.

They're close. It won't be long before they find the motel. You don't want to be there when they do."

Vincent, with a worried look just nods. He drives away as Konrad moves to the passenger side of Candace's Ford Taurus. She is on her knees at the front wheel of the driver's side reaching behind the tire. Before Konrad can ask her what she is doing, she holds her hand in the air and shows him the keys. "A little trick I learned a lifetime ago."

They get into the car and Candace looks at Konrad inquisitively. "Okay, where to?"

He replies, "Take a left to the highway. We're going to the mall on the west side of town."

As Konrad and Candace head west, Vincent heads north, back toward the rail yards and the Romantic Destinations Suites. He thinks as he drives, "Fuck Mr. Smith and his cheater wife. I've got other plans for this cash. The Sahara Suite is reserved for another night thanks to Mr. Smith. I might as well get some use out of it. Some lucky skank is gonna get every inch of Vincent Cabrioni."

He chuckles as he pulls into the motel lot and parks near the office. Vincent gets out of the car and practically trots up to the window yelling, "Hey Harold, give Jocelyn a call. When she gets here tell her Vincent has something hard for her in the Sahara Suite."

Harold approaches the window. That is when Vincent notices the woman standing at the desk. She is middle aged with blonde hair and serious eyes. Vincent looks at Harold and smiles, "You sneaky little bastard. You know we're not allowed to have company in the office. Here, I'll spell you so you can take care of business. We've got room 43 for the whole night. Bought and paid for."

He goes to the glass door and unlocks it with his key. As he enters, the look on Harold's face causes him to stop just inside the door. Harold is sweating profusely and looks terrified. Vincent doesn't feel the taser probes make contact with the back of his neck. He just sees the bright flashing lights inside his head and feels his nose breaking as it makes contact with the floor. His legs seem to float into the air, and he realizes that he is being dragged into the back room. The last thing his mind registers before he loses consciousness is the sound of muffled screaming.

Vincent awakens to a pounding headache. His mouth is dry, and he tastes blood. He quickly looks around and realizes he is in the laundry room of the motel. The lights seem exceptionally bright, his vision is blurry, and the smell of the harsh detergent used to wash the linen burns his fractured nostrils. He tries to move and realizes that his arms and legs are duct taped to the chair he sits in. He wriggles with all his strength, but the bindings are too tight for him to move very much at all. There is tape wrapped around his chest so tight that he can barely draw a breath. He is naked. This is when it dawns on Vincent that he should have taken Mr. Smith's advice.

The blonde woman's face comes into focus, floating across his field of vision. She smiles and touches his cheek, but her eyes are as cold as the grave. Vincent feels the urge to vomit. The woman says with misplaced cheerfulness in her voice, "Good Vincent, you're awake. Do you feel up to answering some questions? That nose really looks like it hurts."

Vincent is frozen like a rat staring at a snake. His mind searches for an angle to get himself out of this situation but comes up with nothing. He resorts to the instinct of the sociopath and decides on indignation. "I'm not answering any of your questions until you untie me bitch. Where's Harold? Do you realize what my lawyer is going to do to you fucks? I'm going to own you. Do you realize who I am?"

The woman reaches up and grabs Vincent's nose between the thumb and forefinger of her right hand, twisting with enormous strength. Vincent sees only stars as he screams, a fresh torrent of blood escaping his nostrils. She looks at him with the same venomous smile. "Now Vincent, there's no need to involve our lawyers in this. Harold is resting and we are just two friends having a nice conversation. Harold told us all about you, so we know exactly who you are. Let's put all that silly talk behind us and get to the subject at hand, shall we?"

Vincent sputters through the blood streaming across his lips, "Okay, look, I want to help you. Just tell me what you want to know."

The woman's face recedes and becomes blurry as Vincent attempts to focus through the tears. He hears lilting laughter and realizes to his horror that she is enjoying this. "Vincent, Harold told us you had some very special guests. A man and a woman who stayed in room 43. My men are cleaning the room right now. Harold said that you gave your special guests a ride somewhere. Where did you take them?"

Vincent begins to weep as he says, "Look, I took them to the truck stop and dropped them off. The guy was throwing money at me, and I did a couple of favors for him. That's it. I swear that's all I know."

The woman slaps Vincent hard across the face. Before he can recover, she grabs his testicles in her right hand in a crushing grip before twisting. Vincent starts to scream but the sound catches in his throat along with the vomit. The deepest ache he has ever felt rises from his groin into his diaphragm, making any attempt at breathing mute. The woman's face comes into focus again. She is still smiling. "Don't lie to me Vincent. What favors did you do for the man?"

Vincent answers in clutching gasps, "Bought, bought a phone and clothes. Please for God sakes, let go of my nuts."

The woman yanks hard without releasing her grip until her rubber gloved hand comes away with a distinct popping sound. Vincent attempts to breath and the woman slaps him again, snapping his head to the side. Where did the man and woman go Vincent?"

Vincent shakes his head back and forth mouthing the words, "I don't know, I don't know."

The woman looks around the room and her eyes settle on a bottle of bleach. Vincent watches in horror as she reaches for the bottle. "Is there anything else you haven't told me Vincent? Think really hard."

Vincent is completely focused on the bleach as he stammers, "Green Ford Taurus. I dropped them at a green Ford Taurus."

The woman leans in with the bleach and removes the cap. "Tag number?"

Vincent desperately searches his memory, looking back and forth, then back at the bleach. "I'm so sorry, I don't know. Please, for God's sake. Please."

A man enters the room. He is solidly built, moving like a large cat. Every movement measured against result. He looks at Vincent and says to the woman, "Room's clean. Some clothing receipts and a burner phone package with a receipt. We sanitized everything."

He looks at Vincent one more time before leaving the room. The woman smiles at Vincent and holds the bottle of bleach close to his face. He recoils as much as he can and begins to sob again. She laughs and says, "You really are a big baby. It's just bleach?"

She puts the bottle back on the shelf still laughing and then moves behind Vincent saying, "You did well Vincent, now it's time for you to get some rest. You have had quite the day. I promise when you wake up, you'll be in a much better place than this laundry room."

The ice pick is razor sharp. Vincent only feels a slight pressure as it penetrates at the base of his skull just above the first vertebrae. His head moves from side to side as the woman wrenches it back and forth, destroying the breathing centers of his nervous system. His vision blurs as blackness takes him, the woman's hand on his chest feeling the last of his life leak away with a shiver of satisfaction coursing through her body. Her burly partners enter the room at just this moment. One of the men winces and says, "We're all set."

The woman, her eyes glassy walks past the men and says as she walks out of the room, "Burn it."

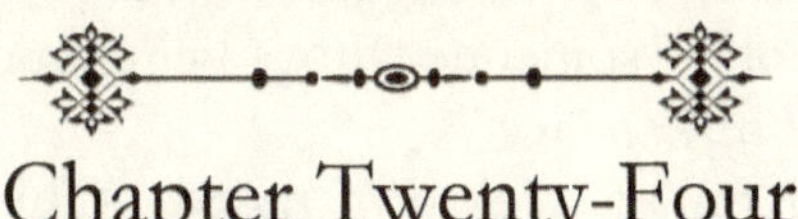

Chapter Twenty-Four

Candace makes the twelve-mile drive to the other side of town in a few minutes by taking the highway bypass. As they travel, Konrad looks around the vehicle and realizes that, for at least part of the time, Candace was living out of her car. He feels ashamed that he was not there for her during her flight. This knowledge also gives him a deeper understanding of the woman he has begun to fall in love with. He thinks as he looks at her, "Maybe I always have loved her in some way, and it was just masked as a deep friendship."

He thinks of his wife Jennifer and again feels ashamed. He reminds himself that, as painful as the thought is, Jennifer and Chloe are dead. The realization strikes him that he may be joining them soon. Candace looks over at him as she drives. "What?"

Konrad smiles a melancholy smile and shakes his head. "Nothing, I'm just glad we're together."

Candace looks back at the road then glances quickly back, smiling. They make the turn into the mall parking lot and find a place to park as close to the middle as possible. Candace looks at Konrad and smiling says, "We'll hide in plain sight."

Konrad smiles and nods. They walk across the parking lot which is full of shoppers and enter the mall, making their way to a shop just inside the door. Candace leads Konrad to a shelf full of sweaters by the shop entrance with a good view of the mall entrance they've just entered by. She leans in and whispers, "Let's watch the door for a few minutes, just to be on the safe side."

They watch the door for five minutes while Candace holds different items of clothing up to Konrad as if shopping. When they're convinced, they weren't followed, they make their way through the crowded mall to the arcade. They hear the deafening noise before entering. Shrill whistles, bells and screams flood their senses as they enter. Konrad begins to move into the interior of the arcade, making it only three steps before Darci grabs him by the elbow. "Konrad?"

Konrad spins and then relaxes. Darci can see the adrenaline in his every mannerism. He has a look she has seen many times before in her short career. The look of someone who is being hunted. Candace steps forward and says, "I'm Candace."

Darci looks at Konrad, eyebrows raised. "This is Candace? The woman who got you fired?"

Konrad looks at Candace quickly and catches her surprise before quickly replying while still looking into her eyes, "It wasn't what I thought. I was wrong about that."

Darci shrugs her shoulders and replies, "If you say so. We need to get out of here. I'm parked in the back near the auto service center. Let's take a drive so that we can talk. They follow Darci out of the mall to a blue Jeep Cherokee with the doors removed. The vehicle has obviously seen many hard miles. It is just the kind of vehicle Konrad had expected Darci to drive. Konrad helps Candace into the back seat and then gets into the passenger side. As Darci gets into the driver's seat, she thinks, "Interesting. He's fucking her. Wonder if that's what changed her from traitor to ally in his mind."

They leave the mall and head south for approximately thirty minutes before coming to a lone gas station and country store. As they pull into the lot, a sign proudly reads, "We sale pecan logs."

Darci pulls to a stop under a tree near the edge of the parking lot and turns to Konrad with an inquisitive look. "Okay Konrad, you said on the telephone that you have proof of what you told me. Do you have it with you?"

Konrad looks at Candace and nods. Candace produces the flash drive and hands it to Darci. For the next hour, Candace and Konrad tell the story of the past few days. Candace also tells Darci her story. She is incredulous. "And you say, all of that is on the flash drive?"

Konrad shakes his head. "No. The flash drive just contains the film of the vaccine attacking the Thai influenza strain and the vaccine's method of combating it."

Darci looks at Candace and then at Konrad as she shakes her head slightly, "This means nothing without someone to corroborate the film. Most people aren't virologists or doctors Konrad. I'll need you or Candace to explain what people are seeing. You'll have to go on air and on record. Are you willing to do that?"

He looks at Candace, then at Darci and nods his head. Darci looks at Candace and says, eyebrows raised, "There's something else to consider here. These people who are chasing you will find you once this hits the news. There can be no room for allegations that the interview or the film have been altered. It will have to be live, in the studio. Are you prepared for that? I can sell it to my producer and Kingman, but you'll be exposed."

Konrad turns his head and looks at the Indiana horizon then looks back at Darci. "Set it up. Everyone needs to know what they've done."

Darci looks straight into Konrad's eyes and says slowly, "What she did Konrad. Candace was a part of it."

Konrad looks at Candace and says, "It's up to you Candace. I'll forget the whole thing if you want."

Candace shakes her head. "No. I'm through running."

Konrad nods his head and then looks at Darci. We're going to need a place to lay low until you get it set up. Any ideas? My house and her apartment are out of the question. So are the motels near the rail yards."

Darci grins and replies, "Well, I've got a finished room in my basement. It's not much but there's a couch that pulls out into a bed and a couple of chairs."

Candace looks down nodding. "That's perfect. Thank you, Darci."

Horace MacGill sits in the kitchen of the safe house on Dallas Drive and broods in the silence. The silence of the place and the silence of the various assets he has in play. He stands and stretches then looks at the young contractors who have been his only company since sending the team to Doctor Pearce's home in case he returned. It hasn't been fruitful. He looks at Peters and asks, "Is there a liquor store around here?"

The burly contractor looks up quickly, eager to please and says, "Yeah. There's a small place up the road. Gas station, pizza place and a liquor store. Do you need something?"

Horace replies, "Makers Mark. A couple of fifths and something made of glass to drink it from."

Peters stands quickly and looks at the other asset, then says, "Sure thing boss, I'll be right back."

Horace opens his laptop. "Both of you go. I need some time to think."

The two assets gladly depart, and Horace's mind begins to visualize all the various angles in play. He is startled from his thoughts by the ringing of his satellite phone. He recognizes the number and answers immediately, "Have you found them?"

The woman's voice replies in her usual monotone, "They were staying at a motel near the rail yards and got some help from an employee. They were dropped off at the truck stop on the east side of town. It looks like they're driving a green Ford Taurus. No tag number. We also retrieved a receipt for a burner phone in their room along with packaging. As before, any link to this place has been sanitized. Some collateral damage but nothing to link us. I'm afraid they could be anywhere now. Any instructions?"

Horace answers in a low tone, "Send me the phone receipt."

The female replies, "Will do. I'm standing by for further assignments."

The call disconnects. In a few minutes, Horace's computer chimes. He opens the message and finds himself looking at a picture of the burner telephone purchase receipt. He picks up his telephone and dials the number of his electronic surveillance unit. The call is answered in two rings by the familiar voice of the asset. "Hello?"

I need to know if you can capture a burner phone from the serial number."

The asset exhales audibly. "That would be tough. If I had the number from the SIM card then yes, but the phone itself is really just a mount for the card."

Horace nods his head and says, "I see."

He disconnects the call and paces the kitchen until he hears a vehicle in the drive and then the garage door raises on rusty tracks. Peters and his partner enter the kitchen a short time later with the bourbon and a crystal glass. Horace smiles and opens the first bottle, pouring the glass full. He takes a long drink of the bourbon, thoroughly enjoying the sweet burning sensation as the liquid makes its way down his throat. He thinks as he takes a second long drink, "Now I can concentrate."

Horace paces the kitchen while drinking and admiring the fine cracks in the drywall. He closely studies the fractures in minute detail as the two assets watch, every so often looking at each other and wondering whether this madman is going to start shooting again. Horace thinks, "Everything has a cause and effect. Every angle puts you closer to the goal. What would I do if I were Konrad Pearce at this very moment?"

He stops and turns suddenly. "Where is Hanes' surveillance notes?"

Peters stammers, "In his pack over there."

Horace smiles a wicked smile and hisses, "Get them for me please."

The asset crosses the room and retrieves a green military notebook from the dead man's pack and gives it to Horace who immediately opens it and starts reading. As he reads, he begins to nod his head and smile, the jumble of angles in his mind forming a structured pattern. A new plan begins to form. One that will lead him back to his timeline. He thinks, "I've got you Candace. You just don't know it yet."

Horace chuckles and dials the electronic surveillance asset. The call is answered, and Horace begins speaking immediately, I need a detailed target workup on Darci Mitchell. She's a reporter. Also, find out who her boss is and get me a package on them too. I need it two hours ago."

He ends the call without waiting for the asset to reply thinking, "At least Hanes had the sense to run the license plates of the good doctor's visitors."

He looks at Peters and says, "Go get the guys at Doctor Pearce's home, we've just regained our advantage."

The two men quickly leave while Horace waits on the target packages. He pours himself another glass of bourbon, takes a sip and smiles. Within the hour Horace's laptop chimes with an incoming message. He opens it and begins to read about Darci Mitchell. As he reads, he starts to feel a certain respect for the young woman and thinks, "A crusader, brave, combat experience and so young. He learns about the loss of Darci's friend to friendly fire, the fact that she volunteered to shadow U.S. Special Forces and the special training she'd received to do that. Horace strokes his chin thinking, "She's a warrior with the mental scars that come along with it."

He continues to read about her isolation after returning to the States. Horace speaks to himself, his voice echoing in the empty house. "No social life. Estranged from her family. Fiercely patriotic. Interesting. I could be describing myself right now."

Horace calls the number of the cleaner and it is answered immediately by the usual monotone female voice, "Hello."

He replies casually, "I'm sending you a package for surveillance only. I want an update every hour."

The female responds in her usual manner, "Consider it done."

The call ends and Horace moves on to the next package. He is staring at the face of Dan Kingman, Head Anchorman for the Green River Morning News. Horace immediately hates the man. The perfect hair and smile. The eyes which indicate nothing but pure ambition. He thinks as he looks at the picture, "You are a weakling, ripe to be exploited and that is exactly what I intend to do."

As Horace reads further, the skeletons in this man's closet begin to emerge. A taste for cocaine and a certain prostitute named Jocelyn Larou. He smiles his reptilian smile, takes a sip of bourbon and says, "Bingo."

As if it was ordained, Horace's laptop chimes and then his telephone rings. It is the electronic surveillance team. Horace answers, "Hello, good news I hope."

The asset reports, "Sir, we've just monitored a telephone call from Darci Mitchell to Dan Kingman regarding an interview with Dr. Konrad Pearce. It sounds like she has convinced him to conduct an interview personally off site."

Horace smiles as his plans seem to come together. "Where are they going to do the interview?"

Horace can almost hear the smile in the asset's voice. "Apparently, they're going to do the interview tomorrow in her basement. Dr. Pearce and Candace Swanson are hiding there. I sent you the recording."

Horace chuckles slightly and replies, "Excellent work. Continue to monitor and report any further developments."

As Horace begins to listen to the recording of the call, Peters and the other three contractors enter the kitchen. They fall silent as Horace turns, greeting them with a stony look. He turns back to the computer. After the recording of the call ends, the young blonde asset says, "Sounds like we know where they are. Want us to go get them."

Horace turns and with a tight grin reply, "No. I have people on them. It's not time yet. We have other things to accomplish.

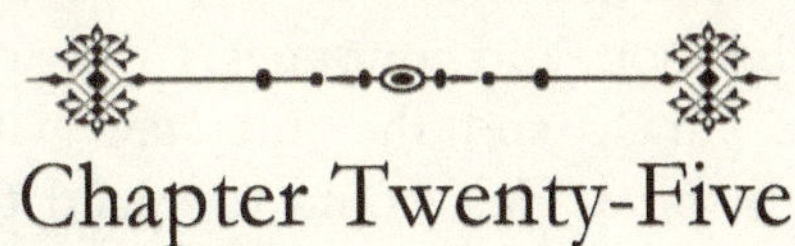

Chapter Twenty-Five

Konrad looks around the room and thinks, "She wasn't kidding." The room is maybe ten feet by twelve with a small sofa bed and two chairs. The only light is provided by a small fixture in the ceiling adorned with a square glass cover and the two small windows at ground level. There are two small end tables at each end of the sofa. Sitting on the far table is a small pot of plastic flowers attempting to serve as a decoration. There is a small television in the corner and a framed poster of an obscure punk rock band on the wall. The concrete floor is covered by green indoor, outdoor carpeting and the air in the room holds a hint of cool dampness. As Konrad and Candace stand in the room looking around, Darci asks from the door, "Well, what do you think?"

Candace smiles and replies, "Its perfect Darci, we're so thankful."

Darci, obviously pleased turns quickly and replies as she heads back upstairs, "I'll get you some linen for the sofa bed."

After Darci leaves Konrad looks at Candace and asks, "Thoughts?"

Candace smiles and moves close to him, putting her arms around his neck. She kisses him and says, "Home sweet home Konrad."

He looks into her eyes and replies, "It's just for a little while. We'll do this interview and then we will leave here forever. We'll find a place to drop off the map. We're going to be alright Candace. I can feel it."

Candace accepts his reassurance with a smile and nod but inside, the little voice that has allowed her to survive this long is screaming for her to notice something. She can't put her finger on it, but something isn't right about this place. She is mentally exhausted and is having trouble focusing on what the voice is saying. As she attempts to review a mental checklist, the feeling of uneasiness stays with her.

Darci returns with the linen and they both turn toward her. She looks at both of them sheepishly and says, "Sorry if I'm interrupting. Here's the linen. I'm not used to guests so please make yourselves at home."

There is an awkward silence for a moment and then Candace replies, "We can't thank you enough Darci."

Darci steps into the room and continues, "Your car should be safely out of sight in the garage and the interview with Dan is set for tomorrow morning at nine. He's going to spend the whole morning report with you. Trust me, it's a big deal. I wonder if I could see the film. Before we go live, Dan wanted assurances that it actually exists. I'm not trying to insult you, but it's both of our careers on the line as well."

Konrad nods his head in an understanding way and replies, "Of course Darci. I'll need a computer."

Darci leaves and quickly returns with a small laptop. Konrad produces the small thumb drive from the waist pack which also contains their dwindling cash supply and hands it to Darci. She expertly brings up the film and Konrad explains the process that they are watching. Darci looks at Konrad and asks, "So, this is the Thai flu?

Konrad and Candace both nod. "It's the deadliest strain I've ever seen. It acts in a manner completely opposite of every other flu virus. It feeds on fever. Millions could die without the vaccine, but millions could also die with it. You can see our quandary."

Darci leans her head to the side inquisitively and asks, "And it just showed up in your lab? I mean, in the sample, but your lab only?"

Konrad looks at Candace, his eyebrows raised in comprehension. "Yes. I don't believe anyone else found it."

Darci smiles slightly, "Pardon me for saying this, but that seems almost mathematically impossible."

Konrad's mouth tightens into a thin line. "Or maybe my lab was better than the rest.

Candace breaks in, trying to stop the argument which is about to occur. "Well, at any rate, the virus does exist, and the vaccine successfully stops it in its tracks. The question is, is it safe?"

Darci nods and replies, "I must warn you Konrad, Dan is a fair man and will conduct the interview ethically, but he won't softball you. He'll ask some tough questions. Are you ready for that? We've decided that I will operate the camera and Dan will come alone. The less people that know your whereabouts, the better. Don't mention me or where you're at. We'll show the film, and you'll narrate. He'll then ask you a series of questions which will probably lead to more questions for clarification. He's not trying to insult you so, please just stay calm and give the public the facts."

Konrad gives Darci a direct look and replies, "I understand completely. Tell Mr. Kingman I'm ready to tell the whole story."

To the south of town, Horace dials the number for the electronic surveillance asset. The call is answered immediately, and Horace begins to speak, "I trust you have Mr. Kingman's cell number?"

The asset replies, "Of course Sir. Would you like for me to connect you remotely?"

Horace chuckles slowly, "No. That might be fun but, I have something more interesting in mind."

He turns toward Peters and asks, "Give me the name of another motel down by the rail yards."

Peters looks up for a microsecond as if the answer is on the ceiling and then answers, "There's the Welcoming Arms Motel. Cash only. A lot of prostitutes work out of the rooms."

He quickly stammers, "Or so I've heard."

Horace smiles an evil smile and responds, "Or so you've heard?"

He turns back to the telephone and says to the electronic surveillance asset, "We're heading to the Welcoming Arms Motel. I'll call you from there."

Thirty minutes later, a dark gray van pulls into the parking lot of the Welcoming Arms Motel. It is a small motel with a line of twenty rooms surrounded by a gravel lot. The office building is separate from the motel room structure. The buildings, originally painted white, are now a dull gray from exposure to years of diesel laden air. Two scantily clad women stand by the drink machine just outside the office door.

They are too thin and obviously bored. As the van pulls to a stop, one of the girls walks slowly forward, stumbling slightly on the gravel as her high heel turns in the rocks. She recovers quickly and brushes a blonde lock of hair from her face. As she reaches the passenger's side window, Horace rolls it down and smiles at the woman. She has dark circles under her eyes and a yellow pallor to her skin. There is bruising on the outside of one thigh. A look of apprehension replaces the inviting smile as she looks at Horace and then past him to Peters. "You boys looking for a date?"

Horace chuckles and replies, "Not at the moment but I'll keep you in mind. Tell me, have you seen Jocelyn today?"

The blonde prostitute wrinkles her nose. "You a cop?"

Horace gives her a cold smile and replies, "No dear. I'm no cop. Just looking for Jocelyn. Have you seen her?"

The girl looks around and then leans on the windowsill while replying in a low tone, "Haven't seen her today, but you can call me Jocelyn if you like. I'm much better than she is anyway."

Horace leans in close to the prostitute's face and whispers, "Like I said, I'll keep you in mind."

The prostitute takes the hint and turns to leave saying over her shoulder, "You don't know what you're missing."

Horace watches the woman walk away. The imitation leather hot pants swaying back and forth in an exaggerated display designed to entice. He thinks as he watches, "I do know what I'm missing, a trip to the nearest walk-in clinic."

Peters looks over, his eyebrows raised. "She might have been fun. You should have taken her up on it."

Horace doesn't look at the man but replies, "Not even with your dick. Go get us a room."

Peters raises a bushy eyebrow and asks, "Okay. They're not really picky here but, what name should I use on the registry?"

Horace looks over at the stocky man and gives Peters a smile that sends chills down his spine. "Why, Dan Kingman of course."

Peters chuckles at the irony as he exits the van. He returns a short time later and says, "Number seventeen."

Horace only nods. Peters drives the van to the room and backs into a space directly across the lot. Horace turns to Peters. "You and blondie stay in the van and keep watch on the lot. I'll take these two with me. You have my number, correct?"

Peters nods and Horace, satisfied continues. Mr. Kingman is going to arrive soon. I want a call when he gets here."

Peters nods and replies, "You got it boss."

Horace and the remaining assets exit the van and enter room seventeen. The room smells of stale cigarettes mixed with the tang of humanity. It is sparsely furnished with a queen-sized bed, two-night stands and a small table with two chairs. The lime green bedspread matches perfectly with the blue green carpeting. Horace looks around the room and thinks, "This place is enough to make you lose hope in the human race."

Horace pulls his telephone from his satchel and dials the electronic surveillance asset. The call is answered immediately. Horace doesn't engage in pleasantries, simply saying, "We are in room seventeen at the Welcoming Arms Motel. I want you to text Dan Kingman from one of your burners. The text is from Jocelyn. Explain that she had to get a new phone. Tell him that she misses him and wants to see him. Tell him she has something special for him if he can get here in the next hour. Tell him there'll be no charge this time. Make it convincing."

The excitement is evident in his voice as the asset replies, "I'm on it, Sir."

Horace looks at the two burly contractors and says, "When he gets here, I want you behind the door. We're going to have a friendly conversation, and I want to make sure he doesn't miss it."

He sits down at the table and pulls a silver flask from his satchel, unscrews the top and takes a long drink of the bourbon. Horace feels the sweet burning sensation as the liquid makes its way down his throat. He closes his eyes and says, "Now gentlemen, we wait."

Several miles away in the heart of downtown, Dan Kingman sits in his office at the Green River Morning Report studios. As the head anchorman and the face of the broadcast, Dan has earned the spacious office which, for all practical purposes, is light years away from the cubicles where the reporters work elbow to elbow.

He sits back in the leather chair with his hands clasped behind his head and admires the plaques and framed awards which adorn the walls. He smiles a contented smile and actually feels the power he now holds, all the while dreaming of more. His revelry is suddenly interrupted by the vibration of his telephone as it sits on his desk. He frowns at the object as if it might react to his disapproval, then picks it up and reads the text message. This immediately elicits a smile as he thinks, "No charge? Maybe she's finally started to appreciate the excellent fucks I give her."

He reaches into the inside pocket of his jacket and makes sure the vial of fine white powder is there then answers the text with a simple, "I'm on my way, baby."

He met Jocelyn a couple of years ago at a function being held at the convention center. His wife had been unable to attend, and Dan considers this to be one of the luckiest nights of his life. It was immediately apparent when he'd seen her standing at the bar that she was a professional and the hour they had spent together after the function proved it. There wasn't anything she wouldn't do to please him. While sex with his wife Samantha was strictly missionary position and very little participation on her part, Jocelyn could do things with her mouth and body which was simply indescribable. Dan thinks as he locks his office door, "I'm as addicted to this bitch as I am coke."

The elevator ride seems much too slow as he imagines what special delights his crimson haired beauty has in store for him. He makes it to his car and sits in the seat, dialing his home number. The call is answered by Samantha, her tone unexcited, "Hello?"

Dan takes a deep breath and replies, "Sorry to bother you babe but I'm still working on this copy for my interview tomorrow. I'm afraid I'm gonna be pretty late."

He waits, barely breathing as the silence on the other end of the line drags on. Finally, Samantha replies in a bored tone, "Well, try not to wake me when you get home. I'm tired and I have a headache."

Dan thinks, "She's consistent if nothing else."

He switches the telephone from the right ear to the left replying, "I won't sweety. Sleep well."

As soon as the call disconnects, he starts the Lexus, and it roars to life. Dan wastes no time leaving the parking lot and heading for the wrong side of Green River. He makes his way through back streets to the neighborhood known locally as "The Avenues." It is an embarkation point. A line between light and dark. The gateway to the poor side of town where Dan's appetites can be fed anonymously. The Lexus crosses through the land of Green River residents, who survive on the precipice of falling head long into abject poverty at any moment and carries Dan to the area of the rail yards where prostitutes and drug dealers practice their trade in the open. He steers the luxury sedan into the parking lot of the motel and feels the familiar aching in his groin as he imagines what Jocelyn has in mind.

Dan parks the car in front of room number seventeen and almost jumps out, not noticing the two men in the gray van, one speaking on the telephone. He walks quickly to the door which stands slightly ajar and enters without knocking, a smile of anticipation on his face. "Honey, daddy is home."

The smile vanishes as the door quickly closes behind him. Dan turns to see an extremely large man with a shaved head and beard standing behind him. There is a coldness in the man's eyes that makes Dan's knees turn to jelly. A sick feeling makes its way into his stomach. Dan knows instantly that he is in trouble as his mind scrambles, searching for a way back through the door. The man blocking his exit outweighs him by at least sixty pounds and it is apparent, the weight difference is made up in muscle.

He smiles a nervous smile, displaying gleaming white teeth and looks around the room quickly before looking at the man and saying, "I'm sorry, I must have the wrong room. I'll just leave. I don't want any trouble."

Dan tries to step around the burly contractor and is grabbed by the shoulder with an oversized hand and spun to face Horace. He looks around the room and sees that the bed has been turned on its side and leaned against the wall. The table and chairs have been moved to the center of the room. There is another man as big as the one who holds him standing in the corner with his arms folded and at the table, a man sits in the opposite chair, patiently smiling a hideous reptilian grin.

As Dan looks into this man's cold eyes the grin widens exposing the sharp canine teeth. At this, Dan almost wets himself. Horace MacGill stands and graciously waves his hand toward the other chair without uttering a word. He looks at the man holding Dan and instantly the news anchorman is almost lifted from the floor by his belt and shirt collar and moved to the awaiting chair. He looks across the table and waits. Horace smiles politely and begins to speak. "Dan Kingman, head newsman for the Green River Morning Report. Thank you for joining me."

Dan tries to smile, his lips quivering and stammers, "I don't want any trouble mister. Really, I want to leave."

Horace chuckles slightly, "Oh, I bet you do Dan. I bet you do. The good news for you this evening is that you will probably survive this if you're cooperative."

Horace pulls the laptop from his satchel and brings the target package on Dan Kingman to the screen. He then turns the computer around so that Dan can see it and gestures with his eyes. "Please, be my guest Dan."

Dan reads about his entire life on the screen. The life everyone sees and the life he leads in the shadows beyond the avenues. He looks up at Horace and says in disbelief, "How in the fuck did you get this? Who are you?"

Horace looks at Dan sympathetically and answers, "Oh Dan, it doesn't matter who I am. What matters is all the things that I can do."

Dan looks around the room again and asks, "Where's Jocelyn? Are you her pimp or something?"

At this Horace gives a raspy laugh and replies, "No Dan, I am not her pimp. You and I have much more important things to accomplish that do not involve a cheap prostitute."

Dan tries to stand from the chair but is pushed back into a sitting position by the contractor standing at his back. "Don't you talk about her like that!"

Horace leans back in the chair and sighs, "Alright Dan, let's move on because our time is limited. We both need to prepare. Tomorrow morning at nine, you are going to do a live interview with Doctor Konrad Pearce in Darci Mitchell's basement."

Dan puts his hands up in a conciliatory gesture. "Look, I don't have to do the interview. I won't, okay?"

Horace shakes his head and replies, "Oh no Dan. I want you to do the interview. In fact, I want you to notify your national contacts, so they'll pick up the story as well."

Dan looks around the room and then back at Horace with a puzzled look. "I don't understand. You want me to do exactly what I was going to do? Why am I here?"

Horace looks at Dan with an evil smile. "Excellent question."

The smile is colder now as Horace turns the computer back around and pulls up the information on Konrad Pearce. He turns the computer around so that Dan can read. "Read it Mr. Kingman and memorize it. I need you to know every little detail about Doctor Konrad Pearce."

Dan begins to read. His focus alternates between the words on the screen and the face of Horace MacGill. For the next two hours Dan reads the file, memorizing every detail as instructed. Finally, he looks at Horace and raises his eyebrows in the unasked question. Horace smiles and asks, "Confident in your memory?"

Dan gives Horace a smug grin and says, "This is what I do. It's memorized. Now, what do you want from me?"

Horace nods and folds the laptop up, putting it in his satchel. He reaches back in the leather bag and pulls out a stack of cash, neatly banded together and puts it on the table. He reaches inside one more time and pulls out a syringe filled with saline. Dan looks at the cash and then at the needle before looking at Horace, concern on his face. Horace leans back in the chair and says, "Mr. Kingman, tomorrow during your interview, you are going to discredit Doctor Pearce. After you are done with him, his reputation will be destroyed. Do you understand? The cash is payment for your services."

Dan looks at the cash and then at Horace in disbelief. "No. I won't do that. You have got the wrong fucking guy. I've been a journalist for twenty years and built my reputation of having integrity through too many shit storms to count. No. No fucking way."

Horace bows his head for a moment then stretches his neck skyward. "That is disappointing Dan. I suppose you should go ahead and empty your pockets now."

Horace glances at the contractor who nudges Dan on the shoulder with his fist. The contractor leans down and whispers in a menacing tone, "Do it."

Dan stands and looks around at the men in the room before emptying his pockets. The last thing he extracts is the vial of cocaine which he sets on the table next to the condom. Horace chuckles slightly and says, "So fucking predictable."

The contractor guides Dan back into a sitting position as Horace stares at the newsman hard. The amiable demeanor is gone, replaced by the coldness of death. "Now Dan, I want you to imagine the sorrow Samantha will feel tomorrow morning as she watches the report of your body being found in this motel room. You'll be unclothed. That condom will still be on your little dick and this needle will still be in your arm. Some sick game of mainlining cocaine while Jocelyn rode you like the pathetic whoremonger you are. It will crush your loving wife. And the shame your daughters will feel. How tragic. Your reputation will be ruined. What a tragic end. Don't you think so?"

Horace picks up Dan's cell phone from the table and holds it out to Dan. "Please put your thumb on the screen."

Dan shakes his head back and forth. "No."

Horace nods at the contractor who grabs Dan's ear and twists. Dan shrieks and recoils but the big man has an iron grip. Dan puts his thumb out and Horace pushes the screen to it. "Thank you, Dan. Now, I'm going to text Jocelyn. Ah yes, here's her number. I'm going to text her and tell her where you are after we're finished with you. She will either find you flush with cash, or she'll find your dead body just as I described. She'll be the face of the last report involving the great Dan Kingman."

Dan, still holding his ear, closes his eyes and nods his head. "I'll do it. I'll do it okay?"

Horace leans forward. "Now Dan, you've seen just a small demonstration of what I'm capable of. If anything goes awry. If the good doctor decides to leave Darci's basement and flee, I'll assume you made a call. I can reach you and your family anywhere and I do mean anywhere. There will be no place to hide. Are we clear?"

Dan nods slowly, the gravity of his situation fully settling in. Horace smiles his usual easy smile, showing the large canines. "There's one more little thing I'll need you to do Dan, and it is very important. The doctor will have a thumb drive that contains the little movie he is going to show the world. You need to maintain control of that drive after the interview. You won't have it for long but I need you to get it. Understand?"

Dan looks at Horace, all the fight having left him. "What am I supposed to do with it?"

Horace stands and walks around the table, putting his hand on Dan's shoulder. "Just hold on to it as if you're holding on to your daughter's lives Dan."

Horace nods to the contractor in the corner who walks over and pockets the needle, leaving the cash. Horace picks up Dan's phone and sends Jocelyn a text then pulls a gold money clip from his pocket and pulls two one-hundred-dollar bills from a stack laying them on the table. "You did well Dan and I'm sure you will tomorrow. Tonight is on me. Jocelyn will be here soon so you'd better clean up. She'll be expecting double the normal rate."

Chapter Twenty-Six

Horace sits in the back of the van and dials the number for the electronic surveillance asset. The call is answered immediately. "Go ahead and initiate the satellite link with my laptop."

The asset replies tensely, "10-4 Sir. Initiating the link. Stand by, and you should be connected."

Horace smiles as he says, "Thank you."

The call is disconnected, and Horace dials a second number. It is answered by the cleaning crew. The voice is, as usual, unmistakable and monotone. "Hello?"

He responds without hesitation. "Any change in status?"

There is a slight pause. "No, no activity all night. One male arrived in a Lexus approximately thirty minutes ago with a camera and equipment as you predicted."

Horace leans back against the cold metal of the van wall and replies, "You have the plan? There won't be any room for mistakes."

The female assassin replies slowly, "I'm well versed in what you want. We always get the job done as you well know Sir."

He hates the woman, but she is a necessary evil. Horace doesn't know anything about her except that she overly enjoys her role and that for him is enough to hate her. He prefers to keep collateral damage to a minimum. He looks at the far wall of the van and thinks of an old quote he'd heard somewhere long ago, "Hell is empty because all the devils are here."

He sighs and replies, "We go on my signal."

The call disconnects and Horace looks toward Peters, who sits in the driver's seat. "Is everyone in place?"

Peters looks over his shoulder and simply nods. Horace takes a deep breath and suddenly realizes that he is tired. Tired of endless operations, of sleepless nights, of bloodshed, but most of all, loneliness. He leans back and reaches into his satchel pulling out the flask and taking a long drink. The whiskey burns all the way down, just the way he likes it.

Konrad sits at Darci's kitchen table and looks at the red light pulsing on the front of the camera. It reminds him of a heartbeat, steadily counting the seconds until he informs Green River, Indiana and the rest of the country of the danger of the flu vaccine and the much larger danger of the Thai Flu. Dan Kingman sits to his left in his khakis, boots and green polo with the news agency logo embroidered on the chest. Dan catches Konrads glance and says with some embarrassment, "The producer thought it might provide a more dramatic visual of the fact I'm reporting an exclusive in the field. What's your opinion?"

Konrad runs his fingers through his hair and says, "The boots are a nice touch."

Dan catches the sarcasm and grins slightly. "We'll be live in a few minutes. If you don't mind, can I have the thumb drive? I'll get the film queued on my computer. I'm going to start off with the local news. While I report that, you'll be off camera. After the news, Darci will pan over to you, and we'll get started on the interview. I guess I don't need to remind you that you shouldn't make any reference to our location and please don't mention Darci's name. I'll introduce you and cover your credentials, then I'll lead off with a few softball questions, after that, we'll get into the meat and potatoes. Any questions?"

Konrad looks at Candace standing behind Darci then shakes his head. Darci looks up from the camera and says, "Five minutes."

Dan looks at Candace and says with a smile, "You know what might make this look more like a friendly conversation, a couple of cups of coffee. Any chance you could get us some Candace?"

She nods her head and heads for the coffee pot, pours two cups and returns with the steaming liquid, setting the cups on the table and returning to her place behind the camera. Dan smiles and takes a sip whispering, "Nothing like being served by a beautiful woman, eh Konrad?"

Konrad gives Dan a deadpan look and visualizes knocking the anchorman's amazing white teeth right down his throat. Darci holds her hand in the air while counting down. "Five, four, three, two."

She mouths "one" and points at Dan. He instantly puts on the famous Dan Kingman smile and shuffles the papers in his hands. "Good morning and welcome to the Green River Morning Report. I'm Dan Kingman with up to the minute news for the Green River area and the nation. I am broadcasting from an undisclosed location this morning to conduct an exclusive interview with Doctor Konrad Pearce, developer of the universal flu vaccine, but first, the news. In local news, officials at Saint Anthony General are reporting that the recent overcrowding of the emergency room is slowing. Public Information Officer Susan Divine stated that while the levels are still higher than normal, the hospital should be able to start taking other than extreme emergencies by the end of the month if the trend continues. Until then, citizens are still encouraged to seek help from larger hospitals in Indianapolis and surrounding areas.

While lines for the universal flu vaccine are still forming outside pharmacies across the nation, as more and more citizens receive the vaccine and supply increases, incidents of violence have dramatically decreased. President Longworth in his latest address to the nation announced enactment of the war powers act in addressing the increased demand for the vaccine. It has been reported from all areas of the nation, that this has resulted in increased vaccine production however other drugs such as insulin are beginning to be in short supply.

On the local scene, my sources at the Green River Police Department tell me on condition of anonymity that the Reginald Emmer homicide is now a closed case with the main suspect, Arnold Jenkins having acted alone in the murder.

The arson investigation into the fire at the Romantic Destinations Suites is still ongoing and authorities are requesting anyone with information to contact them via the Green River Police tip line. They remind the public that all tips are confidential."

Dan leans back slightly in the kitchen chair and takes a quick sip of his coffee as he looks into the camera. With a beaming smile he says, "Now, without further ado, I am extremely pleased to be sitting here with Doctor Konrad Pearce, former head of Research and Development at Emmer Pharmaceuticals and visionary of the universal influenza vaccine. Doctor Pearce, welcome."

The camera pans over to include Konrad in the picture. Although he has combed his hair, he looks haggard. A by-product of being pursued like a wounded animal for days. He looks at the camera with eyes exuding exhaustion and tries to smile and nod. He focuses on Candace. She is the only thing he has left. As he looks into her eyes, he knows what he must do and oddly, his heart is lighter for it as he thinks, "It has to be this way."

Dan begins the interview. "Doctor Pearce, I cannot tell you how long I've wanted to speak with you. Can I call you Konrad?"

Konrad looks at Dan and smiles slightly, "Doctor will be fine."

Dan looks surprised at first but regains his composure, a half-smile, half smirk on his face. "Alright Doctor, let me start off by offering my condolences on the passing off your wife and daughter. What a terrible tragedy. It hasn't been that long ago, has it?"

Konrad quickly looks at Dan and then the camera in surprise. "No, not long but it seems like a lifetime ago."

Dan smiles at Candace and says, "I bet it does Doctor."

Darci looks over the camera at Dan with a look that says, "What the fuck are you doing?"

Candace folds her arms across her chest and looks at the floor, reading the meaning in Dan's smile and knowing what is getting ready to transpire. Dan puts on his trademark smile and continues, "Doctor, will you explain to the audience what the universal flu vaccine is, how it works and what gave you the idea for such a radical approach? You know, I would love to hear your story from the beginning as I'm sure our viewers would also."

As Konrad begins his crucible, Horace sits in the van and watches the live broadcast on his computer, savoring each subtle increment toward Konrad Pearce's destruction. He smiles his evil smile and thinks, "Dan Kingman is good at what he does. The rabbit hole is opened, and Doctor Pearce is getting ready to step in."

Peters looks over his shoulder and says, "Green River PD just parked up the block. One car with what looks like two officers."

Horace picks up his telephone and dials. "We see you. Stand by. I'll let you know when I'm ready."

He ends the call and resumes watching the broadcast on his computer, chuckling intermittently.

Back in Darci's kitchen, Konrad takes a sip of his coffee, his hand shaking slightly. Dan leans in and smiles as he says, "Doctor, the video was very interesting, of course I'm no virologist and I doubt many of our viewers are. How do we know what we're seeing is actually the vaccine at work on the Thai flu? Frankly, there are government entities who deny it exists. How do you explain that?"

Konrad looks back at Dan, his eyebrows raised in surprise at the question. "Well, I have no proof other than the video. The actual samples are at the lab or were when I left. The Thai flu does exist. I discovered it as I said I did."

Dan smiles to himself thinking, "I've still got it. It's like taking candy from a baby. This would be kind of fun if the guy making me do it wasn't such an asshole."

He looks at his notes and asks, "So, you never performed any studies on the vaccine? Just inserted these, uh, nano-bots and released it on the unsuspecting public?"

Konrad sits up in his chair, realizing too late what is about to happen. Candace starts to step forward, but he shakes his head slightly, stopping her. Dan asks, "I mean, it was your lab, correct Doctor?"

Konrad answers, his jaw clenched, "It was my lab, and it was my decision in conjunction with the former CEO of Emmer Pharmaceuticals, Reginald Emmer."

Dan knows he has just put the noose around Konrad's neck. Now, all he must do is tighten it. "How convenient. The same Reginald Emmer who was murdered recently? The reason I'm asking is that Mr. Emmer really can't refute your story now, can he?"

Konrad clenches his fists under the table. He looks at Candace who has tears in her eyes. "Yes, that Reginald Emmer."

Dan waves his hand and says quickly, "Well, we'll get back to that. So, your lab is the only one that found the Thai Super flu in their samples? Your lab, the only lab out of every other pharmaceutical company in the United States? Seems almost mathematically impossible, doesn't it?"

Konrad answers in an exasperated tone, "I can't explain it, but the Thai Flu is real, and the vaccine is real. You've seen it for yourself. I don't know why no other labs identified it."

Dan decides to close the noose. "It is rumored that your employment was terminated by Mr. Emmer. Is that true?"

Konrad is no longer looking at Dan, but straight into the camera, "No, that is not true. I was placed on a leave of absence."

Dan follows up quickly, "Because of your poor work performance. Losing your family in such a tragic event must have been hard. Am I correct?"

Konrad looks at Dan, hate in his eyes. "What do you think?"

It is the final nail Dan has been waiting for. "I think, Doctor Pearce that I would've started taking antidepressants too. No one can blame you. I know that I wouldn't."

Konrad reacts as if he has been slapped. He stands up quickly, spilling the remainder of his coffee. "You son of a bitch! Why are you doing this? This interview is over! I'm done!"

Konrad storms toward the basement with Candace following. Darci cuts the camera off and steps over to Dan. "What the hell Dan? Why did you cut him off at the knees like that?"

Dan smiles as he removes the thumb drive and placing it in his pocket replies, "Darci, you were in over your head with this story from the beginning. Trust me when I tell you to forget this whole mess. If you know what's good for you, you'll keep your mouth shut."

Darci, eyes wide, asks, "What do you mean?"

As the question leaves her lips, a petite, middle aged blonde steps into the kitchen. She has a large semi-automatic pistol with a silencer leveled at Darci. She is followed closely by a large man holding the same type of weapon. The blonde answers the question for Dan. "He means, you have a slim chance of surviving this, but it is a chance so keep your fucking mouth shut."

With this, she steps forward and backhands Darci across the face, sending her sprawling unconscious to the kitchen floor. Dan starts to stand from the chair but the big man who entered with the blonde puts the muzzle of his pistol on Dan's forehead. The blonde turns and says, "I believe you have something that belongs to me."

Dan quickly reaches into his pocket and produces the thumb drive and puts it on the table. The big man picks it up and smoothly puts it into his pocket, his pistol never leaving Dan's forehead. The blonde smiles and moves to the back door, opening it for another very large man to enter. Dan sputters almost in tears, "I did what you wanted. Please don't kill me."

The blonde walks back over to him and whispers, "Where is your special guest?"

Dan looks toward the basement. "They both went downstairs."

The blonde assassin looks at the big man holding the gun to Dan's forehead and says, "Keep an eye on them."

Then she steps over Darci and moves to the basement door followed by the other man.

Meanwhile down in the basement Konrad and Candace listen to what is occurring upstairs. It becomes clear to Candace what the little voice in her psyche was trying to tell her. She looks around and realizes that there is only one way in and more importantly, "out" of the basement. She and Konrad are trapped. As Candace stands by the door of their room, Konrad creeps to the edge of the staircase leading upstairs. As he looks at the door, he sees a shadow fall over the light coming under the door and realizes the very people who have been pursuing them are about to descend the staircase. He looks around for a weapon but sees nothing viable and hurries back to where Candace is standing. It hits him in an instant what he must do and whispers, "The windows. I've got to get you out of here."

She shakes her head and replies, "No. I'm not leaving you."

He grabs her forcefully and then pulls her into an embrace. "I love you. You're all I have left. You can fit but I won't be able to. We're the only ones who know the truth. You have to go, now!"

She looks into his eyes and then nods. They move to the windows and Konrad bends down so that she can get on his shoulders. She unlatches the window. It is a horizontal framed rectangle, much too small for Konrad but Candace's lithe frame slides through with relative ease. Once outside, she turns and says, "Please Konrad, just try. Please."

Konrad takes the waist pack containing their dwindling supply of money and hands it to her. He is about to try and pull himself up when he hears a female voice behind him say, "Don't even think about it Doctor."

Konrad looks at Candace through the open window and says, "Run!"

She mouths the words, "I love you" and then she is gone.

Konrad turns to see the blonde woman from Reginald's house. He looks past the pistol she is pointing at him. She is smiling, but her eyes are cold. Her smile is more like a dangerous animal, showing its teeth. Konrad sees his death in her eyes. At that moment, he accepts his fate. Candace is safe for now and he knows that if he can keep them here long enough, she has a good chance of escaping. He puts his hands up and the woman motions with her head for the large man to approach him. As the man gets within striking distance, Konrad kicks hard at his shin. The man groans and then launches himself at Konrad. The man outweighs him by at least seventy pounds and Konrad knows that he doesn't have a chance. The move was simply to buy Candace time. The big man grabs Konrad by the throat as he says in a deep voice, "You mother fucker! I'm gonna beat the lungs outta your chest."

Konrad screams, "I hope it hurts like hell you bastard."

He barely gets the words out before the big man hits him with two wicked punches to the ribs that double Konrad over. The man releases him, and he falls to the floor gasping for breath. The woman shakes her head and says, "Oh for the love of, are you shitting me? Go easy Ojo. The boss wants him alive. Shit!"

She pulls a phone from her pocket and dials. It is answered immediately by Horace. "I trust everything went according to plan."

The female assassin takes a deep breath and replies, "For the most part. We're secure here. The thumb drive is in our possession. Swanson got out through one of the basement windows. She's on the run but she won't get far."

Horace replies, "Don't bother. She's no threat without the thumb drive and I know where she'll eventually head anyway. I'll pick her up when the time is right. I'm coming in."

Horace walks slowly into the kitchen and looks around the room, like a man on holiday. He smiles as he sees the printer on the kitchen desk. He walks over to it in silence and pulls the laptop from his satchel. Behind him, he can hear Konrad struggling as Ojo manhandles him up the stairs and into the kitchen. Darci has been tied to one of the kitchen chairs with duct tape. Horace doesn't turn around but instead continues to connect his laptop to the printer. Once he's connected, he prints one sheet of paper and then disconnects his device, putting it back in his satchel.

Horace finally turns around, a broad smile on his face showing the wicked canine teeth. "Well, I'm so glad you could all come. We have some business to attend to."

Horace walks up behind Dan and puts both hands on his shoulders. "Dan. Danny Boy. Danski, you did an excellent job. The broadcast was thoroughly entertaining. In fact, I'm very impressed with your interviewing skills. Too bad you're a low life, adulterous piece of shit."

Dan turns his head as far as he can and looks up at Horace saying frantically, "I did what you told me to do. I did it! You've got to let me go."

Horace looks down at him and chuckles. "I don't have to do a fucking thing Dan, but you did keep up your end of the bargain. Sit quiet for now and we'll see how things go."

Dan starts to speak but Horace silences him by grabbing his lower lip and squeezing. "I said, shut up."

Dan whimpers and Horace releases his grip. Darci struggles against the duct tape to no avail, almost tipping the chair over. "You're working for these assholes? You piece of shit! You're through as a newsman. I'm going to blow the whistle on you, you prick!"

Horace looks at the blonde and motions with his head. She moves toward Darci as fluidly as a cat, holstering her pistol and pulling the ice pick from a sheath at the small of her back. It is a wicked weapon with a carved wooden handle, a steel blade and razor-sharp point that gleams in the sunlight coming through the kitchen windows. Darci's eyes go wide as the blonde grabs her by the hair and inserts the point just inside Darci's left nostril. "Don't say another word or I will scramble your fucking brains."

Darci goes limp, her eyes shut tightly, lip trembling as she whispers, "Please, please don't."

Horace nods his head curtly and says, "Good. Now, let's get on with it. Doctor Pearce, I want to commend you on playing your part in our little drama so well."

Konrad looks at Horace with hate in his eyes and replies, "What the fuck are you talking about? Who are you people?"

With a melancholy smile, Horace smoothly replies, "Oh Konrad, haven't you realized it yet? It isn't who I am that is important, it's all the things I can do."

He pulls his telephone from his satchel and dials. "We're ready for you. Come to the front door and we'll meet you there."

Horace looks at Konrad with exaggerated sadness, "I'm so sorry about the loss of your family Doctor. It appears you've had a complete mental breakdown. Don't worry, we'll be with you every step of the way and wish you a speedy recovery."

Konrad looks up from the chair he is being held in with surprise. "There's nothing wrong with me! You're insane!"

Horace laughs a cruel laugh, "Takes one to know one Doctor."

There is a knock at the front door and on cue, Ojo puts Konrad in a half nelson coupled with a wrist lock and forces him to a standing position. Konrad tries to struggle but he is like a child in Ojo's hands.

Horace shakes his head and chuckles as he goes to the front door and opens it. Ojo has walked Konrad behind Horace and stands like an oak tree as he struggles. Two Green River police officers are standing on the porch, their cruiser now parked in the drive. Horace hands one of the officers the form he printed and says in a purely business-like tone, "Doctor Pearce has suffered a complete mental breakdown. Here is the involuntary commitment order signed by Judge Worley. The police officer takes the form and looks it over nodding, then looks past Horace at Konrad. "Doctor Pearce, I have a signed commitment order for you to be admitted to Saint Mary's Behavioral Facility for an indefinite amount of time. I'd advise you to cooperate with us. There's no need to make this any harder than it has to be Doc."

The two officers' step through the door past Horace and grab Konrad's wrists applying handcuffs while Ojo holds Konrad from behind, his big arm wrapped around Konrad's neck. The officer who took the order looks at Ojo and nods as they grab Konrad's arms and start to lead him out. Ojo turns and walks back to the kitchen. As Konrad is led away, he looks back over his shoulder and sees Horace smiling as he slowly closes the door.

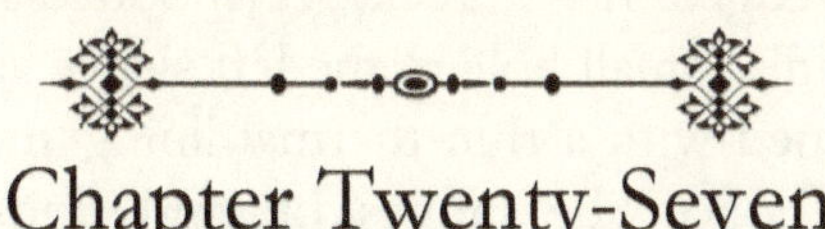

Chapter Twenty-Seven

Candace's lungs burn as she runs through the alleys between Fifth and Sixth Streets. The sound of her ragged breathing fills her ears, muffling the barking of dogs and children playing in the yards on either side as she runs past. She has no idea where she's going. She just knows that she has to get to someplace safe. To someplace where these evil people can't find her. Someplace where she can think and plan her next move. She knows from years of experience that running blindly without a plan is the quickest way to get caught.

She turns left and starts walking, tears streaming down her face as she looks over her shoulder to make sure she isn't followed. After two blocks, she crosses Third Street and enters Sandy Creek Park. The gravel crunches under her feet as she walks quickly along the path which winds past the golf course and soccer field. There are several golfers getting in a lunchtime round.

Their laughter reaching her ears from across the greens. Candace begins to take a mental inventory of her predicament. She has her license but no credit cards. Even if she had them, she couldn't use them. A hotel on this side of town is out of the question. She has cash, but that won't last forever. Her car is gone forever, and she needs to get completely out of this town. Candace thinks of Konrad and wonders if he is even still alive. Her heart aches and a sob escapes before she can stifle it. She exits the park and sees the clothing donation center and attached store and a plan begins to form.

She wipes her eyes on the sleeve of her sweatshirt and enters the store, nodding at the middle-aged woman working the register. The woman looks tired, and it is obvious from her demeanor she has nothing to look forward to but an endless string of days, just like the one before. She pays little attention to Candace who moves straight to the racks which are jam packed with pre-owned clothing. Candace knows exactly the kind of thing she's looking for as she thinks, "I'm going to have to hide in plain sight. Join those who people want to forget."

Candace finds what she is looking for and pulls it from the rack where it is tightly wedged. It is a thick, grey hooded sweatshirt, one size too large for her with a small hole in the left sleeve and some fraying at the bottom. It is lined with a thin thermal lining and on the front, an Indiana University logo. She moves on and finds a pair of black Converse high-tops in her size.

The tread is almost worn smooth. She moves to another aisle and finds a pair of jeans that are in decent condition. Candace moves to the back wall and finds the items which will complete her transformation. She picks up a worn-out gym bag with faux leather handles and a dark gray ball cap. She is about to head to the register when she sees some kitchenware and assorted gadgets on the far-left wall. She heads over and finds a large pair of tailor's scissors. They are six inches long with a sharp point. Candace holds them in her hand and nods her head slightly.

She finds two pairs of thick athletic socks and heads for the register. The woman looks at Candace as she approaches with a look of apathy and asks, "That be all for you?"

Candace looks around the store once more and seeing no one, answers, "Yes. Could you tell me how far the homeless shelter is from here?"

The woman smiles slightly and answers, "You don't look homeless, darlin'. What do you want to know about that for?"

Candace straightens slightly. "Tell me, what does homeless look like?"

The woman just raises her eyebrows and replies, "Four blocks south, toward the prison. You can't miss it, but you better hurry, they fill up quick."

She rings Candace's purchases up and puts them in a bag without another word. Candace thanks her and exits the store, turning right, she begins the four-block walk. After one block, she enters a gas station and asks for the restroom key. The clerk, a pimply faced teenager smiles and says, "Restroom's for customers only."

Candace buys a candy bar and the clerk hands her, her change and the key accompanied by a smirk. It is a typical gas station restroom with off white porcelain tile halfway up the wall. It is dirty, the toilet and sink both stained with a red tinge from the mineral laden water. The floor is tacky. Candace closes and locks the door then looks in the mirror at her reflection. Her eyes drift to the writing scratched into the wall next to the mirror. "Claudine is a man stealing bitch."

She shakes her head and looks at herself, turning her head sideways to get a view of her raven hair put up in a ponytail. A lump forms in her throat as she reaches inside the bag and removes the scissors. Taking a deep breath, she reaches around and cuts the ponytail off three inches below the pony tail holder. After removing the holder, the hair falls around her face. She ruffles it with her fingers, looks in the mirror and nods slightly, her bottom lip quivering.

Candace changes clothes quickly then picks up the extra pair of socks and puts one inside of the other. She puts the scissors inside of the socks and slides them inside the front of her bra, wedging the sheathed scissors between her breasts. She jumps up and down a couple of times to make sure the scissors are secure then puts the sweatshirt over her head. The baseball cap is the final touch. Her other clothes go back in the gym bag then she looks at herself one more time before stepping out of the bathroom, leaving the key in the door as a parting "fuck you" to the snotty clerk. She takes a bite of the candy bar as she walks around the back of the station toward the homeless shelter, thinking of Konrad and vowing to make her pursuers pay.

Back at Darci Mitchell's house, Horace enters the kitchen and rubs his hands together saying, "Well Dan, what shall I do with you?"

Dan's knees go weak as he looks at the muzzle of the pistol pointed at his head. "Please let me go. I swear, I didn't see a thing. I did what you wanted me too. I kept my end of the bargain. Please for heaven's sake, let me go."

Horace chuckles, "Bargain? So, we're partners now. Is that it?"

Dan nods his head emphatically. Horace continues at seeing this, "Okay Danny-Boy. You've seen a lot. Alot of 'secrets.' Can I trust you, partner? I mean, really trust you. Like the lives of your sweet family depend on it?"

Dan nods his head again. "Absolutely man! I swear on my children's lives."

Horace nods his head curtly and says in a serious tone, "Good Dan, because you just did. You just put your children's lives in the balance. If you fuck up, it'll be on you. I won't be the party responsible. Understand?"

Dan nods slowly, realizing the gravity of the deal he has just made. He looks at Darci who is staring at him with pure hatred in her eyes. "What about her?"

Horace looks at Dan and then at Darci replying, "Well Dan, that's touching but Darci and I have our own deal to strike. You, my friend, will have your hands full with yours. Now, you can leave, but remember, there is no place on this earth that I cannot reach you and those you cherish."

Dan stands from the chair on shaky legs as the big man holsters his pistol. He looks at Darci one more time and then starts for the door. Horace takes his gaze from Darci and says, "Dan, don't forget your camera."

Dan moves behind Darci and collects the camera and tripod, then he leaves quickly, his head bowed. The blonde assassin who has been standing by the back door the whole time of Horace's exchange with Dan says in a resolute manner, "Well, that's a disappointment."

Horace snaps his head to look at her. "If you live long enough, you might learn that collateral damage just leads to more loose ends to tie off. I really doubt you'll have to worry about it though."

He turns his full attention to Darci. "Darci, Darci, Darci, what am I to do with you? You know, when I read your packet, I was truly impressed. I foresee a great future for you if you can find it in your heart to be reasonable. There will be positions coming available for a young lady like you within a year or so if everything goes well. Would you like to be part of the future Darci?"

Darci looks up slowly and replies vehemently, "Are you out of your fucking mind? Who are you and why are you here? What do you mean, my packet?"

Horace laughs. It is an unpleasant sound. "That's my girl. Ever the investigator. Darci, it doesn't matter who I am really. What does matter is that I am connected to the most powerful individuals in the world. Nothing is beyond their reach. Nothing is not theirs to give. They know everything about everyone, therefore, I have that knowledge as well. I know about your time overseas, your estrangement from your parents, your deep loneliness. Yes, such bitter loneliness. I know about Roland. Friendly fire, wasn't it? Is that why you immerse yourself in your work? Never letting anyone get close? Is it why you sit at home alone, night after night with no one to share your pain? You see Darci, I am the same as you. You might say we are kindred spirits. I too, have been deployed overseas many, many times and my relationship with my parents was, shall we say, less than loving. I understand the feeling of betrayal Darci. I understand you, my dear."

Darci's eyes go wide as she looks into Horace's eyes. They are cold yet loving at the same time. The voice is a hiss laden with honey. She begins to weep. Horace moves to her and kneels beside the chair, placing two fingers under her chin, gently raising her face to meet his gaze. "There, there now Darci, I'm proud of you. You no longer have to be alone. I'm here now. You see? Your world is going to bloom like a flower in the spring. You'll always be able to count on us. You'll always be able to count on me Darci."

Horace removes a wicked folding knife from his belt and cuts the tape that holds her. She looks at him through her tears and says, "But what about today? What happened here? Why did you do that to Konrad?"

Horace's gaze never leaves her face. He is inches from her. "The future Darci. Our future. We are the chosen Darci, and our future dictated that it had to happen that way. You'll see. Everything will be alright from here on out."

Horace strokes her hair out of her face like a loving father might, then he reaches into his pocket and removes a debit card and a business card with only a telephone number on it. He hands it to Darci. She looks at him with an unspoken question. He holds both of her hands in his and says lovingly, "I want you to take a leave of absence. I'm going to take care of you now until the time is right. The card is limitless. The number is to contact me day or night. Live like you always have Darci. Purchase nothing extravagant. There'll be plenty of time for that later."

Darci looks down at the floor and nods her head. Horace puts his arms around her in a fatherly embrace. "Good Darci. Good. We'll leave now but I'll be in touch soon. Remember to use the number on the card if you need anything. Anything at all."

Horace stands and motions with his head. The three assassins file out with Horace following. He looks back one more time at Darci still sitting in the kitchen chair then he is gone. Darci waits a few moments longer before standing and moving carefully to the door. She peeks out of the window at Horace and the others as they cross the street and get in the vans. She thinks as she watches him, "You forgot to get me to sign my name in blood, you sanctimonious prick. I'll never sell my soul to you or anyone else."

She goes into the kitchen and retrieves her cell phone to inform the station of her leave of absence.

Horace sits in the van as it travels toward the safe house. The assassin's van trails a few cars behind. He thinks about his next move and whispers just under his breath, "Almost there."

His cell phone rings, and he answers it immediately. It is Darci, "I just wanted to say thank you. I called the station and told them that I would be out for a while."

Horace is silent for a moment then replies softly, "Good Darci. I'll be in touch soon."

The call ends and he immediately dials the number for the electronic surveillance asset. The call is answered within two rings. "I want a close eye on everything Darci Mitchell does. Phone, internet, everything. There's a tracker on her car as well. I want daily reports. More if she's doing something unusual."

The asset replies, "I'm on it, Sir."

Horace is about to put the telephone back in his satchel when it rings. He looks at the number and realizes it is the blonde assassin. "Hello?"

Her monotone voice comes over the line. "It's probably above my pay grade, but what was that with the girl?"

Horace smiles his usual smile and asks, "Are you confused?"

The assassin answers after a long pause, "Well, yes."

Horace chuckles, "Good. Don't worry, you still may get your pound of flesh.

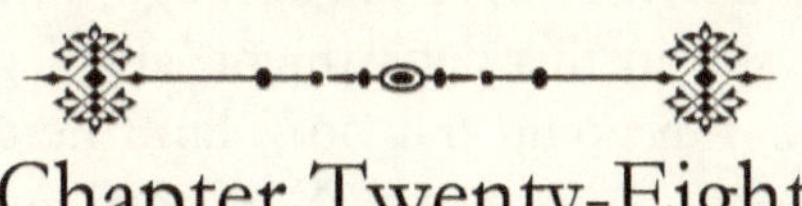

Chapter Twenty-Eight

The patrol car is parked in front of the psychiatric facility and Konrad sits in the back, looking through the expanded metal at the police officer who sits in the passenger seat. He has the feeling he's seen the officer before then it hits him. It is Seargent Jamison. He shifts in the seat to take the pressure off his wrists where the handcuffs are biting into them and asks, "Haven't I seen you before Officer?"

Both of the officers turn slightly in their seats at the sound of his voice, this being the first words Konrad has spoken. The officer in the passenger seat replies, "They'll be out to get you in a second Doc. It'd be best if you just sit back and relax."

Konrad shifts in his seat again. "Why are you doing this and why aren't you wearing body cameras? You're not really on duty, are you?"

The officer in the passenger seat replies, "You might call this overtime Doc. You should've taken my advice."

The driver looks over at his partner and says, "Don't talk to him."

Jamison looks over at the driver with a grin and replies, "It's not gonna matter now Hoyt, you really need to learn to relax."

Then he looks over his shoulder at Konrad and says with a grin, "You too, Doc."

Hoyt is slightly overweight and graying. Konrad figures that he is well into his career as a police officer. He looks at Jamison quickly, "No fucking names. You really need to learn to shut your fucking mouth. You're gonna put us both in the hat."

Konrad senses an opportunity in the division between the two. "Well, like you said Seargent, it doesn't matter now. So, why are you doing this? I mean, the people paying you must be pretty important. So, who is it?"

Jamison turns in his seat and laughs, "Yeah Doc, you're right, it really doesn't matter now. I mean, who's going to believe a word you say from here on out. No offense, but you're a dumbass. You just had to start running your mouth and on national television no less. I'm starting to believe you really belong here. It's pretty simple. I'm in it for the money. I need it and they have it. Although, I'm not sure who they are. Our pay is for shit in this department, and I got a family. It's as simple as that. Now I'm going out on a limb here Doc because you seem like a decent guy, so listen up. You need, and I emphasize the word need, to keep your mouth shut."

Hoyt looks quickly over at Jamison. "Take your own advice, because the welcoming committee is coming down the walk."

Hoyt and Jamison step from the patrol car and help Konrad from the back seat then stand at the curb, waiting for the woman and two orderlies to arrive. She is tall and poised in her approach. There is an heir of friendly authority in her demeanor which exudes confidence. Konrad's eyes follow her down the walk, flanked by the two large orderlies and notices how graceful the woman is. "Looks like I'm getting the V.I.P. treatment."

As she arrives where the three men are standing, she smiles and says, "Well, I guess introductions are in order. My name is Doctor Cindy Cagwell, the director here and one of the therapists. Doctor Pearce, I watched your interview this morning. Very revealing, I must say. My two companions are Lyle and Henry. They'll be assigned to you exclusively Doctor. If you need anything, it will come through them with my authorization. As for me, it seems that I will be taking an exclusive interest in your case as well. We'll meet regularly to see if we can get you feeling better."

She looks at Jamison and Hoyt, raising an eyebrow. "Do you have the order?"

Hoyt reaches quickly into his side pocket and produces the commitment order. Doctor Cagwell reads it carefully and then looks at Konrad while speaking to the police officers. "Everything looks to be in order. You can remove the handcuffs. I'm sure Doctor Pearce would rather walk inside in a dignified manner."

After a slight pause, she smiles slightly and asks, "Wouldn't you Doctor?"

Konrad nods his head slightly and Jamison steps around behind him to remove the handcuffs. As he does so, he says in a whisper, "Remember what I said Doc."

Doctor Cagwell motions for Konrad to walk toward the building while Henry and Lyle move in close in case Konrad has other ideas. He realizes that to resist or attempt to flee would be useless and so, follows her up the walk. When they are almost to the door, Konrad says in a low tone, "Doctor, I shouldn't be here. There's really nothing wrong with me. This is all a set up."

Doctor Cagwell laughs a laugh full of mirth and replies as she glances over her shoulder, "Yes Konrad. I know."

As Konrad Pearce walks through the doors of Saint Mary's Psychological Rehabilitative Facility, Joel Smith, Chief Public Information Officer for the CDC stands behind the couch in his office and watches the television intently. A bead of sweat makes its way slowly down his temple. His bald head slick with moisture and his breathing elevated. He watches as Sandy Smithers reports on the Konrad Pearce interview and thinks, "Why does she keep denying everything. It sounds so desperate. Who's the idiot writing her copy? Fuck! And this Pearce. He's really opened a can of worms. Every time I think I have these conspiracy nuts tied off, something else happens to get them going again. This is going to blow back on me, I just know it. He keeps claiming that he tried to contact the CDC. I wish there were some way to silence this prick. What a pain in the ass."

He picks up his office telephone and dials Warren Densin's number. "Densin! My office, now."

Warren practically runs through Joel's doorway and skids to a stop in front of his desk. "I'm here Sir, what can I do for you?"

Joel walks around his desk and sits down. "Sandy Smithers reported this morning that her network reached out to us for a comment regarding the Thai Flu and these so-called aneurisms. Did she talk to you? Tell me you didn't make a statement to a national news agency without speaking to me first."

Warren begins to wring his hands together and to feel the familiar bladder spasms. "Well, I…."

Joel slaps his hand on the desk. "You did! Didn't you? You idiotic son of a bitch! What did you tell them?"

Warren feels the heat rise into his face. "I told them what the scientists in Influenza Research told me. That there is no Thai Flu as far as we know and there are no verified side effects of the flu vaccine. What was I supposed to tell them?"

Joel steps around the desk. "Are you getting smart with me you little shit? If any of this blows back, it'll be on you. Do you understand? You tell them that we have no comment. You tell them that the CDC is diligently monitoring all possible threats to our country. You purposely give vague responses in case you have to change positions later. Have you learned nothing? Get the fuck out of my sight."

Warren starts to leave but stops when Joel puts his hand up and asks, "Wait. What exactly did Research say?"

He turns to face Joel and responds almost smugly, "They said that there was no Thai Flu and that they wished we wouldn't keep asking about it. They added that we need to leave the science to the scientists."

Joel goes back behind his desk. "How do they explain the film that Doctor Pearce showed in his interview?"

Warren shrugs his shoulders. "It's a nothing sandwich as far as they're concerned."

As he sits down, Joel responds after shuffling the papers on his desk, "Well, no more statements to the press without running it through me first. Am I clear?"

Warren turns to go and replies, "Abundantly Sir. It won't happen again."

After Warren leaves, Joel takes a handkerchief and wipes the sweat from his head thinking, "What he doesn't realize is that a solid denial can come back and bite all of us in the ass. It invites investigation and my head isn't going to be the one on the chopping block."

Warren walks back to his office feeling the effects of the ass chewing. In one sense, he's proud of himself as he thinks, "Well at least I didn't have to run from his office to the bathroom."

In the back of Warren's mind, a little voice has started to whisper, and those whispers are getting louder. Something is terribly wrong with this whole thing. It's no longer a game in which his survival is questionable. Something bigger is going on. He sits at his desk and rubs his eyes, trying to get the anger to subside. He looks at the wall and says inaudibly through clenched teeth, "Maybe it's time that I found out exactly what I'm mixed-up in."

Back in Green River Indiana, Lynn Smith, formerly of the Department of Health and Human Services sits behind the teakwood monstrosity that used to be Reginald Emmer's desk. She looks around the office and smiles, enjoying her new position as Director of Emmer Pharmaceuticals. She thinks back to how she'd run that weakling Emmer right out of his own company. It was a bloodless coup, and she'd enjoyed every minute of it. In fact, she'd been surprised at exactly how easy it was. It was like he had no will to resist any sort of pressure. She'd laid the form on his desk and told him to sign, and he had. All she had to say was that he had no choice. She had the full might of the United States Government behind her. As soon as he heard that, he signed his company away. She takes a sip of cappuccino and thinks, "What a fucking pussy."

She is pulled from her revelry by a knock at the door. Erin, her new personal assistant pokes his beautifully symmetrical face around the door and says, "Sorry to bother you Ms. Smith but Mr. Zwerger is here to see you."

She looks at Erin and wonders what it would feel like to run her freshly manicured nails up and down his toned abdomen. "Sure Erin, show him in."

David Zwerger, Director of Production at Emmer Pharmaceuticals, walks through the door. His lanky frame moving with the fatigue felt only by those locked into a life of servitude to the Lynn Smiths of the world. He positions himself in front of her desk and waits. Lynn looks at him wearing a smile of relaxed amusement. "David, to what do I owe the pleasure?"

David Zwerger looks back at her with dead, beaten eyes. When Reginald was the owner, things had been different. He'd never been disrespectful but was able to at least voice his opinion. Now, he could barely bring himself to look this woman in the eyes. When had he changed? It's as if every bit of backbone has left his body. He feels beaten and small in front of her. "Um, just wanted to let you know, the problem on line three has solved itself."

Lynn's eyebrows rise in surprise. "Really, how so?"

He rubs his face with his hand and looks at the floor. "Mary Finch, the woman who was trying to organize the line workers. She passed away yesterday. One of those aneurysms they're talking about. The rest of the workers have fallen back in line. There are rumors that we're responsible."

Lynn laughs and replies, "How preposterous. Well, don't dispel the rumors. As the famous Roman emperor said, 'Let them hate so long as they fear'. You know David, I just had a thought. We need to send a strong message to the workers. Extend each shift by two hours and cut the breaks to ten minutes instead of twenty. We have to vaccinate the world, David. I have no intention of failing my country. Understand?"

David just nods his head, turns and leaves the office. Lynn smiles a contented smile, looks at the ceiling and slowly spins the oversized leather chair with the special massaging points. "Erin! Be a dear and bring me another cappuccino!"

Chapter Twenty-Nine

The next morning, Candace walks out of the homeless shelter into the sunshine after a long sleepless night. The woman on the cot next to hers had offered her a comb for her hair but she had declined, opting instead to just put the ball cap on. Her plan to get out of the city had solidified during the long hours of thinking and in the end, she was going to follow what she knew. Candace had decided that she would walk back to the truck stop and try to hitch a ride with one of the truck drivers.

She silently prays that she can find a decent one who'll give her a ride without expecting something in return. She knows this plan is inherently dangerous, remembering her days and nights on the run as a teenager, but it is her only option now. She puts the hood of her sweatshirt on her head, looks up and down Third Street and then begins the long walk toward the east end of town.

She walks with purpose and keeps to the less traveled avenues. Within a mile, she realizes that a backpack would have been the better choice instead of the gym bag. By midday, she reaches Twenty Fifth Street and finds a dumpster behind a home improvement store. There is a short length of rope sticking out of the construction and packing materials which overflow from the large metal container. Candace looks around then pulls the rope out and fashions two loops which she runs through the gym bag handles. Putting her arms through the rope, she fashions a makeshift backpack and heads across the large parking lot toward Green River Blvd.

The parking lot is busy and Candace walks with her head down, trying to keep from drawing attention. Shoppers either fail to notice her at all or look at her then quickly away. She thinks as she walks, "I'm part of the invisible now. Good."

As she turns east on Green River Blvd., a city police cruiser pulls into the lot. It slows for a moment as the policemen look her over. She breathes a sigh of relief as it rolls on past without stopping. It takes Candace another hour to walk out of the east end of Green River and reach the truck stop near the highway. She reaches into the waist pack and pulls a twenty-dollar bill out, then zips it shut and hides it back under her sweatshirt. As she enters the truck stop, she heads straight for the restroom, relieves herself then buys a sandwich from the hot bar and a bottle of water. Candace doesn't spend too much time inside the store, but instead, walks out to a grassy area adjacent to the lot and watches for westbound trucks to make the exit and then pull into the lot.

Candace approaches several drivers over the next few hours with no luck. Either they tell her that they're not taking riders, or they make an indecent proposition after undressing her with their eyes. She is sitting in the grassy area, thinking about where she will find shelter for the night when she sees a paunchy middle-aged man walking around his flatbed rig, checking the tires with a tire "billy." He looks over at her and smiles, then begins walking the twenty yards to where she is sitting. His smile is warm, and he looks to Candace to be someone's grandpa. He stops a few yards away from her and says, "Excuse me, Miss. I don't mean to bother you, but you look to me like you might need some help."

Candace looks into his eyes and sees only kindness. She nods her head and replies, "Yes. I need a ride to Colorado. Fort Collins, Colorado. Can you help me? I don't have any money."

The man smiles and says, "Well, it must be your lucky day Miss. I'm headed to Denver. I can get you almost all the way if you don't mind riding with an old man who talks too much."

Candace smiles and swallows the lump in her throat. "I would love to. Thank you so much."

The man makes a waving motion with his hand and says as he turns to return to his truck, "Well, c'mon then. My name's Jack Ragland, and you are?"

She answers him with a slight laugh as she follows him to the truck, "Carol. Carol Smith. I'm so glad to meet you Mr. Ragland."

He waves his hand again. "Please, call me Jack. I'm just coming off my eight-hour break so we have ten hours of driving ahead of us. We ought to be on a first name basis. Don't you think?"

Candace smiles and nods. "Jack it is then."

She climbs into the passenger side of the rig and sits in the large bucket seat. It is like climbing into the cockpit of a jet airliner. The air ride seat bounces as she sits down. Candace thinks, "This is going to be much more comfortable than a bus and much safer."

Jack climbs into the driver's seat, looks over at Candace with a smile then says, "Before we go, I need to make sure you're comfortable."

He reaches down and pulls a lever at the side of his seat allowing the seat to swivel. Then he stands and reaches across Candace. She is alarmed at first but then realizes that he is just pulling her seatbelt across and fastening it. He nods his head and says with a smile, "There you go. Snug as a bug in a rug."

They both laugh as he swivels his seat back and puts the big rig into gear. As they take the on ramp to Interstate Seventy West, the big engine roars as Jack runs through the gears, concentrating as he merges into the heavy traffic. Candace takes the opportunity to take a more detailed look at the rig. She thinks as she looks around, "This is where this man lives, and the devil is always in the details."

It is immediately obvious that the rig is in immaculate condition. There is a faint smell of rubbing alcohol. Candace notices a small picture of a woman holding a small dog hanging from the mirror. She turns and looks back into the sleeper, seeing that the single cot is made up and military tight. The thing that catches Candace's eye is that the cab is pristine. Jack notices Candace looking around and says, "That's Marcie, my wife with our pup, Geronimo."

Candace smiles a polite smile and thinks, "All of the other trucks I looked in today had at least some trash on the floorboards."

What she sees in Jack's truck is an extreme attention to detail and for some reason, this sets her on edge. She replies, her eyes never leaving the man's face, "She's very pretty and the puppy is adorable."

Jack seems to relax and smiles a sad smile, "Yeah, I miss her. She passed away almost two years ago."

Candace looks over at Jack with a sympathetic look. "I'm sorry Jack."

He smiles a crooked smile, keeping his eyes on the road. "I suppose there's a reason for everything."

Horace sits in the darkness of Trojan 34 and stares at the blinking red light on the camera. He dreads these meetings with the Regents, and this meeting will not be any different than the others. He consoles himself by thinking that they are a necessary evil in completing the mission. He leans his head back and takes a deep breath as he enjoys the cool darkness of the room. The safety of Trojan 34 allows Horace to relax. It is the only place he affords himself this luxury. As far as Horace is concerned, when he is outside this room, he is behind enemy lines.

He allows his mind to wander through the past week. The personnel change had been necessary, he's sure of it. Hanes was the traitor, and his removal will undoubtedly be unpopular with the North American Regent but, his men must be loyal only to him. That's the pecking order that must be maintained for compartmentalization and, it's the only real way to get things accomplished. Obviously, the Regents would need to be taught this lesson. Horace smiles slightly with the realization that phase two of his plan is complete. The final phase can begin immediately, and the mission is almost complete. He feels a deep fatigue and realizes that he really wants only one thing and that one thing is the peace of retirement. Horace decided months ago; this would be his final mission. This would be his legacy.

The computer chimes and the light turns blue, indicating that the meeting is about to begin. Horace straightens in the chair and begins speaking to the blank screen. "Thank you all for your attendance. I have a lot to share in this operational briefing, some of which I'm sure you already know. I apologize in advance for any redundancy. The final phase of the operation will begin in the next few days. The Pearce interview had the desired results in pushing worldwide compliance to roughly ninety-four percent. The non-compliant are now so few, their eradication can be left to attrition. They are, in a word 'irrelevant'."

The North American Regent interrupts. "Mr. MacGill, what is the status of your scapegoats? I'm afraid we've been left in the dark on that matter since your trip to Green River."

Horace smiles to himself. It is vindication from the guilty party herself. "I have no doubt of that Madam Regent. I made a personnel change on my arrival in Green River. I handled it personally. We should all remember in the future that I am your sole point of contact for operational details. At any rate, the matter has been irrevocably adjudicated. As for the world population, the sheep are now ready to follow the shepherds."

The Regent from Asia Minor cuts in with a question. "Horace, what of the sheep who refuse to follow?"

Horace takes a deep resigned breath and replies, "Their fate is already sealed Madam Regent. Now, getting back to the 'scapegoats', both are still in play. In summation, operational integrity is still in place. Everything is going according to predicted timelines. I predict that your edicts should be in place within the year. Are there any questions?"

No one speaks. Horace smiles and says, "Thank you for attending this meeting. I'll bid you all a good day."

He watches the light turn from blue to red signifying the end of the meeting and feels good. The meeting ended with him having the upper hand. Horace feels almost as if he had rested control from the Regents. It is a good feeling.

Back in Green River, Darci walks into Dan Kingman's office and sits down in one of the leather chairs in front of his desk. He looks up from the copy he is reading with red rimmed eyes. He is pale and the tangy smell of fear is noticeable in the room. They stare at each other for a long moment, neither of them saying anything. Darci is the first to speak, her voice low with menace, "You son of a bitch. I want to kill you right now."

Dan puts both hands out, palms up. "For God's sake Darci, close the door."

She quickly stands from the chair and slams the door closed. "Why did you do that to Konrad, Dan? You railroaded him and made him look like a fucking nut. And who were those people? What are you mixed up in?"

Dan stands from his chair and walks around the desk. "I had to. You saw what I saw Darci. They had me in a motel room near the rail yards and there was only one way that I was going to walk out and that was to play ball. They're connected. I don't know to who or what, maybe CIA or the Mob, but they knew everything about me. Every fucking thing! That was the packet that spook was talking about. He let me read mine and Pearce's. Listen, they have one on you too. Whoever they are, you don't want to cross them. I've been doing this a long time and I can recognize connected when I see it."

Darci walks closer to Dan and jabs her finger into his chest. "Yeah, well I'm not playing along."

Dan shakes his head. "Don't do it Darci. You'll end up in a ditch with a bullet in your head. I'm telling you. These fuckers mean business. The guy, the spook, he threatened to kill my family. Please Darci, I'm begging you."

Darci looks Dan in the eyes, her eyebrows raised and asks, "You're not going to help me then?"

Dan shakes his head and looks at the floor, "Help you what, get my family killed along with the both of us? No Darci. I'm sorry but no!"

Darci crosses her arms and looks at Dan defiantly. "Well, maybe I'll go to the police."

Dan laughs and says, "The police? Like the two cops that took Pearce away? They own the police, Darci. There's no way you can fight these people so get it through your thick skull and forget whatever you're thinking. You should just be glad you're alive. By the way, why are you alive?"

Darci looks away, "I don't really know. That sick fuck thinks I'm going to be some kind of companion to him. A kindred spirit is how he put it."

Dan snorts, "He has to be some kind of broken to think that."

Darci moves toward the door and turns before she walks through. "I agree, but what he hasn't figured on is that I'm broken too."

Then she is gone.

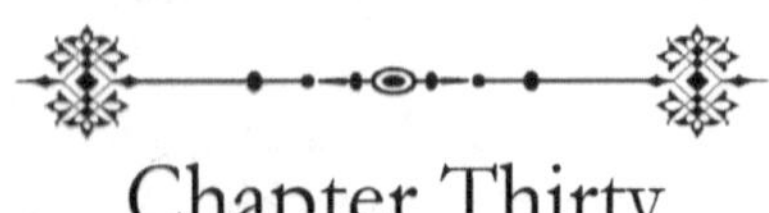

Chapter Thirty

Candace rouses from her slumber as the big truck roars down Interstate Seventy. The conversation between her and Jack had run out about four hours into the drive and she had fallen asleep, the rocking of the big rig causing the stress of her flight to melt away into the air ride seat. She mentally chastises herself for letting down her guard in the presence of a man she really knows nothing about. Of course they had talked about themselves during the ride, but his story might have been as much a fiction as the one she had told him about herself. She learned early on as a teenager on the run, the truth is reserved for your closest friends and right now Candace has none. Jack looks over at her with a smile and says, "You took quite the nap. You must have needed it."

Candace's mouth is dry. She shrugs her shoulders and says, "I guess so. Where are we?"

Jack looks at her with a friendly smile again, balancing his attention between her and the road. "Oh, we're about two hours from Denver. I'm going to take the next exit and top off with fuel. Maybe get a bite to eat. Would you like some dinner? My treat."

Candace realizes that she does need to use the bathroom and is very hungry, having had nothing since the sandwich at the truck stop. "That would be very nice Jack."

Jack maneuvers the big rig off the exit and into one of several truck stops. This one is decorated with a large sign which reads, "Granny's Diner." He pulls the truck around back and expertly backs the rig into a vacant spot in a deserted part of the lot. Candace thinks, "Granny's cooking doesn't seem very popular."

Jack opens his door and exits the truck, Candace following his lead. This area of the parking lot isn't well lit, and Candace stays close to Jack as they walk toward the restaurant. They enter the restaurant and find a booth. The restaurant itself isn't much to look at. The walls, once white, are dingy from years of exposure to the smoke coming off of the grill which snaps and pops constantly. The seats of the booth are red, cracked vinyl that squeaks as Jack squeezes into the booth. There are only a few patrons in the place, most are men who sit at the counter. The one waitress looks to be in her sixties with tired eyes and dyed blonde hair pulled back in a ponytail exposing the grey roots. Candace excuses herself and heads to the restroom. She returns to find that Jack has ordered for both of them and the food is waiting. "I hope you like breakfast for dinner. I just took a chance. The food here is great."

Candace smiles and replies, "I love breakfast for dinner."

This pleases Jack and he begins to devour his meal. He finishes well ahead of Candace and has time for two refills of coffee before she is done. Jack stretches and says, "Well, I don't mean to eat and run but we should probably get going."

Candace raises her eyebrows and smiling just nods as she gets up from the booth. Jack pays for the meal, and they head back to the truck. Jack helps her up into the rig, then goes around and climbs in the driver's seat. Candace looks over at him with a smile and says, "Thank you Jack. I really enjoyed the meal."

He looks back and replies, "I was hoping you would."

His phone chimes and he tilts his head to the side with a look of amusement then says as he removes the telephone from his pocket, "I almost forgot to take my medication. I take it after dinner."

He reaches into his sweatpants pocket and pulls out a pill bottle. In an overly dramatic movement, Jack fumbles the bottle, and it slips from his fingers landing in the floor board in front of Candace's seat. He looks over apologetically and asks, "Would you mind."

Candace looks down at the bottle and then at Jack's smiling face. The little voice in her psyche is screaming that something isn't right, but Candace brushes it off. After all, Jack has been so kind. She reaches down with her right hand and retrieves the bottle, reaching over to give it to Jack.

He reaches across, still smiling but something in his eyes has changed. It isn't the fatherly smile any longer. Candace sees it too late. His hand is quick, as he grabs her wrist, pulling her out of the seat and into the floor between the seats. She doesn't see the handcuff but feels the burst of pain as the steel strikes her wrist bone. Jack ratchets the handcuff down tight on her right wrist. He quickly fastens the other half of the cuff to the steering wheel with practiced efficiency. Candace looks up into eyes that exude pure evil and screams, "What the fuck do you think you're doing? Let me go!"

Jack laughs a hoarse laugh and says through clenched teeth, "Go ahead and scream all you want. The cab muffles sound, bitch. She tries to get her legs under her and strike him with her left hand, but he wards off the blow and slaps her across the face with a wicked backhand. Her ears ring and she tastes blood. He swivels his seat and partially stands, pulling his sweatpants down exposing his erection. "Now you stop that shit right now. You owe me for fuel and dinner and you're going to pay up. You're going to swallow everything I give you and like it, bitch."

Jack grabs Candace by the back of her head, lacing his fingers in her hair. She reaches up and tries to pry his fingers loose, but his grip is like iron. He shakes her head violently and yells, "I said to stop that! Now suck it!"

He pulls her face within inches of his throbbing penis. Candace whimpers and says, "Okay, okay, please don't hurt me. I'll do it."

He relaxes his grip slightly as he sits back down on the driver's seat. Smiling, he replies, "That's better. Now do it."

Candace feels as if she is going to vomit as the smell of his unwashed groin reaches her nose. She pulls her knees under her as if she is going to relent to his vial demand and at the same time reaches under the sweatshirt with her left hand, retrieving the scissors still hidden between her breasts.

She has the scissors out in a microsecond and jabs hard, aiming for the area between the base of Jack's penis and his scrotum. Jack shrieks and gags as if he is going to vomit then tries to stand but the sharp point of the scissors has him pinned to the seat. He releases his grip on her head and raises his hand to punch her, but she sees what is about to happen and screams, "If you hit me again, I will cut your balls completely off you rapist piece of shit!"

He opens his clenched hands and says shakily, "Okay, fuck, okay. Holy shit!"

She says through gritted teeth as she leans her weight on the scissors, twisting them slightly for good measure, "Take this fucking handcuff off my wrist. Do it!"

Jack reaches slowly with shaking hands and removes the ignition key. Finding the handcuff key on the ring, he removes the handcuff saying, "Alright, I did it, now be a good girl and pull those scissors out of my ball sack."

Candace looks up at Jack and smiles. "Sure daddy."

She raises her right hand quickly and hammers down on the scissors, driving them up to the hilt into the seat. Jack screams as his testicles are pierced. Candace stands quickly and grabs Jacks telephone from the dash, then scrambles from the truck. She runs. Candace runs as fast as she can across the parking lot and into the adjacent wooded area.

She stops only long enough to vomit, Jack's screams still echoing in her head. She knows that she must get away and get away quickly. She exits the other side of the wooded area, scurries under a barbed wire fence and continues on, crossing a pasture. Before long, she comes to a two-lane black top road and begins to walk through the inky blackness. The wind cuts through her sweatshirt, chilling her to the bone.

Candace comes to a sign which reads, "Welcome to Idania. We're really something special."

She continues until she sees the lights of a small motel with a flickering neon sign. Sandy's Inn boasts seven rooms and the best pot roast in Idania. The parking lot is almost empty with only two cars parked toward the end of the row of rooms. Candace steps through the glass door into the small lobby. It is dark with wood grained tile flooring and dark wood molding. The counter is made of the same wood, the scars indicate that this place has been here for many years. There is an overweight woman sitting behind the counter looking at a magazine. A cigarette burns in the ashtray near her hand.

Candace steps to the counter and tries to smile but her mouth hurts. The woman looks up, concern immediately on her face. "Can I help you, sweety?"

Candace smiles a half smile, feeling the swelling of her lip. "I need a room for the night. Can you help me?"

The woman smiles a knowing smile, "Sure honey. You know, you don't have to take that. He's got no right to treat you that way. Want me to call the law?"

Candace shakes her head, playing the role offered. "No, no police. I just slipped and hit the door on my way out. He didn't lay a hand on me."

The woman just nods her head. "Uh huh. I bet that door had knuckles. You got some ID?"

Candace thinks of Konrad and the tears she needs come forth. "No, I left it at the house when I ran out. I can't go back tonight."

The woman replies in a resigned tone, "Don't worry about it honey. Just sign the register. I'll put you in room one. Close to the office so I can keep an eye on you."

The woman looks at the register as Candace signs. "Alright Miss Mary Beth Pinkley, I'll get you some ice for that lip. Are you hungry?"

Candace looks down and shakes her head. "No, I don't think I can eat. My jaw hurts."

The woman shakes her head resignedly. "Well, sweety, that'll be twenty-five for the night if you can afford it. Call it the MTAA discount."

Candace looks up and replies quizzically, "MTAA?"

The woman smiles, her eyes bright with mirth. "Yeah, the 'I'm married to an asshole' discount."

She laughs and hands Candace a key. "Room number one darlin'. Checkout is at eleven."

Candace pays the woman, thanking her before walking out of the office with her small baggy of ice. She stops by a soda machine and inserts two dollars for a drink before heading to room number one, a short walk away. The room is small with a double bed, dresser and nightstand. The television on the dresser is secured with a cable. The television remote is secured to the night stand in like fashion. The carpet is light brown, matching the forest print bed spread nicely. Everything is out of date, but it is at least clean. Candace closes the door behind her and exhales deeply. She sits on the bed and genuine tears begin to fall as she thinks, "I've come full circle."

She regains control of herself and picks up Jack's telephone, swiping her finger across the screen. It is password protected, and she just doesn't have the energy to try and break the code. Candace throws the telephone in the trash and moves to the telephone located on the nightstand. She dials the number from memory, hoping that it hasn't been changed. One, two, three rings and a fragile female voice answers with a simple, "Hello?"

Candace takes a deep breath and says, "Mary Beth? It's me, Candace. Mary Beth? Are you there?"

Mary Beth Willows sighs and replies, "Yes Candace, I'm here. Are you alright? It's been ages."

She replies, her voice breaking, "Mary Beth, I'm at a motel called Sandy's Inn in Idania and I'm in trouble. I really need your help. Can you come and get me? Please."

Candace sobs as she waits for Mary Beth's reply. After a long pause Mary Beth replies, "Of course dear. I'm on my way."

Back in Arlington, Horace MacGill sits on the sofa in his apartment and takes a long drink from the glass tumbler full of bourbon. He closes his eyes, enjoying the burning sensation as it makes its way down his throat. He looks out the sliding glass doors and thinks of his retirement. He thinks of Darci and smiles as he thinks, "A kindred spirit. My kindred spirit."

He'd always pictured the chalet that the Regents were providing as being a place of solitude and loneliness but, he just might have someone to share it with. As his mind wanders through a future he hadn't planned on, his telephone rings. Horace answers it in his usual manner, "Yes, good news I hope."

The fragile voice on the other end of the line replies, "She just called. I'm going to pick her up now. What do you want me to do?"

Horace smiles as he replies, "Just do as you always have Mary Beth, welcome her home."

Chapter Thirty-One

General Alejandro Cuispe stands at the window of his penthouse apartment and looks out over the New York skyline. His home, the place he has resided in over the long months in this city which never sleeps, is seventy-six floors up with a view of Central Park and the East River. He pulls the silk robe closed over his midsection and tightens the belt, flexing his feet in the lamb's skin slippers that he wears.

The city, his favorite, seems much cleaner from up here in the sky, high above the people, the vermin. He thinks of them and decides it is fitting, him up here and them down there. It has been two years since he was approached by the Regents. Two years of accepting menial placements at the World Health Organization until he was finally moved like so many chess pieces into the influenza advisory role and now this. This final indignity and Alejandro Cuispe, descendent of royalty will not accept it. He balls his thick hands into fists and thinks, "I know too much. They can't make me take this vaccine. I won't do it. I won't."

It was as if a mass insanity had taken over the organization after the riot in Times Square due to the dwindling supply of vaccine doses. The mandate had come from the top. "Every soul at WHO would be vaccinated. No exceptions and no exemptions." WHO would set the standard for the world and be one hundred percent vaccinated within two weeks.

What tortures Alejandro is that he held a pivotal role in obtaining support for the world vaccination program as it currently exists. This was his sole purpose and usefulness to the Regents. His job now accomplished, he is to be treated exactly as the masses, as so many sheep. The message from the North American Regent had arrived through the usual channels. An unmarked envelope sliding from under his door, making a hiss as it crossed the parquet floor. Inside was the simple yet unmistakable message which read, "Do not draw attention to yourself. Comply."

Along with the note was a prescription with unlimited refills for propranolol. The medication would be necessary to keep his pulse rate down. Tears had filled his eyes when he had seen it. It was the irrevocable pronouncement of a life sentence. Once he had accepted the vaccination, he would need the drug forever. Alejandro has heard the saying many times that ignorance is bliss. He is anything but ignorant, being an insider from the start.

He knows a high pulse rate is what starts the chain reaction and once it starts, there is no stopping it. He could run and had even considered that course of action, but where do you go to escape those who control the world? Alejandro realized the minute the thought had crossed his mind that he wouldn't make it a day before they found him. He sighs resignedly and leaves the living room, walks through the kitchen full of gleaming cooking utensils and stainless-steel appliances never used, entering the bedroom and finally, the master bath.

He looks around the white marble bathroom and senses the coldness. In this realization, he thinks, "I really should have decorated."

The garden tub is full of hot, soapy water, calling him to step in, which he does after removing his clothes, folding them and putting them on the sink. There is one candle at the end of the tub, its flame burning like a beacon to entertain the consciousness of the damned. Alejandro concentrates on the flame and calms himself, first seeing the flame and then mentally moving inside of it.

The warmth encircles him like his mother's embrace and his eyes fill with tears as he thinks of her, long dead. He closes his eyes and enjoys the warmth, feeling his pulse quicken as his veins and arteries expand in response to the heat. He thinks of the soldier's minute and realizes that this is what it must have felt like before charging from a trench into a hail of machinegun fire for honor alone. Alejandro picks up the straight razor and turns it in front of his face, marveling at how the candle flame dances on the surface of the razor-sharp blade.

His movements are precise, and the blade moves through the flesh of his inner thigh meeting little resistance. The only pain being the initial cut through the layer of nerves toward the surface of the leg, then just a dull, deep ache as the femoral artery is finally found and severed. Alejandro knows the second he has found his target because the water immediately turns crimson. He lays the razor on the side of the tub and concentrates on the candle as his life quickly drains away with each beat of his heart. He takes note of his racing pulse in the last moments before blessed sleep takes him and smiles as he thinks, "The Regents be damned."

Back in Green River, Konrad Pearce sits at the small mauve colored table with matching chairs and waits. Several other patients sit around the room at tables which look just like the one at which Konrad currently finds himself. The air is cool in the big room and Konrad feels the chill distinctly through the paper-thin scrubs he was issued after being strip searched on his arrival.

The scrubs, a distinctive marker in this place that he is a suicide risk and requires one on one monitoring at all times, do nothing to insulate from the constant chill. Henry, his constant companion, stands by the entrance to the commons area watching, his eyes never leaving Konrad for a second. He looks at the man and imagines the cruelty he might be capable of if given the order. Their eyes meet and the two men stare at each other, Konrad studying Henry and Henry looking right through Konrad.

He remembers the advice he was given by Jamison and thinks, "He's just waiting to knot a sheet around my neck."

His thoughts are interrupted when he sees Gloria and David approaching the commons through the security glass. Henry opens the door and in true David Smith style, David barges through two steps ahead of Gloria, a scowl on his face. Konrad thinks in the brief seconds before David reaches his table, "How in the fuck did Jennifer survive a childhood with this asshole."

As they reach his table, Konrad stands and smiles a rueful smile, "Hello David, Gloria."

Gloria, full of emotion circles the table and embraces Konrad. "Oh Konrad, we're so sorry this has happened. How are you?"

Konrad looks over Gloria's shoulder into David's eyes and sees no compassion there before whispering, 'I'm fine. This is all a big mistake. I'll be out of here before you know it. Please, let's all just sit down. I don't want to draw any attention."

They all sit and there is a brief pause before David begins to speak, Gloria looks down at the table, knowing what is coming and powerless to stop it. "You'll be out before we know it? You do understand what an indefinite commitment order is, don't you? I mean, Konrad, after what you did. It's all over the news, local and national. As for drawing attention to yourself, hell, you've done a bang-up job of that."

Konrad leans forward and speaks in a low urgent tone, "What I did? What are they saying? I've done nothing David. That's what I'm trying to tell you."

Gloria interrupts, "Konrad, honey, the news is reporting that after your interview with Dan Kingman, you went completely berserk. They had to call the police. They said that you were rambling about people chasing you. Honey, don't you remember?"

Konrad runs his hands through his hair in exasperation. "That's a lie Gloria. I didn't do any of those things."

He leans forward and whispers, "There were people chasing me and they caught up with me at the Kingman interview. He sold me out. They're the ones that gave me to the police. They were dirty cops who were working for the people chasing me."

David can take no more and leaning in says, "Dammit Konrad, enough. Are you listening to yourself? You've lost it. There are no secret figures after you and there's no big fucking conspiracy. You've had a mental breakdown. The sooner you acknowledge that, the better."

Konrad replies through gritted teeth, "I'm as sane as you are, you sanctimonious prick."

David stands and puts both hands on the table. "You're a fucking disgrace, a coward. I'm just glad Jen isn't here to see this."

Konrad stands suddenly, the chair sliding backward and falling on its side. "Don't you throw Jennifer up in my face."

Gloria stands and puts her hand on Konrad's arm. "For God's sake, both of you, stop!"

The two men glare at each other from opposite sides of the table, neither one willing to concede. The tension is broken by Henry who appears at Konrad's side. With a sideways grin he says, "I'm afraid the visit is over folks. Doctor Pearce has a counseling session scheduled in a few minutes. It's time to say goodbye."

Gloria moves in quickly and hugs Konrad tightly whispering, "We'll always be here for you Konrad."

Konrad looks over her shoulder at David and mouths the words, "Fuck you."

David's upper lip quivers as he says, "Time to go Gloria."

Konrad and Henry remain at the table and watch as David walks out, Gloria a few steps behind. They do not look back. Henry leans over and whispers, "Looked like you might've needed a little help Doc. Doctor Cagwell wants a word."

Konrad looks over at Henry, eyebrows raised and replies, "Imagine that."

Henry motions for Konrad to start walking and says, "After you Doc."

It is apparent that Konrad doesn't have a choice. It is a short walk to the second floor where Cindy Cagwell's office is located. There is no conversation between Konrad and Henry on the way. They make it to her office and Henry steps past Konrad, knocking twice. Henry opens the door after hearing Doctor Cagwell say, "Come in."

The office is small and unbefitting a director as far as Konrad is concerned. Several bookshelves line the wall, all jam packed. There are two office chairs positioned in front of a standard metal desk. The walls are adorned with certificates of achievement and credentials in cheap frames. Cindy Cagwell sits behind her desk and smiles as Konrad enters. She looks at Henry and says, "You can wait outside. Doctor Pearce and I will be fine, but don't go too far. This won't take long."

Henry nods and looks at Konrad as he replies, "I'll be right outside Doctor."

Henry closes the door, and Konrad sits in one of the metal office chairs. They aren't made for comfort. Konrad looks around and says, "Nice office."

Cindy smiles and leans her head slightly to the side. "Not really, but we never know what the future might hold, do we."

Konrad nods his head slowly and replies with a polite grin, "Is that your compensation for participating in this travesty? You get a big promotion and an office to go with it?"

Cindy laughs and replies, "Interesting question, but I'd rather talk about you Konrad. Is it alright if I call you Konrad?"

Konrad nods slightly. "Fine. Can I call you Cindy?"

She shakes her head slightly. "I'd rather you didn't, therapist, patient relationship. I'm sure you understand."

Konrad nods. "Alright Doctor, why am I here?"

He leans back in his chair and crosses his arms, waiting. Doctor Cagwell also leans back. "I was watching the cameras. Your visit didn't seem to go well. How does that make you feel? I mean, everyone thinking you're unbalanced. Of course, your interview with Mr. Kingman didn't help matters. Kind of contradictory, don't you think? The vaccine works but isn't safe. It will save millions but also might kill millions. Which is it Konrad?"

Konrad looks to the side and answers tightly. "Both. It wasn't tested, but it works. What can I say?"

She raises her eyebrows and replies, "Konrad, Emmer Pharma has verified the testing of this vaccine and even provided the clinical trial documentation. Don't you think it's about time we start you on your journey to wellness? Would you consider that your current troubles might be related to the loss of your wife and daughter?"

He leans in toward Doctor Cagwell. "My 'current troubles' as you put it are the result of trying to bring a conspiracy into the light. Don't patronize me with this therapy crap. I'm being held prisoner here to shut me up. It's as simple as that and you're a part of it."

Doctor Cagwell looks down and smiles before staring hard into Konrad's eyes. "Well, that is unfortunate Konrad. With that attitude, I would suggest that you get comfortable. Until you accept the fact that there is no conspiracy against you, I'm afraid treatment can't even begin and without treatment, you'll never leave this place."

The realization hits Konrad at that moment. He stands and says, "Well if we're through here Doctor, I have some thinking to do."

She smiles a disarming smile and stands. "Of course, Konrad. Go back to your room and think about what we've talked about today. Remember, I'm always here to help you."

He turns to leave, but before he reaches the door, he looks over his shoulder and asks, "Am I going to die here?"

Doctor Cagwell chuckles. "That is not likely Konrad. It seems that you have a guardian angel."

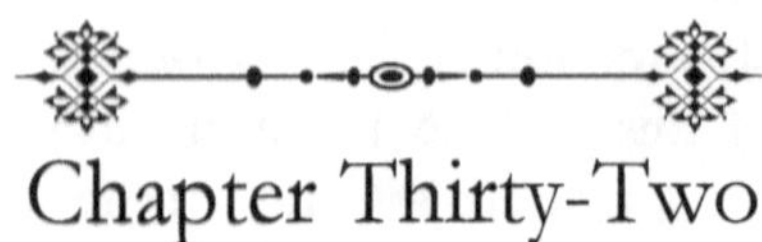

Chapter Thirty-Two

Darci carries the last of several bags of groceries into the house and puts them on the kitchen table. The grocery order, paid for with the card given to her by Horace, is slightly more than she usually buys on her monthly trip to the grocery, but she thinks, "What the hell, I might as well enjoy the benefits of being owned by that asshole."

That is how she has felt since fate put her in Horace's way. Darci feels like he owns her now, but had she declined his offer, she has no doubt that she would have been "disappeared," never to be seen again. She stands in the kitchen and looks at the plastic grocery bags and asks herself, "What fucking choice did you have Darci? You survived and that's all you can ask for in that situation."

It has been a month since she took the card and the telephone number from Horace's pale, cold hand. Four weeks of sitting in her home and brooding over her situation. A situation in which there seems to be no escape. After many hours of plotting and reflection on various options, she knows in her heart that Dan was right and without some type of outside intervention, she has no way to escape from the monster that seems to have plans for the rest of her life.

Horace has been in contact with her twice since they first met. Both times were to seemingly check on her welfare and discuss 'the future'. As she puts the food away into various cupboards and the fridge, she talks to herself, "Fucking plans. How can I be a 'companion' to that monster? I can't stand the thought of being in the same room as the bastard. So, what are you willing to do to survive, Darci? Live the rest of your life in a mountain chalet with a fucking reptile? God help me."

She thinks back over the telephone conversations between the two and wonders what caused Horace to pick her. What made him single her out? Was it the fact that she was a loner at heart? Her grit? The fact that she had no family ties? The questions were endless and maddening. Horace had referred to her as a kindred spirit, a companion, never as a "lover." The thought of being with him sexually turns her stomach, but

Darci doesn't think that's what he wants from her. At least, she vehemently hopes that isn't the case. She puts a pot of coffee on and pictures the barrel of a gun in her mouth thinking, "Suicide would be infinitely more attractive than crawling into bed with that monster."

She mentally files it away as a viable option and pours herself a cup of coffee. Her telephone rings and she answers blandly, "Hello."

A familiar voice comes through the phone. "Darcy, it's Dan. I was just calling to check on you. How are you holding up?"

She chuckles, "Kind of out of character for you, isn't it? What do you really want?"

Dan stammers, "Well, I was just wondering about you. The Personnel Department is asking whether you're coming back. Are you? They said that they haven't been able to get in contact with you and are considering letting you go. I guess I was a last-ditch effort to make contact."

Darci answers in a muted tone, "I know they've been trying to reach me. I don't see a need to talk to them really. You know what my situation is better than anyone. Just tell them that I won't be back. Tell them whatever the hell you want. It makes no difference."

She ends the call before he can respond and takes a sip of her coffee then looks around the kitchen and pictures a life without purpose. She sees the gun again and must force the image from her mind. Darci finishes the coffee and then goes into the hall bathroom to pee. She returns to the kitchen and freezes in the doorway, her breath caught in her throat. Sitting at the table is the middle-aged blonde, her dead eyes showing an uncharacteristic mirth. She says in a monotone voice, "I hope you don't mind Darci. I poured myself a cup. The coffee is delicious, please, have a seat. You and I have something to discuss."

Darci moves slowly into the kitchen, her eyes scanning the rest of the room. The blonde reading the question in Darci's eyes says, "He's not here. We're alone, now, please sit."

She takes a deep breath and calms herself before moving to the table and retrieving her cup, pours herself a refill before sitting opposite the blonde. Darci looks at the other woman and remembers the swift brutality that the assassin is capable of. She raises her eyebrows and asks, "Well, what do we have to discuss?"

The blonde taps a file folder on the table which Darci just now notices and says, "Would you like to have your life back Darci, pitiful as it was?"

Darci isn't sure if this is a test, trick or something else so, decides to be noncommittal. "I'm not sure what you mean."

The blonde laughs a laugh that raises the hair on the back of Darci's neck. "You're not sure what I mean? That's rich. No one knows that I'm here Darci. At least, no one that really matters. The person who holds the ultimate power of your life, or death is interested to know, would you like your life back?"

Darci nods her head slowly, her eyes never leaving the assassin's. The blonde pushes the file across the table and says, "Read it. Read it slowly and memorize every detail. You know Darci, you've been taken notice of as a person who might be able to solve a very unique problem. Read the file."

Darci opens the file slowly and gasps as she sees the contents. She begins to read every line, committing it all to memory. After all, that's a skill she had to have as a combat reporter. Remembering details of incidents which happened in microseconds while under extreme stress. Darci was good at what she did. It takes Darci only thirty minutes to read the contents of the file, the blonde studying her with those dead eyes the whole time. She looks up, tears in her eyes. "But how can I? I mean, how do you expect me to...."

Her voice trails off. The blonde reaches across the table and collects the file. "Your value Darci is your resourcefulness. That trait has not gone unnoticed. The offer is a simple one, really. You buy back your life with this one task. I just need an answer. Think about it carefully because you're now dealing with the devil herself. Make no mistake, once you make the deal, it is irreversible."

Darci looks into the dead eyes of the woman sitting across from her and feels the bile rise in her throat. She nods slowly. The blonde smiles a flat smile and reaches into the pocket of her overcoat, briefly exposing the butt of the large pistol concealed in its shoulder holster. She tosses a cell phone across the table. "The number is programmed in. You'll only be making one call on the phone. Make it when the task is complete. Do you have any questions?"

Darci looks at the phone and shakes her head, a bewildered look in her eyes. The blonde nods as she reaches into the other pocket of her coat and pulls a different phone out. She dials and speaks into the telephone, "She understands and has accepted the assignment."

The assassin stands and asks, "Want some advice?"

Darci nods. The blonde looks around the room before looking into Darci's eyes. "Relax and play your role until the time comes. Don't over think it. You'll know when the time is right. Trust me."

Then she turns and walks out of the back door without saying another word. Darci tastes the bile again, runs to the bathroom and vomits.

Five hundred miles away in Atlanta, Georgia, Warren Densin sits in his office and chews on his thumbnail. He picks up the business card with the telephone number that he has memorized, contemplating the finality of his intended actions. Over the many weeks, it has become harder and harder for him to look at himself in the mirror because he knows what he will see there is not the man Sandra deserves. Warren has fallen deeply in love and plans to ask her to marry him. He's just been waiting for the right time. He thinks as he flips the card through his fingers, "Time to unload the baggage. I can't marry her with this hanging over my head. It's time that I ended it."

He dials the number on the card and Horace's familiar voice answers, "Warren, it has been a while. Good news I hope."

Warren stammers, "Well, I think so. I'm going to ask Sandra to marry me."

Horace chuckles, "Well, congratulations Warren, but why are you reporting this wonderful news to me?"

There is a long pause and then Warren blurts out, "I can't work with you anymore. I can't be a part of this, whatever 'this' is. I just can't. I don't want to start my marriage in a lie."

There is silence on the line and Warren continues quickly, "Please understand."

Horace exhales audibly before replying in a low tone, "Warren, you don't work with me. You work 'for' me. What a disappointment. Are you sure about this because every action has consequences. Have you forgotten our first meeting? No Warren, you aren't quitting anything. I own you, so get your fucking head on straight."

Warren feels the heat rise into his face as he blurts out, "Consequences? Like what happened to Leonard? I know you had something to do with that you son of a bitch, but I'm through being scared. Do you hear me? I'm not afraid anymore. I'm going to come clean at the weekly briefing tomorrow and then I'm going to resign."

Horace replies in almost a snake like hiss, "I see. What a disappointment you are Warren. I'll be in touch."

The line goes dead, and Warren feels the urgent need to urinate. His pulse is racing, and he is sweating profusely as he thinks, "Oh fuck, fuck, what have I done? What the hell was I thinking? As if that monster would have even an ounce of gratitude for what I've already done for him. I'm a dead man."

That night Warren goes home and confesses everything to Sandra. He shows her the ring while the shock of what he's told her is still on her face. She stands from the couch and walks across the room without giving Warren an answer. As she turns to face him, she says, "So, let me get this straight. You've been working for this what, secret agent type, secretly because he has something on you? What does he have Warren?"

Warren shakes his head. "What they have is bullshit. They hacked my phone and put some bad stuff on it. I don't want to tell you what but I'm innocent. I didn't want our marriage to start with secrets Sandra, but now, they've threatened you too. You must leave honey. Go someplace safe for a while until this blows over. I don't want to know where, but you must go."

She looks at him, tears brimming and replies, "Marriage? I love you Warren, but as far as I can see, you're going to be unemployed as of tomorrow and you want me to just up and leave? Throw away my life?"

Warren looks at her from the couch, desperation in his eyes. "Please Sandra, I know I can make this work. I have to get free from this guy and the people he works for. Afterwards, we can leave and go someplace he'll never find us."

Sandra looks at the floor, her voice thick. "Warren, you're forgetting one thing, he found you the first time."

She walks into the bedroom and starts packing.

The next day, Warren walks into his office, straightens his tie and makes his way to the large conference room where members of the news media are waiting for the weekly briefing. He makes his way to the small podium feeling lifeless inside. Sandra packed and left him without even a parting kiss. If any of the reporters had bothered to look into Warren's eyes, they would have noticed the deep sadness there. He stands in front of the small crowd of regulars and fills his lungs with air, letting it out slowly thinking, "Take a few minutes Warren. There's no hurry."

He looks over at Joel, who looks back with the usual concern on his face. Joel mouths the word, "Well?"

Warren smiles thinking, "I've got a surprise for you this morning, you sanctimonious prick. It's all going to be on me, huh. We'll see about that."

He looks around the room at the reporters with disdain and says, "Good morning, everyone. I'm going to start the briefing this morning with a statement, then, if you have any questions Mr. Smith will be glad to answer them. After all, he is ultimately responsible for everything which transpires in this office."

Joel's head snaps around to look at Warren so quickly, perspiration flies off. The fear in his eyes is readily apparent. Warren looks directly at him with a look of menace as he continues, "I'm sure that you have all seen the interview with Doctor Konrad Pearce regarding the influenza vaccine and the Thai strain. It is true that Doctor Pearce did try to contact the CDC and make us aware of his concerns. His efforts were ignored and even actively thwarted."

Gasps from the reporters can be heard as twenty cell phones are ripped from pockets to get the information to editors across the country. Joel steps forward and screams, "What the hell do you think you're doing! No, listen everyone, he's crazy. He's lying!"

Warren screams, "Quiet! Now, Mr. Smith will be glad to take questions."

Warren turns to leave but a voice from the crowd can be heard yelling, "Mr. Densin! Mr. Densin! I have a question for you!"

Warren stops and turns to look at the crowd as a middle-aged man, well dressed in a suit and tie walks up to the podium. Warren looks at the man as he stands there filled with self-confidence and exuding authority. There is a badge hanging from his breast pocket. Warren nods toward him, a cold feeling in his gut. The man takes another step toward Warren. The other reporters, having noticed him now, have fallen silent, the drama thickening. "Mr. Densin, I wonder if you would place your hands behind your back? You're under arrest."

Joel Smith falls to the floor, blood streaming from his nose.

Chapter Thirty-Three

Mary Beth Willows stands at the old gas stove in her small bungalow located in Fort Collins. It is well before sun-up, but Mary Beth has always been an early riser and doesn't mind the change in her usually solitary morning routine. She stands in her flannel robe and expertly flips the eggs in the skillet. "Would you like cheese on your eggs Joshua?"

The man seated at the table smiles exposing a gleaming set of teeth with unusually large incisors. He answers her in a smooth sounding voice. So smooth, it is almost a hiss. "I would love cheese on my eggs Mary Beth. Thank you so much for cooking me breakfast like this and for taking such good care of Candace."

Mary Beth turns and looks at the man she knows as "Joshua," smiling, she replies quickly, "Oh, I've been cooking breakfast early and taking care of Candace off and on for a long time. She's like a daughter to me."

When Horace had first approached Mary Beth at the diner, she used to wait tables at, he had introduced himself as Joshua. A benefactor with unlimited resources, his only intention to help those who needed it and Candace needed it badly. He also knew what Mary Beth needed more than anything in the world. He'd told her that Candace was on the run again and might show up on Mary Beth's doorstep like she had so many times before. The proof of his amazing generosity was the payment of all her debts and a sizeable lifetime annuity so that she could finally retire. It was truly a miracle because, in truth, Mary Beth Willows was tired to the bone. He'd only asked one thing in return, "If our girl does contact you, let me know so that I can help her out of the trouble she's found herself in."

A small favor, right in line with what Mary Beth had been doing for what seemed like her whole life, helping Candace out of trouble. Mary Beth had sat with "Joshua" for nearly an hour, just talking. His looks were a little off putting but, he was such a caring, thoughtful man and now, here he is, her guardian angel, descended from Heaven, only to land in her cozy, warm kitchen. As Mary Beth sets the breakfast plate in front of Horace, Candace appears in the doorway of the kitchen, her black hair framing her face in a tussled way. "Mary Beth, I smelled bacon."

As Candace finishes this sentence, she freezes, her eyes locked on Horace. He smiles a relaxed smile with concern in his eyes. "Good morning, Candace. I thought we might have breakfast together. Please come and sit with me so that we can talk."

Mary Beth looks at Candace and sees the fear in her eyes, then into Horace's eyes, seeing the concern there. "Candace honey, this is Joshua. He's here to help us."

Candace starts to turn but Horace says in a low, firm tone, "No Candace. It's time to stop running. Konrad is waiting for you."

She turns back to face him with a look of surprise. "Konrad? He's alive? Where?"

Mary Beth sits down at the table, her body tense and takes a sip of coffee, her hand trembling slightly. "Konrad? I don't understand Candace. Your boss at the lab? What does he have to do with this?"

Candace looks at Mary Beth apologetically and shakes her head. "I'm so sorry I've brought this mess to your home. This man isn't who he seems to be."

And then to Horace, "How do I know you have Konrad. How can I be sure he's even alive."

Horace eases back in his chair and replies, "Candace, you're just going to have to trust me on this. I've been more than reasonable. Konrad is safe in Green River and I'm here to take you to him. It's that simple."

She looks at Mary Beth, then back at Horace. "I'm not going anywhere with you, you fucking monster."

Mary Beth stands quickly. "Candace! Joshua is just here to help you! He's the reason that I don't have to slave away in the restaurant ever again. I'll not have you talk to him like that. Now sit down and here him out."

Candace looks around the kitchen and seeing no one else, slowly moves in and sits at the table. Mary Beth takes a deep breath and smiles, "Good. Now, would you like some breakfast?"

Candace shakes her head slowly, never taking her eyes from Horace. He puts both hands on the table palms down. "Candace dear, I am here to help you believe it or not, because you helped me, and I am a man who knows the meaning of gratitude. Right now, Konrad Pearce is safe and sound under my complete and utter protection, just as Mary Beth is. I would appreciate your cooperation. If I don't have it, I'm afraid things here and in Green River will have to go another way."

Candace remains silent, her gaze never leaves Horace's face. He sighs almost inaudibly and says slowly, "I need for you to at least nod that you understand Candace. The future now rests in your hands. I need to know that you understand."

Mary Beth is silent as she watches a drama play out in her kitchen that she has no understanding of. Time stands still in the small, warm kitchen as Candace grasps the full meaning of Horace's words. Then, she slowly stands and looks at Mary Beth with tear filled eyes saying, "I'll go and get my things."

The next day and eight hundred and forty miles away from Mary Beth Willows' tiny home, Konrad Pearce is escorted from his room inside the secure perimeter of Saint Mary's Behavioral Rehabilitation Center to a private visitation room used exclusively for visits with legal counsel. Lyle, Konrad's ever-present companion on Henry's days off walks closely with his hand lightly touching Konrad's elbow. It is a subtle signal, letting Konrad know that he isn't a free man. As they approach the room, he sees Cindy Cagwell standing near the heavily reinforced door with her hands folded in front of her and the ever present demure smile. They reach her, Konrad forcing a smile and Lyle nodding. She leans in toward Konrad and whispers whimsically, "Good luck."

Lyle unlocks the door and Konrad steps inside. He hears the tumblers of the lock engage, snapping him from the mental fog brought on by long hours of forced isolation. The complete lack of hope Konrad has felt since his counseling session with Cindy Cagwell disappears in an instant when he looks into Candace's eyes. A sob escapes her as she stands and moves around the table toward him. Konrad rushes to meet her, catching her in a tight embrace. She whispers into his ear, "Oh my darling, I was so worried. I didn't know if you were even alive."

Konrad tightens the embrace and kisses her cheek then looks past her to the man still seated at the small round table. "It's going to be alright Candace. I love you."

She sobs, "I love you too."

Horace stands and says, "This is all very touching, but I really must interrupt. I have a plane to catch, so please, have a seat. We have a lot to discuss, Konrad."

Candace steps away from Konrad, a look of warning in her eyes and moves back to the chair she was originally sitting in. Horace motions for Konrad to sit in the chair on the opposite side of the table and says with a smile, "Please."

Konrad moves to the chair and sits, his eyes never leaving Horace, who also sits with a long sigh. "I don't mind telling you Konrad, I am absolutely exhausted. Before we start, I want to let you know that Candace is here to demonstrate my sincerity. I am a man of my word, but she isn't here to participate in our little parley. The decisions you must make have to be yours and yours alone. Those are the rules."

Konrad looks into Candace's tear-filled eyes then at Horace and nods slowly. He looks around the room and asks, "What do you want? You obviously hold all the cards, so, what is it?"

Horace makes the sound of a hissing chuckle. "Right to the point, I like that. We've been watching you for many months Konrad. You should feel privileged that the individuals I'm associated with chose you. You, out of all the scientists in America. Do you have any idea what an honor that is?"

Konrad sits forward and replies, "Chose me for what? To ruin my life? Lock me up like a criminal? Ruin Candace's life? Please tell me because there has to be some meaning too this."

Horace smiles exposing the large canine teeth. "I needed you Konrad, to bring order to the world. A man who has always craved order in chaos. A man of science with a dream of saving humanity. A man people would listen to."

Konrad bows his head. "I don't understand."

Horace sighs. "Don't you see it Konrad. We have accomplished something truly amazing that will change the world. We've vaccinated most of the world's population in a matter of months. We did it with a vaccination that will end needless wars and bring humanity to the human race. Humans can now be guided in one direction by those who know what is best for them. We have initiated the creation of a utopia."

Konrad looks at Horace and smiles. "You're insane. It's just a flu vaccine designed to combat a deadly strain. That's it. We conquered influenza. It won't change humanity."

Horace laughs as he continues, "That is where you're wrong. Have you considered what a marvelous discovery the nanobots were, Konrad? A programmable protein molecule so small it can be placed into a vaccine and enter a human cell. Have you wondered what else it might be programmed to accomplish? Humans are unpredictable with their opinions and beliefs. Imagine a human whose actions were not influenced by such things. Imagine someone who could and would be guided through life gladly."

Konrad sits up in his chair and looks directly at Horace. "What did you do?"

Horace moves his head to the side slightly and replies with a slight grin, "I didn't do anything. You and Candace did it, and beautifully I might add. Oh, I gave you the tools, but make no mistake, it was your decision."

He looks at Horace with hate in his eyes and replies tightly, "We did nothing but try to save people from the Thai strain and you know it."

Konrad pauses and then it's as if a light comes on in his eyes. "The Thai strain. I know it was real. I saw it. That was you?"

Horace laughs out loud. "You're getting it now. Wonderful!"

Konrad runs his hands through his hair. "And you released that on humanity? You're a fucking madman."

Horace sits back in his chair. "Konrad, I'm not a total asshole. No, the Thai strain only existed in your lab and you, or I should say Candace did exactly as we'd hoped you would. You followed your dream and in so doing, told the world about the strain. Don't you see Konrad, you were the one who sowed the panic. Confused the sheep as it were. Confused sheep always follow the herd, the shepherd."

Konrad looks at the table as he asks flatly, "What else do the nanobots do?"

Horace leans forward and smiles an evil smile. "They stop human aggression and the will to resist, Konrad. They bring order to the world, something you've craved your whole life. That's why you became a scientist, isn't it? The purity of the process? The nanobots take control of the oldest part of the human brain, the amygdala. Burdock was fond of Latin and named it 'the almond' of all things. Think of it, no more aggression. No more resistance to order. A passive human population ready to be guided into the future."

Konrad looks at Candace, tears in his eyes. "My God, what have we done?"

She shakes her head but before she can speak, Horace says, "No Candace, you know the rules."

Then to Konrad, "You've saved humanity Konrad. That's what you've done."

Konrad shakes his head and replies, grinning slightly, "You won't be able to control everyone, you bastard. Each person's physiology is different. The bots won't be able to subdue every person. Not 'every' person. Don't you see that?"

Horace sighs deeply and replies, "An astute observation. That variable was considered and the bots, of course, served as our answer. An almond that refuses to be tamed will result in a fatal aneurysm, plain and simple. You'll need to know that before you make your decision. A high pulse rate is the trigger, the chain reaction irreversible. Now, I really must be getting along, and I can't have you muddying the waters in the future so, you'll be vaccinated. Do you understand? You will take the vaccination. I'm not an ungrateful person and to tell you the truth, we couldn't have accomplished this without you, but we must know you'll stay in line."

Konrad stands and asks, "And if I don't?"

Horace looks into Konrad's eyes with a cold stare. "You should know that whatever decision you make for yourself will also be made for Candace. Your futures are now completely intertwined. If you refuse, I'll have to go another way. You need to understand that."

Konrad sits back down and looks into Candace's eyes, seeing the truth there. Without looking away, he nods. Horace stands and with a sardonic grin says, "Very well, I'll leave you two love birds to live your lives."

He starts to move toward the door but stops and puts his hand on Konrad's shoulder. "I gave her the same option and she didn't hesitate. You're a lucky man Konrad. She truly loves you."

Horace moves toward the door and knocks twice. Konrad says quickly, "Wait. Who are you?"

Horace turns with a sardonic grin and sighs another deep sigh, "I suppose it makes no difference now. My name, Konrad, is Horace MacGill but that really isn't important, is it? What really matters is what I'm capable of."

He chuckles, turns and walks out.

A week later Darci stands in the luxurious mountain chalet located just outside of Telluride, Colorado, which she now must call home. Horace had called her and informed her that it was time for them to start their retirement together. Her bag was already packed. A short flight and then a long drive through the snow-covered mountains had brought the two to this oasis fifty miles from nowhere. She looks around the expansive kitchen with all the modern conveniences and marvels at the extravagance.

Under other circumstances, she would have been thrilled. The house, decorated in pine accents with large windows all around, is big enough for ten people to live comfortably. The family room is furnished with heavy leather furniture and several quilted throws. All the bedrooms are furnished in a like manner. Every aspect of the chalet is a reflection of opulence. A heated pool adorns the back of the house with a Jacuzzi on the deck.

She looks out at the snowy countryside, appreciating the picturesque view thinking, "Such wasted beauty on a prison."

Her worst fears had not been realized and to her relief, Horace indeed just wanted a companion. Another soul to share his loneliness. Darci has her own room which is as big as her whole house back in Green River. She already misses the familiarity. A bottle of bourbon stands on the granite countertop along with a crystal tumbler. For a week, since arriving, Darci has been listening to Horace's self-aggrandizing rants about the new "utopia" he has created.

His plan, or so he says, is to wait for the societal change at the chalet which he has assured her over and over is coming. Once the world has fallen in line, he and Darci are to begin living the "good life." As extravagant as the chalet is, the place doesn't run on its own. So far, the two cohabitants have worked together with household duties. The arrangement might not be so bad if it weren't for the fact, Darci absolutely despises the man she is being forced to live with. She wasn't given many options.

This morning, Darci had made breakfast while Horace had used the small hatchet by the fireplace to split some kindling and get a fire going. The chill had left the air inside long ago, being replaced by comfortable warmth. After breakfast, Horace as usual had stepped out onto the deck in his parka where he has spent every morning sipping bourbon since arriving. Darci pours from the bottle, her hand trembling as she hears Horace say in a voice loud enough to be heard from the deck, "Darci, I'm still waiting on my refill."

She picks up the tumbler of bourbon and wills her hand to be steady as she walks across the expansive family room toward the double doors leading to the deck. On her way to the doors, she walks close to the fireplace and picks up the small hatchet which lies on top of the kindling pile. It is small, weighing only one and a half pounds. As she walks it dangles limply at her right side. She walks numbly, stopping at the door to put a smile on her face. As she steps out, the icy wind cuts through her sweater like a knife. Her grip tightens on the hatchet, but her arm remains relaxed. She walks quickly and stands just behind Horace's left shoulder saying, "Here you are Horace, just the way you like it."

He turns slightly, smiling, "Thank you. I'm so glad you decided to come. Would you look at that view? Our lives together are just going to keep getting better and better from here."

Horace takes a deep sip of the bourbon, enjoying the burning sensation as it makes its way down his throat. He lets out a deep, appreciative sigh. Darci smiles back and putting her left hand on his shoulder says, "I'm certain they will Horace."

He continues to look out over the snowy mountains and says, "You know Darci, I hope that we can get to know each other. I mean, I really don't know who you are, as a person. I want that."

Darci looks at Horace with dead eyes, and softly replies, her voice lacking any emotion, "It really doesn't matter who I am. Not really. What matters is what I'm capable of."

Horace's body tenses but he is too late. The arc of the hatchet is small but swift as the blade comes down striking him at the apex of the skull. The momentum burying the blade to the handle, the tip of the blade resting deep in the brain. His body jerks as he drops the bourbon and spasms. Horace tries to turn his head to look at Darci, but the handle of the hatchet wedges against the chair.

Blood pours from his nose and mouth, a deep gurgle emanating from his throat. Darci backs up quickly and watches Horace's death throws numbly until he ceases to move, his sightless eyes still staring at the beautiful mountain vista. She turns and walks back into the house, retrieving the telephone from a shoe in her closet and dials the preprogrammed number. It is answered after one ring by a monotone female voice. Darci says, "It's done."

She disconnects the call and throws the telephone into the fireplace then goes to the bedroom and packs her bag. Her mind is racing as she runs into Horace's room. Opening the closet, she finds the safe and pulls on the handle, finding it locked. She curses inwardly, seeing the biometric readers that will require Horace's fingerprints before it can be opened. She runs to the kitchen and grabbing the meat cleaver from the knife block heads for the deck thinking, "Oh fuck. Please be warm, please be warm."

She gets to Horace's dead body and grabs his right hand without hesitation. His is one of many bodies she has seen. Darci had stopped fearing the dead long ago. She pulls hard and his body falls sideways from the chair, landing face down on the deck, sending specks of blood onto the front of her sweater.

To her relief, she feels a semblance of warmth remaining in his hand and raises the cleaver high above her head, bringing it down on the wrist. The cleaver sticks into the wood of the deck as the hand is severed from the arm. She quickly grabs the hand and races to the safe, placing the fingers on the biometric pads. Darci breathes a sigh of relief as she hears the metallic click of the safe bolts disengaging.

She tosses the hand aside and opens the safe, finding a stack of neatly bundled cash. She smiles slightly as she also finds two tubes of gold Krugerrands and a chrome Walther PPKS .380 pistol. Finding a small satchel, Darci empties the safe of any valuables then places the pistol in the bag as well thinking, "A little insurance never hurts."

Walking to the Land Rover parked in the drive, she looks down and sees the flecks of blood on the front of her sweater. No matter, she gets in, turns the key and the vehicle starts, a sob escapes but she shakes her head and says, "No."

She takes one last look at the chalet and thinks of Konrad Pearce and his amazing story, realizing that the chase is all she has left. Darci drives away wondering what the weather in Karachi is like this time of year.

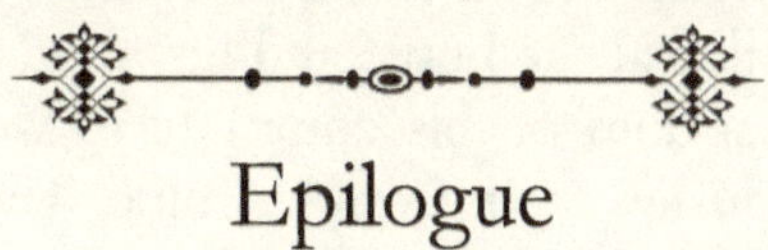

Epilogue

onrad Pearce sits in his company car, a bead of sweat snaking its way down his temple toward the inevitable destination of his collar. The Ford Fiesta's air conditioning is barely keeping up with the summertime heat in Green River, Indiana and he is sweltering. Konrad holds the wheel with both fists and practices the deep breathing exercises given to him by his therapist. He puts the small sensor which he uses to monitor his pulse on his index finger and reads the LED display thinking, "Ninety-three. Not too bad considering."

He knows that he is probably going to be late for work but this morning, it can't be helped. He looks ahead at the long line of cars slowly moving through the construction site on Fruitridge Avenue and curses under his breath at the automatic traffic arms as they rise and lower in their slow dance. The line of traffic moves through dutifully, five cars at a time. No honking horns or shouts of profanity come from the passing traffic, just an orderly movement of drivers staring straight ahead. This will be the first time Konrad has been late since landing the job as supervisor of testing at Fola Labs. He'd been recruited for the position shortly after his release from Saint Mary's. He was enormously overqualified for a position in a franchise blood testing facility, but apparently, he'd come highly recommended.

Of course, Konrad had said yes when they'd contacted him. He no longer believes in chance or good luck. He now knows all too well, the world is a large chess board with only a few players moving the pieces. Konrad knows also, pieces can be removed from the board without warning. Traffic begins to move slowly forward and stops after five cars move through the construction area. Konrad takes advantage of the stop to uncap the medication bottle and take his morning propranolol with a drink of decaffeinated coffee. He looks at the bottle, something nagging at his psyche. As a scientist, Konrad knows from many years of research that the devil is always in the details. Sometimes the most impervious aspect of a virus can be the very agent of its undoing. The same could be said for a vaccine. He shakes his head slowly. "What is it? What are you trying to tell me?"

He continues to stare at the bottle and his mind wanders to Jennifer and Chloe as it often does on his commute to work and as he does every time, Konrad pushes them from his mind. They are the one thing that can overrun the effects of his medication. For a fleeting second, he wonders if they are looking down on him and if so, what are his wife and daughter's thoughts. It is too painful to dwell on. The arm goes up and he moves five cars closer to entering the construction zone. He can clearly see the workers standing by their truck now, drinking coffee and he wonders if theirs is decaffeinated too. He stares at the traffic arm with its red flashing eye, a warning beacon, reminding him to stay calm. The flood of aneurysms around the globe has slowed to a small trickling stream. Every once in a while, a case is reported in the Green River news, but not often. Konrad thinks, "The culling of the flock must almost be complete."

He thinks of Candace and how much he loves her, and she him. He feels an immense feeling of gratitude. The part the two played brought them together like a mountain mist slowly drifting through the branches of a pine forest. They are inseparable now. The line of cars moves again bringing him up to the traffic arm. He stares at the red eye, blinking its taunting message, over and over. "I control you."

Candace will be waiting for him after work. She'll have supper cooked in the tiny apartment they share. The apartments were built where the subdivision his home had been located in used to stand. The family homes bulldozed, and the apartments constructed. Hundreds of the prefabricated squares stacked one on top of the other. The home he'd shared with Jennifer is gone like so many others. The LED on his monitor reads one hundred two. Konrad takes a deep breath and closes his eyes.

They'd filled the pond and constructed a market, pharmacy and workout center. Soon they would add a movie theatre. Everything a person needs within walking distance. Soon Green River would be a city made up of many small cities. Cities that are guarded by security officers who scan your identification as you come and go. Konrad decides to think about something else and turns on the radio. Dan Kingman's voice comes through the speakers reporting peace and security across the ten regions of the globe. "The Secretary General of the United Nations was quoted as saying, "The human race is now ready to move into the future as one.""

Konrad quickly turns the radio off. His pulse rate registers one hundred five. It is still well below the limit but he begins to panic and reaches for the medication bottle. The arm raises but Konrad's vehicle does not move. He's preoccupied with the bottle. One of the construction crew members appears at his window. "Hey buddy, are you okay? The arm's up."

Konrad apologizes and slowly presses the accelerator. People have forgotten him, and he doesn't want to draw attention. He is just another member of the flock, one of many, blindly following the shepherd. As he coasts through the construction zone the nagging feeling becomes a whisper and that whisper is something he dare not listen to. He gets past the construction zone and accelerates, rolling the medicine bottle back and forth between his thumb and fingers. Konrad has begun to form an idea and ideas have power, but he realizes with every fiber of his being, true power can never be seen, it must be felt.

About the Author

A. Sappington II is a Christian and veteran of the United States Marine Corps. After being honorably discharged, he pursued a career with the Federal Bureau of Prisons and served honorably for twenty-three years until his retirement. He is still active as a public servant. Arthur enjoys spending time with his family and his best friend, "Buddy."

www.ingramcontent.com/pod-product-compliance
Lightning Source LLC
Chambersburg PA
CBHW030132010826
48973CB00002B/521